Woman Miss

LOCAL WOMAN MISSI

Local Wo

SSING MISS

MAN MI

LOCAL WOMAN MISSING

LOCAL MISS

Local Woman

n Miss

SSING CA

LOCAL WOMAN MISSING

MAN

LOCAL WOM

Local Woman Miss

OMAN MISSING

man Missing SING

LOCAL WOMAN MISSING

Also by Mary Kubica

The Good Girl
Pretty Baby
Don't You Cry
Every Last Lie
When the Lights Go Out
The Other Mrs.
Just the Nicest Couple
She's Not Sorry

MARY KUBICA

LOCAL WOMAN MISSING

PARK
ROW
BOOKS

PARK
ROW
BOOKS™

Recycling programs
for this product may
not exist in your area.

ISBN-13: 978-0-7783-8773-2

Local Woman Missing

First published in 2021. This edition published in 2025.

Park Row Books
22 Adelaide St. West, 41st Floor
Toronto, Ontario M5H 4E3, Canada
ParkRowBooks.com

Printed in Lithuania.

MIX
Papper | Bidrar till
ansvarsfullt skogsbruk
FSC® C021394

For Addison and Aidan

PROLOGUE

There's a smudge of lipstick on the collar of his shirt. She sees it. She says nothing about it. Instead, she stands there, bobbing the crying baby up and down like the needle of a sewing machine piercing fabric. She listens to his lame lies, his same, dispassionate *Sorry I'm late, but*s he reels off almost every night. He must have an arsenal of them amassed, and he uses them in rotation: a bottleneck on the expressway, a coworker with car trouble, getting stuck on the phone with some apoplectic policyholder whose house fire wasn't covered because of insufficient documentation of the damage. The more specific he is, the more sure she is of his betrayal. Still, she says nothing. If she presses him on it, he gets mad. He turns it around on her. *Are you calling me a liar?* For this reason, she lets it go. And also because it would be a double standard for her to make a big deal of the lipstick.

"It's fine," she says, taking her eyes off the lipstick.

They eat dinner together. They watch some TV.

Later that night, she puts the baby to bed, feeding her at the last minute so that she won't wake hungry while she's gone.

She tells him she's going for a run. "Now?" he asks. It's after ten o'clock when she steps from the bedroom in running clothes and shoes.

"Why not?" she asks.

He stares at her too long, his expression unclear. "When people do dumb shit like this, they always wind up dead."

She's not sure what to make of his words, whether he means running alone late at night or cheating on one's husband. She convinces herself it's the first one.

She swallows. Her saliva is thick. She's been anticipating this all day. Her mind is made up. "When else do you expect me to go?"

All day long, she's home alone with their baby. She has no time to herself.

He shrugs. "Suit yourself." He rises from the sofa and stretches. He's going to bed.

She goes out the front door, leaving it unlocked so she doesn't have to carry keys. She runs only the first block so that if he's watching out the bedroom window, he sees.

At the corner, she stops and sends a text: On my way.

The reply: See you there.

She deletes the conversation from her phone. Is she as transparent as her husband? Is what she's doing as obvious as the lipstick on his shirt? She doesn't think so. Her husband is hot-blooded. If he had any idea she was sneaking out to hook up with some guy in his parked car on 4th Avenue, where the street dead-ends a hundred feet from the last house, he'd have beaten her to within an inch of her life by now.

She walks along the street. The night is quiet. It's the only time of day she looks forward to, lost in the anticipation of some guy she hardly knows indulging her for a while, making her feel good.

He isn't the first man she's cheated on her husband with. He won't be the last.

After the baby was born, she tried to quit, to be faithful, but it wasn't worth the effort.

This guy says his name is Sam. She's not sure she believes it. She's been seeing him off and on for months, whenever he or she gets the urge. She met him when she was pregnant of all things. To some guys, it's a turn-on. He made her feel sexy, despite the extra weight, which is far more than she could say for her husband.

Like her, Sam is married. And he isn't the only guy she's been seeing on the side.

The few times they've been together, "Sam" takes his ring off and leaves it on the dashboard, as if that somehow mitigates what he's doing. She doesn't do the same. She isn't one for feeling guilty. She's made herself believe that it's her husband's fault she does what she does. Turnabout is fair play.

The sky is full of stars. She stares at them awhile, finding Venus. The night is cold and her arms are covered with goose bumps. She's thinking about his car, how warm it will be once she gets inside it.

She's looking up at the stars when she hears something coming at her from behind. She spins around, eyes searching the street but coming up empty in the darkness. She chalks it up to some wild animal rummaging through trash, but she doesn't know. She turns back, goes back to walking, picking up her pace. She's not one to get scared, but she starts thinking of what-ifs. What if her husband is on to her, what if he is following her, what if he *knows*?

She tells herself he doesn't know. He couldn't know. She's a very good liar; she's learned how to silence her tells.

But what if the wife knows?

She isn't sure what "Sam" tells his wife when he leaves. They don't talk about things like that. They don't talk much at all except for a few preliminary words to kick things off.

Don't you look pretty.

I've been waiting for this all day.

They're not in love. No one is leaving their spouse anytime soon. It's nothing like that. For her, it's a form of escapism, release, revenge.

Another noise comes. She turns and looks again—truly scared this time—but finds nothing. She's jittery. She can't shake the feeling of eyes on her.

She starts to jog, but soon trips over an untied shoe. She's uncoordinated and nervous, wanting to be in the car with him, and not alone on the street. The street is dark, far too dark for her liking.

She senses movement out of the corner of her eye. Is something there? Is *someone* there? She asks, "Who's there?"

The night is quiet. No one speaks.

She tries to distract herself with thoughts of him, of his warm, gentle hands on her.

She bends over to tie the shoe. Another noise comes from behind. This time when she looks, car lights surface on the horizon, going way too fast. There's no time to hide.

PART ONE

DELILAH

NOW

I hear footsteps. They move across the ceiling above my head. My eyes follow the sound, but there ain't nothing to see 'cause it's just footsteps. That don't matter none, though, because the sound of them alone is enough to make my heart race, my legs shake, to make something inside my neck thump like a heartbeat.

It's the lady coming, I know, 'cause hers are the bare feet while the man always wears shoes. There's something more light about her footsteps than his. They don't pound on the floor like the man's do. His footsteps are loud and low, like a rumble of thunder at night.

The man is upstairs now, too, 'cause I hear the lady talking to him. I hear her ugly, huffy voice say that it's time to give us some food. She says it like she's teed off about something we've done, though we've done nothing, not so far as I can tell.

At the top of the stairs, the latch unlocks. The door jerks suddenly open, revealing a scrap of light that hurts my eyes. I squint, see her standing there in her ugly robe and her ugly slippers, her skinny legs knobby-kneed and bruised. Her hair is mussed up. There's a scowl on her face. She's sore 'cause she's got to feed Gus and me.

The lady bends at the waist, drops something to the floor with a clang. If she sees me hiding in the shadows, she don't look at me.

This place where they keep us is shaped like a box. There's four walls with a staircase that runs up the dead center of them. I know 'cause I've felt every inch of them rough, rutty walls with my bare hands, looking for a way out. I've counted the steps from corner to corner. There's fifteen, give or take a few, depending on the size of my steps and if my feet have been growing or not. My feet have, in fact, been growing 'cause those shoes I came with no longer fit right. They stopped fitting a long time ago. I can barely get my big toe in them now. I don't wear no shoes down here anymore 'cause I stopped wearing those ones when they hurt. I got one pair of clothes. I don't know where they came from but they ain't the same clothes I was wearing when I got to this place. Those stopped fitting a long time ago and then the lady went and got me new ones. She was put out about it, same as she's put out about having to feed Gus and me.

I wear these same clothes every day. I don't know what exactly they look like 'cause of how dark it is down here. But I do know that it's baggy pants and a shirt that's too short in the sleeves 'cause I'm forever trying to pull them down when I'm cold. When my stink reaches the lady's nose, she makes me stand cold and naked in front of Gus while she washes my pants and shirt. She's got words for me when she does. *Ungrateful little bitch,* 'cause then she's sore she's got to clean my clothes.

It's pitch-black where we are. The kind of black your eyes can't ever get used to because it's so dang black. Every now and again, I run my hand in front of my eyes. I look for movement but there ain't none. If I didn't know better, I'd think my hand was gone, that it up and left my body, that it somehow tore itself off of me. But that would've hurt and there would have been blood. Not that I would have seen the blood on account of how black it is down here, but I would have felt the wetness of it. I would have felt the pain of my hand getting tore from my body.

Gus and I play chicken with ourselves sometimes. We walk from wall to wall in the darkness, see if we'll chicken out before we run face-first into the wall. Rules are we got to keep our hands at our sides. It's cheating if we feel with our hands first.

The lady calls down from the top of the stairs, her voice prickly like thorns on rosebushes. "This ain't no restaurant and I ain't no waitress. If you wanna eat, you've got to come get it for yourself," she says.

The door slams shut. A lock clicks and there are the footsteps again, drawing away.

The lady wouldn't bother feeding Gus and me but the man makes her do it 'cause he *ain't gonna have no blood on his hands.* I've heard him say that before. For a long while, I tried to make myself not eat, but I turned dizzy and weak because of it. Then the pain in my belly got to be so bad that I had to eat. I figured there had to be a better way to die than starving myself to death. That hurt too much.

But all that was before Gus came. Because after he did, I didn't want to die no more, 'cause if I did, then Gus would be alone. And I didn't want Gus to wind up in this place all alone.

I push myself up off the floor now. The floor is rock hard and cold. It's so hard that if I sit in the same spot long enough, it makes it so I can't feel my rear end. The whole darn thing goes numb, and then after numb, it tingles. My legs are worn out, which don't make no sense 'cause they don't do much of anything except sit still. They've got no reason to be tired, but I think that's why they're so tired. They've plumb forgotten how to walk and to run.

I slog to the top of the stairs, one step at a time. There ain't no light coming into this place where they keep Gus and me. We're underground. There's no windows here, and that crack of light that should be at the bottom of the door ain't there. The man and the lady that live upstairs are keeping the light all to themselves, sharing none with Gus and me.

I feel my way up the stairs. I've done it so many times I know what I'm doing. I don't need to see. I count the steps. There's twelve of them. They're made of wood so rough sometimes I get splinters in my feet just from walking on them. I don't ever see the splinters but I feel the sting of them. I know that they're there. Momma used to pull splinters out of my hands and feet with the tweezers. I think of these splinters living in my skin forever and it makes me wonder if they fall out all on their own, or if they stay where they're at, turning me little by little into a porcupine.

There's a dog bowl waiting at the top of the steps for Gus and me to share. I don't see it, either, but I feel it in my hands, the smooth round finish of the dish. There was a dog in this house once. But not no more. Now the dog's gone. I used to hear it barking. I used to hear the scratch of nails on the ceiling above me, and would make believe the dog was gonna open the door one day and set me free. Either that or eat me alive 'cause it was a big mean dog, from the sound of it.

The lady didn't like it when the dog barked. She'd tell the man to shut it up—*either you shut it up or I will*—and then one day the barking and the scratching disappeared just like that, and now the dog's gone. I never did lay eyes on that dog, but I imagined it was a dog like Clifford, big and red, on account of the gigantic bark.

Inside the dog bowl is something mushy like oatmeal. I take it back downstairs. I sit on the cold, hard floor, lean against a concrete wall. I offer some to Gus but he says no. He says he ain't hungry. I try and eat, but the mush is nasty. My insides feel like they might hurl it all back up. I keep eating, anyway, but with each bite, it gets harder to swallow. I have to force myself to do it. I do it only so that my belly don't hurt later on, 'cause there's no telling when the lady will bring us more food. My mouth salivates, and not in a good way. Rather, it salivates in that way it does right before you're about to throw up. I gag on the mush, vomit into my mouth and then swallow it back down. I try to make Gus eat some, but still he won't. I can't blame him. Sometimes starving is better than having to eat that lady's food.

They've got a little toilet down here for Gus and me. It's where we do our business in the dark, hoping and praying the man and the lady don't come down when we're on the pot. Gus and I have an agreement. When he goes, I go in the other corner and hum so I can't hear nothing. When I go, he does the same. There ain't no toilet paper in this place. There's no place to wash our hands, or any other part of us for that matter. We're dirty as all get-out, but things like that don't matter no more, except for when our filth makes the lady mad.

We don't get to take no real bath in this place. But every now and again a bucket of soapy cold water arrives and we're expected to strip down naked, to use our hands to scrub ourselves clean, to stand there cold and wet while we air-dry.

It's damp down here where they keep us, a cold, sticky wet like sweat, the kind that don't ever go away. The water oozes through the walls and trickles down sometimes, when it's raining hard outside. The rainwater pools on the floor beside me, making puddles. I walk in them puddles with my bare feet.

In the dark, I hear something else splashing in them puddles sometimes. I hear something scratching its tiny claws on the floor and walls. I know that something is there, something I can't see. I got ideas, but I don't know for sure what it is.

I do know for sure that there are spiders and silverfish down here. I don't ever see them, either, but sometimes, when I try and sleep, I feel their stealth legs slink across my skin. I could scream, but it wouldn't do any good. I leave them be. I'm sure they don't want to be here any more than me.

I'm not alone down here, not since Gus came. It makes it better, knowing I'm not ever alone and that someone is here to bear witness to all the things the lady does to me. It's usually the lady doing the hurting, 'cause she don't got an ounce of goodness in her. The man has maybe an ounce 'cause sometimes when the lady ain't home he'll bring down a special treat, like a hard candy or something. Gus and I are always grateful, but in the back of my mind I can't help but wonder why he's being kind.

I don't know how old I am. I don't know how long they've been keeping me here.

All the time I'm cold. But the lady upstairs couldn't give two hoots about that. I told her once that I was cold and she got angry, called me things like *ornery* and *ingrate*, words that I didn't know what they mean.

She calls me many things. If I didn't know any better, I'd think my name was just as easily *Twit* or *Dipshit* as it is Delilah.

Come get your dinner, Dipshit.

Stop your whining, you little twit.

The man went and brought me a blanket. He let me sleep with it one night but then he went and took it away again so that the lady didn't find out what he'd done.

I don't know the difference between daytime and nighttime anymore. Long ago, light meant day and dark meant night, but not down here it don't. Now it's just all dark all the time. I sleep as much as I can because what else is there to do with my time than talk to Gus and play chicken with the walls? Sometimes I can't even talk to Gus 'cause that lady gets mad at us. She screams down the stairs at me to stop my yammering before she shuts me up for good. Gus only ever whispers 'cause he's scared of getting in trouble. Gus is a fraidy-cat, not that I can blame him. Gus is the good one. I'm the one who's bad. I'm the one always getting into trouble.

I tried to keep track of how many days I'd been down here. But there was no way of doing that seeing as I couldn't tell my daytimes from my nights. I gave that up long ago.

The sounds upstairs are my best measure of time. The man and the lady are loud now, trash talk mostly 'cause they ain't ever nice to each other. I like it better when they're loud, 'cause when they're quarreling with each other, then nobody's paying any attention to Gus and me. It's when they're quiet that I'm scared most of all.

I set the dog bowl aside. I did the best that I could. If I try and eat any more I will vomit. I offer some more to Gus but he says no. I'm not sure how Gus has made it this long on account of how little he eats. I never get a good look at him in the darkness, but I imagine he's all skin and bones. I've caught glimpses of him when the door opens upstairs and we get a quick scrap of light. He's got brown hair. He's taller than me. I think he'd have a nice smile but Gus probably don't ever smile. Neither do I.

The spoon chimes against the bowl. I reach down and take ahold of it in my hand. For whatever reason, I get to thinking of the way that lady comes downstairs sometimes. I don't like that none. She only comes when she's hopping mad and looking for someone to take her anger out on.

Gus must hear the jingle of the spoon. He asks what I'm doing with it. Sometimes I think Gus can read my mind.

"I'm keeping it," I say.

Gus tells me that a round spoon isn't going to do nothing to hurt no one, if that's what I've got my mind set on, which it is.

"You're just gonna get yourself in trouble for not giving the lady back her spoon," he says. I can't ever see the expression on his face, but I imagine he's worrying about what I'm gonna do. Gus always worries.

I tell him, "If I can figure out a way to make it sharp, it'll hurt."

I'm banking on that lady being so soft in the head she'll forget all about the spoon when she comes to get her bowl. I put the rest of the mush down the toilet so she don't get angry and call us names for not finishing her food that she made. I put the empty bowl at the top of them steps and start thinking on how I'm going to make this round spoon sharp as a spear.

There ain't much to work with in this place where they've got us kept. The man and the lady don't give Gus and me no stuff. We've got no clothes other than the ones we're wearing, no blankets, no pillows, no nothing. The only thing we have aside from the floor and the walls is each other and that icky toilet on the other end of the pitch-black room.

It's only after I try to sharpen my spoon on the walls and the floor that I decide to give the toilet a go.

I don't know a thing about toilets other than that's where I do my business and that ours has never once been cleaned. The darkness is a blessing when it comes down to the toilet 'cause I don't want to see the inside of it, not after all this time that we've been crapping in there and no one's been cleaning it. The foul smell alone is enough to make me gag.

"Where you going?" Gus asks as I take my spoon to the toilet. Gus and I have a way of knowing what the other is doing without ever really seeing what the other is doing. That comes from living down here long enough and getting to know each other's habits.

"You'll see," I tell him. Gus and I speak in whispers. I'm pretty sure the man and the lady who live upstairs aren't home right now 'cause I heard the doors opening and closing not too long ago. I heard their loud footsteps go suddenly quiet. There's no one up there talking now, no one screaming, no noise from the TV.

But I can't be sure. 'Cause if they are here, I don't want them listening in on Gus and me and knowing what I'm doing with my filched spoon. I'd get a whipping if they did—or worse. I ain't ever tried to run away before or make myself a weapon, but common sense says that's gotta be a worse punishment than not finishing the lady's nasty dinner or telling her I'm cold.

I let my hands float over the toilet awhile. I feel it up for a sharp spot. But the toilet is smooth as a baby's bottom. I almost give up, not thinking I'm going to find a spot to sharpen my spoon here. It's all one part, except for the top of it, the lid, which I discover by accident comes off. I hoist it up in my arms. It's heavier than I thought it'd be, all dead weight. I almost drop it.

"What's the matter?" Gus asks, panicked over some noise I make. I think that Gus is younger than me, on account of how chicken he is, even if he is taller. But anyone can be a chicken, no matter what their age or size.

"Nothing's wrong," I tell him, not wanting to think what would have happened if I did drop the lid. I set it gently upside down on the floor. I tell Gus, "Don't worry about it. Ain't nothing the matter. Everything's fine."

Gus is a worrywart. I wonder if he's always been that way or if the man and the lady have done that to him. I wonder what kind of boy Gus was before he got here. The kind who climbed trees and caught frogs and played ghosts in the graveyard at night, or the kind who read books and was afraid of the dark. We tried talking about it once, but then I got sad and wound up telling Gus I didn't want to talk about it no more. 'Cause most of my earliest memories have that man and that lady in them, and in them, they're doing wicked things to me, things that I don't like.

That man and the lady saved the newspaper from when I went missing. The lady read those stories out loud to me, telling me what happened to my momma, showing me pictures of my daddy standing in front of our big, blue house, crying. She told me how the police was looking for me. But then, soon after, she rubbed it in and gloated, saying that the police weren't looking for me no more. She told me then that I was old news and that they got away with taking a kid that wasn't theirs.

"Stealing kids," she said, "is the easiest thing in the world."

I go back to investigating the toilet. I discover that that tank is full of nasty water, which I mistakenly plunge my whole arm into, right up to the elbow. I cringe and shake it dry, not knowing if it's pee or what. Then I get down on the ground and run my fingers along the inside of that toilet tank lid.

The inside is much different than the whole rest of the toilet. It's gritty and coarse, not the same baby's bottom smooth. My fingers come across a jagged ridge on the inside of it, like a lip. That jagged ridge might just do the trick.

Gus is worried sick that whatever I'm planning won't end well. I've tried for a long time to make him see we ain't got no other options if we ever want to get out of this place. But that there's the problem with Gus. He'd just as soon stay here than risk getting caught trying to leave.

I run the edge of the spoon back and forth on that ridge. I get my knuckles caught on it time and again, and feel them getting scraped up. It burns like heck, but I keep at it. It takes a long while, but eventually the ridge of the toilet tank lid begins to mangle the spoon. Not spear-sharp, but uneven, the kind that promises to get sharp the longer I work with it.

"You shouldn't be doing that," Gus says.

"Why not?" I ask.

"They'll kill you."

I run my finger along that botched edge, feeling hopeful for the first time in a long while.

"Not if I kill them first," I tell Gus back.

I ain't ever thought about hurting or killing a person before. That's not my way. I don't got a mean bone in my body, or at least I don't think I did before coming to this place. But being locked in the dark does bad things to a person's mind. It changes them. Turns them into something new. I'm not the same person I was before that man and that lady stole me.

If it wasn't for Gus, I wouldn't have survived so long in this place. Gus is the best thing that happened to me.

I don't know for certain when Gus arrived. All I know is that he showed up out of the blue one time when I was dead asleep. I went to sleep and when I woke up, he was there, crying in the corner, worse off than me.

That man and that lady, he told me, had opened up the basement door, shoved him down them steps, locked up behind him. Gus was twelve at the time. Only God knows if he's still twelve.

What Gus told me when he stopped his crying was that they used that big red Clifford dog of theirs to cajole him into their car, just like fishing bait. Poor Gus liked dogs. And he couldn't help himself when the lady smiled kindly at him and asked if he wanted to pet her dog, which was sticking its big red head out of the car window.

Gus had been at the playground that day, playing ball with himself when they stole him. Shooting hoops. There wasn't anyone around to see them go. His ball got left behind. I wondered why Gus was playing ball alone, and if that meant he didn't have any friends, but I never asked him. Things like that don't matter anymore, anyway, 'cause now he's got me.

Day and night, I continue to work on my spoon. I don't know how long I've been going at it, but I've whittled it down enough that I've gotten myself a point. It ain't the best point ever. It's jagged and uneven, but at the top of that spoon, the metal thins to a sharp tip. When I stab it into my finger it hurts. I'm too chicken to stab it hard enough to make it bleed, but before too long I'm gonna have to. I've got to test it. I've got to know if it works.

I lost track of how long I've been carving this dang thing. Long enough that my hand's tired as all get-out. Gus offered to do it for me, but I said no 'cause I didn't want him getting in trouble. I know he doesn't want to help 'cause he's scared half to death of what I'm doing. He was just trying to be nice, but if someone's gonna take the fall for this spoon, it's me.

I hide that spoon when I ain't working on it. I hide it inside the toilet tank, put the lid back on and cover it up.

But it's not hidden now 'cause now I'm working on it, even though the man and the lady are right upstairs. I ain't got no other choice if we're ever gonna get out of here. I've got the lid off the toilet. I'm going at it full tilt with my spoon when I hear the lady declare to the man that she's got to feed us. There ain't no warning then because the door yanks suddenly open, and there it is again, that thin scrap of light that hurts my eyes.

All at once that lady's at the top of them steps. "Come get your dinner," she says, and I don't make a move to go 'cause usually when she says it like that, she just sets the dog bowl there at the top of them steps and leaves it for us. But not tonight. Because tonight, when we don't come, she says, "How many times have I told you before that I ain't your dang waitress and this ain't no dang restaurant? You better get your ass up here and get your dinner in five seconds or else. Five," she barks out, keeping count.

I look at Gus, but he's scared stiff. I got to be the one to do it 'cause Gus is frozen in fear. He can't move.

"Four," she says, and before I know it, the lady's counting down faster than I can get my spoon back in the toilet, get the lid quietly on and push my sleepy legs up off the floor and run.

I'm not dumb. I know how many seconds it is till she reaches one, and it's not many. I remember how to count and do math, 'cause my minute math worksheets are one of them things that I do in my head when I'm bored to death. I know that the lady will be at one in no time flat.

"Three," she's saying. I ain't ever gonna get there in time. My hands and legs are shaking. My heartbeat is thumping loud. I catch a glimpse of Gus out of the corner of my eye as I go running by. He's sitting on the floor with his legs pulled into him, scared as heck, wanting to cry.

The lady reaches one right around the same time my feet hit the bottom step. She's up there at the top of them steps, looking down at me. I got to squint my eyes to see her because my eyes ain't used to the light. She's standing up there holding her nasty meal in the dog dish.

I hear her ugly laugh when she gets to one. She's delighted in having me run scared.

"You ain't hungry?" she asks, standing smugly at the top of them steps, like a know-it-all. She don't wait for an answer. Before I can get a word out, she asks, "You think I got all day to sit around here and wait for you to come get your food?"

"No, ma'am," I say, my lips quivering.

"No, ma'am, what?" she asks sharply.

"No, ma'am, I don't think you got all day to sit around and wait for me to come get my food," I say, the words rattling in my throat.

"You ain't hungry?" she asks, and I got to think a minute about what the right answer is. I am hungry. I'm just not hungry for her food. But if I tell her that, she'll be angry 'cause she went to the trouble of making me food.

"I am hungry, ma'am."

That lady tells me, "It would be good for you to show some gratitude from time to time. I ain't gotta feed you, you know? I could just leave you here to starve to death."

"Sorry, ma'am," I say. My eyes stare hard at the floor so I don't have to see her ugly face.

She asks me, "What were you doing down here that it took you so long to come?" I don't like the way she's looking at me, like she knows something she shouldn't. My stomach churns, thinking maybe she knows I've been up to no good. I feel myself stiffen there at the bottom of the steps. But my spoon is tucked away inside the toilet where she won't ever find it. My spoon is safe and because of that so am I, for the time.

I lie and say, "I was sleeping."

"What's that you say?" she snaps, suddenly madder than she was before. Up there at the top of the steps, her face turns beet red.

I realize my mistake too late.

"I was sleeping, *ma'am*," I tell her. I ain't ever supposed to say anything without saying ma'am at the end. I'm supposed to show some respect for all that she does for me, otherwise I get punished.

The lady's quiet for a long while. She's just looking at me, staring. I don't like the quiet because when she's quiet, she scares me most of all.

"Looks like someone ain't gonna eat tonight, after all," she says, and then she mutters under her breath, "Ungrateful bitch."

She turns away from me and takes her slop with her. At the top of them steps, she slams the door closed and turns the lock. I step backward and drop down from the wooden step to the concrete floor, thinking that if that's the worst she's got for me—taking away Gus's and my dinner—then I got off pretty easy this time.

But I'm no dope. I know that's too good to be true.

That lady hasn't fed us since that day I forgot to say ma'am, not that I want to eat her nasty food. But just because I don't want to, doesn't mean that I'm not hungry. It doesn't mean that I don't need to eat. I don't know how much time has passed since that day she tried to feed us last. It feels like weeks.

At first I was hungry as could be. But then, strange enough, that feeling of being hungry went away, only to be replaced with something else. Something worse. For the first couple of days, all I thought about was food, until I was sure I could smell and taste the foods I was thinking about. Now I don't think about it much anymore. Now I just think about what it will be like to starve to death. I wonder if I'll just go ahead and die in my sleep, or if I'll know the moment I stop breathing and my heart stops beating 'cause I'll be gasping for air or something.

The lady hasn't brought us nothing to drink, either. I'm thirsty as all get-out. Gus and I went without water long enough that we got to drinking that dank water in the back of the toilet tank because it was all that we got. We've been taking baby sips only, not knowing if or when it will run out. We don't ever drink nearly enough to quench our thirst. We're still thirsty as heck.

I'm not the only one around here who's hungry. Gus is hungry, too. I hear his tummy grumbling, but Gus don't say nothing about being hungry, though we both know it's my fault he is.

Gus is sleeping now. I'm trying to sleep. But I got too much on my mind to sleep. Now that the lady's starving us to death,

I know we got to get out of here if we don't want to die. We got to take the next chance we get to run, if we ever get another chance. I been doing my calisthenics. It ain't easy because after all this time not eating, I'm weak as can be. My legs don't work right, and if I'm gonna stand a chance of running away from here, I got to get them ready. I've been spending my time jogging in place, leaning down to touch my toes, marching laps around Gus and my dungeon while he watches on, asks what I'm doing, begs me to stop. Gus don't like the idea of us running away 'cause he's scared as heck we're gonna get caught.

I shrugged when he said that, and said, "Maybe we will, maybe we won't. But how do we know if we don't try?" I told him that when I go, he's got to make sure he's right behind me. He can't drag his feet 'cause we're better off dead than getting caught.

I sit now with my spoon in my lap. I keep it close. It's not a spear. I don't think it'll ever be a spear, but it's mangled enough that it's got a chiseled point and could stun someone, if not kill. Stunning someone might be as good as it gets, but it's better than nothing.

All of a sudden, the door creaks open. I hold my breath. It ain't the lady coming. It's the man. I can tell by the sound of his footsteps, though he's trying to be quiet, which tells me the lady is somewhere up there, too, but she don't know he's coming down to see Gus and me.

I grip my spoon. The last thing I want to do is hurt the one who's been nice to me—or nicer, 'cause keeping kids in your basement ain't ever nice, even if you aren't the one hitting them. But sometimes you got to do what you got to do, and the man is the least suspecting of the two. I'm ready, or at least as ready as I'll ever be. I've thought this through a gazillion times. In my head I know what to do. But still, that don't mean that my heart isn't going hog wild. My arms and legs is shaking and I know I've got to get ahold of them if I'm going to do this right. I take a deep breath, count to ten. Release it.

"Where you at?" the man is asking, hissing his words out into the darkness.

Gus says nothing. "Right here," I say, gripping my spoon so tight it hurts my hand.

He comes to me. He says he's got a candy bar for me to eat. I hear the sound of him unwrapping it. "Far as she's concerned, we might as well leave you down here to starve to death. But don't worry. I won't let nothing bad happen to you." He's trying to sweet-talk me, to make up for her not feeding us for all this time. He feels badly about it. He slips the candy bar into my hand. "Go on," he says, "eat it." This ain't the first time the man's brought me chocolate. He brought me a cupcake once, 'cause he said it was my birthday. I don't know if it was.

I bring the candy bar to my mouth. I set my lips on it and taste the chocolate. It's richer than I've ever tasted before. I sink my teeth slowly in. This candy bar is the kind with nuts. It's got something gooey inside. That gooey something falls to my chin, tasting so sweet that I want to cry. I can't remember the last time I ever ate something so sweet in my whole life. I nibble at it 'cause I want this candy bar to last forever. I should save some for Gus. Gus would love this candy bar. And Gus needs to eat far more than I do. He's wasting away. But I don't want the man to think I'm ungrateful. He's probably got another one for Gus, anyway.

I take another bite. The sweet sugar rushes through my bloodstream. I make a sound.

"You like that?" the man asks, standing so close I feel his breath on me when he speaks. It stinks.

"It's good," I say back with a hunk of chocolate in my mouth. It sticks to my teeth, that gooey something like glue.

The man is trying to wheedle me. He talks soft, buttering me up, and I don't know if it's 'cause he feels bad about the lady starving me or if it's 'cause he's got something else on his mind.

"I got more where that came from. Whenever you want, it's yours. All you've got to do is ask."

The man is standing so close. Wherever the lady is at, she don't know that he's here.

There may never be another chance as good as this.

I'm nervous, 'cause I'm thinking about all the things that could go wrong when I try and stab him with my spoon. The fear almost gets the best of me. I almost talk myself out of it.

But then I get to thinking about Gus spending the rest of his life in this place, and know I've got to do it for him. I've got to get Gus out of this place if it's the last thing I ever do.

I hold the spoon tight, wrapping my fingers around the belly of its handle. I got only one chance to do this right. I don't plan to aim for anything in particular. It's too dark to see where I'm aiming, anyway. I just got to stab and see where it lands.

The man is telling me what a pretty girl I am when I take a deep, terrified breath and reach out and jam that spoon as hard as I can into him. If I had to guess, I'd say I hit somewhere around the side of the man's neck because of where he's standing. When I stab him, the tip of the honed spoon goes into him; I know 'cause it don't feel like a dead end when I touch skin. It don't go far, but it goes, leaving behind more than a scratch. The man lets out a screech.

It ain't a knife I have. It's something far lesser than a knife. One run-through isn't going to work. I grab my spoon out of this man's neck and spear him again and again. I don't know how much damage I'm doing, but by the sounds he's making, it hurts.

The man falls to the ground, taking me down with him. He's grunting, clutching himself, calling me names. I try rising up to my legs. As I do, he reaches out and tears at my hair with his sweaty hands. I pull away, feeling some of my hair go with him. I let out a cry and keep going.

The man reaches out again, but this time I'm standing upright. He gets my leg and tries tugging on it to keep me from leaving. I kick at him. I got only my bare feet, so that don't hurt none, but I kick hard enough that his hands let go 'cause he can't hold on to me no more.

I got him on the floor. From the sound the man's making, he ain't gonna be quick to get up and follow me.

I call to Gus, "Come on," as I go charging up them steps. I must've dropped my spoon 'cause I don't have it anymore.

At the top of them steps, I lay my hand on the door handle and turn. I hear Gus's scared footsteps on the stairs behind me. He's walking from the sounds of it, when I need Gus to run. I tell him to hurry up. There's a pounding in my head, a ringing in my ears. Gus is crying.

The man downstairs is making a sound. It's not so much a scream as it is a bellow. But it's loud enough that I'm starting to wonder how far it carries. Far enough that the lady will hear?

Once upstairs, I have no idea where I am. I have no idea where I'm going. The only time I've ever been up here before was when they first brought me to this place, for those first two seconds before they pushed me down the steps and locked up tight behind me. I don't remember it. It's dark upstairs but, unlike downstairs, it's not black as pitch. Here and there is a faint glow of light that helps me see.

I call to Gus to hurry up. I don't know how far he is behind. One quick glance over my shoulder tells me he's there, but lagging behind. I know Gus is scared to death, and I try and reassure him that everything will be all right. "This ain't no time to be scared, Gus," I say, trying not to be mean about it, but firm. "We got to go. You got to run." I reach back and grab ahold of his hand, pulling him with me. His hand is cold as ice. Gus says nothing but every now and again I hear him cry.

I hear that lady's voice somewhere in the distance, half-asleep and confused. "Eddie?" she's calling out. "What's the matter, Eddie?"

The man is making his way up the stairs now. He figured out how to get himself up off the floor, though he's still groaning as he chases after Gus and me. I hear the man scream to the lady, breathless and mad. "That little bitch got out," he's saying. "She's getting away."

"What?" the lady asks. "How, Eddie? How in the hell did that happen?"

That man lies and tells her, "I don't know how." He's telling the lady they got to find me, that they can't let us get away.

I find a door on the wall. I can just barely make out the square shape of it in the faint nighttime glow. I reach for the handle, but the door is locked up tight. My sweaty hand feels up the door, landing on the lock.

The man and the lady are getting closer. I know 'cause they're still screaming at one another, telling each other which way to go to find Gus and me. Calling one another idiots, telling each other to turn on a light so that they can see. Their voices feel close enough to touch.

They try and negotiate with me, saying things like, "If you tell us where you are, we'll give you a cookie," as if I'm dumb enough to fall for that. No cookie is good enough to live here the rest of my life.

But then, in the blink of an eye, they go from negotiating to mean, 'cause right after their offer for a cookie, they're calling me a bitch again, saying, "I'll kill you when I get my hands on you, you little bitch, you dumb twat."

They know this is my doing. They know Gus ain't so naughty as to try and run on his own.

My sweaty hand turns that lock and the door miraculously opens. There's a rush of air on the other side of it. It's hot and sticky, hitting me like a wall. It comes barreling into me and I freeze 'cause I ain't ever felt it in all these years that I've been here. Fresh air.

The outside world immobilizes me at first. But then I get ahold of myself 'cause if I don't I'm easy prey. 'Cause when the front door opened, an alarm on the house started screaming. If the man and the lady had any question about Gus and my whereabouts before, they know now.

The lady hollers that we're getting away.

I force myself outside. I start running. I've still got Gus's hand in mine and I pull on it, dragging him with me. There's fear in being outside as much as there is in staying inside. I haven't been outside in a long time. I nearly forgot all about outside.

The heat and the darkness swallow me whole and I run faster than I ever have in my life. I drop Gus's hand by accident, but I pray that he can keep up. Gus hasn't been doing his calisthenics like me, so there's no telling what kind of a runner he is. But sometimes being scared makes you do things you didn't know you could do.

My bare feet run across pebbles first and then the grass. The pebbles cut into my feet, hurting, making them bleed, though I'm not paying any attention to things like that. The grass, when I get to it, is soft and wet, tickling my feet. But I can't feel that, either, not really, 'cause I'm just running.

I see something shining in the sky. The moon. Stars. I forgot all about the moon and stars. I hear the buzz of nighttime bugs around me. I want to stop and stare and listen, but I can't. Not yet. Not right now.

"Stay with me, Gus," I scream back over my shoulder, knowing we've got to get far, far away from this place before we stop to look back. For all I know that man and that lady are just twenty paces behind and they'll catch us if we stop for a breath. I ask Gus if he's coming, if he's okay. I tell him to stay with me. To not slow down one bit. "We're almost there, Gus," I say. "We're almost free."

For a while I hear that man and that lady calling after us. They're quiet mostly because they don't want to cause a commotion. They got flashlights with them, though, 'cause I see the glow of those flashlights moving through the trees. Every so often the light falls on Gus and me and I duck away from it, veer off in some different direction so that soon I'm all turned around and couldn't find my way back to that house if I wanted to.

But then, after a while, I can't hear the man and the lady no more, which is a relief, but it also terrifies me. I wish they'd make some sort of noise so that I'd know where they are. Have we lost them? Or are they hiding in the trees, waiting for me?

It's dark outside mostly, still nighttime. The moon and the stars light the world a bit, make it so I can somewhat see. After all that time in the basement, our eyes are accustomed to the darkness. It gives us an advantage over the lady and man. They're not used to seeing in the dark, like Gus and me.

I don't know where we're at. There are houses, a street. But there aren't too many houses and what there are is broken up by trees. The trees are big and tall, but not the kind that are big enough that Gus and I can hide behind. The houses are tucked into the trees, and they're dark, hardly a light on anywhere. The grass everywhere is overgrown. It reaches right up to my knees and is chock-full of prickly weeds that scratch at my bare feet and legs. They're knifelike, stabbing me and making me bleed.

I run headlong into a tree branch, stunning myself. For a minute, I see stars. My knees lock and I freeze in place, trying to get my bearings. "What happened?" Gus asks. But before I have a chance to tell him, I hear the snap of a tree branch from somewhere behind and know we've got to keep running if we're to survive.

I say, "Let's go." I take off again. I hear the sound of Gus's heavy breathing behind me. After a while, neither of us says another word 'cause we got to conserve our breath for running.

I trip over a felled tree. I go soaring to the ground, where I land on my hands and knees. It hurts, my knees mostly, but I can't lie there on the ground and cry about it. I get myself up, dust off my hands and knees and keep running. "Watch out for the tree," I whisper to Gus as I go, knowing he's got to be just steps behind me, though his breath is getting harder and harder to hear over the sound of mine.

My legs are getting worn out from all the running, my feet heavy as lead. My heart is beating hard, on account of being short of breath, and my fear. I'm scared as hell, wondering what that man and that lady would do to us if they caught us.

Now that I got a little taste of freedom, I don't want to die.

I run fast past houses. I cut through yards. I run down the road.

A ways down, my legs become tired as all get-out. Gus and I ain't got a lot of options. There are a handful of houses, but what are the odds that anyone would open up for us if we knock on their door in the dead of night? I'm not sure we can risk it. We're sitting ducks if no one lets us in.

Hiding out seems like the better choice. I start looking for a place to hide. My running has slowed down some. We're no longer being tailed by the flashlights, but I'm not so dumb as to believe the man and the lady plumb gave up and went home. They're playing games with Gus and me.

In the backyard of one of them houses, I spy a shed tucked beneath a gnarled tree.

"Come on, Gus," I call, knowing the shed would be as good a place as any for us to hide. "In here," I tell him, spotting a padlock on that shed door, but seeing that it ain't locked up tight. We can still get in.

I silently remove the padlock from the metal loop and open up the hasp. The shed door pipes when I open it up, so I don't open it all the way. Just enough to get in. I slip inside, make room for Gus. But Gus doesn't come. He must have fallen farther behind than I thought. I got to wait for him to catch up.

Only when I'm in, tucked behind the shed door, do I allow myself a look back. I hold my breath waiting for Gus to materialize in the yard in the darkness of night and join me in the shed. But Gus ain't there.

I look all around and call quietly for him. Gus ain't nowhere.

I hear footsteps. I hear the mashing of leaves beneath someone's feet, like someone's chomping on chips. I hear the sound of breathing, of heavy huffing and puffing, and though I hope and pray it's Gus, I know it ain't, 'cause that's the same huffing and puffing that man was making when he was first chasing after me.

I'm in that shed. I got the door pulled to. It ain't closed up tight 'cause I was looking out for Gus when the footsteps came. I slinked back into the blackness of the shed when they did. I wasn't quiet enough 'cause that man heard something. Something brought him to me.

Now he's inches away. I'm crouched down into the corner of the shed, tucked behind a big old garbage can. There ain't a whole lot of room in this place 'cause it's chock-full of stuff I can't make sense of in the dark.

I can feel my whole self shaking. I got to sit on the wood floor, pull my knees into me and wrap my arms around them to keep from shaking so much I rattle the stuff around me. I'm wondering where Gus is. I'm thinking that if the man is here, then that means he don't have Gus. But maybe the lady has Gus. Or maybe Gus is hiding in his own shed, 'cause even though he's a scaredy-cat, Gus ain't an idiot. He can take care of himself.

The man's footsteps encircle the whole entire shed. They come to a stop right there by the door. His heavy breathing makes me breathe faster and louder, so that I got to hold my breath to keep from giving up my hiding place. I got to press my hands to my mouth so that the noisy air can't get in or out.

The heartbeat inside my neck is going so wild it makes me dizzy. I got a cold sweat going on. I feel like I could pee my pants. I can't hold my breath forever. I take one small, quiet breath, and then press my hands to my mouth and hold it.

The moon on the other side of the shed door is bright. It lights up the man, shines on him standing there just outside the open doorway. It makes him glow. I see the shape of him. I see his pointy chin and his straggly hair. His big nose. He's an ugly man, just like the lady's ugly. He ain't super tall, not nearly as tall as my daddy was when I remember him.

The man turns toward the shed door and opens it up all the

way. The door whines, sad that the man is coming in. With that door all the way opened up, the moon comes worming into the shed, too, brightening it some. Not a ton, but enough to scare me 'cause with the moonlight on me, I'm not as invisible as I thought.

I close my eyes and burrow my head into my knees, try and make myself small.

I hear the click of the flashlight turning on. Through my closed eyelids, I barely see the blaze of light as it goes roving around the inside of the shed, bouncing off walls. I ain't ever been so scared in my whole entire life.

The garbage can is tall and wide, taller and wider than me. I'm crouched so low my body hurts. I got myself rolled into a ball, just like pill bugs. I ain't breathing much, just enough as I have to do to keep from turning blue. But they're half breaths that I take, never letting enough air in or out, so that my chest aches and burns. I pee myself. My soft pants fill with it, turning soggy.

The light from the flashlight moves on and gets dimmer, but it doesn't go completely away. He's investigating some other part of the shed. The moments tick by at a snail's pace. With my eyes closed up tight, I can't see nothing, but I imagine the man investigating every crevice, every nook and cranny, in that whole entire shed, looking for me.

I start wondering, worrying that I got a foot stuck out, that the sleeve of my shirt or a clump of dirty hair is somewhere where he can see. 'Cause even though I'm hiding behind that garbage can, what if all of me ain't tucked neatly back?

The shed door squeals open even wider.

One loud footstep tromps into the shed with me. Then another. Then another.

He's coming inside the shed. Next thing I know, he's all the way inside the shed with me. I hear that man's heavy breathing. I smell his rank breath.

He's saying words, telling me he knows I'm there.

"Come out, come out, wherever you are," he singsongs, and if it wasn't for that, I'd think he did see me. But I'm no idiot, whatever that lady thinks. I'm no twat. If he knew where I was, he'd have me by now. But a hunch is all the man's got.

He swears blind that he ain't gonna hurt me none. "Just come on out, little girl, and I'll take you home."

I don't believe him. Or maybe I do. Except home is not my home. He don't intend to take me back to Daddy. No, this man intends to take me back to his home and lock me back in that dungeon of his, after he teaches me a lesson about stabbing people with spoons.

I curl more tightly into my pill bug ball. I hold my breath. I bite my lip and clench my eyes shut tighter, 'cause somehow not seeing makes it feel less real.

Something inside that shed goes crashing down. I start. It takes everything in me not to scream. Whatever it is, the man knocked it from its place, trying to scare me out of my hiding place. Something else falls. He's knocking things down on purpose. I peek one eye open and see a box of nails spilled on the wooden floorboards. They're sharp as daggers.

I think of all the bad things this man could do to me with them nails. He's madder than I've ever seen him. I brought out the devil in him when I went and stabbed him with my spoon.

I hear the lady's voice hissing from the other side of that shed wall. She's calling for the man, telling him to stop making such a racket 'cause someone will hear.

"You see her?" the lady asks. "She in there?"

The man lets out a big long breath, then says, "Not in here."

The flashlight light falls away from me. His footsteps retreat and he goes outside.

On the other side of that wall they're talking quiet-like, making a plan about how they're gonna find me. He's gonna go one way, she's gonna go the other.

I make a plan, too. I'm gonna stay right here.

The man asks, "Everything good back home?" and I know that's when he's talking about Gus.

"All good," the lady says, and I know then that that lady did snatch Gus and bring him back. Now Gus is locked in the dungeon without me. Or maybe he's dead. 'Cause that's the best way they could punish me for what I've done, by hurting or killing Gus.

I want to cry, but I can't cry 'cause crying would give me away. I could give myself up and go back to living in that dungeon of theirs with Gus, but I can't. One of us has got to live through this ordeal and tell the rest of the world where we've been all this time. For Gus's sake, now more than ever, I've got to live.

Light noses its way into the shed with me. It comes in through the slats of the wooden boards. It's a golden yellow, something I ain't seen in years. Seeing the sunlight nearly makes me cry, but I don't cry 'cause crying won't do me any good. I've got to keep my wits about me if I'm going to try and find my way home.

The shed, now that I see it in daylight, is old and rickety. There's a lawn mower and a ladder in here, and a bunch of broken bikes. I rise up to my feet, try and step around them, but my legs are half-asleep on account of the way I've been sitting. I never did sleep, all night long. I spent the whole night crouched into a ball, waiting for that man to come back.

At some point in the middle of the night, it started raining. I heard them raindrops pounding on the roof and, every now and again, a stray raindrop snuck into the shed with me, landing on my arms and face. I tried to gather that rain into the palms of my hands and drink it, but there wasn't ever more than a couple drops of it. I'm so thirsty. My throat is bone dry. I ain't drank in days. My lips is dry, too. They're split so that, on them, I feel blood. I run my tongue over that blood and taste it.

When it was raining, it took everything in me not to go outside, to leave the safety of the shed, and turn my face up to the sky with my mouth open wide. But I was scared to death the man was waiting for me on the other side. So I settled on just drinking one stray raindrop at a time.

My body hurts now, from running the way I did. There's dried blood on my hands and legs. That's from tripping over the tree. My feet are covered in blood, too. There's wood chips and pebbles stuck in them. It hurts to walk, but I do, anyway, 'cause I got no other choice. In the sunlight I see scars on my arms, from who knows what. Probably all the times that lady went and hit me with her belt, or the time she threw hot water that smelled like a swimming pool on me. That hurt like heck, when it wasn't itching half to death.

I go to the front of the shed, but I don't go straight outside. I stand in the doorway first, looking out, surveying my surroundings. I don't know where I am. I don't know that I'm alone, that I'm not being watched.

There's a house outside. It's big and white and falling down. It's got a slant to it, the porch is uneven and a broken window is patched up with red tape. Smoke comes from the chimney, which is the only way I know that the house isn't abandoned, that someone still lives there.

The world outside the shed is wet from the rain, though it ain't raining no more. The sun is just starting to come up. The sky is full of puffy clouds in shades of pink and blue. Seeing colors like that makes me gasp. I haven't seen colors in nearly forever. I have to think a minute to remember the names of them. There's yellow beneath the clouds, the sun sitting there where the sky meets land.

The earth itself looks fuzzy to me, like there's clouds coming up from the ground, too. The world is overwhelming and big. I find myself missing the darkness of the enclosed basement, 'cause even though it was the worst place in the world, something about being shut in made me feel safe. There was only one way in or out. No one was gonna sneak up on me without me knowing. But here, bad things can come at me from any direction. The sun is getting to be so bright I can just barely open my eyes. I feel danger everywhere, lurking, hiding out where I can't see it.

The shed feels safe and enclosed to me, like the basement. I have half a mind to lock myself inside and stay put. I got to give myself a good talking-to to work up the nerve to leave.

I take a hesitant step out. I put my bare foot on the wet grass. There's a puddle there. It's mud-splattered and warm, but still, I drop to my belly and take a big, long swig of the dirty water before standing back up.

I decide right away that I'm not going to go to that house and see if anyone is home. Because I don't know who lives there, and what kind of people they are. I don't know if they're the kind of people who would snatch up children that ain't theirs and keep them.

Instead, I move unnoticed across the yard and to the street on the other side of it. The street is at first dead quiet. There's more than one house, but they're all the same, big and white, and run-down. They're spread apart, with land between them, so that I got to walk awhile to get from one house to the next. I don't walk in the street. Instead, I walk in the ditch beside it so that when a rare car comes soaring past, I drop down in that muddy ditch and hide.

I don't know where I am. I don't know where I'm going. I've never been in this place before, not so far as I know. But I don't know where the house is that the man and the lady kept me; I don't know what it looked like from the outside. With all my running last night, I got turned around. I couldn't ever find my way back, which makes me think that the man and the lady could be living inside any one of these houses here; that Gus could be inside any of these houses here; that the shed where I spent my night could have just as easily belonged to them.

I'm worried about Gus. But I don't got any idea what to do. All I know is that I got to save myself first before I can save Gus. The thought of that knocks me sideways. It just don't feel right leaving Gus behind, though I know if I go back to the man and the lady, we're both dead.

I try and memorize my surroundings. If I'm ever gonna find my way back I got to remember things like the fence, which sits waist-high and is brown, falling down. I got to remember them smokestacks billowing not so far in the distance. I got to remember the houses, which are old, every single one of them, with paint that flakes off. There are trees on one side of the road, but on the other there's a field, with crops that grow. I go to the crops and snatch an ear of corn for myself. For a moment, I hide myself in the field and take a bite of that corn, not remembering the last time I ate, but especially not remembering the last time I ate something that wasn't mush. The corn is hard and starchy. It ain't tasty at all. It hasn't been cooked. But that don't matter at all. I'm so hungry I'd eat dirt if it was my only choice.

I rise back up to my feet when I finish that corn. I'm tired, but I don't got time for napping. I trudge on through the edge of the cornfield, which hides me some. It's not easy on the feet. The ground here is mushy from last night's rain, and soon the bottom half of me is covered in mud.

The sun keeps coming up. After a while, it dries the puddles some. It warms my skin so that I go from cold to hot real quick. The fields thin and, little by little, trees crop up so that soon I'm marching through a forest. Like the cornstalks, the trees hide me, too, though I hear the street not so far from here. I hear the cars go zooming past. In the woods, I cross a little crick. I pause for a sip of water. I splash a handful of it on my face and hands, cooling me down, washing the caked-on blood away. I rub it over my arms. It feels good, but it don't do nothing to get rid of the scars.

The sun is hot now. It burns my eyes. I keep them trained on the ground, 'cause looking anywhere up hurts bad. My eyes aren't used to the sunlight.

I don't see the lady and her little girl and dog come walking through the woods at first. It's the dog that sees me. I turn sharply at the sound of its bark, rise up quickly from the crick and think about running. Energy floods my legs and I nearly bolt.

But the dog is small and white. It yaps more than it barks, its tongue hanging out sideways. Its little tail wags like it thinks that seeing me is the best thing in the world. The girl says hi. She says it about a gazillion times, like it's a new word she's learned and she's trying it on for size. They put me at ease. I don't bolt, because the dog and the little girl are pleased as Punch to see me.

The woman is slack-jawed. Her eyes are wide and she's pulling on the leash, trying to stop the dog from running to me. But then, by accident, the leash slips from her hand. The dog breaks away and comes running. At first I flinch 'cause it's been a long time since I've seen a dog, and here this dog is jumping on me, licking me, peeing.

"That's Cody," the woman says. Her voice is kind. "He won't hurt you. He just gets excited when he meets new people," she says, coming closer to pick up the dog's leash, but she leaves him where he is 'cause the dog is nice, and after a quick second, I'm not scared of it no more.

The woman is looking strangely at me. I have no idea what I look like. All I can see is my arms, my chest, legs and feet. I can see my hair, too, 'cause it's long, but I can just see the part of it that dangles. I got no idea what it looks like on my head. In that dungeon where they kept me, it used to fall out in clumps for no good reason at all.

"Are you new?" the woman asks, 'cause she knows she ain't ever seen me around here before. I shake my head. Her eyes go to my bare feet, which is bleeding. There's a thin stream of blood coming real quick. There's still blood on the knees of my pants and I ain't bathed in weeks. My breath and my underarms is raunchy. I keep my arms down so the woman can't smell what I smell when I lift them up. The little girl is still saying hi.

"Are you hurt?" the woman asks. She doesn't wait for me to tell her 'cause she can see for herself that I am. I'm hurt bad all over. "You're hurt," she says. "You're bleeding," she says, pointing at my feet and then my knees. "Right there. And there. How old are you?" she asks, and when I don't answer right away, she starts rattling off numbers. "Eleven? Twelve? *Fourteen?*"

I nod at fourteen 'cause I've got no idea how old I am. Fourteen is as good an age as any.

It hurts to stand or walk, 'cause my feet on the underside is all torn up. My legs are sore and my belly aches.

The woman is still staring at me. She's got yellow hair like the sun. She smiles at me, but I can tell that it's not a real smile. It's a worried smile. The woman don't know what to make of me, though soon she ain't looking at my face anymore 'cause she's looking at my hands and my arms and my knees and my feet.

I like the sound of her voice. It's soft and kind. "Are you lost, sweetheart?" she asks me, her eyes coming back to mine. I say nothing.

"Do you live around here?" the woman asks.

I shrug my shoulders. I open my mouth to speak, but my voice is just barely there. I got to stop and start over a time or two. "I don't know, ma'am," I say, 'cause truth be told, I got no idea where I live, other than that the house is blue. But I couldn't find that blue house if my life depended on it.

"You don't need to call me ma'am, honey," she says. "You can call me Annie." But of course I can't do that 'cause when I don't say ma'am I either get a beating or I get starved. "You're really lost, aren't you? What happened here?" she asks, meaning those scars on my arms.

I just stare dumbly when she asks. I don't say nothing but I feel tears pooling in my eyes.

The woman asks, "Can I call your parents for you? Do you know their phone number?"

I shake my head. I don't know nothing about that.

I can see the worry in her eyes. She looks me up and down. I feel uncomfortable with her looking at me like that, so I look at my hands instead. There's gravel buried into the palms of them. I pick at the tiny pebbles with my dirty fingernails so I don't have to look this pretty woman in the eyes.

"What's your name, sweetheart? Would you be willing to tell me that?" She takes a breath when I say nothing. She says, "You don't have to if you don't want to."

I'm scared as heck, wondering what she wants to know my name for. But I tell her, anyway, 'cause I don't know what else to do and 'cause the woman seems kind. She don't seem like the kind of lady who would snatch kids that aren't hers and keep them in her basement.

"Delilah," I tell her, my voice rattling.

I see in her throat that she swallows hard. There's a bulge that moves up and down. The little girl is tugging on her hand now, asking again and again, "Who dat? Who dat, Mama?" but the pretty woman don't answer her.

"Delilah what?" the woman asks me. She got her eyes set on me now. She's not looking at my feet or my knees, but now she's looking at me. Her eyes have gone from wide to wider and her skin is suddenly white-like. The dog's yapping up at her, trying to get her attention, but she pays it no mind.

"Delilah Dickey," I say.

The woman don't say nothing this time, but her hand goes to her mouth and she gasps.

PART TWO

KATE

May

There's a knock at the door. It's loud and insistent. It's after nine o'clock at night. It's dark outside, the moon and stars hidden behind storm clouds. The only time I can see outside is when lightning strikes, flooding the world with a sudden burst of light.

I'm in the kitchen, home late from a long day of work. I've just opened a bottle of wine and am waiting for leftovers—Bea's stuffed shells that she made hours ago, when I was still under the impression I'd be home on time—to warm in the microwave when the knock comes. I look up from my glass at the sound of it, my blood running suddenly cold.

People don't show up out of the blue at nine o'clock on a stormy night.

Bea is out back in the detached garage that she uses as a music studio. Her phone lies on the counter beside my glass of wine. From the kitchen window, I look out into the backyard, where it's dark and raining. The rain pours down from the sky, a sudden blitz. I have trouble seeing out the window because of the rain. It hasn't stopped raining for days. It's unlike anything I've ever seen. I'm not the only one who's contemplated building an ark. Even Bea, the more even-keeled of us, has contemplated building an ark. Severe flooding is expected, and every day of the next week calls for more rain. Rivers have overflowed their banks, wreaking havoc. The grocery store parking lot is a swimming pool. Roads are impassable, and some of the schools have been closed. There was footage on the news of canoes in towns not far from ours, paddling down the middle of the street.

There's talk of the apocalypse, a quiet hysteria arising that maybe these rains are indicative of the end of times. I'm not some doomsday prophet, but still, I went to church and told the priest my confession just in case. You can never be too careful about these things.

The wind has picked up in the last few hours. I turn on a light in the backyard, flicker it a few times. Outside the branches of trees sway, scratching against the side and the back of our house. It's horrible to listen to, the stuff of nightmares, the rasp of tree limbs like claws against the wood siding, scraping to get in. Outside, trees lose their leaves in the storm, getting blown about. Power is out in parts of town, due to downed lines. Thankfully we still have ours, though there's no telling how long that will last. We stocked up on candles, flashlight batteries, just in case. By now, they're impossible to find in stores.

This morning there were fallen trees in the street, casualties of last night's violent storm. In the middle of the night, the tornado sirens howled. Bea and I sat crouched in the first-floor bathroom with Zeus in our arms, waiting for the storm to pass. Zeus hates to be held almost as much as he hates thunder. There are marks on my arms because of him.

I continue to flicker the backyard light, but Bea doesn't notice because the door to the garage is closed. The only window is in the attic portion of the garage, where Bea doesn't go.

It comes again then, the same insistent battering on the heavy wood. My teeth clench; my shoulders tense. I tell myself that it's nothing to worry about. Bea is the more bold of us. If she were here, she'd answer the door unflinchingly. But without Bea, I force myself to be an adult, to go to the front door and open it up. Zeus is on the bottom step when I come into the hall. He runs upstairs at the sound of another knock to hide, an incompetent guard cat.

The front door is edged by windows. I turn the porch light on and have a look out the window before opening up the door. A man stands there in the glow of the porch light. He's dripping wet. At first my heart starts, but then I breathe a sigh of relief when I see that it isn't some stranger showing up unsolicited at this time of night.

My body physically relaxes at seeing him, the tension I was carrying in my shoulders melting away. Josh is our neighbor. He lives next door with his wife, Meredith, and their two kids.

I pull open the door and the wind rushes in. The rain has drenched Josh and his son, Leo, who stands at Josh's side shivering and wet. Both of their hair is limp, falling onto their faces. Water runs down their foreheads and cheeks. Their clothes hang heavy, shapeless. The rain can't reach them under the porch's wide roof, but that doesn't matter now that they're thoroughly soaked. They've walked here in the rain. It's not far, but they must have a good reason to be out on a night like tonight. Josh has his arm around Leo's shoulders and he's pulling him into his leg, Leo's head barely surpassing Josh's knee in height.

Leo isn't crying. But I can see on his face that he'd like to cry. Leo is four. We celebrated his birthday with Josh and Meredith last month, at a circus-themed party in their backyard, where they hired a clown and a man who made animals out of balloons. People came in costume.

Josh says hello. There's a half smile, but it's weighed down with something like worry. He's wearing his work clothes, though Josh, invariably, is home by dinnertime. He keeps bankers' hours when he isn't wining and dining clients, so that by now he should be relaxing in front of the TV in pajamas.

"What's going on?" I ask, seeing that something is wrong. I pull the door open wide enough to let them both in, to get them out of the rain. But Josh, with a firm hand on Leo's shoulder, doesn't come.

He looks to his house and then back at me. "Have you heard from Meredith, Kate?" he asks. "Do you know where she is?"

Lightning flares behind Josh and Leo, the kind that stretches from the sky clear down to the ground. A second later, thunder booms. Leo leans in closer to Josh, clinging to his leg now. The rain pummels the porch roof, gathering in the gutter, running out the downspout and onto the lawn, where it collects.

I shake my head. "No. I don't know. I haven't heard from her," I say, speaking loudly over the sound of the pelting rain. "You can't find her?" I ask, and my gut reaction isn't the same worry as Josh's. Meredith works odd hours. She's a doula, always disappearing in the middle of the night to help support some woman in labor. At a pinch, Bea or I—though mostly Bea, who works from home—have watched Leo and his sister because Meredith needed to run to a birth and Josh wasn't home. It's not uncommon.

Josh tells me that he can't find Meredith and he hasn't heard from her.

"She must be at a birth," I say.

Josh's reply is irresolute. He's of two minds about it, saying, "Maybe. I don't know. But I don't think so. She would have called me if she was heading to a birth. She always calls. And then there's Delilah..." he says, voice trailing.

I ask him, "Where's Delilah?" Delilah is Josh and Meredith's daughter. She's six.

Josh is shaking his head, the rainwater spraying off. "I don't know," he says. "I don't know where Delilah is, either." There's a panic to his voice. He shouts over the rain.

I ask him again to come inside, but he won't. His eyes swing back and forth from his house to me, and I know that he's watching for Meredith, waiting for her to come home.

Josh goes back to the beginning. He fills me in on the details of the day. He was at work, he says. He took the train home and went to the babysitter's house to pick up Delilah and Leo, same as he always does. He took the 5:46 out of Chicago, which gets into town at 6:26. "It was probably around 6:45 by the time I got to the sitter's house," he says. The sitter lives in the neighborhood, about a mile from here. Bea and I don't have kids, but I know where she lives. I know which house is hers.

"When I got there," he says, "the sitter told me only Leo was there. She said that Meredith had kept Delilah home for the day because she was running a fever. She said Meredith had called Delilah in sick to school, and had canceled her own classes."

Meredith teaches at a yoga studio in town. She does it to supplement the income she makes as a doula, not that she and Josh need it because Josh does well enough for both of them. He works in wealth management, dealing with high net worth clients. But Meredith's schedule is irregular, with peaks and valleys. Some weeks are overladen with births. Then she goes weeks without a single birth. She used to complain that she needed stability in her life, a sense of purpose during those times she had nothing to do. That's what drew her to yoga.

"You tried calling?" I ask.

"Ten times at least."

"When is the last time you talked to her?"

He looks at me and runs his fingers through his dark hair. "When we went to bed last night," he says. He tells me he saw her this morning. She was there lying in bed beside him, but she was asleep. He didn't want to wake her. He kissed her on the forehead before he left. His day was busy; it got away from him. He never had time to call or text Meredith but, to his defense, she also didn't call or text.

"That's not unusual," he says. "That's the way it is with Meredith and me. Sometimes we're filling each other in on the minutiae of the day. Other times we don't have time to check in. I didn't see Delilah today, either," he says regretfully. "I left for work before she was up. For the life of me I can't remember if she looked run-down last night. I've been racking my brain trying to remember."

Josh is getting emotional now, worked up. He isn't crying. But I can see the weight of worry in his eyes and in the lines of his forehead. "It isn't like Meredith not to call. Not after all this time."

I feel it in my gut then: something is wrong. I'm not just thinking about Meredith and Delilah. Because it would be one thing if this was an isolated incident, then maybe I wouldn't feel so concerned. But there's Shelby Tebow to consider, a young woman who went for a jog in our neighborhood ten nights ago and never returned.

"What are you thinking, Josh?" I ask, setting a hand on his arm.

"I wasn't worried when the sitter told me Delilah wasn't there. Not at first," he says. He thought it was weird that Meredith hadn't called to tell him about the fever—or at least tell him he didn't need to pick Delilah up. That seems like something Meredith would have done.

"But Delilah," he says, "gets sick all the time." Kindergarten wreaks havoc on an immune system. They call her a germ magnet because of it. And maybe, he rationalized, Meredith's day had gotten away from her and she hadn't had time to call, because she was too busy taking care of Delilah.

"When I left the sitter's, I was sure I was going to come home and find Meredith and Delilah there. So I didn't think much of it. Truthfully, Kate," he says, "it didn't cross my mind that they wouldn't be home. I tried calling Meredith before I left the sitter's, to ask if she needed me to pick anything up from the pharmacy. Medicine, juice. Popsicles," he says, telling me how much Delilah craved red Popsicles when she was running a fever. It was the only thing she'd eat.

"What happened?" I ask.

"It went to voice mail," he says.

He drove home. He pulled down the alley and opened the garage out back, finding it empty, though he knew he would because the house was also dark. The sun hadn't yet set. But with the storm, it was dark enough outside to warrant turning a light on, especially since Delilah is afraid of the dark.

That's when the worry set in for him, about two hours ago. He parked the car and ran inside to find the house empty. Only the dog was waiting for Leo and him, food and water bowl both empty, like he hadn't been fed since morning.

"Now I'm thinking the fever is way worse than the sitter made it out to be," he admits. "It seems too late in the year for the flu. But what about meningitis? A burst appendix? Sepsis?"

"Or an ear infection," I offer, thinking of a less frightening alternative to his.

I squat down to Leo's height and ask in a soft voice, "Hey, Leo. Can you tell me what Delilah was like today? Was she not feeling well?" I ask. "Do you remember if anything hurt?"

Leo just stares, gripping his wet security blanket in his hands, saying nothing. He's shy. But he's also four, maybe too young to know or remember if Delilah was sick. The fever is concerning to me. But so, too, is what happened to Shelby Tebow, who still hasn't been found. There are also the weather conditions to consider. The thunder, the lightning, the threats of tornados. Add to that the fact that the current river levels are high. We've been under a flash flood warning for days, so long it feels like it will never lift. I've been hearing reports on the news that cars have been getting stuck in water on the streets. Flooded roads, the reporters keep saying, can be extremely dangerous. It only takes a couple feet of water to carry a car away. In the last few days, a month's worth of rain has come down. In the city, raw sewage is leaking into people's homes. It's awful.

Suddenly I hear movement in the hall behind me. I turn to see Bea making her way to us through the arched doorway that cuts between the kitchen and foyer. Bea is barefoot as always, the calves of her jeans wet from the rain. "I thought I heard voices," she says, smiling down on me because Bea is tall. I haven't seen her since I left for work this morning. Today was long, nearly twelve hours spent on my feet. There were surgeries, a euthanasia. Then, just as I was about to leave, a dog walked in with a rectal prolapse. I could have sent the owners to the after-hours emergency clinic, but I didn't, prevailing instead on a couple vet techs to stay and help me push the tissue back in and suture it up, saving the owners hundreds of dollars. Those emergency clinics aren't cheap, and they didn't have the money for it. I doubted they would go. I imagined the dog in that condition all night, how uncomfortable he would have been.

Bea was in her studio when I came home; I didn't want to disturb her. Most days Bea and I are like ships that pass in the night, because even tonight, long after Bea goes to bed, I'll be working on my records. *Leave it for the morning,* she always says, wanting me to go to bed with her. But if I leave it for the morning, I'll forget.

A cold gust blows in from outside. It's late May. It should be much warmer than this, but it's an El Niño year. The summer is expected to be cooler than normal, and wet. So far, the weather forecasters have been right.

Bea tugs the sleeves of her shirt down to the wrists. Her hand settles on my lower back. It's warm, a nice contrast to the cold air. She kisses me on the top of the head.

I look at Bea. "Josh can't find Meredith and Delilah," I say. "You haven't heard from them today, have you?"

Bea thinks. "Meredith came by this morning," she says. She looks at Josh. "You were out of milk," she says, and he asks her what time that was. "It was early, maybe eight o'clock. The kids wanted cereal for breakfast. *Cinnamon Toast Crunch,* wasn't it, Leo?" she asks, smiling down on him. He smiles shyly back. "Meredith left them at home and ran over to grab a cup."

"Did she say anything about Delilah being sick?" he asks.

Bea shakes her head. "She came quickly. Just grabbed the milk and left. The kids were home alone—she didn't want to leave them more than a minute. She apologized for being a bother. I told her you two are never a bother. Delilah's sick?" she asks, looking concerned.

I fill Bea in on the details of the babysitter. I tell her about Delilah's fever. "I'm so sorry, Josh. Meredith didn't say anything about it. I'm sure it's nothing. Could her cell phone be dead?" she asks.

Josh says, "It is. But that still doesn't explain why they aren't home now."

"You found her phone?" I ask, surprised. It isn't like Meredith to leave her phone behind.

"No," Josh says. "We have that app, where we can track each other's phones. It was the first thing I checked. It says her location is unavailable, so her phone must be dead, I think, or shut down. But Meredith's clients are so dependent on her. She wouldn't shut her phone down. Not on purpose."

Josh looks at his watch to see what time it is. Delilah, he tells us, goes to bed by seven-thirty most nights, eight latest. It's nearing nine-thirty now. "By now," Josh says, "both kids should be asleep, and Meredith and I should be catching up on TV."

Josh tells us that in the last two hours he called the pediatrician's office to see if Delilah had been there. But it was late; the office was closed. All he got was their answering service, who didn't have access to the schedule and wouldn't have told him even if they did. He called the hospital in town and a handful of convenient care clinics, but there are dozens of those. He doesn't know if he got them all, and even those he connected with weren't willing to give patient information over the phone.

I go back to the possibility of a birth. If Meredith had a client in labor, would she have taken Delilah with her if she had no other choice? Childbirth can be fast and furious, not that I would know. But on the nights that Josh, Meredith, Bea and I shared a drink on the porch after their kids were asleep, Meredith

MARY KUBICA

regaled us with her most bizarre tales of birth: the women who
refused to push, the fathers who threw shit fits when their sons
turned out to be daughters. There were times Meredith missed
or nearly missed births, when a laboring woman advanced from
two centimeters to ten in the blink of an eye. Maybe this was
one of those times. Meredith didn't have time to call Josh or to
leave Delilah with Bea. She had to go.

"Still," Josh asks, "if the birth was fast, wouldn't she be home
by now?"

Bea looks at Leo standing there in the glow of the porch
light. He looks so small. Every time lightning strikes or thunder booms he shudders, clinging tighter to Josh's leg. But Josh
is so concerned about Meredith and Delilah, he doesn't notice.

Bea says to him, "Hey, buddy. I made cookies. You like chocolate chip?" and he nods a hesitant yes. "They're in the kitchen.
On the counter. You go help yourself, okay? You know the way."

Leo looks to Josh for approval. Josh forces a smile. "Go on,"
he says. "Just take your shoes off." Stepping timidly inside our
home, Leo does as told before scampering off in wet socks for
a cookie, his blue blanket trailing behind.

With Leo gone, Bea asks Josh, "Did you call the police?"

Josh shakes his head. There's something frantic about it. His
eyes are wild.

"Josh," she asks, "did Meredith have a reason to leave?" Bea
doesn't mince words. It's not her way. She gets right to the point,
asking, "Were you guys fighting?"

His reply is resolute. "We weren't fighting," he says. "Not
like you might think. But Meredith wasn't herself lately. She
was stressed out all the time. She was quiet. I wanted to know
why. She wouldn't tell me. All she'd say is that it was nothing,
that she was fine."

"How long had this been going on?" I ask.

"I don't know," he says. "Maybe two weeks." It's been about
two weeks since I last saw Meredith. I remember that night,
Bea's thirtieth birthday. I don't remember Meredith being par-

56

ticularly quiet or stressed. That said, we all put on a good face when we need to.

"It's not like Meredith to keep secrets from you," I say. Josh and Meredith have a marriage others would envy. By their own account, they've always tried to be honest with each other. They made a promise before they got married to never go to bed angry. It's the kind of promise most couples make and then easily break. But not Josh and Meredith.

That said, I overheard the occasional snarky remark from time to time. Sometimes, in summer, with windows open, the sound of angry, arguing voices carried from their house to ours. But that's a marriage. They're not all happy, all the time. Bea and I argue, too.

"Meredith came from a broken family, you know," Josh says. "I did, too. We wanted ours to be different. But I could tell something had her down lately."

"Like what?" I ask.

"I don't know," he says. "I thought maybe she was seeing someone else. Maybe she was falling out of love with me."

His eyes move from Bea to me and back again. He's looking for one of us to either substantiate or disprove his theory. I can't honestly do either because I don't know. Neither can Bea. We know Josh and Meredith well enough, but not enough to know if she was being unfaithful. We're not that kind of friends, and we're just as close to Josh as we are to Meredith. We don't have a loyalty to one over the other. If Meredith was cheating, it isn't the kind of thing she'd tell us.

"That's unlikely," I say. I say it to appease him, but the truth is I never had any reason to believe Meredith wasn't madly in love with Josh.

"Even if that's the case and—worst-case scenario, Meredith is leaving you—why would she take Delilah and leave Leo behind?" Bea asks. "She wouldn't do that, Josh. She adores those kids. Both of them. You know that."

Josh shakes his head. He's at a loss. He asks, "You think I

should call the police, or is it too premature for that? Maybe I should give it the night and see if she comes home on her own. I don't want to blow this out of proportion."

Bea tells him, "If you're worried, Josh, I don't think a call to the police would hurt."

I echo Bea's sentiment. Between the fever, the weather, Meredith not answering her phone, there's plenty of cause for concern. The sudden scourge of missing women also has me worried. I can't get Shelby off my mind.

We convince Josh to come inside. With one last glance at his own home, he grudgingly does. He sits down on our sofa, and while Bea disappears into the kitchen to keep Leo company, Josh calls the police and reports his wife and daughter missing.

MEREDITH

March

The text comes from a number I don't know. It's a 630 area code. Local. I'm in the bathroom with Leo as he soaks in the tub. He has his bath toys lined up on the edge of it and they're taking turns swan diving into the now-lukewarm water. It used to be hot, too hot for Leo to get into. But he's been in there for thirty minutes now playing with his octopus, his whale, his fish. He's having a ball.

Meanwhile I've lost track of time. I have a client in the early stages of labor. We're texting. Her husband wants to take her to the hospital. She thinks it's too soon. Her contractions are six and a half minutes apart. She's absolutely correct. It's too soon. The hospital would just send her home, which is frustrating, not to mention a huge inconvenience for women in labor. And anyway, why labor at the hospital when you can labor in the comfort of your own home? First-time fathers always get skittish. It does their wives no good. By the time I get to them, more times than not, the woman in labor is the more calm of the two. I have to focus my attention on pacifying a nervous husband. It's not what they're paying me for.

I tell Leo one more minute until I shampoo his hair, and then fire off a quick text, suggesting my client have a snack to keep her energy up, herself nourished. I recommend a nap, if her body will let her. The night ahead will be long for all of us. Childbirth, especially when it comes to first-time moms, is a marathon, not a sprint.

Josh is home. He's in the kitchen cleaning up from dinner while Delilah plays. Delilah's due up next in the tub. By the time I leave, the bedtime ritual will be done or nearly done. I feel good about that, hating the times I leave Josh alone with so much to do.

I draw up my text and then hit Send. The reply is immediate, that all too familiar ping that comes to me at all hours of the day or night.

I glance down at the phone in my hand, expecting it's my client with some conditioned reply. *Thx.*

Instead: I know what you did. I hope you die.

Beside the text is a picture of a grayish skull with large, black eye sockets and teeth. The symbol of death.

My muscles tense. My heart quickens. I feel thrown off. The small bathroom feels suddenly, overwhelmingly, oppressive. It's steamy, moist, hot. I drop down to the toilet and have a seat on the lid. My pulse is loud, audible in my own ears. I stare at the words before me, wondering if I've misread. Certainly I've misread. Leo is asking, "Is it a minute, Mommy?" I hear his little voice, muffled by the ringing in my ears. But I'm so thrown by the cutthroat text that I can't speak.

I glance at the phone again. I haven't misread.

The text is not from my client in labor. It's not from any client of mine whose name and number is stored in my phone. As far as I can tell, it's not from anyone I know.

A wrong number, then, I think. Someone sent this to me by

accident. It has to be. My first thought is to delete it, to pretend this never happened. To make it disappear. Out of sight, out of mind.

But then I think of whoever sent it just sending it again or sending something worse. I can't imagine anything worse.

I decide to reply. I'm careful to keep it to the point, to not sound too judgy or fault-finding because maybe the intended recipient really did do something awful—stole money from a children's cancer charity—and the text isn't as egregious as it looks at first glance.

I text: You have the wrong number.

The response is quick.

I hope you rot in hell, Meredith.

The phone slips from my hand. I yelp. The phone lands on the navy blue bath mat, which absorbs the sound of its fall.

Meredith.

Whoever is sending these texts knows my name. The texts are meant for me.

A second later Josh knocks on the bathroom door. I spring from the toilet seat, and stretch down for the phone. The phone has fallen facedown. I turn it over. The text is still there on the screen, staring back at me.

Josh doesn't wait to be let in. He opens the door and steps right inside. I slide the phone into the back pocket of my jeans before Josh has a chance to see.

"Hey," he says, "how about you save some water for the fish."

Leo complains to Josh that he is cold. "Well, let's get you out of the bath," Josh says, stretching down to help him out of the water.

"I need to wash him still," I admit. Before me, Leo's teeth chatter. There are goose bumps on his arm that I hadn't noticed before. He is cold, and I feel suddenly guilty, though it's mired in confusion and fear. I hadn't been paying any attention to Leo. There is bathwater spilled all over the floor, but his hair is still bone-dry.

"You haven't washed him?" Josh asks, and I know what he's thinking: that in the time it took him to clear the kitchen table, wash pots and pans and wipe down the sinks, I did nothing. He isn't angry or accusatory about it. Josh isn't the type to get angry.

"I have a client in labor," I say by means of explanation. "She keeps texting," I say, telling Josh that I was just about to wash Leo. I drop to my knees beside the tub. I reach for the shampoo. In the back pocket of my jeans, the phone again pings. This time, I ignore it. I don't want Josh to know what's happening, not until I get a handle on it for myself.

Josh asks, "Aren't you going to get that?" I say that it can wait. I focus on Leo, on scrubbing the shampoo onto his hair, but I'm anxious. I move too fast so that the shampoo suds get in his eye. I see it happening, but all I can think to do is wipe it from his forehead with my own soapy hands. It doesn't help. It makes it worse.

Leo complains. Leo isn't much of a complainer. He's an easygoing kid. "Ow," is all that he says, his tiny wet hands going to his eyes, though shampoo in the eye burns like hell.

"Does that sting, baby?" I ask, feeling contrite. But I'm bursting with nervous energy. There's only one thought racing through my mind. *I hope you rot in hell, Meredith.*

Who would have sent that, and why? Whoever it is knows me. They know my name. They're mad at me for something I've done. Mad enough to wish me dead. I don't know anyone like that. I can't think of anything I've done to upset someone enough that they'd want me dead.

I grab the wet washcloth draped over the edge of the tub. I try handing it to Leo, so that he can press it to his own eyes. But my hands shake as I do. I wind up dropping the washcloth into the bath. The tepid water rises up and splashes him in the eyes. This time he cries.

"Oh, buddy," I say, "I'm so sorry, it slipped."

But as I try again to grab it from the water and hand it to him, I drop the washcloth for a second time. I leave it where it is, letting Leo fish it out of the water and wipe his eyes for himself. Meanwhile Josh stands two feet behind, watching.

My phone pings again. Josh says, "Someone is really dying to talk to you."

Dying. It's all that I hear.

My back is to Josh, thank God. He can't see the look on my face when he says it.

"What's that?" I ask.

"Your client," Josh says. I turn to him. He motions to my phone jutting out of my back pocket. "She really needs you. You should take it, Mer," he says softly, accommodatingly, and only then do I think about my client in labor and feel guilty. What if it is her? What if her contractions are coming more quickly now and she does need me?

Josh says, "I can finish up with Leo while you get ready to go," and I acquiesce, because I need to get out of here. I need to know if the texts coming to my phone are from my client or if they're coming from someone else.

I rise up from the floor. I scoot past Josh in the door, brushing against him. His hand closes around my upper arm as I do, and he draws me in for a hug. "Everything okay?" he asks, and I say yes, fine, sounding too chipper even to my own ears. Everything is not okay.

"I'm just thinking about my client," I say. "She's had a stillbirth before, at thirty-two weeks. She never thought she'd get this far. Can you imagine that? Losing a baby at thirty-two weeks?"

Josh says no. His eyes move to Leo and he looks saddened by it. I feel guilty for the lie. It's not this client but another who lost a baby at thirty-two weeks. When she told me about it, I was completely torn up. It took everything in me not to cry as she described for me the moment the doctor told her her baby didn't have a heartbeat. Labor was later induced, and she had to

63

push her dead baby out with only her mother by her side. Her husband was deployed at the time. After, she was snowed under by guilt. Was it her fault the baby died? A thousand times I held her hand and told her no. I'm not sure she ever believed me.

My lie has the desired effect. Josh stands down, and asks if I need help with anything before I leave. I say no, that I'm just going to change my clothes and go.

I step out of the bathroom. In the bedroom, I close the door. I grab my scrub bottoms and a long-sleeved T-shirt from my drawer. I lay them on the bed, but before I get dressed, I pull my phone out of my pocket. I take a deep breath and hold it in, summoning the courage to look. I wonder what waits there. More nasty threats? My heart hammers inside me. My knees shake.

I take a look. There are two messages waiting for me.

The first: Water broke. Contractions 5 min apart.

And then: Heading to hospital.—M.

I release my pent-up breath. The texts are from my client's husband, sent from her phone. My legs nearly give in relief, and I drop down to the edge of the bed, forcing myself to breathe. I inhale long and deep. I hold it in until my lungs become uncomfortable. When I breathe out, I try and force away the tension.

But I can't sit long because my client is advancing quickly. I need to go.

LEO

NOW

To be straight, I never thought they were going to find you. I gave that up a long time ago. In all honesty I kind of wish they hadn't 'cause Dad and I were getting along just fine without you. It took him long enough to get over you in the first place. Now you've gone and reopened the wound, made him mourn for Mom all over again as if she's only just died.

The truth is, Dad was never much of a dad to me until he got over missing you. But now you're back and, in his eyes, you're all that matters.

That's not to say I didn't think about you. I thought about you a lot when you were gone, though all I ever knew was the absence of you. I knew I was supposed to have a big sister, but didn't. I knew that compared to you, I was second-tier.

There's a room in our house that's yours. I don't ever remember anyone living in there. It's pink, that's all I know, 'cause I'm not supposed to go in there and mess it up. It's off-limits. Dad pretends it's something sacred and holy, but all it is, is an old dusty room.

At school they treat me like some abnormality because of you. Everyone's supposed to be nice to me because I'm the kid whose mom is dead and whose sister is gone. The truth is, nobody's nice to me. They treat me like a freak instead.

I don't remember having a sister. I can't be sad about it. When you were gone, I tried to remember. I wanted to remember. But turns out, kid memories are weird. I spent probably too much time trying to learn about implicit and explicit memories, like why I can't remember us playing together when we were little, or Mom singing me to sleep, but the smell of bacon always comes as a punch to the gut, and I don't know why.

Dad tells me you used to push me on the swing in our backyard. We still have that swing. It's no ordinary swing but is instead a scrap of wood with two thick strings that hangs from a tree. You probably don't remember this, but when I was three—and you were five—you pushed me so hard I fell face-first off the swing. I don't remember it, either. But Dad's told that story so many times it's like I do. It's like I can convince myself that I remember what it felt like when I let go of the strings, fell forward and face-planted to the ground. It left me with a scar over my eye. The scar I've still got, but the memory of it is gone. They're not false memories because they really happened. They're just false to me. There's a difference.

I don't know why I'm telling you this. You probably don't care.

When you were gone and I wanted to feel close to you, I Googled your name. You're all over the internet, you know. A recap, mostly, of the last few days before you went missing. Details about the search and what happened to Mom, potential sightings that never panned out, like the lady who said she saw you at some IHOP in Jacksonville, right across the street from the used-car dealer where she worked. Dad booked a flight that very night, left me behind and went to Florida where he searched for you for days. You never turned up. Not a year later, some man said he spotted you at a Safeway in Redwood City,

California, and after that, a truck driver swore he saw you at World's Largest Truck Stop. Dad went to those places, too, but every time he came back empty-handed and sad.

There's a reward for your return, you know. There's nothing people won't do for money, even lie.

Online there are the conspiracy theories, too. My favorite is the newspaper article from the Macy's Thanksgiving Day Parade, 2015, where people swear some girl in the background of a black-and-white photo is you. That photo is all over the internet now. That girl, whoever she is, in famous, or infamous, or whatever. The cops were never able to identify her, and yet there are whole sites devoted to that picture, like *Find Delilah*, which some obsessed nobody started up in the hopes of finding you and earning that reward.

Ten grand the reward is up to now. That woman who found you hit the jackpot.

But for as much as people think the internet knows everything, the one thing it doesn't say is that the girl who came back isn't the same one who disappeared.

KATE

May

Bea is in bed when the police finally come. It takes over an hour. With weather conditions as they are, emergencies abound. The police and paramedics have been kept busy lately, rescuing people from flooded roads and homes.

The officers arrive without lights and sirens. They slip nearly invisibly down the darkened street, pulling to the curb and parking in front of Josh and Meredith's house.

When he called to report Meredith and Delilah missing, Josh was told that an officer was on his way, and so he'd left Bea and me and carried Leo home, to get him to bed before they came.

When will Mommy be home? Leo had asked as they left, chocolate on his fingers and lips, woozy with fatigue.

I open the front door and step out onto the covered porch with a throw blanket wrapped around me, my feet bare. I leave the porch light off, feeling invisible in the darkness, though I stay alert. It's hard not to be scared after all that's happened. I have to wonder if some monster is stalking women in the neighborhood, or if what's happened to Shelby and Meredith are two isolated incidents. I back myself into the corner on the porch, where nothing can come at me from behind. The wooden porch is damp on my feet. It's still raining, but the rain is slower now, the night more tame. It's quieted down to a peaceful drizzle. I stand in the darkness, staring through the trees that disrupt my view of the street. I watch as two officers make their way to Josh and Meredith's house, where Josh pulls the front door open before they have a chance to knock and wake up Leo.

I hear their voices, one male and one female. They introduce themselves. Josh says hello and tells them his name. He invites them inside. The officers step in and he closes the door. The blinds are open in their house, so I can see Josh and the officers, but I can't hear what they say. There's a chill to the night air, and soon I'm cold. I wait outside awhile, until five minutes turns into fifteen, and I step back in, watching through a window until, forty minutes later, they finally leave.

I wait in vain for Josh to call or text with news. I think about calling him, but don't want to overstep. I try and work on my records, but my mind is too agitated to focus. All I can think about is Meredith and Delilah. It's after eleven o'clock and they still aren't home. After this many hours missing and this late at night, it's hard to believe something innocuous has happened. My mind gets flooded with images of Meredith's car submerged in the river or Meredith and Delilah taken along with Shelby. The thought terrifies me, and I force back tears, telling myself no, that whatever happened to Shelby is far different than what's happened to Meredith and Delilah.

It was ten days ago that Bea and I first woke to the news. We hadn't known Shelby, but it was all over Facebook and then, later in the day, in the paper and on the news: *Local Woman Missing*.

Bea and I watched as police cruisers surveilled the neighborhood, as police dogs went in and out of the Tebow home to pick up and track Shelby's scent. The police came around asking questions. Until I saw her face on the news, I didn't know what Shelby looked like; I'd never heard of her before. Ours is a large suburb, with a population that tops a hundred thousand. You can't know everyone.

According to her husband, Shelby had gone for a run that night. From what we read, it was after ten when she left. It was dark outside. Bea and I both thought the same thing: that was too late for a woman to be out running alone. But, according to her husband, they had a new baby at home. Shelby stayed home with the baby. Her husband worked long hours. When he came home that night, they had a late dinner together and then she hung around until the next time the baby needed to be fed. This wasn't the first time she'd gone running late at night, because some days it was the only time she had to herself.

Needless to say, she never came home.

Shelby's husband, Jason Tebow, was the first to come under suspicion. The first and the only, as far as we know. He's still a suspect. Secrets were quickly smoked out by reporters and the police, and became common knowledge. Friends of Jason's reported that Shelby had a flair for the melodramatic. They said she was a liar and a con. There was plenty of gossip all over the social media sites. The police department posted the details of Shelby's disappearance to their Facebook page. The comments were ruthless. *That girl wouldn't know the truth if it hit her in the face*, someone said.

Shelby's side fired back. They accused Jason's friends of slander. Shelby, they said, was none of these things. She's kind, loving. She always put others first. They said instead that Jason had been unfaithful since the baby was born, and probably before. Fatherhood was apparently not his cup of tea, and neither was monogamy.

It was easy to assume he'd done something to her.

But now, in light of Meredith and Delilah's disappearance, a thought sows fear into my mind. What if it wasn't domestic violence? What if there's a serial kidnapper on the loose?

MEREDITH

March

The hospital parking garage is empty when I leave. It's three-thirty in the morning. I was with my client for nearly seven hours, helping her deliver a beautiful baby boy that she and her husband named Zeppelin. It's horrible. He's only hours old and already I'm imagining him being made fun of at school. But no one asked for my opinion. The husband, Matt, is an amateur guitar player and a diehard fan of '70s rock. They'd made up their minds weeks ago.

All night my phone was quiet. The only person to text was Josh, who said good-night before he went to bed and told me he loved me. He doesn't ever ask how things are progressing or what time I'll be home. He knows better than to ask. He knows I don't know. Childbirth is rarely predictable.

This delivery was relatively quick, as firstborns go. My focus was on my client and her baby. It was a welcome reprieve. I didn't have time to think about anything else, like those awful texts.

But now, as I step onto the fourth floor of the parking garage, they come rushing back to me. I spot my car on the other side of the garage. I move quickly, a speed walk, just shy of a run. There are only a handful of cars here. Visiting hours ended eons ago. The cars still here belong to patients and hospital staff. Everything about the parking garage is cliché. It's poorly lit, dirty and claustrophobic. There's a foul smell to it because the garage walls are solid, with little ventilation. Even without the texts, the garage sparks fear. It belongs in a movie scene. It always scares me, but tonight especially so.

I reach into my bag. I carry pepper spray with me because long ago Josh made me. He's always hated the idea of me out on the street or in abandoned parking garages late at night. I told him he was being ridiculous. I swore nothing bad was going to happen to me. But now I'm grateful for the pepper spray. I've had the same canister for years. It's probably expired, the ingredients degraded so that they wouldn't be much help if I needed them. But the weight of it in my hand is a relief. It's better than nothing.

I keep my head up as I walk. I stay alert, scanning the parking garage with every step. There's no one here. The parking garage is empty. Still, there are darkened voids where I can't see, like in the corners of the garage where the lights don't reach. There are stairwells at each corner; the doors are open, only a blackened hollow remains. If someone was there, standing in that blackened hollow, three feet back from the open door, I wouldn't know. I also wouldn't know if someone was behind me. I try to listen for footsteps. But there is some sort of supply or exhaust fan whirring in the garage. It dampens all other sounds. All I can hear is that fan. Twice I glance back to see if someone's there, and no one is. Still, it doesn't fully suppress the fear. As soon as I turn back, the fear of being followed returns.

I dig again into my bag. I find my cell phone, grip it in my hand. I don't want to call and wake Josh; I'd never hear the end of it. If he knew I was scared, he'd want to send a whole brigade with me to every birth I went, to make sure I was safe.

I consider a call to Kate or Cassandra or Bea. It would be a great comfort to have someone on the other end of the line, keeping me company. But it's three-thirty in the morning. I can't call and wake someone up.

I hasten my pace. By the time I'm halfway across the garage, I've broken into a run. I'm sweating, my breath coming so fast that I have trouble catching it. My pulse pounds in my ears.

I reach the car. I yank open the door and nearly dive into the driver's seat. I slam the door closed. I tap the button and activate the locks, but that's only a partial relief because there's still the fear that when I look in my rearview mirror, someone will be there. My fears aren't unfounded, because of the text messages. *I hope you die. I hope you rot in hell.* I have every reason to be scared, though I've tried my best to convince myself that the texts are only a prank, that someone with a sick sense of humor is sending them, though I don't know anyone like that.

I thrust my keys into the ignition. I start the car. Before I can throw it into Reverse, there's a tap on my window. I scream, seeing only blackness filling the glass. Someone is standing beside the car. I can't make out a face. I grab for the pepper spray. The only other things I have to use are an ice scraper and my keys.

The figure squats down and there in the window is Jeanette, the midwife.

I throw my hand to my heart. "Oh God," I say, lowering the window and forcing myself to smile, to relax, "you scared the shit out of me, Jeanette."

I take a deep breath. Jeanette is here in the parking garage with me. No one will hurt me while Jeanette is here.

"Sorry!" she replies, still on a high from the birth. They can be vitalizing sometimes, especially the ones like this that don't take twenty-four hours only to wind up in surgery. "I thought you saw me," Jeanette says. "I've been trailing you for a while. I called out for you."

I tell her, "I didn't hear you or I would have stopped."

Then she gets a mischievous grin on her face and says to me, *"Zeppelin,"* and we both laugh. "The kids will have a field day with that."

"I feel sorry for the poor boy," I say. "He'll grow up hating his parents for it."

"Whatever happened to Thomas and James?" Jeanette asks. Jeanette is older than me. She's more traditional.

"Come on, Jeanette," I say. "Don't you know that Thomas and James have fallen out of rotation in recent years? These days it's all Jacobs and Noahs and Masons."

"And apparently Zeppelins."

"It's an atrocity," I say. We have a good laugh.

"It's getting late," Jeanette says. In just a few hours, the sun will rise. "You better get home and try and sleep before your own babies are up."

We say our goodbyes. I watch as Jeanette makes her way to her car parked farther down. Once she's safely in, I spin out of the parking garage, going fast. The relief washes over me when my car finally reaches the street outside. On the street there are other cars, building lights, streetlights. It's still hours away from dawn, but the moon is nearly full, giving off additional light. A twenty-four-hour McDonald's calls for me, and though I'm usually not a fan of fast food, I consider a run through the drive-through because it's been hours since I've had a thing to eat. I'm famished, craving something greasy and quick.

The relief is short-lived because soon after comes the familiar ping of my phone. A text message. It could be Josh, wanting an update. Now that Tuesday has become Wednesday, childcare arrangements may need to be made. He leaves for work early, by six o'clock. He'll need to find something to do with the kids if I'm not home by then, though I will be; he just doesn't know it yet. He's being proactive.

I grab my phone from the passenger's seat to see what he's said.

But the text message isn't from Josh. It comes from the same unfamiliar number as the rest.

Get home safe, it says.

LEO

NOW

Dad took home videos of us when we were kids. Hours of them. Some nights, when he's being especially pathetic, he makes me watch. The girl in those videos is giddy, silly. She smiles a lot. She's always giggling. You, on the other hand, are dead serious. You look shook, scared. You're nothing like that girl anymore. You're someone new.

I'm at school when Dad gets the call from the police. He comes to get me. It's fourth period honors algebra when he comes, which most people hate but I like because it comes easy to me. Apparently I'm good at math. Not that you care. The whole stupid class gets fired up when they call me down over the intercom because they think I'm in trouble. The truth? No one likes me. I'm the weird kid, the freak, the loser. I have you to thank for that. I don't get in trouble, though. The only time I get in trouble is when the other kids tell lies about me.

Dad's waiting in the office when I come down. His eyes are red and watery like he's been crying, which is embarrassing as fuck: when kids at school see your dad cry. Todd Felding walks by and sees and I know I'm never going to live this one down.

Dad and I leave and, together, we go get you. They've got you in a room at the police station, and it's just you and the lady cop. She has a name. It's Detective Rowlings. I just don't like calling her that. Dad calls her that sometimes, but mostly he calls her Carmen. I'm not entirely sure, but if I had to guess, I'd say Dad and the lady cop have hooked up before. She's been there from the beginning and is, as Dad says, *invested*. Dad's so blind that he can't see she's got the hots for him. He thinks it's all about solving a cold case. Instead, it's about trying to get into his pants, which I'm sure she has more than once.

Dad doesn't know it but I've read the texts the lady cop sends him. They're mushy, sloppy, sentimental. They make me want to vomit. She massages Dad's ego, tells him she admires how brave he is, how gentle, how honest. I've been thinking about you, she sometimes texts. You and Leo are on my mind all the time.

Gag.

They've got a plate of food for you. You're eating. Except that it's like you forgot how to eat 'cause you're doing it all wrong.

You're thin. You've got pale skin. Your hands shake. Dad is so sure you're you that he rushes right up to you and gives you a hug. You go stiff. It looks to me like you stop breathing. You try to pull back, but Dad won't let you. He's crying. He's holding on for dear life. The lady cop has to lay a hand on his arm and tell Dad to give you some room. I'm embarrassed for him. I feel my own cheeks get hot because of the way he acts.

"You look just like your mom," he says, cupping your face in his hand and, from the pictures I've seen, you do. You both have red hair, which is something because only about two percent of people have red hair.

I hang back, by the door. I don't know you.

Dad and the lady cop talk a long time. They stand too close. A DNA test is pending, but that doesn't matter because Dad already knows it's you. The lady cop suggests you get checked out by a doctor. She wants to check for evidence that you've been sexually abused. Dad looks like he might be sick when she says those words. *Sexually abused.*

"Like a rape kit?" Dad asks.

I've heard of that before. The lady cop says yes. She touches his hand, her voice going soft. "It's precautionary, Josh. We don't know for sure that she's been sexually abused. But if we can find the person who did this to her, it will help convict him." She says that there might be DNA evidence on you that will aid in their investigation. I don't like that she calls Dad Josh. I also don't like that she touches his hand when she says it.

Dad's torn. He wants to help the police, but he doesn't want to traumatize you. The line between these things is thin. Eventually Dad says yes and we go to the hospital, where we sit in the lobby and wait. You go into the exam room with the nurse alone. Dad offers to go with you, to hold your hand, which is weird as fuck. The lady cop tells him no. She says it gentler than that. "I don't think that would be a good idea, Josh." You're not six years old anymore, but try telling that to Dad. The lady cop sits with us during the whole entire exam. "You shouldn't be alone," she says to Dad, though he isn't alone. He has me. I wish that she would leave.

It takes so long I think it will never be done.

They confiscate your clothes. They send you home with something else to wear.

There's never any question of if you are who you say you are, though the DNA results won't be back for another day. Child services could take you for the night. Child services is supposed to take you for the night. But after all that you've been through, the lady cop breaks the rules and lets Dad and me take you home.

She tells Dad what you told them about where you've been. Dad nearly goes through the roof. "It doesn't make sense," he says, and he's right, seeing as how Mom was found dead of a self-inflicted knife wound with a note: *You'll never find her. Don't even try.*

The note went on to say that you were safe, that you were fine.

If what you say is true, you weren't fine. You were far from fine. But maybe you're lying. No one thinks about that but me.

We leave with promises to take you to a shrink and to our own doctor for a follow-up. They're worried about malnutrition, muscle atrophy, physical abuse; they're worried about your eyes. You have to wear special sunglasses because you haven't seen daylight in eleven years. At home, we're supposed to keep the blinds closed. They're worried about your feet. They're wrapped in bandages. If you had shoes, they took those, too.

They're also worried about your mental state. It's clear to see you're not all there. You're not right in the head. You're scared as heck, wasted and emaciated. You should be seventeen but no one would ever think you're seventeen. You could pass for ten. You've got no boobs. You're about four and a half feet tall. You weigh maybe eighty pounds.

We drive home. You ride in the back seat. You say nothing.

It's a media circus when we get home. That's what Dad says as he steers the car through a crowd of reporters. *A media circus.* It makes me think of the reporters as clowns, as circus freaks, which they are. They step back so Dad doesn't run them over. Still, they take pictures through the car window; they shout questions at you. Those farther back crane their necks for a measly look at you. There are a butt load of them. They fight each other for a square foot of our lawn, which Dad says they aren't supposed to be on, anyway, because that's trespassing. He lays on the horn and they step farther back from the car. At the sound of Dad's horn, you spaz out, getting all twitchy. I feel sorry for you. But I don't know what to say to make it better, so I say nothing.

I ask Dad how they know you're here. Dad says some shyster at the station or the hospital probably leaked to the media that you were back. Otherwise how would they know? Your miraculous return is supposed to be kept on the down-low.

Dad's angry about it because if what you told the lady cop is true, then there's still someone out there looking for you. And if that's the case, these reporters will lead them right to our door.

MEREDITH

11 YEARS BEFORE

March

Dawn comes quickly. The morning after a birth is never easy. I wake to Josh leaning over me, kissing me before he leaves.

"What time is it?" I ask, bleary-eyed. I try to shade my eyes from the morning sun that streams in through the break in the curtains.

"Six," he says. "There's coffee on the table beside you. What time did you get home?"

"Around four."

When I got home, it took me a while to fall asleep. I was scared, wondering if the same person who texted me had also followed me home. I thought about waking Josh and telling him what happened. But I didn't want to worry him unnecessarily. Josh already worries. He's said it before, how he doesn't like me driving home alone in the middle of the night after a birth. Many, if not all, of the hospitals I visit have sketchy parking garages. Some of the hospitals are in the city, in rougher neighborhoods that I have to walk through to get to my car. There aren't many people on the street after nightfall. I've always been dismissive of his concerns. If anything, I've agreed to the pepper spray, to downloading some app on my phone that tracks my whereabouts all of the time. Josh feels better because of it. *This way,* he said—when he convinced me to download the app and accept his friend invite—*if you go missing, I can find you.* He said it in jest and we both laughed at the time. But now it's not funny.

It works both ways. I can keep tabs on Josh, too, though I never have.

Josh has suggested before that I shut down my private doula practice and teach yoga full-time. He likes that yoga classes are held during business hours. That the hours are predictable. That the clientele is primarily female. I don't tell Josh about what happened last night because he'd want to reopen this discussion. That's not an argument I want to have. I love the practice of yoga. But teaching yoga can be repetitive, mundane. I couldn't do that for the rest of my life. I love what I do. I love the miracle of birth.

"What'd they have?" Josh asks, and I tell him a boy.

"Zeppelin," I say.

He pulls a face. "As in the blimp?" he asks.

I laugh. "As in the band," I say, not sure it makes it any better.

"Do you want me to wake the kids?" Josh asks, but there's no need because I hear them down the hall, their feet hobbling toward our room. They appear in the doorway, all bedhead and out of joint. Delilah clutches her doll, Leo his beloved blue blankie. He never goes anywhere without that thing. He hangs on Delilah's arm, and already, at six in the morning, she's whining at him to stop touching her. Leo deifies Delilah. He can't get enough of her. All he wants is to be with her, in any capacity. He'll play hours of school, of house. Delilah, on the other hand, wishes he was a girl, a big sister preferably.

"Come on, guys," Josh says as he stands before the floor mirror, tying a half-Windsor knot into his houndstooth tie. Josh always wears a tie to work. He's always well groomed. He wants to look good for his clients because looking good fosters confidence and respect. I get that. I stare at his reflection in the mirror. My husband is incredibly handsome. *How did I get so lucky?* I often wonder.

The kids jump into bed with me. Before Josh leaves, he tells them to be good for Mommy. Delilah finds the remote and turns the TV on. Together we sit quietly in bed watching *Bubble Guppies*. Delilah lays her head on my lap and Leo snuggles in closely beside me. I wrap my arm around him, wishing we could stay like this all day. Ever since Delilah started kindergarten, our days go by exceptionally fast. I miss the long, lazy days we used to have, when they were younger. But before nine o'clock comes, Delilah will be in school, Leo at the sitter's and me at work.

I reach for the coffee Josh has left me and take a sip. An hour of sleep is never enough. The exhaustion wears me down, makes me feel physically ill.

My phone is on the table beside me, volume turned up because it has to be. I never have the luxury of powering it down at night, because a client might need me. I reach for it in the hopes that I somehow misunderstood the text messages from yesterday. I take a look, ever hopeful, yet there they are, just the same as they were last night, instantly evoking fear.

I hope you rot in hell, Meredith.

KATE

11 YEARS BEFORE

May

The next morning when I wake up, Bea is already gone. It was nearly one o'clock by the time I went to bed. I only got five hours of sleep, and even that was intermittent at best, because I kept thinking of Meredith and Delilah, hoping that by morning there'd be good news. Hoping that by morning they'd be found.

Now I take the servant stairs down to the kitchen and find that Bea is in her studio, working again because the back door is open. There are two staircases in our house, one in the front, and this one, which is narrow, curved and tucked away in back, a passageway from the second floor to the kitchen, dating back to times when servants weren't meant to be seen. It's one of the reasons I first fell in love with the old home, for its history.

Bea must have taken her own breakfast out to the studio to eat while she works. She's left me a plate. The cool, humid morning air comes in through the open door.

Bea had the detached garage converted into a music studio

when she moved in with me. It's a charming place, though one I rarely go inside because it's Bea's workplace, much in the same way that she doesn't ever show up at my office. Boundaries are important in a relationship.

Bea writes her own music in the garage. She records it. I know I shouldn't, but still I try and listen in sometimes because Bea has a sexy voice. It's husky and rich and thick. You'd think she smoked a pack a day by the sound of her voice, but she doesn't. But unless she leaves the door open by mistake I can't hear inside.

I met Bea six years ago at a bar in the city where she was performing. It was the summer before vet school. I was working as a cocktail waitress to earn extra cash for school. We fell in love. Two months later, I left for school. We kept in touch; Bea came to visit me. After graduation, I came back, got a job, bought a house.

When Bea moved in with me, she didn't want to piss the neighbors off with her music. It's the reason we had the garage converted, making it soundproof. She figured the neighbors would already be pissed off enough with two gay women living on the street. The idea of a house in suburbia made Bea's skin crawl; she wasn't that type. But she did it for me. The house was close and convenient to my work. Bea could work anywhere.

The house is a yellow 1904 Italianate in our town's historic district. It sits just a stone's throw away from a college campus, in an area more liberal than conservative. It's romantic, with brick walkways and hundred-year-old trees. But that doesn't mean there isn't the occasional hatred and bigotry. Because no matter where you go, you can't get away from that.

Bea no longer performs in bars. These days, the only time I hear her sing is in the shower. For someone who loves to perform for a crowd, she's strictly against private performances.

When Bea is writing music, she disconnects from the rest of the world. She tunes it completely out. It's when she's gone the longest that I know she's lost herself in her music and I'm happy for her because of it. Bea is a born musician. She taught voice and guitar lessons for years, performed in bars and nightclubs. But that didn't satisfy her. It wasn't what she saw herself doing for the rest of her life. Now she's working on an album.

That said, Bea isn't some freeloader. She carries her weight financially. She's sold some of the songs that she's written and has a nice inheritance from a dead grandma who was apparently rich. I never met her. She was dead before I met Bea. Not only did Bea get her money from her; she also got her name, Beatrice, which is one of those vintage names someone else might hate, but not Bea. She adored her grandmother. A picture of them together sits on Bea's nightstand.

When my back is turned, Bea steps inside. She closes the door and comes to me, wrapping her arms around me from behind. I turn to her, let her envelop me. Bea is in her pajamas still, the cotton shorts and Kurt Cobain shirt she wore to sleep. Her dark hair hangs long and straight because somehow, inexplicably, Bea never gets bedhead.

"I want to jump in the shower before they get here," she says, *they* meaning the subcontractors who are working on our home. The house is old and we're in the midst of a messy renovation. The house is full of historic elements, which we love: the ceiling medallions; the original, oversize windows; the library with its built-ins; the servant stairs. They tell a story. But the bathrooms and the kitchen are seventies-era, thanks to some previous owner who did a hack job on them. They lack the charm the rest of the house still has. We're getting those redone, brought back to a modern version of their original state, to restore the history and authenticity of the home.

There's a combination lockbox on our front door. The workers come and go whenever they want. Their workday starts as early as seven a.m. If we aren't quick to shower in the morning, they catch us in our pajamas. These men know their way around our house because they're here even when Bea and I aren't. It had never bothered me before, but now, in light of what's happened over the last twelve hours, it does.

The contractor came recommended from Josh, who had work done on his own home, a 1890s Queen Anne. Apparently they're whizzes at keeping the integrity of historic homes. Meredith, though pleased with the final result, hated the invasion of privacy. She couldn't wait for their renovation to be through, she'd told us, saying how glad she was to have that lockbox removed from her door, to regain sole possession of her home afterward. I'm thinking now that Bea and I should take it a step further than that and have the locks replaced, because who's to say one of the subcontractors couldn't have duplicated the key? It makes my stomach hurt to think about someone besides Bea and me having a key to our home.

"Any news from Josh?" I ask. It's early. I don't expect Bea to have heard from him, but as it turns out, she has.

"I just saw him," she says, telling me that he was in the backyard, letting his dog out.

"What did he say?" I ask Bea, measuring out the coffee and pouring it into the filter. I hope for good news, but it's not.

"Meredith still isn't home," she says.

"He hasn't heard from her?"

"No," she says. "Not a word. The police came last night."

"I know. I saw them. What did they say? What are they doing to find her and Delilah?"

"Not enough, according to Josh. He's trying to organize a search party himself," Bea says. "He was outside, making calls this morning, appealing to family and friends to help. I told him we'd help," she says.

I nod and say, "Yes, of course. Anything. Whatever he needs."

I have the day off work. But even if I didn't, I would stay home and help search. Meredith and Delilah need me now. Finding them is all that matters.

LEO

NOW

That first night in our house you hardly speak. You don't say anything unless Dad says something first. You keep your head hung low. You don't look at us.

You call Dad *sir*. He tells you not to, but you do it, anyway, 'cause you can't stop. Every time you say it, Dad dies a little inside. I see it in his eyes.

You cower in the corner of rooms, looking scared as hell. You don't know what to do with yourself, with your hands, with your eyes. Dad tells you to have a seat because he's so worried about your feet, which were full of glass and thorns and flint when the cops got to you. Docs had to pick it all out with tweezers. You didn't flinch, 'cause I'm guessing that's not the worst thing that's ever happened to you.

When Dad tells you to have a seat, you drop to the floor. We're in the kitchen when it happens, in a room with six chairs. Yet you pick the floor. Dad looks shook but goes on as if it's no big deal because he doesn't want you to feel all weirded out by calling you out for it. So instead he makes turkey sandwiches and we all eat on the stupid floor, except you don't eat much because two sandwiches in one day is like five hundred more calories than you're used to, and your stomach can't handle it. You try to eat. You look hell-bent on eating, but you also look like you could puke.

I tell you, "You don't have to eat it if you don't want to," because I can see in your eyes that you think you do.

When Dad goes to take your plate away, you pull back fast. You whimper a little, like you think he's going to hit you. It gives Dad pause. Sure, we both know you got roughed up while you were gone. That goes without saying. But knowing it and seeing it are two different things. I feel bad for you, thinking all the time that someone's going to sucker punch you. I've been beaten up by kids at school before. I know what it's like. Except that at school there's always some teacher there to pull kids off me, though that's not necessarily a good thing 'cause I still get in trouble for fighting, and then I get crucified by kids for being a sissy. A one-two punch. But at least I don't get killed.

I doubt you ever had anyone to stand up for you.

I can't help myself. I stare at you. I don't remember what you used to look like, but I've seen videos and the pictures. You look almost the same as you did before, except you're bigger now, though hardly, and what were baby teeth are big and yellow and crooked. Your hair is bald in spots. I see Dad trying not to look at the bald spots, but they're hard to miss. Kids aren't supposed to be bald.

Later I ask Dad why he thinks you're going bald. I ask if he thinks you have cancer. He gets mad at me for that. He says of course you don't have cancer but he never says why he thinks you're going bald. I take my question to the internet. You might have alopecia. But more likely, you're compulsively pulling your own hair out or it's falling out because of stress. When I read that, I feel like a jerk for thinking you have cancer. I tell myself not to stare at the bald spots anymore because I don't want to give you a complex. I wonder if you even know the bald spots are there.

You talk like a redneck. Which is weird as fuck since you come from an upper-middle-class neighborhood in the Midwest. But you haven't been to school since kindergarten. And whoever had you was probably some redneck meth head, and everything you know, you learned from him.

Though mostly you don't talk, you just say *yes sir* and *no ma'am*.

That night, the cops keep watch on our house. They sit parked in their police car, same as the news crews do, everyone vying for a piece of you.

MEREDITH

March

I've just stepped outside. The day is expected to be unseasonably warm, nearing sixty degrees. The morning starts off cold. It's only March. There are robins in the trees, making their way back from their winter homes.

The kids and I are running late. We're rushing. I glance at the time on my phone. It's eight-thirty. I have to get the kids where they need to be, and make it to my yoga class on the other side of town by nine o'clock. I'll never make it.

Cassandra is outside with Piper and Arlo. I see them, heading off to school. The school is a couple blocks away, the distance short enough that the school doesn't provide a bus. We have to walk. Either that or I have to drive Delilah to school. I never like to drive because the drop-off line is a nightmare. Some days I drive just close enough and then let Delilah off, letting her walk the rest of the way alone. I never feel good about it. She's only six years old. But there are other mothers and other children there, and also a crossing guard. Nothing bad will happen to her with so many people around. Delilah is street smart; she knows the way to go. She knows better than to talk to strangers or to be lured in by things like candy or kittens.

But today I won't have to do that. I glance up at Cassandra, Piper and Arlo across the street, heading out of their own home. They look like something out of a magazine. They're completely put together and holding hands as they trot down their stone walkway and to the sidewalk. They're a picture-perfect family. Arlo is a toddler, yet he'll walk the distance without complaint. No one makes a fuss of holding hands.

I look to my own children. Today Delilah wears a dress. I combed her hair and found the elusive part, using a water bottle to tame the flyaway hairs. I managed a shower, and Leo got dressed all by himself, with his pants on the right way for a change. We don't look half-bad ourselves, considering. On the outside, we're put together, too.

But inside I'm all wrought up, my panic and agitation tucked neatly behind a smile. I'm getting by somehow on an hour of sleep.

"Hey, Cassandra," I call out, waving across the street. We speed walk to her and the kids. "Hi, Piper. Hi, Arlo," I say too eagerly. Delilah beams at her friend. She offers a shy wave, one that's only waist-high. She's shy because of Cassandra and me. If there were no adults here, Delilah would be uninhibited. She's the extrovert in our family. I don't know where she gets it. It must be from Josh, not me.

"I'm so glad I saw you," I say. "Perfect timing. Do you mind if Delilah tags along with you to school? We're running late," I say, knowing that Cassandra never has any issue with walking Delilah to school.

"Please," Piper pleads.

Cassandra says, "Yes, sure, of course," which I knew she would. It wasn't like Cassandra was going to say no. They're headed in the same direction that we need to go and, really, one more child isn't a burden.

Delilah tries to run off without saying goodbye. "Come back here, missy," I tease.

She giggles. She rushes back, wrapping her arms around my legs, and I hug back, inhaling the smell of her, a combination of syrup and shampoo. I remind her to be good, to do as Miss Cassandra says. "Okay, Mommy," she says.

I watch them walk away, missing Delilah before she's gone. I remember her first day of day care, that sick feeling in the pit of my stomach at leaving my child with a person I didn't know well. It's lessened over the years, but has never gone completely away. It was hard for me to go back to work after the kids were born, even though it was something I needed to do for myself.

Delilah has broken up the formation. Now Delilah and Piper skip ahead, laughing, while Cassandra and Arlo lag behind, still holding hands.

I feel somewhat guilty for unloading Delilah on Cassandra. Walking the kids to school is a favor I rarely get to repay. But Cassandra is autonomous. She's independent. By her own admission, she doesn't like to ask for help. I never get the chance to reciprocate.

I take Leo to Charlotte's. I head to work. On my way, my phone pings and I break out into a cold sweat. I glance at the phone with reluctance, knowing I have to. It might be a client in labor.

It's not. What it is instead is a variation of the same text I received last night. I gasp and drop my phone, but not before I've read the message.

I know what you did. You'll never get away with it, bitch.

KATE

11 YEARS BEFORE

May

Bea and I meet Josh in his yard just shy of eight o'clock. It's early in the morning, but already he's gathered about a dozen people to search for his missing family. There are more on the way. Still, ours is a grassroots effort. We gather in a circle and talk about places Meredith and Delilah might be. Some ask for details about yesterday, and Josh, rubbing at his forehead, fills them in. He looks wired and high-strung, but also exhausted. His eyes are bloodshot. He's twitchy. I doubt he slept much, if at all. I look around. Leo isn't here. Josh left him with the sitter, Charlotte, I assume. Charlotte watches many kids in the neighborhood. Even Bea and me, without kids of our own, know who she is. She's a staple around here. We see her and the kids out when the weather is nice, parading around the neighborhood. Charlotte is in her late fifties, sixty, maybe. She lives alone with her husband.

I wonder if Leo knows what's happening, if Josh told him.

Does he know that Meredith and Delilah are missing? I doubt it, thinking that would be indigestible to a four-year-old boy. Crayons go missing. Puzzle pieces go missing. Moms and sisters do not go missing. I wonder where Josh told Leo that they are. He would have had to be confused when he woke up and Delilah wasn't there.

Among our search party is the woman who owns the yoga studio where Meredith works. Josh goes to her and apologizes for Meredith's absence yesterday. He says, "I hope it wasn't too much of an inconvenience."

She says it was no inconvenience at all, that she and another teacher split Meredith's classes among themselves, same as they did last week when Meredith was sick, and the week before.

Josh is taken aback, as are Bea and me. We exchange a glance. "What do you mean?" Josh asks, because as far as any of us know, yesterday was the first time Meredith called in sick. I watch Josh's reaction. He's a tall man, a brunette with cool blue eyes. His eyes are moist, the blue turning somehow even more blue because of his tears. Leo, wherever he is, has the same eyes.

The woman feels stupid. She turns red. She's misspoken. She fights for words, saying, "It's just that yesterday was like the third time in two weeks that Meredith has called in sick. You didn't know?" she asks Josh, and he shakes his head. "We were worried. Until a couple weeks ago, Meredith was always so conscientious. This wasn't like her. We thought there was some real health crisis, like cancer or something," and it sounds to me as if she's trying to make light of that—Meredith having cancer—though I wonder if cancer would be preferable to whatever's happened. With cancer she'd have a fighting chance. With this, I don't know.

Another woman speaks. She introduces herself as Jeanette, a midwife with whom Meredith works on occasion. "If I may," she says, explaining that Meredith had very recently made the decision to cut back on her workload, to spend more time with her family. She told Jeanette a week or so ago that she'd be taking on fewer clients, and asked for recommendations of other doulas that she could send inquiries to.

I see in Josh's reaction that he didn't know this, either. His expression turns thoughtful, contemplative, but also sad. He runs his fingers over a mustache and beard. Frown lines appear between his eyes, one deeper than the other. Josh, like Meredith, must be in his midthirties, just slightly older than Bea and me. He's not yet forty. I remember a conversation about whether they would go somewhere exotic when they both turned forty. It wasn't around the corner, but something they had time to think about and decide, years away but still on the horizon.

Bea is the one who comes up with a strategy. It's so like Bea to take charge and be a planner. She divides us into groups with plans to search the town. Bea tells people to drive around looking for Meredith's car, to stop in restaurants and shops and see if Meredith or Delilah has been there recently. Josh gives us the make and model of Meredith's car, as well as the license plate number. The volunteers carve up the town among themselves, using major roads as their guide. Bea and I will stay and canvass the neighborhood, because we live here. Because we know the neighbors, and we know our way around.

Before anyone splits, Bea takes cell phone numbers. She starts a group chat, so we can update each other with news. Josh sends a picture of Meredith over the group chat so we have it to show around. He gets choked up when he scrolls through and finds the image on his own phone. It's a picture of Meredith with Delilah and Leo, taken recently. Meredith is a beautiful woman. In the picture, her hair is gathered into a loose bun on the top of her head. Her skin is fair, covered in freckles, and her eyes are a stunning mineral green. She's clearly of Irish descent, dressed in some kind of embroidered shift dress that's as red as the hair on her head.

I feel a pang of sadness at seeing the image of Meredith, with little Leo and Delilah wrapped beneath each of her slight arms. I pray nothing bad has happened to her or Delilah, who sits beside Meredith in the photograph, tiny and nearly toothless, staring lovingly at her mom and smiling so sweetly it makes my heart hurt.

I may never have kids. Bea and I talked about the possibility of using donor sperm to get one of us pregnant. We got so far as to discuss which of us would be better equipped to carry a baby—Bea, who's larger in stature but also more maternal than me—and whether we'd want a sperm donor we knew or if we'd prefer to keep it anonymous. I wanted to keep it anonymous, but that was too impersonal for Bea. Too cold. She wanted to use the sperm of someone we knew, which felt weird to me. Bea and some man we knew having a child together. That's where the conversation ended.

My eyes move to Bea's now. She stares over my shoulder at the picture. Her eyes are misty like mine.

"They'll turn up," she says, her hand on my arm, and though she sounds so certain, she's thinking the same thing as me: What if they never come back? We've grown close to Josh and Meredith over the years; we've grown close to their kids. "They're fine. They have to be fine," Bea says, voice trembling, fighting tears, and I wonder if it's only wishful thinking.

Are they fine? My gut tells me they're not.

One by one people get in their cars. They pull away, dispersing in different directions. Bea and I turn and move slowly down the sidewalk. We're quiet, each processing what's happening. The idea of something bad having happened to Meredith and Delilah is unfathomable. I won't let my mind go there, no matter how much it keeps drifting. I have to stay positive, for Josh's sake. For Bea's sake. For mine. As we walk, Bea slips her hand into mine. It feels good, having something to hold on to.

We make our way to the first home. I knock and, when Roger Thames answers, I ask if he's seen Meredith. Roger is limping. He threw his back out working on his car, he tells us. That was last week, and he's hardly left the sofa since. He hasn't seen Meredith.

"What's the matter with her?" he asks abruptly.

Bea says, "If you see her, can you just let Josh or us know?" I've never liked Roger much.

We turn and make our way back down the walkway and to the sidewalk, moving on.

"Could she just be at a birth?" asks Gwen, the woman who lives on the opposite side of Meredith and Josh. Gwen is a widow. For three years now, her husband has been dead. Lou Gehrig's disease. I didn't know him well, but I remember that he went quickly. To me it seemed like I'd no sooner heard the news than I read the obituary in the paper.

I tell Gwen no, that we don't think Meredith is at a birth because of the fact that Delilah is also missing. "Little Delilah?" she gasps, her hand going to her mouth.

"I'm afraid so," Bea says. Delilah is high-spirited. She's full of life. Everyone adores her.

"Delilah colors pictures for me on my sidewalk with chalk. I find bouquets of dandelions on my front porch from her. Last year, when I broke my hip, she carried my mail to the door every day. She's a darling girl." Her voice cracks as she says it. "I'm afraid I haven't seen Delilah or her mother for a couple of days. The weather," she tells us, "has kept me inside."

I say, "The weather has kept many people inside, I fear." Because of the relentless rain, everyone has been cooped up for days, blind to what's happening on our streets.

Bea tells Gwen the whole story. As she does, Gwen's eyes fill with tears.

"You'll let me know when there's news?" she asks. Gwen would join the search party if she could, but Gwen is nearing eighty and not as mobile as she used to be.

"We'll let you know the minute we hear a thing," I say.

Most of our immediate neighbors know Meredith. Though no one has seen her, they almost all want to talk. They step out onto their front porches and ask for details.

"Has something happened to her?" they ask, everyone concerned. Meredith, like Delilah, is well liked throughout the neighborhood. She's been known to drop everything to help a neighbor in need. When Gwen's husband was gravely ill, she helped get him in the car and drove him to doctor appointments when she could. When the Timmonses' little dog got out, Meredith walked miles around town, pushing Delilah and Leo in the double stroller, until she found it.

Bea and I share the little we know with our neighbors, but the information we gather in return is unremarkable. Jan Fleisher remembers Meredith's car parked in back; Tim Smith saw her pull down the alley.

"Were the kids with her?" I ask Tim. He doesn't know. He didn't get a good look inside the car because there was a glare. He just knows that it was Meredith's car.

"What time was this?"

He shrugs. "Eight, maybe. Or nine." He thinks hard. "I had an appointment at eleven so I left the house around ten-thirty. It was before that. Sometime before ten-thirty, I'd say," he decides, apologizing for being unintentionally vague. He feels badly for it, knowing he may have been one of the last to see her before she disappeared.

Bea and I move on. This morning it isn't raining. Still, the sky is full of heavy clouds. We feel the moisture in the air. The trees drip rain from last night's storm down on us, making us wet in spots. We carry umbrellas, but we don't need them, not yet, though the humid weather does nothing for my hair.

There are twigs everywhere, torn savagely from the trees and tossed to the street by the rain and wind. The sidewalk is riddled with puddles; Bea and I part ways and step around them. It's chilly outside, no more than sixty degrees, but the gray skies, the threat of rain and the relentless wind make it feel more like fifty. I didn't think to bring a coat, and I regret it.

We cross the street and go to the house directly opposite Josh and Meredith's. It's a gray house that belongs to a young couple with kids. Bea and I don't know the Hanakas well because families with kids tend to bond better with other families with kids, and Bea and I don't have any kids. But I've met them once.

The Hanakas are friendly with the Dickeys. I've seen Delilah and Leo riding bikes on the sidewalk with their daughter. I've seen Meredith and the other woman, Cassandra, talking on the street, laughing. Meredith likes Cassandra, I can tell. She speaks of her often on the nights Meredith, Josh, Bea and me share a drink on the porch. It's never anything much, but somehow her name always makes its way into a conversation. *Cassandra said the new bakery on Jackson has the best cinnamon scones. Cassandra and Marty are planning one of those Alaskan cruises next summer, with the kids. Cassandra told me that a little baking soda and vinegar in the drains will get rid of those annoying fruit flies.*

Josh teased Meredith about it, said she had a *girl crush* on Cassandra, before looking mortified and apologizing to Bea and me, as if he'd said something to offend us.

I don't know much about Cassandra and her husband, Marty. Most of what I've heard is secondhand from Meredith. I know that they moved from the city. I know that, like Bea, they didn't relish the idea of suburban living. Yet, as their daughter approached school age, they had to choose between an extortionate private school education, a shoddy public school system or moving to the suburbs. They came here.

Bea and I step up to the door and knock. Cassandra comes. When she draws the door open, the house behind her is quiet, still.

"I hope we're not bothering you," Bea says.

"No," Cassandra says, "not at all. I just put my little guy down for a nap." A cat circles her ankles. Cassandra scoops it into her arms and invites us inside. "You two look cold. Let me get you some coffee," she says, and we step out of our shoes and follow her down the hallway and to the kitchen. Cassandra's home is tastefully decorated. Everything is in neutral tones and a touch too nice to belong in a home with little kids. It's also immaculately clean. Cassandra seems like the type. She's immaculate herself.

She sets the cat on the ground. "You're here about Meredith," she says, taking the glass carafe from the coffeemaker and filling it at the sink. Cassandra is tall like Bea. She's blonde, with shoulder-length hair that parts at the center and frames her face. She wears a maxi dress that a woman my height could never get away with. I envy her for it.

Cassandra knows about Meredith. Of course she does. She, like us, would have been one of the first people that Josh went to when he realized Meredith was missing.

"It's awful what's happened," she says, back at the coffeemaker, generously scooping ground coffee into the filter. "I can't believe that she and Delilah are just—" she pauses, a pregnant pause "—gone." She reaches inside a cabinet and pulls out three matching mugs. She sets them on the countertop. As the coffee begins to percolate, Cassandra suggests that we sit down at the kitchen table and talk.

"I haven't seen her in a few days if that's why you're here. This weather," she laments, sliding gracefully into a wooden chair across from Bea and me, "is ridiculous. We've hardly been able to get outside at all. Piper has been begging for a playdate with Delilah. She absolutely adores her. Just this morning, Piper was asking if Delilah could come over after school. I put her off, told her I thought the Dickeys had plans this afternoon and that Delilah wouldn't be able to play. I've never lied to my kids before. But I didn't know what else to say. Piper is inquisitive, always asking questions. She wanted to know what the Dickeys were doing that Delilah couldn't play. I said they were going to the dentist. She asked if Delilah had any cavities. I said I didn't know. I hate lying to her. If Delilah doesn't come home soon, I don't know how I'll ever be able to tell Piper that something terrible has happened to her little friend," she says.

This would be hard for a child to understand. It's hard for me to understand. The area where we live is an area of low crime.

Compared to national statistics or even the statistics of suburbs nearby, crime is nearly negligible.

"I'm so worried," Cassandra says about Meredith and Delilah. "Josh must be beside himself."

"He's organized a search party," I say, and she tells us she knows, that she plans to join the search just as soon as Arlo is up from his nap.

Bea tells her that Josh is in the process of pulling together a list of phone numbers for Meredith's clients, family and friends. "When he does," Bea says, "there will be people to call. Perhaps you can help with that while your son is napping."

"Of course. Anything I can do. They'll be okay, won't they?" Cassandra asks. Neither Bea nor I reply. We're quiet, contemplating the question. Will they be okay? No one knows. No one can say for certain. But Cassandra is staring at us, asking earnestly whether Meredith and Delilah will be okay. A tear leaves her eye, weaves down her cheek. I'm moved by the sudden show of emotion.

Cassandra pushes herself from the table and goes to the coffeemaker. She fills the mugs, asks how we take our coffee. She gathers the sugar and milk.

With her back turned to us, she says, "I saw something."

Her words are quiet but charged, full of meaning. They send a sudden shiver up my spine. I find myself wanting, desperate for more.

Did Cassandra see something having to do with Meredith and Delilah's disappearance?

She goes on, back still to us. "I'd forgotten all about it," she says. "It came to me only after Josh called to tell me Meredith and Delilah were missing."

"What'd you see?" Bea asks. Only then does Cassandra turn back to face us.

"Someone outside their house. In the middle of the night," she says, and then she makes the first of three trips to the kitchen table to deliver the coffees.

"When?" I ask.

"A couple weeks ago," she says.

"Did you tell Josh?" I ask.

"No," she admits. "I haven't. Not yet. I forgot. I only remembered late last night, when it was too late to call and wake him." This morning her daughter, Piper, was around and so she couldn't call and tell Josh then; she didn't want to scare Piper. By the time Piper went to school, the search was in full swing. Cassandra didn't feel right stealing Josh's attention away from the search.

"Arlo, my son," she explains, "he's a lousy sleeper. We're trying to sleep train, but easier said than done. Anyway, that night—the night that I saw someone—he was wide awake, crying. I was in his room trying to rock him to sleep. His room faces the street," she says, and without her saying it, I understand that Arlo's bedroom has a bird's-eye view of Josh and Meredith's home. "We never do pull the shades. We didn't when we lived in Chicago. You know what they say about old habits."

"They die hard," I say. There's a tremor to Cassandra's voice when she speaks. Whatever she witnessed out Arlo's bedroom window that night has her suddenly spooked.

"What exactly did you see?" Bea prompts. My pulse quickens in anticipation. I wrap my hands around my coffee but I don't drink it. I hang on to Cassandra's every word.

"It was dark out," Cassandra says, "a moonless night. The streetlight outside has been out a month or two. My husband, Marty, called the city about it a while ago, but it still hasn't been fixed. Our tax dollars," she quips, "hard at work. The only light came from whatever porch lights were left on overnight.

"For as dark as it was, I still saw movement in Josh and Meredith's yard. At first I thought it was my imagination. That I was seeing things. It was late and I was tired. Then, when it didn't go away, I told myself it was their trees or a deer. A coyote, maybe. But the longer I watched, I realized it was someone, *people*, in

Josh and Meredith's yard. I watched for a while, not sure what they were doing, wondering if I should call the police."

"Did you call the police?" Bea asks, knowing the answer.

"I wish I had," Cassandra says regretfully.

"How many people did you see?" I ask.

"Two," she says. "It didn't look like a break-in attempt. The people I saw, they weren't flush against the house. They were farther back, away from the door. I convinced myself—once I knew that what I was looking at was *human*—that they were college students heading home from the bars. It was after one. The timing felt right," she says.

Bars in town close at one o'clock during the week. There is student housing, both off-campus housing and residence halls, just blocks from our home. It's entirely possible that whoever Cassandra saw that night were overserved college students heading home from a night at the bar—in which case they were most likely doing something stupid but harmless that didn't require intervention by the police. I probably wouldn't have called the police, either.

"Did you get a good look at them? Do you know what they look like?"

She shakes her head. "It was so dark."

"What were they doing?" I ask. "Could you tell?"

"I couldn't," she says. "But whatever it was, it didn't last long."

"How long?"

"I don't know for sure," she says. "Arlo had me distracted. He was all worked up, totally inconsolable that night. I was worried about him waking Piper, and then having to deal with two crying kids in the middle of the night. I thought about opening the window a crack to see if I could hear something, but with Arlo crying," she says, "it would have had the adverse effect. He would have just scared them away. I should have called the police. Or, at the very least, thought to tell Josh and Meredith about it the next day."

"Why would you?" Bea asks, trying to buoy Cassandra up.

"Drunk college kids is hardly news. They probably stopped to take a pee on the lawn."

"But what if it wasn't just drunk college kids?" she asks.

"Listen," Bea says, reaching out to lay a reassuring hand on Cassandra's arm. "Don't beat yourself up about it. The police will be at the Dickeys today. I'll talk to them. Maybe someone on the block has a home security system they can pull. Video surveillance."

I tell her, "That's a good idea, Bea."

I don't know that any of our neighbors have video surveillance on their homes. Even if they do, I don't know how much storage those cameras have. I don't know if they keep footage for weeks, or if it's the kind of thing that disappears after a day or two. But it's worth a try because maybe it was drunk college kids heading home from a night in the bars, or maybe it was someone else.

Bea and I drink our coffees quickly. I'm anxious to get back on the street and continue the search. We say our goodbyes. Cassandra walks us to the door, stepping outside with us. She watches us leave.

We move on, following a path of stepping stones through her sodden lawn, leaving Cassandra on her front porch alone. We stop at other homes on the block. When we reach the end of it, we turn the corner and keep going. Along this next block, many of the houses belong to the college. Some are administrative buildings or the private homes of professors, while others, the more unkempt of them—those with sofas on porches and beer bottles in plain sight—belong to students. Graduation was a few weeks ago; the summer session hasn't begun. Most of the houses we come to are vacant; no one is home. We keep walking.

It's midafternoon when, a few blocks from our own home, we come to the house of Shelby Tebow. We know which is hers because it's been all over the news. Hers sits outside the historic district, and is one of the last original homes that remains on a block of teardowns. It's midcentury, surrounded by brand-new custom homes that start in the seven figures. There are yellow ribbons tied to the trees up and down the street. A street pole bears Shelby's face, the word *Missing* in big, black print, the sign itself encased in a plastic sheet protector to save it from the rain. I've seen this same sign around town, in store windows and on restaurant doors. There are flowers laid on the sidewalk just before her home. A kind gesture and also a grim reminder of what's happened here.

I tell Bea that I think we should skip the Tebows' house. Something about going to the home of a missing woman to inquire about another missing woman feels in poor taste. But Bea disagrees. "We should go to their house *because* of the similarity, not despite it," she says, and I know then that she's right.

I've heard Jason Tebow has a temper. I've seen it in press conferences on TV. But Bea isn't scared. She takes the lead and, again, I envy her assertiveness. Bea is a born leader. With hesitation, I follow her down the narrow walkway, up a single stoop and to the front door. She knocks on the storm door. The sound of it is empty, hollow. It would never get someone's attention. She rings the doorbell instead and immediately the sound of footsteps on the other side of the front door startles me. I'd been wishing no one was home.

The door pulls abruptly open. Jason Tebow stands there before us. There's an infant in his large arms, drinking from a bottle that Jason holds. He's bullnecked. He's not tall, but he's well built and wide. He fills the doorway, the storm door still separating us.

I can tell straightaway that he's annoyed we're here. He huffs, curses under his breath. "For fuck's sake," he says, words full of vitriol, and instinctively I step backward. Bea doesn't. She's not scared. I don't think there's a thing in the world that could scare Bea. He scowls and asks, "What's the problem? Can't you read?" while pointing to a No Soliciting sign on the front door. Truth be told, I didn't see the sign. But I don't know that it would have stopped Bea if she did. He looks us up and down, taking in our sweatshirts and jeans, our sneakers.

"We're sorry to bother you," Bea says. "Mr. Tebow, isn't it?" she asks, introducing herself and then me. I watch the manner in which he holds that baby. It's awkward and stiff. He doesn't know what to do with it.

"Our friend," Bea begins, "has been missing for almost a day. Since yesterday morning. We're out knocking on doors, to see if anyone has seen her."

At this, Jason Tebow turns gray. He swallows hard, his Adam's apple prominent in his neck. I watch him. Jason is built like a bodybuilder. His arms are as big as my thigh.

"Is this some kind of fucking joke?" Jason asks, stepping outside, letting the storm door slam shut, as the baby begins to cry. The bottle has moved from its mouth and is dripping milk onto its cheek. I don't know if the baby is a boy or girl because the onesie it wears is white but dirty, stained with spit-up.

There's hardly a person in town who doesn't think that he did something to hurt his wife. Twice that I know of he's been hauled down to the police station for questioning. At random times, police cars are parked in the street outside his house, watching him. He thinks we're harassing him, baiting him.

I speak up. "You don't understand. This has nothing to do with your wife, Mr. Tebow. Our friend, our next-door neighbor, didn't come home last night. Neither she nor her little girl. Her husband is worried sick. His little girl, Delilah, is only six years old. You, more than anyone, can understand what he's going through. We're just trying to help find them. We've been to every house for three blocks, asking if anyone has seen them. Meredith Dickey," I say, reaching into the back pocket of my jeans for my phone, so I can show him the picture. We're a few blocks from where we live. Jason Tebow wouldn't know who she is.

But he does. The recognition is evident right away. He falls a step back, turns slowly to me and asks, "Did you say Meredith?"

I take a breath. "You know Meredith?"

He pauses. As he does, his anger wanes. His tone softens, becoming civil, less vitriolic. "I know Meredith," he says.

"How?" I ask.

"She was Shelby's doula," he says.

I stiffen. My stomach churns.

"She was?" I ask, my mouth like cotton. It's gone suddenly dry at the realization that Meredith and Shelby knew one another. I try and swallow but the saliva gets stuck in my throat. Meredith and Shelby had a connection. Now they're both gone. Is that a coincidence? Or is that something more?

"How long had Shelby known Meredith?" Bea asks.

Jason shrugs. "Not too long. A few months."

"They were friends?"

"Not really. Shelby liked her, sure," he tells us. "But it was a business arrangement. Shelby was worried about giving birth. This was her first, and she doesn't have a high threshold for pain."

"So you hired a doula?" I ask, and he nods. "Why Meredith?"

He shrugs. He doesn't know how Shelby came upon Meredith.

"How old is your baby?" I ask.

"Six weeks. Grace, 'cause that was Shelby's middle name. Shelby Grace," he says. His use of his wife's name in the past tense isn't lost on me. "This one here is Grace Eloise."

"That's lovely," I say.

Bea asks if Shelby and Meredith kept in touch after Grace was born. "Some," Jason says, shrugging. From what we know, Meredith remained close to many of her clients even after they'd given birth. They'd call with questions on breastfeeding, diaper rash. Meredith humored them because she's a selfless person, though contractually she wasn't required to do anything after the baby was born.

"Were you at the birth?" asks Bea.

"Yeah," Jason says. "It was a fucking nightmare."

"A nightmare how?" I ask.

"It just was," he says, turning reticent. "I can't talk about it." His eyes drop to the baby in his arms, and only then does he see the spilled milk, does he notice that the baby is fussing. He inserts the nipple back into the baby's mouth and the baby settles. Her squirming limbs become inert. When Jason looks back up at us, his eyes are wet.

He asks about Meredith and Delilah. "How long have they been gone?"

"Her husband saw her yesterday morning. That was the last time," Bea says.

"Shame," says Jason. From his tone, I can't tell if he's being sincere. I find myself watching him. I wonder if he's the kind of man capable of hurting his wife. And if he is, is he the kind of man capable of hurting Meredith and Delilah? But why would he?

What kind of person hurts a child?

There are holes in his story about the night Shelby disappeared. There are accounts from friends and neighbors that Jason and Shelby fought often, that Shelby was seen with bruises on her arms and legs. Jason's excuse was that Shelby was on medication that made her easily bruise. It seemed he had an excuse for everything. Why had she gone out running so late that night? She'd just been given permission to exercise and was trying to shed the baby weight. According to Jason, Shelby thought that she was fat; after the baby was asleep was the only time she could run. The way he said it came off as misogynistic. *I told her not to go*, he said then. *It's not my fault that she's gone.* In essence, what he meant by that, was that it was Shelby's fault. He tried to retract that later, in a press conference, when asked by a reporter. He said it wasn't what he meant to say, that he wasn't actually trying to blame his wife for her own disappearance. But by then, it had already run in the paper. There was no taking it back. Public opinion of him had already formed.

"Any leads on Shelby?" Bea asks.

"The cops used their dogs to track her scent a couple of blocks. Then it disappeared. They think that was where she was snatched. They used luminol and found blood there, on the street. Someone tried to clean it up. Or the rain washed it away."

"No idea who?" she asks.

"None yet, but I've got my ideas."

It surprises me. "You do?"

"Shelby didn't have many enemies," he says, "but she had one."

"Who?" I ask, on edge. I don't know Shelby. I don't know what kind of person she is or was, or if she was the kind to make enemies.

He thinks awhile. He isn't quick to say. He looks around, as if we're being watched. "Dr. Feingold," he tells us in time, his words weighty.

"Who's that?" I ask.

He waits a beat. He's already said more than he wants to say. But then he says, "Her obstetrician."

"Why were they enemies?" I ask.

"I can't talk about it," he says, and our conversation ends abruptly there. Jason decides that he needs to get the baby back inside, out of the rain, which only then begins to fall. It starts as a drizzle, but soon comes down in sheets. Bea and I watch as Jason Tebow turns with that infant awkwardly in his arms and pushes his way through the door. He lets it slam loudly closed, startling both the baby and us. On the other side of the door, the baby begins to scream.

We turn and make our way back down the walkway. "What do you think he means by that?" I whisper as we reach the side-walk.

Bea shakes her head. She isn't sure.

We move on. We go to more houses; we knock on more

doors. No one has seen Meredith or Delilah. The lack of information, of answers, is wearing on us. We're getting nowhere.

But then, at nearly noon, a text comes through the group chat. A body has been found.

MEREDITH

March

I just barely make it to my nine o'clock vinyasa flow class on time. I start by grounding my class. I ask them to find any comfortable position. There we focus on breath. I invite my students into a deeper awareness of their current mental and physical state. I focus on mine. I use this time to try and shake off the fear I feel after having just received another threatening text. I'm not used to feeling so out of control, so frantic. But these text messages have me all worked up. I tell my class to breathe in through their noses. To let the air fill their bellies, then their chests. When they exhale, I want to hear them. I breathe as they do, trying to force myself to relax. There's no one in the world who should want to hurt me. No one has any reason to wish me dead. I'm an extremely conscientious woman. I've done nothing wrong.

I lead my students in a short, guided meditation. We move into our warm-up. We work our way toward peak pose. I move around the room. I help my students find proper alignment, trying hard to distract myself from the thoughts inside my head.

The lights in the studio are turned down. The classroom is heated, the thermostat set to ninety degrees. There are humidifiers. Everyone sweats, including me.

We say, "Namaste," and then everyone leaves.

After class, I have a meet and greet with a potential new doula client and her husband. Our plan is to meet at eleven. It's standard protocol, to see if they like me and vice versa. We've made arrangements to meet at a public spot—a coffee shop— in case they turn out to be dodgy. For all the horror stories you hear about Craigslist—people being lured to strange homes by classified ads, only to be murdered when they arrive—it seems smarter this way. It makes me feel safer to meet in a public spot.

The coffee shop is new to me. It has scuffed wood floors, tin ceilings and tables the size of postage stamps. I spot my prospective client when I arrive. She's easy to see. She's the anxious, uncomfortable-looking one with a belly the size of a basketball. She waits at a table, alone. I go to her and shake her hand.

"Meredith Dickey," I say, smiling.

"Shelby Tebow," she says, shaking mine. "You want some coffee?" she asks. I do. The fatigue is taking over. Without caffeine, I don't know how much longer I can last on my feet.

We drift in the direction of the counter. We order our coffees. Mrs. Tebow offers to buy mine. I don't object. She asks if I want something to eat. I get a cinnamon scone because, on top of tired, I'm famished. I can't remember the last time I ate, or if I even ate this morning. I remember feeding the kids and doing their dishes. I don't remember having anything myself.

Mrs. Tebow gets nothing. "You're not having something to eat?" I ask, feeling guilty all of a sudden. I take the scone from the barista.

She shakes her head. She harrumphs. "Look at me," Mrs. Tebow says, showing off her very pregnant self. "I'm fat. The last thing I need is a pastry."

"You're not fat," I scold. "You're pregnant."

We take our coffee to a table and sit. The coffee shop is quiet, small. There are only a handful of people here, professionals on laptops mostly. These meetings are as much about me trying to impress potential clients, as they are the other way around. If we like each other at the end of it, a contract gets signed.

"My husband says I'm never going to lose all this weight. I've gained thirty pounds," she says. She says it like it's grotesque, but thirty pounds is average. I gained at least that with each of my kids.

"Is your husband on his way?" I ask. I didn't have time to change after class. I wear my yoga clothes, with a sweater on top. My eyes are heavy, the lost hours of sleep catching up with me.

Shelby fiddles with a ring on her finger. "He's not coming," she says uneasily.

"I'm sorry to hear that. He couldn't make it?"

Husbands don't always make it. Sometimes they're at work, or on a business trip, and sometimes they're uninvolved. It's okay. Because the women who need me most are often those with husbands who show disinterest or inefficacy.

Shelby looks sheepish. She lets go of her ring. She rearranges herself on her chair, takes a sip of her coffee, which I overheard her order and know it's not decaf. I don't judge. I didn't drink caffeine when I was pregnant. But every pregnant woman is different. Maybe a little caffeine is the one thing that gets her through the day. I've seen a lot of women over the years. Single mothers. Women who've been raped, but want to keep their baby. Women who choose to abort a fetus based on the result of genetic testing. Being unbiased is important. Every woman is not me.

Shelby shakes her head. Her hands are also shaking. Tiny ripples form in her coffee, ruining the latte art. "I didn't tell him I was meeting with you," she says. She's nervous. There could be a million reasons why. Maybe she's just timid or is trying to impress me. Maybe she feels badly about her husband or she's terrified of the impending birth.

"Oh?" I ask. I don't want her to feel strange. I reach across the table and pat her hand. Research shows the importance of touch on a person's emotions, their physical well-being, the way they respond to others. Tactile stimulation is one of the most important.

I say, "That's not a problem. It happens all the time, Shelby."

"Really?" she asks. Only then do her eyes move to mine.

"Of course it does. It can be hard to get those men on board. It's not like they're the ones pushing a baby out of their bodies," I say with an empathetic smile. Across the table, Shelby visibly relaxes. "After we talk," I tell her, "you can talk to your husband and decide what you want to do. How far along are you?" I ask.

She says, "Thirty-six weeks."

Most of my clients come to me newly pregnant. Rarely do they come at thirty-six weeks. She tells me why, how she and her husband just moved to town. She had an obstetrician she loved, but now she's two thousand miles away. She also had a close family, a large support system, but now they're gone, too. In essence, she's alone with the exception of her husband.

I tell her why I became a doula. I tell her about my experience giving birth to Leo. What I remember is that the hospital staff didn't pay much attention to me that night. Josh had to beg and plead for a nurse to check on me. I felt alone. I felt like I was a burden. After it was done, I wished I had had someone to advocate for me, someone other than Josh, whose emotions were running on high like mine.

I've since seen things happen in a labor room that appall me. My own birth experience was a cakewalk in comparison. A common belief during labor is that a baby's needs supersede that of the mother's. Women don't always know they have options. Or they aren't given a choice in their care. If they are, they aren't allowed ample time or information to come to a decision themselves. Choices are made without their consent. Too many women don't want to be a burden and so they say nothing. The mistreatment is subtle, too, and falls under the guise of medical care.

Doctors do things that verge on sexual assault to me. They stick their hands inside a woman's vagina without telling her first. They disregard a woman's pain. They use forced or invasive practices. In the labor room, *no* doesn't always mean *no*.

Most times labor ends with a happy ending. Women put aside whatever negative feelings they experienced during birth because they got what they wanted in the end: a healthy baby. That doesn't make it right. One of the reasons I do what I do is to advocate for women during birth.

"Continuity of care is important. To have someone who is there for you and only you during your labor." I leave it at that.

We talk about a birth plan, what she wants out of this birth. "A healthy baby, that's all," she says. She reaches down to set a hand on her midsection. I ask questions. I learn that Shelby doesn't want to deliver at home. She wants to deliver in a hospital. "I don't need any of that new age crap," she says. "I mean, I want the epidural. I don't want a C-section, unless I need it. Then I want it. But I won't be eating my placenta any time soon."

That gets a laugh out of me. It feels like the first in days.

There isn't any definitive research into the benefits of placentophagia that I've been able to find. But if a client wanted to eat her own placenta, I wouldn't stop her.

We talk awhile. As we do, I find that I like Shelby Tebow. I really like her. She's practical, not pretentious. She's matter-of-fact. She's young, and it shows. I was once young, too. She has dreams for the rest of her life. She likes helping people. She's not working now that she and her husband have relocated. But when she's able, she wants to get back to work. Her husband doesn't want her to work. He likes it better when she's home.

"Tell me about your husband," I say. It feels like a good transition.

"What about him?"

"Oh, I don't know," I say. "Anything."

Her husband is an insurance agent, she tells me. He was a linebacker in college. He wanted to go pro, until a knee injury sidelined him. He's still bent out of shape about it. He's three years older than her. They started dating in high school, when she was a freshman and he a senior. When she turned eighteen, they got married. Shelby never went to college. She tells me how much he loves kids, how he'll be a great father one day. I just don't get the sense that *one day* means four weeks from now, when their baby is due to arrive.

After a while she gets down to brass tacks. She isn't sure she can trust her husband to be there for her during the birth— physically, emotionally or otherwise. He's kind of *hard core*, as she calls him. I'm not sure what she means by that. But it's why she needs me there.

The next time I see Shelby is two days later. We meet again at the same coffee shop. This time I offer to buy her coffee, but she says no; she can't stay. She's jumpy. She brings the signed contract. She presses it into my hand. I take it. Both she and her husband have signed the document.

"You were able to get him on board," I say, smiling.

"He had his reservations," she says. Shelby doesn't smile.

"Like what?"

She waits a beat before she tells me. "He thinks you're a con. He thinks you're ripping us off. He looked up people in your line of work. He wants to know why you charge so much. At first he said I was out of my damn mind if I thought we were going to pay that much for a babysitter."

An image of her husband forms: cynical, candid, lacking trust.

I've been asked this question before. I'm not agency-based or hospital-based. I work alone, which is the reason my fees may be more than most. I provide services not everyone provides. You don't get just any doula when you go into labor, dependent on who's on call. You get me.

"He found one online that charged only three hundred dollars," Shelby says. "But I said I didn't want that one. I want you."

"Why's that?" I ask. Shelby doesn't know me from a bar of soap. Why would she pick me over any other doula?

She shrugs. She smiles. "I like you," she says. "But Jason said if I could talk you down to a thousand, that would be even better."

"Talk me down to a thousand?"

"Or even eight hundred. I mean, he's right. It's a lot of money for one day of work."

I have a sinking feeling in the pit of my stomach. I don't like where this conversation is headed. It's not one day of work. It's a prenatal appointment, meetings like this, the labor and delivery, a postnatal visit, endless phone calls and texts. It's also my livelihood, me putting my own life and family on hold for hers.

I don't tell her that.

"I'm sorry, Shelby, but I don't negotiate on my fees."

Another shrug. Another smile, this one far more brazen. I get the sense that there's more to this woman than I originally thought. For as nervous as she was the other day, there's none of it today. Today she is assertive and sure. Which side of her am I to believe is true?

"Yeah, well," she says, "it doesn't matter. I got him on board either way, didn't I?"

What I notice is that Shelby wears sunglasses, though we're inside and outside the day is gloomy and gray.

KATE

11 YEARS BEFORE

May

There's a river in town. It's bordered by landscaped trails that curve around the water's edge in an area known as the River-walk. The Riverwalk is the crown jewel of town. On weekends, people flock to it by the hundreds to visit. They walk on the brick paths, toss coins in the fountain, get their pictures taken on any number of the covered wooden bridges that pass over the river.

In the heart of downtown, the paths are maintained with ample lighting, an abundance of flowers and pristine landscaping. Nary a weed grows there. The streets nearby are all upscale boutiques. The number of bars and restaurants in our downtown nears fifty. On weekends, it's exasperating trying to find a place to park.

But the farther from downtown you get, the river's edge turns woody. The wide, well-kept paths metamorphose into a desire line created by years of erosion from people who pass through, feet wearing away the land. The path becomes narrow, just a ribbon of dirt that cuts through the grass and weeds, enmeshed in trees.

This time of year, the area is mosquito-infested. The excessive rain and flooding are the cause of this. Mosquitoes breed in damp conditions. They lay their eggs in stagnant water, like puddles. Because of the heavy tree coverage, the puddles never have a chance to fully dry out, and so the land stays muddy, mossy, the ground littered with the moldy debris from trees.

This is where the body was found.

Our group meets back at Josh and Meredith's house. Everyone is talking fast, sharing what they know. It's frenetic. The air hums with the sound of voices, a constant drone.

I look around. Josh isn't here. But there are police officers here. Their cars are parked just outside, while an officer stands guard at the door. Other officers are inside the house, searching through Josh and Meredith's things.

"Has anyone seen Josh?" I ask.

"He's gone to the river," someone says, "to see the body." We all fall momentarily silent at the mention of that word: *body*. My heart is in my throat, hoping and praying that it isn't Meredith or Delilah they've found.

We stand in a circle on Josh and Meredith's lawn. The entire group is on edge and feeling anguished and defeated. The rain has slowed to a steady drizzle. Those of us that have them hold umbrellas over our heads to repel the rain. The rest just get wet.

"How do we know there's a body?" Bea asks.

"My wife and I heard about it," a man says, stepping forward.

"How?" she asks.

"We were on the Riverwalk, showing Meredith and Delilah's photo around, asking if anyone had seen them. There were a couple runners there. We showed them the photo. *No*, they said. They hadn't seen them. But they'd heard that the cops were just a couple miles downriver, trying to identity a body that was found. *Hope that's not who you're looking for*, they said."

"We continued to dig for details," the wife says. "We asked around to see if anyone knew anything."

What they derived, she tells us, fighting tears, was that the body had been discovered early this morning by a man walking his dog. It was half-buried in the earth. The head and the torso were concealed underground, while the rest of it poked obscurely out. It had likely been buried better, some surmise, but last night's rain may have washed the mud and the leaves away. The dog found the body first, driven there by the offensive scent. The river there is high, on the verge of overflowing; a day or two later and the body would have been at risk of floating away.

"Any signs of foul play?" a woman asks.

The husband and wife exchange a glance. They tell us they heard the body was unclothed, and, collectively, we gasp. Our minds go to the same place.

"Oh God," Bea, beside me, says, taking my hand into hers and squeezing it tightly. Our eyes meet, thinking of what might have happened to our friend before her body was left abandoned and alone, thinking of Delilah. Praying that the naked body does not belong to Delilah, but also wondering, if it is Meredith, then where is Delilah? Death might be preferable to being taken by someone we don't know.

Because of our close proximity to Josh's house, Bea and I go home and gather snacks to pass around to the search party, which now nears thirty in number. When we step into the house, the workers are there. The music is loud, something techno with a low bass that makes the entire house shake. They're hard at work, but they stop when we come in. They stop and stare.

"Excuse us," I say, begging their pardon for being in my own home. I feel a man's eyes on me as I collect strawberries from the refrigerator, wash and slice them in the kitchen sink. It's unnerving. Bea grabs two bags of chips and as many bottles of water as her arms can carry. We go back, grateful to get out of there.

Everyone politely declines our offer of food. No one wants

to eat. Everyone feels the same sickness in their stomach, a sadness and unrest, not knowing what's happening down there by the river. It's all anyone can think about. I, myself, try and imagine the scene: police and evidence technicians, reporters, yellow caution tape. A body being exhumed from the bramble.

After a while, I watch as Bea pulls the midwife aside. I see them talking on Josh's front porch, where they're sheltered from the rain.

I'm in the middle of talking to the woman who first heard about the body late this morning. She and her husband, she tells me, tried to make their way to the body, to see it for themselves, to see if it was Meredith or Delilah. But they got only so far before the local community service officers got in their way, blocking them and anyone else from getting too close. Many people had the same idea, fueled mostly by morbid curiosity: to see a dead body.

I excuse myself. I make my way to Bea, extending a hand to the midwife and telling her that my name is Kate. The midwife is midfifties with tender eyes and a kind smile. Her hair is long, graying, woven into a single braid down her back.

"Kate is my partner," Bea says.

The midwife replies, "Yes, of course. Meredith spoke of you often. Good things only. I'm Jeanette," she says, shaking my hand. "Meredith and I worked together on occasion."

As a doula, Meredith worked in a variety of settings. She worked home births, often with the help of a midwife. She worked in hospitals. She went where her clients went, whether they gave birth in a bathtub or a hospital bed.

Bea is in the middle of telling Jeanette what we learned from Jason Tebow. "He said Meredith was their doula. It sounds like something went wrong with that birth, but he wouldn't say what. He suggested some animosity toward the obstetrician."

"Dr. Feingold," Jeanette says, nodding thoughtfully. "Nobody likes him much," she says.

"Why's that?" I ask.

"He doesn't have the best bedside manner. He can be un-compromising. He wouldn't have appreciated Meredith being there, questioning him, undermining his decisions. To Meredith, clients came first. She didn't care who she pissed off in the process." She explains to us the role of a doula: to be there for emotional and physical support, to empower the mother, to ensure the labor and delivery were the best experience they could be. "Meredith is a wonderful doula. There isn't anything she wouldn't do for her clients," she says. "We talked a lot about our clients, even those that we didn't have in common. Labor and delivery can be overtaxing. The long, unplanned hours, the physical and emotional fatigue. It's heady and exhilarating from time to time, but also the kind of career that can run someone into the ground. We relied on each other for support. Meredith is a good friend."

"She is," I say, thinking of all the times Meredith had been there for me. A thought comes to me. "Why would Shelby see an obstetrician like him, if he's so unlikable?" I ask.

Jeanette says, "Shelby was already late into her pregnancy when she started seeing him. Very few OBs like to take a patient on that late in the game because they don't have a full knowledge of the patient's history. But Dr. Feingold did. Dr. Feingold was also one of the few who didn't already have a full practice, which should have been a red flag."

"Do you know anything about this particular birth?" asks Bea.

"I do," Jeanette says. She breathes deeply, holds the air in. At first she's reluctant to tell us. But then she does. She exhales slowly and says, "The baby isn't right."

Bea and I exchange a glance. We've both seen the baby. The baby didn't look not right to us. "How so?" Bea asks.

"She suffered irreparable brain damage during the delivery. The Tebows are suing Dr. Feingold for malpractice. Dr. Feingold should have opted for a C-section, which Meredith suggested. The mother was exhausted. But Dr. Feingold wouldn't listen; he wouldn't be told what to do. He cut an episiotomy and used forceps instead, applying too much pressure to the infant's fragile skull."

"But she will be all right?" I ask, worried for baby Grace. The fact that Shelby is suing for malpractice concerns me. Lots of doctors get sued. As a doctor myself, it's one of my biggest fears. Many malpractice suits are settled or dismissed before they ever get to court. But still, it has lasting effects on a doctor's finances and reputation. If Dr. Feingold is the type of man Jeanette paints him to be, I wonder what kind of reaction he'd have to being sued.

Jeanette shrugs. "We may not know for some time. Some of these children are diagnosed with cerebral palsy. Some seizure disorders. Still others have developmental delays. Meredith planned to testify against Dr. Feingold. She was to give a deposition this week," she says, and for a second I don't breathe. I think that this doctor did something to silence Meredith so she couldn't speak out against him. The timing is significant. First Shelby went missing and then Meredith, the two women who were witness to his negligence.

We go quiet, each lost in our own thoughts. In time, Jeanette drifts away, standing under a tree in the distance, staring upward at the clouds. I watch her for a moment.

"I have a bad feeling about this," Bea says, stealing my attention away from Jeanette.

The rain picks up and then slows down. Dusk seems to come sooner than usual because of the rain. By late afternoon it's turning dark, the clouds heavy and gray. Tonight there will be thunderstorms, some violent, newscasters predict.

Later, early in the evening, we watch as Josh's car pulls down the street. He parks in front of the house. He stays there, not getting out, while the rest of us watch on, expectantly. We hold our collective breath, wondering what Josh knows that we don't. Is Meredith dead?

I see him through the windshield. He sits in the car awhile, bent over the steering wheel. Is he crying? Or is he just collecting his breath? I think about approaching, of going to the car, knocking on the window and getting his attention. But Josh deserves this second of peace. He's been gone for hours. It's nearing five o'clock. For the last few hours, the rest of us have been gathered on his lawn, holding a near-silent vigil. Everyone stayed. Even with the weather as it is, no one left. No one would leave until they knew what was happening down there by the river.

When he steps from the car, Josh's body sags. He trips over the curb, stumbling like he's been drinking. But Josh isn't drunk. His shoulders round forward, his head dropped so far his chin practically touches his chest. He has been crying. Though his tears are dry now, the evidence is written all over his face: the redness and the swollen eyes. He looks a decade older than he did this morning, and entirely spent. There's dirt on his hands and on the knees of his pants.

He makes his way to us. But partway across the lawn he stops. He leans heavily against a tree, burying his face into his hands as if he can't go on. There he sobs, his whole body convulsing, and, twenty feet away, Bea wraps her arms around me, steadying me so I, too, don't collapse.

The worst has happened. Meredith is dead.

No one goes to him. We all stand by and let him have this cry. Many among us begin to cry, too. My hand goes to my mouth, expecting all the emotion that's welled up inside me to come flooding out. But it doesn't. I hold it inside, focusing instead on what needs to be done. We need to find Delilah. The search for her needs to be amped up. We can't stand around and mourn Meredith's loss when we have Delilah to find.

Behind me, Bea quietly cries. We've switched roles. Usually I'm the more emotional, Bea the logical, the one orchestrating plans. But Bea and Meredith were close. Bea and Delilah were close.

There will be a funeral. Arrangements will have to be made. Bea and I will help Josh with the arrangements. He shouldn't have to do that alone. He'll be completely beside himself now that Meredith is dead.

Those words get trapped in my head. They're incomprehensible to me. Meredith is dead. They don't belong together.

But when Josh finally manages to collect himself, he tells us.

"It's not her," he chokes out.

"What do you mean it's not her?" someone asks.

"The body," he says. "It wasn't Meredith. It was that Tebow woman," he cries out, and, God help me, I feel the greatest sense of relief. My knees buckle, and only then do the tears come. Tears of relief that it's Shelby and not Meredith.

He tells us how Mr. Tebow came down to the station and identified her body. "What happened to her?" someone asks. "How did she die?"

It's a question we all want to know. But only one of us has the nerve to ask.

"We won't know until after the autopsy," Josh says. But he tells us that Shelby's death is being investigated as a homicide. It was clear that foul play was to blame. Everyone gasps, then falls silent.

Just then a plainclothes officer steps out of Josh and Meredith's house, a woman, a brunette with strong features: an angular jawline, straight nose, jutting cheekbones. Her lips are thin, her eyes narrow, cheeks taut. She could be pretty if she smiled. She wears a pantsuit, a holster with a handgun tucked beneath the jacket of it. The wind blows, pulling the plackets of her jacket apart and I see it: the gun. She crosses the lawn for Josh, some male detective with a lesser paygrade following behind. Stupidly I think that she is going to comfort Josh, to give him some statistic, to say something reassuring about investigations like this.

But instead, when she speaks, her voice is flat and comfortless. "Mr. Dickey," she says. "Detective Rowlings." She flashes a badge. "If you wouldn't mind stepping inside with us for a minute?" while making a motion toward Josh's home behind him. I look. It's a beautiful home, a blue Queen Anne, over a century old. It's large and ornate, with round towers and cone-shaped roofs that give the impression of a small castle. As long as we've lived here, Josh and Meredith have lived here.

Josh stands upright. He wipes at his eyes, dries the remaining tears. Everyone else stands at attention and leans in to listen.

Josh looks around. He sees the mass of people waiting there for news. Every man, woman and child here has set aside their own day for Meredith and Delilah.

"If you have something to say about my wife," Josh says, fighting for composure, "you can just say it. Everyone is here for the same reason. To find my family."

"There's no news, sir," Detective Rowlings says grimly, shaking her head. "We have some questions for you."

"What kind of questions?" Josh asks.

"If you wouldn't mind," she says, "we'd prefer to discuss this inside."

A van pulls down the street. It comes to a stop behind Josh's car. We watch as a man and a woman in Tyvek get out of the van and head for the house. I swallow against a lump in my throat. They've found something.

"I have to pick up my son," Josh says. He looks at his watch. "I have to pick him up from the babysitter. I told her I'd be there by five. I'm already late. Can this wait?" he asks.

"Couldn't you make other arrangements for your son?" Detective Rowlings asks, promising this won't take long. She's unsympathetic. I doubt she has children.

Bea steps forward. "We'll get him," she says to Josh. "Kate and I will get him and keep him until you're done." She touches Josh's arm.

"That'd be a big help," Josh says over his shoulder. "Thank you, Bea."

While dozens watch, Josh, with his head hung low, follows the detective to his house and closes the door.

LEO

NOW

Dad tells you you'll sleep in your old room, 'cause where else would you sleep? Still, it's weird having someone in that room. No one's been in that room for as long as I can remember.

Dad has to show you where your room is because you don't know.

You also don't know my name. After half a day of assuming, it becomes evident you don't know. Dad tells you I'm Leo. "You remember Leo, don't you?" he asks, and you shake your head, which doesn't surprise me, because I'm not so memorable.

"He was smaller the last time you saw him," Dad says.

You don't have any clothes other than the ones you're wearing, which came from the hospital's clothes closet. They were donated. I can tell by looking at them that they're not new. You're wearing someone else's old clothes. But the only clothes in your closet are a kids' size six, because that's the size you wore when you were taken. They're not going to fit. Dad is tall, so he says to me, "Leo. Find something in your closet for your sister to wear."

I still can't wrap my head around it, how when Dad says *your sister*, he's talking about you. You're here in the same room as me. You're home. Or at least some version of you is home.

I go to my room. I find a shirt I don't wear anymore. I find a pair of sweatpants. I bring them to you. "Here," I say, holding them out.

You take them. You say back, "Thank you, sir." I can't even bring myself to laugh because it's pitiful that you think you need to call me, your kid brother, *sir*. Talk about fucked up.

"Just call me Leo already. Old people are *sirs*."

You stand in your doorway holding my shirt and pants in your hands. There are things I want to know. Questions I want to ask you, but can't. Questions about Mom. I know the story the police came up with. What I want to know is if that's really the way it went down.

Dad asks if you want him to tuck you in, after you get dressed. His eyes get wet when he does. They're hopeful, desperate. I can hear it in his voice. He's begging you to let him tuck you in. It's been eleven years.

You stare back. You say nothing.

Dad stands down because of your silence. "If there's anything you need," he says, "just ask." Dad is as good as a stranger to you. It would be pretty messed up for him to tuck you into bed. You're also too old for snug as a bug in a rug. Dad stopped tucking me in when you disappeared. He was too busy crying himself to sleep to notice me.

I lock my door when I go to sleep. I don't know what kind of person you are.

The lady cop said you escaped because you made your own shank. Except she didn't say shank. She said an improvised weapon. You stabbed somebody with it. There was blood on your clothes when they found you. It was his.

How do I know you won't stab me, too?

I try to sleep. I can't get comfortable. I think I won't sleep. But then, before I know it, I hear Dad calling for you, screaming out your name. I look at the clock. It's two a.m. Somehow or other, I slept.

I scramble from bed. I unlock the door and stumble from the room. When I find him, he's in the hall. He's out of his mind. His breathing is heavy. He spins in circles in the dark hall as if you're right there, two feet behind, but he can't get there fast enough to see you.

I go for the light switch, turn it on. The bright lights hurt my eyes. I use a hand to shield them. Dad's sweating. He's got a hand pressed to his chest like it hurts. I'm not so sure he isn't having a heart attack.

"She's gone," Dad says, coming to a stop in front of me. He's wearing pajamas. Dad doesn't usually wear pajamas. Usually he wears boxer shorts. But tonight he had the wherewithal to put something more appropriate on, because of you. Except that the pajamas are long-sleeved. He sweats because of them.

I ask, "What do you mean *she's gone?*"

Dad grabs me by the shoulders. He gives me a shake and says, "She just is, Leo. She's not here. She's gone. Delilah is gone."

I think he's had a bad dream, something about you disappearing. It would be understandable. I go to your room to see for myself, but he's right. You are gone. The blankets and sheets are pulled all the way up like no one's ever slept in the bed. My clothes are on the floor. You didn't put them on.

I check the window first. It's closed and locked. Wherever you went, you didn't go out that way. I think you ran away, but maybe your kidnapper came and got you. "The fucking reporters." That's what Dad's muttering, 'cause anyone watching the news now knows what town we live in, what our house looks like, and they know that you're here. A ten-year-old with internet access and a bike could find you.

I leave your room. I check the bathroom, and then Dad and I race downstairs to scout out places you might be. We come up empty. There's no sign of you on the first floor. The front door and the back door are shut and locked.

Dad's on the phone, calling the lady cop because he has her number programmed into his phone. It's the middle of the night, but that doesn't stop him. There are cops sitting right outside, but Dad doesn't bother with them or with 911.

The lady cop answers immediately. "Carmen. It's me. Josh," he says, breathlessly. His informality makes me want to gag.

I leave. I go from window to window, trying to figure out which way you went. You have no shoes. So whichever way you went, you went barefoot. But that's nothing new to you.

I make the rounds. The windows are shut. They're all locked. You didn't go out any of them. I head back toward the kitchen. I pass by the basement door on the way there. I don't know why I look, except that I'm running out of options. I open the door. It's black down the steps. The basement is unfinished because even though Mom hoped to finish it one day, it didn't happen before she tried to slash her wrists. *Tried* being the operative word, because she failed. The cuts were shallow, not enough to bleed out. There were a whole bunch of them, but they only got the surface veins. Mom didn't get down to either of the main arteries, the ones that would have killed her. According to statistics, most people who try to slash their wrists fail. Because it hurts.

That's when Mom turned the knife around and stabbed herself in the abdomen. Easy and quick. According to coroner reports, she managed to get her own liver and bleed out. She had a nasty lump on the back of her head, too, from whacking something on the way down.

I turn on a light. The basement becomes yellow. I go down the steps and there you are, sprawled on the concrete floor.

At first glance, I think you're dead.

But then I see that your chest is moving. You're breathing. You're not dead; you're asleep.

You passed on a soft, warm bed to come sleep on the cold, hard basement floor in the dark. Because for eleven years, it's all you've known. In some effed up way, you find comfort in it, being down here in our dark, dingy basement.

It doesn't get much more fucked up than that.

MEREDITH

11 YEARS BEFORE

March

In the middle of the night, my cell phone pings. It's been four days since I've received a threatening text. Somehow, I've put them out of my mind. Since nothing bad has happened to me, I've convinced myself they're some stupid teenage prank. Some kids must've gotten ahold of my name and number and are having a field day messing with me.

When the text comes, my first thought isn't that it's a threat. My first thought is that it's a client in labor. I have two women due soon. I never go to bed with the guarantee that I'll be able to sleep the night through without having to go to a birth. It's a hazard of the job.

Beside me, Josh stirs at the sound of the phone. It's a preprogrammed response; he's gotten used to this. He rolls away from me. He pulls the covers over his head.

I reach for the phone. I glance down at it, the light from the screen burning my eyes.

I'm scared, it reads.

The text comes from Shelby Tebow. I sigh. I prop myself on my elbows to reply. Shelby is scared of giving birth. Many women are. I was, too, for both Delilah and Leo. It's a fear that doesn't necessarily go away, even after your first. With Delilah everything went right. With Leo it all went wrong. If I was to have a third, I'd still be scared.

But the middle of the night is not the ideal time for a pep talk. Some clients don't toe the line. They think that because they're paying for my services, they have access to me around the clock. Such is not the case. My rules are laid out in the contract. If they're in labor, then I'm at their beck and call. But if they have cold feet, they'll still have cold feet during normal business hours. This is something I'd be glad to talk about tomorrow.

I write back, All first-time mothers get scared. It's normal. Try to sleep. You need your rest. Let's talk tomorrow. xo.

It's an empathetic response, but one that hopefully puts the kibosh on a lengthy discussion. I'll call her tomorrow, ask if she wants to meet for coffee and discuss. We'll make a list of her fears and tackle them one by one.

Shelby doesn't write back at first. It's three in the morning. She took the hint and went to bed.

But just as I'm about to return my phone to the nightstand, it pings.

I'm scared of my husband, it says this time.

I stare at those words. I read them through twice. I haven't met Shelby's husband. I don't know who he is. I do know that his name is Jason, and the few things Shelby told me about him.

I don't wake Josh. Josh would tell me to drop this client. He'd say that I don't need to be getting myself involved in some sort of domestic dispute.

But I'm already involved, aren't I? Shelby paid her deposit. She and I both signed the contract. I put a copy in the mail for her yesterday.

That said, the check still sits on the kitchen counter. It's waiting to be deposited. I suppose I could just give it back. I could say I've bitten off more than I can chew and can't take on another client. I have another eight women due next month, same month that Shelby is due. The odds of two of them going into labor at the same time is good. I could apologize, recommend another doula. Shelby might leave me a bad Yelp review. But that would likely be the end of it. That's the worst she could do. I don't think she could sue.

That said, the last thing I want to do is make someone else shoulder the burden. Besides, it's women like Shelby who need me the most. Women like Shelby are the reason I got into this career, to be there for women with no or unsupportive partners.

I take a deep breath. I peek at Josh to be certain the covers are still over his head.

Did he hurt you? I ask. I remember the sunglasses the last time I saw her. She was hiding something, either red, swollen eyes from crying, or a black eye.

I think of all the things that she could say in reply. She could tell me that yes, he hurt her. That he hit her. That he has a temper. That he screams and throws things.

But abuse isn't always physical. It can be emotional, too. Name-calling, throwing insults, controlling her behavior, monitoring her whereabouts at all times, asserting financial control. Shelby used to work. She no longer does. She no longer has her own source of income. We think that victims of abuse should leave their spouses. We judge them for *not* leaving but choosing to stay in abusive relationships. But with no job and a baby on the way, what are women like Shelby to do? She's reliant on Jason.

Physical abuse worries me more than emotional abuse. But the fact that Shelby doesn't reply is most disconcerting of all.

I think the worst: that he saw her texting and now he's mad. Is everything okay, Shelby? I ask.

When again she doesn't reply, I consider going to her house to see if she's all right. The Tebows' address is on the contract.

They don't live far. They live quite close actually, in our neighborhood. It might be how Shelby heard of me.

Now that I think of it, I don't know how Shelby heard of me. Sometimes OBGYNs recommend me. But Shelby's is leery of doulas. I haven't worked with him before, but his reputation precedes him. He wouldn't have recommended me or anyone else in my line of work.

I have a website. There is a database of doulas where she could have found me. The fact that I can walk to her house may only be coincidental.

But it would be rash for me to go to the Tebow house now, by myself. It's the middle of the night. And what would I do when I got there? Just knock on the front door? If her husband isn't mad now—if he doesn't know what Shelby told me—he would be.

Besides, how am I to know he wouldn't answer the door with a shotgun? People have them. I am a mother. I have my own kids. I can't put myself in harm's way for Shelby's sake.

I could call the police then, ask them to do a welfare check. But what if that would only make things worse for her? Her husband would be angry if the police showed up. He'd want to know why they were there. There would be backlash.

And besides, not long ago a woman called in a welfare check on a neighbor whose door was left open overnight. When police arrived, they got spooked. They inadvertently shot the neighbor in her own home. She died as a result. I wouldn't want something like that on me.

In the end I do nothing. Indecision paralyzes me. I go back to bed, clutching the phone to my chest in case, later on, she needs me.

LEO

NOW

We don't need the lady cop anymore. Our crisis was averted when I found you asleep in the basement. Still, Dad doesn't call her off. He lets her come, though it's the middle of the night and her arrival sparks much interest from the hacks outside. There are lights and cameras on our house because of her.

"Josh," she says as Dad ushers her quickly in and closes the door.

"Carmen."

She takes Dad in her arms. They hold each other too long. It's embarrassing to watch. "I came as soon as you called. You must be beside yourself with worry."

Dad pulls back. The lady cop isn't in her usual detective getup, but the most put-together version of someone who's just rolled out of bed. I smell her perfume from halfway across the room. "We found her," Dad says, "Leo did," and then they look at me, as if they only just then realized that I was here.

"Oh, thank God. Where was she?"

Dad tells her.

Her hand goes to her heart. "Oh my God."

Dad couldn't stand the idea of you sleeping on the basement floor, so he woke you and sent you back upstairs. You did as told, though you were disoriented when you awoke. You weren't so sure you weren't still in that other basement. You panicked. "It's okay, it's okay," I said when you did, careful not to touch you like Dad had. "It's just Dad and me. Leo. You're home. You're safe. Remember?"

You're not sure what *safe* means. Still, you climbed the stairs and went back up to your bedroom. You closed the door. I wonder how long you'll stay there.

"Good for you, Leo," the lady cop says now.

I shrug. "It's not like she was that hard to find."

Dad tells her, "I should have called and told you you didn't need to come. But we just found her a couple minutes ago. There wasn't time." I silently call bullshit. It's been at least fifteen minutes since Dad sent you upstairs. Plenty of time to call the lady cop off.

"No, it's fine. You know I'm always here for you whenever you need me, Josh."

She's staring at him. Their hands are still touching. Inside I gag. I don't announce that I'm going to bed. I just leave, though there's no chance I'm going to sleep.

I don't go into my room. I take a seat at the top of the stairs instead. I listen to what they say. One thing I've figured out about the lady cop is that she has two voices. She has her cop voice, in which she thinks she's pretty badass. That's the one I always hear at the police station. And then there's her lady voice, which is the exact opposite of this. It's eager to please. Tonight her lady voice showed up.

"So tell me. How's it been going having Delilah home?"

Their voices are hushed from the distance. Dad's chilled out some from his near heart attack upstairs, but I can tell that his nerves are still frayed. After he got you back upstairs, he cracked open a cold one and finished it in two minutes flat. "I'd be lying if I said everything was perfect. It's far from perfect. She's not right, Carmen."

"Of course she's not."

"She's suffered greatly."

"She has. And you have, too."

No one mentions me and my suffering.

"It's been over a decade that she's been gone. She's not my little girl anymore. Don't get me wrong. I'm ecstatic to have her home. Relieved and overjoyed. I keep having to remind myself that this is real, that Delilah is actually home. That this isn't just another dream I'll wake up from in the morning, as I have hundreds of times since she disappeared. She's here, and no one's ever going to take her away from me again. We'll get there," he says. "We'll get to a place where things feel normal."

"A new normal. Things may never be how they used to be."

"You did this, you know?"

"Did what?"

"This. You brought my baby girl back home to me. You never gave up on her, on us. You told me you'd keep looking until you found her, and now you have. I can't ever thank you enough for this, Carmen."

"I was just doing my job."

"You went above and beyond. You are still," he says, and then it's quiet for a long time. Too long. In my perverted mind, I see them sucking face, even though I've never actually witnessed anything more intimate than their sappy texts and the occasional hug. But how would I know what they do when left to their own devices? They're two lonely grown-ups, after all. The man has needs, even if the idea of it makes me want to puke.

You're making noise in your room. I don't know what you're doing in there, but I know you're awake. I push myself off the floor. I go to your door. I knock. And then because I think me knocking might scare the bejesus out of you, I call through the door. "It's me. Leo."

Your side of the door goes quiet. If I had to guess, I'd say you're standing there, trying to talk yourself into letting me in. How do you know that you can trust me? How do you know I'm not here to do something bad?

I don't blame you for being scared.

I knock again. It takes some time for you to open up the door.

You don't say anything when you do. You just stand there, looking uptight. "Why aren't you asleep?" I ask. You don't say. You're still wearing the hospital clothes. For whatever reason, you don't want to put mine on.

"What are you doing in here?" I ask. I look around to see what you've been up to. But the room is mostly dark. I can't see much.

You give your head a little shake. Your hair falls into your eyes. It's schlumpy. You've got a smell to you. You need a shower, but Dad thought you'd had enough for one day, so a shower will have to wait until tomorrow. "Nothing, sir," you say.

"Leo," I tell you, getting annoyed now. "It's Leo. Le-*o*," I say, 'cause maybe you don't know how to pronounce it or something. I could wear a nametag to help you remember, but I don't want to be a dick and assume you know how to read. "Say it with me. Le-*o*."

You say my name. I think there's going to be something déjà vu-ish about it when you finally do, but there's nothing. Not the spark of recollection I'd been hoping for.

"See? That wasn't so hard, was it?"

You don't say either way.

"Why aren't you sleeping?"

You don't tell me.

"Just can't sleep?"

You don't say.

I think it would be hard trying to sleep in a place that's brand-new, surrounded by people you don't know. You were asleep in the basement, until Dad went and put an end to that.

"Stay here," I say. "I'll be right back."

I go to my room. Kicked to the back corner of the closet floor is my old security blanket. It's blue. The silk edge is torn. Why

I still have this stupid thing is beyond me. I used to go every-where with it. I'd cry without it. According to Dad, Mom used to have to dupe me to get it out of my hands long enough to wash it. Once, it got left in the grocery store shopping cart and my world almost came to an end.

I'm thinking maybe you need my blanket more than I do.

I half expect your bedroom door to be shut and locked when I come back. It's not. I thrust the blanket at you. "Take it," I say.

"What is it?" you ask, feeling the texture of it, the weight. The thing's been washed so many times it's anything but soft. It's thin. It isn't the kind of thing that would keep anybody warm. It doesn't look like much.

"My old blankie. My blanket. Some kids have them. Maybe you did, too. I don't know. I couldn't sleep without that thing as a kid."

You don't say anything. You just hold my blanket in your hands, staring blankly at it, then me, then it, 'cause you can't hold someone's stare more than a second at best. "I thought maybe it would help you, you know, sleep. It used to be the only thing that made me feel better when I was sick or sad." I turn my back to you and start walking away.

Three steps later, you say, "Don't you need it?" Then you tack on, "Leo." The way you say it is unsure, like you're not a hundred percent sure you should say it. It gets a smile out of me, though you don't see. I keep walking.

"I think you need it more than me."

KATE

11 YEARS BEFORE

May

As promised, Bea and I drive to the babysitter's to pick Leo up.
We park on the street, then walk to the door, sharing an umbrella. When we reach the door, it sounds like mass chaos on
the other side. I rap my knuckles against the door. When that
fails to get anyone's attention, I pound. Charlotte, the babysitter,
comes. As she draws the door slowly open, I catch a glimpse at
the anarchy on the other side. A TV is on, volume loud, but no
one watches it. Instead, a group of kids play Simon Says, while
another plays tag. They chase each other in circles around the
living room, leaping on furniture whenever necessary to get
away from *It*.

It's madness to play tag inside, and yet it's raining outside.
And even if it wasn't raining, the ground is sopping wet from
days of rain. It's too wet to play in.

I try and get a head count. But the children are constantly on
the move; they're impossible to count. If I had to guess, I'd say

more than a dozen, including the one who hangs from Charlotte's leg, wanting a ride. The kids are hysterical, slaphappy.

I have to look a while to find Leo. He sits by himself at a small table in the corner of the room. He pieces together a puzzle, alone. The kids run circles around him. One knocks into the table. It's by accident only, and yet it's careless, insensitive. It's a little girl who does it, taller than Leo by a head. If she knows what she's done, she doesn't apologize. She keeps running, laughing, while Leo's puzzle goes flying to the floor. The pieces separate. No one but Leo and me notice. Leo's face falls, but he doesn't cry. He looks so small in comparison to the others as he scooches his chair out and drops to his knees, reclaiming the fallen puzzle pieces.

"Can I help you?" Charlotte asks, peering at Bea and me through the screen. I let my gaze fall from Leo, feeling sad. Charlotte's hair is gray. Her eyes are gray. She has deep-set wrinkles around her mouth and under her eyes, made worse when she smiles, which she does. She has a kind smile.

"We're here to pick up Leo," I say, "Leo Dickey," in case, in this mayhem, there's more than one Leo.

"Yes, of course," she says, "Josh called and told me you'd be coming. The weather," Charlotte complains, leaning in closer to be able to speak over the noise. "Usually I'd have the kids downstairs, but the darn sump pump went out yesterday, and the basement flooded."

"Oh, no, how awful," I say. "What a mess."

"We had a new one put in, but the basement is in the process of drying out. It will take a while. There are fans everywhere, but even after it's dry, we'll need repairs before the kids can go back down. Being cooped up inside like this," she says, turning to look at the kids, "it's making the children stir-crazy. All that pent-up energy. They need to get outdoors and play."

She calls across the room for Leo. He's still on his knees, picking up fallen puzzle pieces. He glances up at the sound of Charlotte's voice, seeing Bea and me through the screened door. A slow smile spreads across his lips, and Bea waves. Like a good boy, Leo finishes gathering his puzzle to put it away before he leaves.

Charlotte hugs him before he goes, confessing to Bea and me, "He's my favorite. I wish all the kids were as well behaved as him." I wonder if she says this to all of the kids.

Charlotte opens the door and Leo steps outside with us. We make our way to the car. Leo is quiet, as always. He doesn't ask about Josh, Meredith or Delilah. Still, Bea says something glib about why we're not going to his home.

"Delilah's sick," Leo tells us at random.

Bea says, "Yep, buddy. That's right. Delilah's sick." It doesn't feel right lying to Leo.

At home, Bea makes dinner for Leo and me. She lets Leo help. They make pasta. Bea serves it with milk for Leo, a glass of wine for me. She makes an extra plate to save for Josh, not that he will eat it.

We sit at the table and eat. Bea tries to get Leo to open up about his day. He isn't very forthcoming. When Bea asks if he likes it there at Charlotte's, tears well in his eyes. He doesn't answer with words. He doesn't need to.

I finish my glass of wine and Bea brings me another. She switches topics to something more light. She and Leo get lost in a discussion of superheroes with the best superpowers. I don't join in. My mind is elsewhere, circling on three things: What is happening at Josh and Meredith's house? Who did Cassandra see on the Dickeys' lawn that night? How can I meet Dr. Feingold for myself?

We're playing charades when Josh comes for Leo. We're in the living room. The TV is on but muted. For the last hour or so, Bea and I have watched the news ticker at the bottom of the screen warn us that we're under a severe thunderstorm watch. As I open the door for Josh, I see that the world outside has turned ominous. It's late and dark; he was with the police for hours.

I welcome Josh in, pressing the door closed against the weight of the urgent wind. Josh rushes to Leo, where he scoops him into his arms. They talk about Leo's day. Leo asks where Mommy is. Josh hesitates, and I feel for him, having to come up with an answer to Leo on the spot. As with Bea, it's a lie. The truth would be too much for Leo to handle right now, especially when none of the adults in his life know what the truth is. Where is Meredith?

"Mommy is at work," he says.

"When will Mommy be home?" he asks. His voice is small, discreet, like he doesn't want Bea and me to hear.

"You know how it goes, Leo," Josh says. "Sometimes we don't know when Mommy will be home from work. But she'll be home as soon as she can. I promise you that."

We let Leo pick out a cartoon. Once he's fully immersed in it, Bea, Josh and I slip into the kitchen where we can speak in private.

"What happened?" I ask Josh. I go to the refrigerator, offer him a beer. Bea warms his dinner and brings it to the table, though, as expected, he doesn't eat. Josh looks beat, disheveled, undone. He hasn't shaved in two days. I'm not entirely sure he's slept or showered.

He says reluctantly, "They found Meredith's pills." I know what he means by this. I know what the implication is. They're blaming the victim.

I get angry for Josh and Meredith. "Did they have a warrant to search your house?"

He shakes his head, says remorsefully, "They didn't need one, Kate. I gave them permission to search. I didn't think we had anything to hide. We *don't* have anything to hide."

I get it. For Josh, the invasion of privacy was worth it if it meant the police finding something that might tip them off about Meredith and Delilah's whereabouts. He just didn't expect them to draw certain conclusions when they found Meredith's pills in the medicine cabinet. Meredith struggled with postpartum depression after Leo was born. She wasn't ashamed of it. She didn't try and keep it a secret. In fact, she was unapologetic and unreserved, appreciating how her own experience made her better at what she does. Meredith saw a therapist for a while, and was put on antidepressants. The antidepressants helped; she was in no rush to get off them, because if they were working, then why would she be?

"So what?" I ask, wondering what Meredith's antidepressants have to do with anything.

"They asked a lot of questions. About her mental health. About whether she's ever tried to hurt herself or one of the kids."

"My God," Bea says, her hand going to her heart. The media has sensationalized postpartum depression, made it out to seem like all women who suffer are the kind to kill their children. It's not true. Postpartum psychosis is something else. It's different and rare, and even of those affected, only a small percentage do something violent. I know because Meredith told me. She talked once about writing a blog about the experiences of women, and this was one of the things she considered writing about. Postpartum psychosis both fascinated and saddened her.

"What did you tell them?" I ask.

"I told them no, of course not. Meredith is the most sound person I know. Ask anyone, I said," Josh tells us, and it's true. Meredith has always been the glass-half-full type. She teaches yoga, she meditates. She rarely has a bad thing to say about anyone else. She's a good person. She's not capable of hurting her kids, under any circumstance.

"The police are way off base if they think Meredith has done something to Delilah," I say. I'm getting worked up. I'm angry. The wine hasn't helped because I feel less inhibited, free to say whatever I want. But the police are wasting time if they think Meredith did this.

Josh takes a big, long swig of his beer and says, "There's more." He's guarded as he says it. Quiet. He sinks back into his chair, takes another long drink from the bottle and sets it slowly down.

He wipes at his mouth with the back of a hand, his eyes focused on the wood grain of the table, avoiding Bea and me.

"They found blood," he says, and only then do his blue eyes rise slowly up.

There's a sudden heaviness in my stomach. I push my glass of wine away, no longer able to drink from it. Josh's words make me instantly sober up. *Blood.* "Where?" I ask. Bea leans forward to hear.

"In the garage."

"You hadn't noticed?" I ask.

Josh shakes his head. "It's dark in the garage. One of the bulbs is burned out. I keep forgetting to fix it. It's not what you're imagining," he explains. "There wasn't a ton of blood, Kate. Even after the police pointed it out for me," he says, "it was still hard to see."

"But it was there," I say, voice drifting.

"What do they think?" Bea asks. She's standing at the head of the table, hands on the top rail of the backrest. Beside Josh, I sit. I reach my hand out and touch his. He takes my hand into his and holds it for a minute. Neither of us speak. I can't imagine what he is going through. His hand trembles in mine. I doubt that Josh has had anything to eat all day and a beer, on an empty stomach, can't be good. I let go of his hand, push his plate of pasta closer and encourage him to eat.

To appease me, he takes a couple of bites before setting the fork down. "They're seeing if it's Delilah's or Meredith's," he says, about the blood. "We should know soon."

I wonder what good knowing this will do. I think, if anything, it will make Josh, in addition to Meredith, look bad. More victim blaming.

It's as if Josh can read my mind. He confesses, "They asked where I was that day, if someone at work could vouch for me."

"An alibi?" Bea asks, and he nods his head. "They think you did something to her?"

"I don't know what they think," he tells us. "They're just

doing their jobs," he says, and I admire his diplomacy. It would be easy to understand why he might get upset. I would be upset. I would be raging. But Josh doesn't get upset. "I have an alibi, if that's what you're wondering," he says, but he's tight-lipped about it, unforthcoming. This suggests to me that Josh was doing something he shouldn't have been doing.

My heart hurts. Was Josh seeing someone else? Was Josh cheating on Meredith?

"What were you doing?" Bea hesitantly asks, thinking the same thing as me.

"It sounds so shallow in retrospect," he says, and she has to ask again, more insistent this time.

"Where were you yesterday, Josh?"

He takes a deep breath, slowly exhales. "Playing tennis," he says, describing for us the very chichi exclusive club where they play. He's ashamed, knowing now that while something terrible was happening to Meredith and Delilah, he was having a doubles match with a prospective client. He wasn't having an affair.

"I won, not that it makes any difference now." He swallows hard, keeping his emotions at bay. I don't think he'd cry with Leo just in the next room. For Leo's sake, he has to be strong.

"You can't beat yourself up about it," Bea tells him, relieved like me to know that he wasn't with some other woman, not in the way we thought at least. "You didn't know."

"There's no way you could have known," I echo.

Bea changes the subject. She brings up the body found down there by the river's edge. Shelby's body. Josh says it's something that will haunt him for the rest of his life; he won't ever get that image out of his mind. An autopsy would still need to be done, but speculation was that she'd been dead at least a couple of days. I've seen animals dead a couple of days. It must have been horrific for Josh, seeing Shelby's whole body expanded in size due to the buildup of gases inside. I just thank God it wasn't Meredith he had to see that way.

"Do they think her husband killed her?" I ask.

"No one said."

"We heard she was naked."

"Mostly, yes," he says. "But she was covered up with a blanket."

"A blanket?" Bea asks. She's surprised, as am I. It's unexpected. It strikes me as an affectionate, intimate thing to do, not the kind of thing a ruthless killer would do. Unless of course the murderer knew his victim and had a fondness for her. Then he might do something like cover her up with a blanket.

I think of Bea and my conversation with Jason Tebow, with the midwife and what we learned about Dr. Feingold.

"How much does Meredith tell you about her clients?" I ask.

"What do you mean?"

"Did you know Shelby was a client of hers?"

The look on Josh's face is clear. He didn't know. "Meredith left her clients' names out of it when we talked about them. Their privacy was important to her. She'd tell me when a husband was being an ass, or about a baby born with some abnormality, but she never called them by name."

"Then you didn't know that the Tebows are suing their obstetrician for malpractice. Meredith is to testify in a deposition against him," I say.

The color fades from Josh's face. "How do you know?" he asks, and I tell him. He looks at us in disbelief, his eyes going back and forth between Bea's and mine. He asks, "You spoke to Jason Tebow? You should be more careful. He could be dangerous. What if he killed Shelby?" he asks. "How do you know he wouldn't have killed you, too?"

Bea and I say nothing. Josh runs his fingers through his hair. The realization that Meredith might have gotten herself into something high-risk scares him. I can see the disbelief in his eyes. The worry. Once upon a time, Meredith told him everything. Even if she kept her clients' confidentiality, testifying against this doctor was something she should have told him.

"What do you think, then," he asks, "that this obstetrician did something to both of them, and Delilah, too?"

"I don't know," I say. "We're just telling you what we know, Josh." I say it softly because I know that he's scared. He's beside himself, barely keeping it together. He isn't trying to be argumentative or defensive. I'm scared, too.

He inhales deeply, slowly lets the air out. "Maybe," Josh says, thinking aloud, "that's what Mr. Tebow wants you to think. Maybe it's a lie."

It's possible, of course. I don't know Jason Tebow. I have no reason to believe anything he said was true. In my mind, both men are equally culpable. But Jeanette the midwife corroborated much of what he said. What reason would she have to lie?

"We don't know what to think, Josh," Bea says. "God willing, Meredith and Delilah are fine. Completely and absolutely fine."

"Still," I say, hating to be the alarmist, but it's something that can't be ignored. "The connection between Shelby and Meredith. The fact that they knew each other. It's concerning, right?" I ask.

They both look at me and stare, no one wanting to face the fact that it's more than just concerning. What it means is that, with Shelby now dead, Meredith and Delilah are in serious trouble. We need to find them soon, if it's not too late for them already.

MEREDITH

11 YEARS BEFORE

March

"Good morning," Josh says as he appears in the kitchen doorway in a slim-fit dark gray suit. He smiles at me, looking smart,
competent. I stand at the stove, already showered and dressed,
making pancakes and bacon for Josh and the kids. Josh comes
to me. He wraps his arms around me from behind and I get a
whiff of him, of his shaving cream and his cologne. "How'd
you sleep?" he asks me.

"Okay," I say, though I didn't sleep well. Now I'm up early,
feeling anxious, wanting to know if Shelby is all right after her
text last night. I keep checking my phone, but it's quiet. It has
been since shortly after three a.m. "How about you?" I ask,
turning to face him. "How'd you sleep?"

"Like a baby," he says, kissing me. His kiss isn't rushed. It goes
on far longer than the usual peck, which is all we ever have time
for before we're interrupted by kids. His kiss is tender, unhur-
ried, and I find myself thinking how much I miss this, some-

thing as commonplace as kissing my husband. Everything else falls by the wayside. For one blissful minute, the anxiety of the last few days abates.

And then, from upstairs, I hear a toilet flush: the first sign of life. Delilah or Leo, whoever is up, will be down soon. Josh draws slowly away, still smiling.

"What do you have on tap for today?" I ask and he tells me.

"Finalizing a deal with a prospective client. Hopefully." He and his team have been working on this pitch for some time. It would mean the world to Josh and his career to land this client.

"What time is the meeting?"

"Eleven."

"Good luck," I tell him. "Not that you need it." Josh is incredibly good at what he does. He's climbed the corporate ladder more quickly than most.

"Thanks," he says, then asks, "Do you have a client in labor?"

"No. Why?"

"Your phone," he says. "I heard a text come in in the middle of the night."

"Oh." Of course he did. I remember him drawing away, pulling the covers over his head to block the phone's light. "Braxton-Hicks," I lie, saying that a client thought she was in labor, but she's not. It can be confusing, for first-time mothers. The contractions are not as intense as real contractions. They don't come at regular intervals; they don't progress. I often have to talk these women out of thinking they're in labor.

It doesn't matter, though, because it's a lie. None of my clients is currently experiencing Braxton-Hicks contractions.

I don't like lying to Josh. It isn't something that happens often. In fact, it never happened, not until about six months ago when Josh started to get more apprehensive about my job. It began with a random carjacking. A young woman was stopped in town, at a red light near midnight. During the day, it's a busy intersection. There's a grocery store, a gym, Walgreens. But at that time of night it was vacant. Everything around was closed.

Two masked men approached the car at gunpoint. They made the woman get out of the car. They assaulted her first, before stealing her car. They left with her phone, her purse, her ID. She couldn't call for help. She walked three miles home in the dark. They never found the people who did it to her. It left Josh scared for my safety. He's overprotective as a result. He wishes I was a stay-at-home mom like Cassandra. *We don't need the money*, Josh has said. It's a conversation we've had often. He does it because he loves me. Because he doesn't want anything bad happening to me. I get that. I love him even more for it. But I also love my job.

"Is she okay?" Josh asks, meaning my client with Braxton-Hicks.

"She's fine. It's unsettling," I tell him. "The unknown. But she's forty weeks yesterday. She'll go into labor soon."

"How long did she keep you up?" he asks, looking at me, sizing up my eyes. They're tired, heavy. I'm on my third cup of coffee.

"Not long."

"You're a good person," Josh says before he leaves for work. I hate how we're always rushing off in opposite directions.

I also feel guilty for lying to Josh. But what he doesn't know won't hurt him. I'm lying to protect him. To protect Shelby. To protect my career.

Through the window, Delilah sees Cassandra, Piper and Arlo leave for school. She gets upset because of it. She wants to leave, too. She wants to walk to school with Piper. But we can't leave yet, because I can't find one of Leo's shoes.

"Help me look," I tell Delilah, and she does. She finds it hidden behind the kitchen curtains. Leo won't sit still long enough for me to put it on. By the time we make it outside, Cassandra and family are gone. They're too far ahead to catch even if we ran.

"Don't worry. You'll see her at school," I tell a pouting Delilah.

Leo and I walk Delilah the few blocks to school. We take her to the corner where parents congregate, watching as the crossing guard gets the children across the street and to the redbrick building on the other side.

Delilah makes us walk quickly to try and catch Piper before she crosses the street. She wants to walk into school with her. But by the time we arrive, Piper has already crossed the street. Even worse, she's walking hand in hand with another little girl from school, Lily Morris. Lily Morris is in Piper and Delilah's kindergarten class.

Delilah is upset because she has to wait for the crossing guard to allow her to cross. But the crossing guard is letting traffic pass now; she has to wait. I feel badly for her, having to watch these other girls walk into the building without her, feeling left out. Friendships are hard. I lean down and whisper in her ear, "You'll catch up with them in class. It will be fine, honey. You'll see."

Cassandra and Arlo stand at the corner. I'd go over and say hello, but Cassandra is caught up in a conversation with Lily Morris's mother, Amber. I don't like Amber any more than Delilah likes Lily. Lily, according to Delilah, is not nice. She's mean. She won't ever play with Delilah. She makes fun of the kids. She calls them things like *stupid* and *dumb*.

I watch as Piper and Lily make it inside the building. Their mothers turn away, stepping past me. I hear the word *playdate* as they do, and I stiffen in reply. Piper and Lily are having a playdate without Delilah. I don't want to get caught up in kindergarten drama. But she's my daughter. If she's being excluded, she'll be sad. Delilah's happiness means everything to me.

"Hi, Cassandra," I say. I reach out to touch her arm as she sweeps by. It's a reflex.

Cassandra turns to me and says, "Oh, Meredith. I didn't see you there." I find it hard to believe. There are only a dozen parents at the corner. And even now that she has, she doesn't stop and talk to me. She keeps walking, with Lily's mother. I feel a stab of jealousy, of resentment. Because Amber used to be the one Cassandra and I would talk about over coffee. How she's so overinvolved in the PTO. How she thinks school bake sales are the end-all and be-all of life. Her grandiose sense of self-importance.

The tables have turned. I'd bet my life they're talking about me. I try not to dwell on it. I have enough friends. I don't need Cassandra to be my friend, though I like Cassandra. I like her a lot. I'd be sad to lose her as a friend.

The only reason Cassandra has for being angry, anyway, is one too many canceled coffee dates. It's a hazard of my job. Childbirth can't be planned. Cassandra knows this. She's always been tolerant, until now. It's not like she could know about her husband, Marty, and me. Unless he told her, but he wouldn't do that. We'd agreed to keep things secret, for Cassandra's and Josh's sake.

Leo and I watch Delilah walk across the street, and then we walk back to the house. We get in the car. I drive him to the babysitter's house. I put Cassandra out of my mind for now.

I park on the street. Leo leaves his blanket in the car, though he never likes to be apart from it. He does so reluctantly, with the promise that I'll keep it safe while he's gone. I walk him to the front door. When the sitter Charlotte comes, Leo throws a fit. This happens, sometimes, though it's relatively new. Some-days Leo goes willingly. But other days he doesn't want to go to the sitter's house. He wants to stay with me.

"Mommy has to work," I say soothingly. I peel his arms from my leg and gently shove him into Charlotte's open arms. It feels awful to do this, to push my crying child away. In Charlotte's arms, his crying intensifies. My heart aches. Leo tries squirming away, coming back to me. There's a hitch to my voice. I choke back my own tears as I say, "You'll have fun. You'll play with the other kids. Before you know it, Daddy will be here to pick you up, and then you'll be having so much fun you won't want to come home."

It's only lately that Leo has had stranger anxiety. Of course

Charlotte is not a stranger. He's known her for months. She's far from a stranger. But these days Leo only wants to be with Josh or me. We talked to the pediatrician about it. She said to give it time, that, like most things in our kids' lives, it's a passing phase.

"He'll be fine," Charlotte says. "He always is after you leave."

It's the same thing that the pediatrician said. Saying goodbye is the hardest part. I take comfort in that as I stand alone on her front porch, watching as Charlotte carries my crying child away and closes the door. From the other side, I hear him wail.

Delilah and Leo have been coming to Charlotte's house since Delilah started kindergarten this year. Before that, they attended a different day care. I didn't love it. It had a clinical feel, nothing homey like this. Things got complicated, too, when Delilah started school. Then I needed a sitter who could pick her up at the end of the day, who could keep an eye on her until Josh came home. The school didn't provide a bus. Charlotte was that sitter, parading there with all the kids to pick them up, pulling the little ones in the red wagon. Until recently, the kids have been happy with her. I think of what the pediatrician said: a passing phase. This, too, shall pass.

I turn my back to Charlotte's house. My next stop is Shelby's. I need to see with my own eyes if she's okay after her texts last night.

I drive to Shelby's home. I leave my car on the street, behind a red sedan that's parked on the curb. I step out. I make my way to the front door and quietly knock.

Shelby peels the door slowly back. She's still in her pajamas, from what I can tell, though the door blocks most of her body. I examine her face for signs of bruising. There are none. That said, she looks washed-out. She wears no makeup. In the coffee shop, she had makeup. Today she looks like she just rolled out of bed. I'm grateful to see her alive and seemingly unharmed. I breathe a sigh of relief. I never would have forgiven myself if something bad had happened.

"What are you doing here?" Shelby asks. She's unable to hide the surprise. I'm the last person in the world she expected to see. Her voice is quiet. It's little more than a whisper.

I'm relieved that there are no visible bruises. But I've heard that abusive spouses can be masters at hiding their handiwork. There may be bruises that I can't see or, if her husband is abusing her, it could be emotional rather than physical.

I'm not only worried for Shelby's sake. I'm worried for her unborn baby. A kick or a punch to her gut could easily end its life. I looked up photos of Mr. Tebow online. He's a large man. He looks mean.

I say, "You didn't text back last night, Shelby. I was worried."

Shelby looks vacant. Either she doesn't know what to say, or she doesn't know what I mean. Her hair is mussed up, thrown into a sloppy ponytail. Her roots are shades darker than the rest of her hair.

She says nothing apropos of what I've said.

Instead, "How did you know where I live?" It's accusatory, almost. As if she thinks I've crossed a line. As if she thinks I'm stalking her.

"It's on the contract, Shelby," I say. I can hear the patience in my voice start to wane. "You wrote your address on the contract."

"I did?" she asks.

"You did."

"Oh," she says. "Right. I did. I just didn't think that you'd show up at my door."

I tell her, "I don't usually show up at my clients' homes. This is a first for me. But I was worried," I say again. "After your texts last night, I came to make sure everything was fine."

I hear a man's voice in the background. It startles me. My insides tighten. I see the shadow of him loom at the top of the stairs. I swallow against a bulge in my throat. That must be him, her husband, Jason. I hadn't expected him to be home.

He calls for her, asks her to grab him a drink on her way up.

The gap in the door gets smaller. Shelby is inching the door closed, inadvertent or not.

His tone is brusque, but not necessarily mean. *Hey, Shel? Bring me something to drink, would you?*

"I'll be there in a minute," she calls up the stairs. She looks to me, says anxiously, "I have to go." She fully intends to close the door in my face. Before she can, my foot inches forward. It happens unintentionally, before I can think it through. My foot fills the door's narrowing crack so that she can't close it when she tries.

"What are you doing?" Shelby asks, surprised. She looks down at my wedged foot. Her voice stays quiet, words hissed. She doesn't want him to know that I am here.

I say flatly, "You didn't tell me if you're all right."

"Why wouldn't I be?" she asks, her tone immature. Shelby is in her early twenties. I thought I'd reached adulthood when I was that age. Now, over a decade later, I realize that at twenty-three or twenty-four, I didn't know much of anything. I still had so much growing up to do, so much to figure out about how the world worked.

"Because of your text messages, Shelby. You told me you were scared of your husband."

"Oh. That," she says. "I shouldn't have sent that." She runs her hands through her hair, pulls the rubber band out. Her hair falls around her shoulders. She shakes it out. "We had a stupid fight, that's all. I fired off some stupid text. I didn't mean it."

"Then why did you say it?" I ask, not sure if I believe her.

"I was mad," she says.

"You said you were scared."

"He was yelling at me."

"About what?" I ask, not sure that she'll tell me.

"It was stupid," she says. I say nothing. I wait, seeing if she'll continue, and she does. "I spend too much money. He said I have crap for brains because I went and bought some new maternity shirts and got one of those prenatal massages. He says we're broke and I can't be wasting money like that, but he has no idea what it's like to be carrying around a baby all the time. He doesn't give a shit that I've outgrown my clothes."

"Did he hurt you, Shelby?" I ask.

"He was really pissed off," she says.

I ask again. "Did he hurt you?"

"Do I look hurt to you?"

She doesn't. I don't know what to think. Maybe he did and maybe he didn't.

"You coming, Shel?" he calls again, more brusquely this time, losing patience. "I haven't got all day to wait."

"It's really nice of you to come check on me, Meredith," she says. The rest of her words come quickly out, tumbling like a waterfall. "No one does kind things like this for me."

I lean in and whisper, talking fast, "Did he hurt you? You can tell me if he did. I can help." I don't know what I'd do to help other than go to the police. But I'd do that for her. She doesn't answer. "You can talk to me." I breathe the words through the doorway, withdrawing my foot to reach in and set my hand on hers. Her hand is cold. "I'm here for you," I say.

The grin on her face is very Stepford wives. "You're sweet, Meredith. Really sweet. I'm glad I found you," she says. She drops my hand. She goes again to close the door. She still hasn't told me if she's all right.

I try to stop her. Before I can, the door is shut.

LEO

NOW

Dad takes you to a shrink. The shrink came recommended by the lady cop, because she's worked with trauma victims before.

I go because Dad needs my help getting you to the car. The reporters are hungry, and the walk to our garage, where the car is parked, is long.

We leave out the back door. We make a run for it, but the reporters are ready and waiting. They're like vultures. They close in on us the second we're out the door. They call out questions. Dad tells them, "Your first amendment rights don't give you permission to trample our lawn."

He's cheesed off, but trying not to fly off the handle because the reporters would only get that on video and show it on TV.

Still, Dad threatens to press trespassing charges. It takes a while for the two fat cops to get out of their car, shut down the reporters' inquisition and get them off our lawn.

Between Dad and me, you shake. You're not used to the pandemonium, to the sunlight, to the noise. Dad's got his hooded parka on you, and you hide beneath the hood like Little Red

Riding Hood, looking scared as hell 'cause the wolf is about to eat you alive. You've got my blanket with you, which makes me feel all sorts of things I've never felt inside. But I don't point it out because I don't want you to feel weirded out. And besides, externalizing feelings isn't my thing. So instead I pretend that I don't see the blanket.

When we get to the shrink's office, Dad and I stay in the waiting room, much to his chagrin. He planned to go in with you. But the shrink says no, that it would be better if Dad stays put. We never know what you talk about or don't talk about with her. She's got a white noise machine on the floor, so Dad and I can't hear what you say. I see Dad looking at it. I read his mind. He's thinking about pulling the plug, but he never does.

This is what you told the police: you were kept in a locked basement by a man and a woman, who the cops now need to find. You don't know how you got there. You don't know much about your life before. You've blocked most of it out, though you have hazy memories of our house, Dad's face, the fact that Mom is dead. Dad's hoping the shrink can squeeze the rest of it out of you, especially your last minutes with Mom. He needs to know once and for all what happened. Dad's willing to try just about anything to make it so: medicine, hypnosis.

We go back to the police after seeing the shrink. The lady cop is waiting for us when we get there. "Can I talk to you, Josh?" she asks, and they disappear. I'm left with you. Someone else might try and make small talk with you. But I just stand there like some dope, not sure what to say. I should say something to make you feel better, but I can't find the words. Anything I might say would sound stupid. So I say nothing. Dad and the lady cop stand in the far corner of the room. She holds a file folder in her hands, but she never opens it. She does all of the talking. Dad's head nods.

"What was that all about?" I ask when Dad comes back.

"The DNA results."

"What about them?"

"It's her. She's your sister."

I thought we already knew that.

Today, when talking with the lady cop, you remember that the man's and the woman's names are Eddie and Martha. They're the ones who kept you. The lady cop asks if you can describe them, and you do, but it's fuzzy at best, things like brown hair and a fat face. She gets a sketch artist to sit with you. Then she talks to Dad. She asks whether Mom knew anyone named Eddie or Martha. Mom didn't, as far as Dad knows. The lady cop thinks maybe this had something to do with money. Maybe Mom owed money to someone and so they took you as payment. She asks Dad if Mom was in debt to anyone, if Mom had gotten in over her head. Did she have a history of gambling, a drug addiction? Was she selling? There's a thing with some suburban moms: selling prescription drugs like Vicodin and their kids' Adderall to make ends meet. It's been on the news.

Dad has doubts. Even after all that's happened, he still hero-worships Mom. Sure she took you, she ended her own life. I kinda hate her for it. But he idolizes her.

"Meredith wouldn't have done that."

"I know that's what you want to believe, Josh. But we have to consider the possibilities."

Mom hadn't been herself before it happened. Something went down that made her want to kill herself. We don't know what.

Dad wonders aloud about a middleman. What if Mom put you somewhere safe, and then that person gave you away? That's the only way he can think that you would've ended up with Eddie and Martha.

In an instant Dad becomes obsessed with this idea of a middleman.

There never was much of an investigation into what happened to Mom. When she was thought to be missing, there were a few suspects, like Dad. But as soon as it became apparent she offed herself, they were all suddenly innocent. Only Mom was to blame, even though there were things found during the investigation that the cops swept under the rug. After the coroner said suicide, the focus shifted to finding you. Except that Mom's note—*You'll never find her. Don't even try.*—made the cops think Mom had given you to someone she knew. Someone she trusted.

The cops spoke to everyone Mom ever knew. There were never any leads.

Back then, there was never any question of if someone stole you. Dad took comfort in that, even though he wanted you back. He stuck with that story my whole life, telling me and anyone who would listen how my big sister, Delilah, was in safe hands because Mom never would have let anything bad happen to you. It's the only way he could sleep at night.

I'm starting to think that's not the way it went down.

MEREDITH

11 YEARS BEFORE

March

Dinner is in the oven. With classes to teach in the afternoon, I got a late start. Josh comes home from work with Delilah and Leo in tow, having picked them up from Charlotte's on the way home.

"How'd everything go with the kids?" I ask. What I really mean is how did everything go with Leo. Delilah would have been fine, because she's always fine when she's away from us. She's playful and unreserved, always able to find a friend. But I want to know how Leo was when Josh picked him up. Had he stopped crying after I left? Of course he had. Charlotte would have called and told me if he hadn't, wouldn't she? I would have canceled my classes, gone back and picked him up. It would have broken my heart for him to cry at Charlotte's all day.

"Everything was fine," Josh says. He's nonchalant about it. I have the disadvantage of dropping Leo off. Of seeing him cry.

Of having to push him into another woman's arms for comfort. Josh gets to be the one to pick him up and bring him home.

"What were they doing when you got there?" I ask.

"Playing outside," he says. This week is springlike: sunny, warm. Winter has left us, though maybe not for good.

"How long until dinner will be ready?" he asks.

"About thirty minutes," I tell him, asking how the pitch went today. It went well, Josh says, grinning from ear to ear. They landed the client.

"I meant to call," he says, "but the afternoon got away from me. There was a lot of celebrating." I imagine they cracked open a bottle of champagne after the deal was finalized. I can see how thrilled Josh is, and I'm thrilled for him as a result.

"It's fine," I say. I go to him, feeling terrible that I didn't think to do something more special for him tonight, knowing when he left this morning that this deal was nearly a sure thing. I should have made his favorite dinner. I should have called the sitter and made reservations for Josh and me at the steakhouse in town. Instead, I'm making a rather prosaic baked chicken recipe that feels suddenly inadequate for Josh's good news. "I'm just so happy for you," I say.

"Happy for us," says Josh, still grinning.

"We'll have some champagne with dinner," I say.

"Sounds perfect."

He excuses himself to go upstairs and change.

While waiting for the chicken to bake, I run a bath. Delilah goes first. She's in a mood. "Stupid Lily Morris," she says, pouting. "I hate her." Delilah plops herself down into the warm water. She does it with such ferocity the water splashes outside the tub.

"What did she do?" I ask.

"She's trying to steal my friend. She's a thief, Mommy. A friend thief."

"Oh, honey," I say, my heart breaking for her. I wish I could tell her that in five, in ten years from now, none of this will matter. That when she's sixteen, she won't even remember this little disappointment. But I don't want to trivialize her pain. Words like that are of little comfort to a sad six-year-old. "I'm sorry she upset you. Friendships can be hard." I ask, "Do you think you could all be friends?"

"Lily Morris doesn't like me," she complains.

"She doesn't know you, that's all. She'd love you if she got to know you. How could she not?" I ask, smiling at her. "Maybe we could invite both Piper and Lily over for a playdate," I say. I tell her that we could make cookies, do a craft. I don't know when we'd find the time to do that. But Delilah likes that idea. It settles her. It gives her something to look forward to. We'll find the time. We'll make the time.

Leo is up next. With Leo naked in the tub, I see the bruise on his bottom. It's about the size of a baseball.

"What happened?" I gasp. I run a finger over it and he winces. It hurts to touch. The bruise is red. It's fresh. The area around it is swollen. It hasn't had a chance to turn purple. This bruise happened today.

"Did you bump into something?" I ask Leo. He stares in reply. He says nothing. Either he doesn't know, or he won't say. "Do you remember, Leo, how this happened?" I ask again. This time he shakes his head.

Leo asks for his bath toys. I get them for him. But this time when he lines his whale and fish up on the edge of the tub, they don't gracefully swan dive into the water as they usually do. Instead, they kick one another into the tub. It's aggressive. Mean. The much bigger whale uses its big blue fin to firmly kick the tiny, unsuspecting red fish into the water. The fish falls, becomes submerged. But only for a moment. It floats back to the surface.

Leo grabs the fish. He sets it back on the edge of the tub. It happens all over again.

"Leo," I say. My voice is more firm. "Did someone do this to you?" I ask, pointing for a third time to the bruise.

Leo doesn't answer with words. Instead, he lifts a finger to his lips, says, "Shh."

Suddenly my heart is in my throat. Did someone do this to him and tell him not to tell?

After I get him out of the bath, I call Charlotte. Charlotte should have told Josh at pickup if something happened to Leo. I ask Josh. She didn't. He goes to see the bruise for himself.

Charlotte answers on the third ring.

"Hi, Meredith," she says. Her voice is singsong. Charlotte is older than me. She was a teacher once. She taught at an alternative school in town. It's what they call an "in lieu of expulsion" program. Kids that would otherwise be expelled from their current schools get transferred there. Burnout is high. Charlotte didn't last long before she started her own in-home day care.

I tell Charlotte why I'm calling. I say what I saw in the bath. I ask, "Did Leo fall at your house? Did he get hurt? Do you know?"

"Let me think," she says. Charlotte watches a number of kids. They range in age from eighteen months to twelve years. The older kids, like Delilah, are in school most of the day. But at three o'clock, Charlotte and the others walk to pick them up. Then her number of charges doubles. It's organized chaos whenever I'm there.

"No," Charlotte says after a short hiatus. "I don't remember anything happening to Leo. I didn't see anything happen. Leo didn't tell me if he got hurt." There's a pause. She asks, "Is that what he said, Meredith, that he fell at my house?"

"No," I tell her, "he didn't say that. But I was just wondering, since he hasn't been home all day, and he didn't have the bruise this morning." I don't mean for it to sound accusatory.

"I'd like to think Leo would have told me if he was hurt," Charlotte says. "We could have put some ice on it."

The way that she says it touches a raw nerve. She's blaming Leo. Maybe not for what happened, but for not coming to her for help.

That said, I don't want to make more out of this than there is. He is a kid. Kids bump and bruise themselves all the time. Besides, Leo is the shrinking violet type. He would never have gone to Charlotte for comfort. That's outside his comfort zone. The only way Charlotte would have known is if Delilah saw it happen and told.

Charlotte came recommended from nearly everyone in the neighborhood who has kids. She's a patient, loving, grandmotherly type, though she isn't a grandmother because she never had kids of her own. People that we know called her a godsend, an angel. *The best*. It doesn't get better than that.

I say, "I know you would have, Charlotte. I'll talk to Leo, make sure he knows he can tell you if he ever gets hurt at your house again."

I do talk to Leo, but it only settles me somewhat. Because the realization that harm can come to one of my kids when I'm not there to protect them still terrifies me.

KATE

May

The next morning, Bea walks in on me when I'm on the phone. I'm in the bedroom. I thought she was outside in her studio working, and so I didn't even try and be quiet. I had no intention of telling her what I had planned, knowing she'd try and talk me out of it if I did.

"Did I get that right?" she asks from behind. I spin to face her. I hadn't heard her come in. She looks disappointed in me. She stands there, showered and dressed, while my own hair, still wet from a shower, air-dries. I'm in a towel, hurrying to get dressed before the workers arrive and find me this way.

Bea asks in disbelief, "You made an appointment with Dr. Feingold?"

I go to my dresser. I riffle through it for something to wear, putting Bea off. I don't know how to respond to her, though it's not worth a lie. Bea and I aren't the type to lie to one another. But more than that, Bea heard what she heard. She knows what I've done.

I step into a pair of underpants and jeans. "Didn't you know?" I ask, keeping my voice light. "Surprise!" I say. "I'm pregnant."

"Kate," she says, shaking her head in dismay. She knows as well as I do that I'm not pregnant. She asks, "And what exactly are you going to say when he tests you at his office and it comes back negative?"

My answer is immediate because I've thought this through. "A false positive. Home pregnancy tests are good, but they're not foolproof. It happens," I say.

Last night I couldn't sleep. How could I possibly sleep, with all that's happening? My mind was consumed with thoughts of Meredith and Delilah, wondering where they were. As I was sleeping in my bed, all I could think about was where they were sleeping, if they were sleeping. I thought about Shelby sleeping forever. I imagined what she must have gone through in the moments before she died. I wondered what exactly someone did to take her life. Was she stabbed, shot, suffocated? No one has said. My mind drifted then to the blood the police found in Josh and Meredith's garage. Was it Meredith's blood? Delilah's? How did it get there? My thoughts then shifted to Dr. Feingold, the malpractice suit, two figures hiding in the darkness of the Dickeys' home that night, weeks ago, when Cassandra saw. Was it Dr. Feingold that she saw? Did he do something to Meredith and Delilah? At some point in the middle of the night, I knew that I needed to meet this man. I need to see for myself if he's someone capable of murder.

"Then I'm going with you," Bea decides.

"You can't," I say.

"Why the hell not?" she asks. She's angry because she's worried for me.

"Because two women can't conceive on their own," I say. "It would raise questions. Dr. Feingold would want to know why we didn't just go see our fertility specialist if we were pregnant."

"We don't have to tell him we're gay," she says. "We'll tell him I'm your friend. This baby is the result of a one-night stand with some man. I'm not letting you do this alone. He could be dangerous, Kate. We don't know. Either I go with," she says, giving me an ultimatum, because quite often that's what Bea is in our relationship, the decision maker, "or you don't go."

Bea won't be talked out of it. She's decided, and so I agree. I finish getting ready and follow Bea downstairs, where I sit down at the kitchen counter and research symptoms of early pregnancy on the laptop. I won't have to fake the nausea because, with Meredith and Delilah still missing, I feel constantly sick to my stomach. I can hardly keep anything down.

MEREDITH

11 YEARS BEFORE

April

Over the weekend, a client goes into labor. It's Saturday. Ordinarily Josh would be home. But on this particular Saturday, he's entertaining clients at a Cubs game. They have a suite on the first baseline. The weather is terrible: windy and cold. But they'll be indoors. They also have access to as much food and beer as they can eat and drink. Josh asked if I minded if he went. He was excited, like a kid on Christmas Eve. How could I say no?

I was hoping my client wouldn't go into labor today, not with Josh gone and the kids home with me. I need to make arrangements for them. I go to Cassandra's first. I bring the kids with me, out into the inclement weather. It's not raining. But the skies are portentous. The wind spins the hair around our heads. It's like walking into a wall. It's hard to walk at all. I grab the kids by the hand and pull them across the street. The wind tries to push us back.

I could call Cassandra. But refusing in person is harder to do than over the phone.

Marty answers the door. The surprise is evident. He hadn't expected to see me. "Meredith," he says, glancing down at the cold kids, then back up at me. "What's up?"

Josh and Cassandra know that Marty and I both went to the same college in Indiana. What they don't know is that we were friends, that we lived in the same coed dorm our freshman year.

They also don't know that we dated, that we were hot and heavy for a while, until we weren't. Marty and I lost contact after college. He's originally from Indiana. He stayed there and attended grad school after I left. We didn't talk again after that. I didn't think we ever would. In fact, I forgot all about Marty, except for those random thoughts that come to you at random times, like how I lost my virginity to him. I thought about him mostly in terms of Delilah, knowing that one day my daughter would grow up, go to college and discover handsome, charming, smooth-talking boys like Marty Hanaka, the kind you could never say no to.

I didn't want that to happen. I wanted someone more like Josh for Delilah: sturdy, honest, dependable.

When, ten months ago, Cassandra and Marty moved into the house across the street from ours, I couldn't believe my eyes. Marty isn't one for social media. It's not like we were Facebook friends. He isn't on Facebook at all. He could have been dead and I wouldn't have known.

By the time he moved across the street, he had a master's degree and was working as a market research analyst in Chicago. He was no longer twenty-two. Now he was thirty-six, married, with two kids.

"I'm sorry to bother you," I say.

"You're never a bother," he says. He smiles. Marty has a way of putting me at ease. He's still just as handsome and charming as he's always been. Sometimes when we speak, it's like fourteen years hasn't passed since I last saw him. "What can I do for you?"

"Is Cassandra home?" I ask, looking past him. There is noise and activity deeper inside the house.

"She was out shopping," Marty says, "but I think I just heard her come in the back door. Let me see," he says, but he doesn't need to.

"Oh, Meredith," Cassandra says, suddenly appearing in the doorway from the kitchen. She wears a coat, but her cheeks are pink. Forty degrees and gray is much more appropriate for this time of year than the weather we've been having. Still, it comes as a blow. One step forward, two steps back. Everyone hates it, our eternal winter.

Cassandra takes a look at the kids and knows exactly why I'm here. "I didn't know you were stopping by," she says. "I've been out running errands. Just popped back in for a minute because I forgot a return," as she makes her way to a coat closet, opens the door and draws out a shopping bag.

Marty looks incredulous. "You're heading back out?" he asks. He looks at his watch. "I thought you'd be done by now. I told you, I need to go to the gym." I'm embarrassed to be witness to their tiff. The kids and I still stand outside, on the stoop, freezing cold. No one has invited us in.

"Yes," Cassandra says to Marty. "I have a few more stops to make. It's not like I can easily do this during the week with the kids, and you're never home."

In this way she's able to dodge my question altogether. It would be wrong of me to ask her to run her errands another day. She knows I'm not that forward.

But she also knows I wouldn't leave my kids with Marty. Marty doesn't know them and vice versa. Cassandra thinks I don't know Marty, that our encounters are limited to the rare barbecues and progressive dinners our street throws. She's wrong.

It wasn't my decision not to tell Josh and Cassandra about our past. It just happened. Josh and Cassandra were right there when we first saw each other after all those years. It was last summer. Someone in the neighborhood had thrown a barbecue. Josh met them first, then brought them over to meet me. Marty thrust out a hand. He introduced himself as if he was someone I'd never met. I went along with it. I don't know why we did it that way. But we couldn't take it back after the fact.

"What's Josh up to today?" Cassandra asks.

I say, "Cubs game."

"Must be nice," she says. "You and the kids didn't go?"

"It was for work," I say.

"He should bring you and the kids along on his fun outings," she says.

"I don't know how fun they are," I say. It's a lie. Josh always enjoys himself at events like this, though they're chock-full of schmoozing clients. It would be a terrible place for the kids. "He's working when he's there," I remind her. "Trying to get to know prospective clients." Trying to convince prospective clients to trust him with their millions of dollars.

"Of course," she says. "You didn't say why you stopped by," Cassandra remembers.

"Oh," I say, feeling awkward. It's not like I can ask her or Marty now to watch the kids, not after their little row. Neither of them wants to be home with their own kids. They want to be out, doing things. I can't burden them with my kids, too, especially not when there's this sudden untold strain on Cassandra and my friendship.

"It's about Piper," I say.

"Oh?" she asks. Beside me, Delilah looks up at the mention of her friend's name.

"Yes," I say. "Delilah was wondering if she would like to come over for a playdate this week. We were thinking about inviting little Lily Morris, too."

"Oh. Yes," she says, "that would be lovely."

"Wonderful," I say. "I'll call Amber and set a date."

We leave. I go to Bea and Kate's house next. I try not to worry about whatever is going on with Cassandra. She's being snippy. But maybe it has nothing to do with me. Maybe it has something to do with her, with her marriage. If I was a better friend I would ask her about it. I would bring baked goods and ask her if everything was all right. I will do that when things settle down and I have more time.

I ring Bea and Kate's bell. Bea opens the door. Bea is a beautiful woman. She's as tall as Josh. At first glance, she seems unapproachable. But she's not, not at all. Bea has tattoos, too many to count. They mean things. A bird in a cage. A woman's name written in Old English font. When she's had a few drinks, she tells you what they mean. The woman's name, contrary to what I first thought, is her sister, who has special needs.

Bea's eyes light up when she sees Delilah and Leo. "How are my two favorite people?" she asks. Bea dresses in an effortlessly cool grunge style. I could never pull it off. If I tried, it would look all wrong on me. But not Bea. Ripped jeans, Doc Martens, a newsboy hat.

At Bea's feet, Delilah giggles. She tells Bea that they are good. She's bubbly as she says it, the word mixed up in her laugh. Shy Leo says nothing. But he grins, the kind of grin that spreads to his eyes. He's happy to see Bea.

Bea looks to me. "What's going on?" she asks.

I groan. "I hate to bother you," I say.

Bea doesn't let me get the rest out. "You've got a client?" she asks.

I say, "Yes. Her water just broke. She's on the way to the hospital. It's her third, so…"

Bea stops me there. She takes charge as Bea does; relief overwhelms me. I admire Bea's can-do attitude. She's a problem solver. She says to the kids, "I've had my heart set on pizza for the last hour, but there was no way I can eat a pizza all by myself, and Miss Kate's at work." She looks pleadingly at Delilah and Leo. "You think you could help me out with this?"

There's nothing my kids love more in this world than pizza. Delilah screams, "Yes!" Leo nods his head.

"God, Bea," I say, setting a hand on her arm, "you're a life-saver. I can't thank you enough for this."

She tells me, "You'd do the same for me."

The four of us walk back to our house. Delilah and Leo gather a few of their things to bring with them. I say I'll walk them back, but Bea says no. "I've got it from here. You need to go," she says, and I do. The phone in my pocket pings every few minutes. It's my client. She's in the passenger's seat of her husband's car, texting updates. **On the expressway. Traffic.**

"Give me a hug," I tell the kids. "You're going to stay and play with Miss Bea today." The kids do as they're told. Bea grabs them each by a hand and leaves. Leo has no qualms in getting left with Bea. He goes with her willingly, without a backward glance in my direction. It's telling. Something about Charlotte's house has him spooked. Seeing Leo with Bea warms my heart. I feel at peace, watching him walk voluntarily away, blue blankie dragging through the grass.

The birth is quick. My client nearly delivers without me. Sometimes this happens.

As I'm leaving, Josh calls. He's on his way home from the baseball game. "Oh," he says. "I didn't think you'd answer. I was going to leave a message."

"Why's that?" I ask, wondering why he didn't think I'd answer his call.

"You're at a birth," he says. I find my car in the hospital's parking garage. I get in and lock the doors. I keep my eyes peeled to the rearview mirror. I don't like not knowing what's behind me, if anyone is there.

"Just leaving," I say. I start the car and shift into Reverse, glad to be moving. "How did you know?" I ask. I would think that he's spoken to Bea, except that if Josh didn't know I was at a birth, he wouldn't have called Bea. Unless Bea called him for something, I think, hoping the kids are all right.

"The app," he says. "I see that you're at the hospital."

"Oh," I say. "Right." His words leave me feeling exposed, like someone is watching me, because he is. I picture Josh looking at the app on his phone. I picture the little thumbnail image of my own face on the map. I imagine it moving as I leave the parking garage and pull out onto the street, Josh all the while watching.

I ask Josh about the baseball game and what time he'll be home. He'll be there sooner than me. He'll get the kids from Bea. We say our goodbyes, and Josh tells me, "Drive carefully." I end the call.

I'm driving through the intersection when my phone pings the arrival of a new text. I shouldn't look when I'm driving, but I do. It's from the same 630 number that's been sending me threatening texts. Just seeing the number strikes terror into me. I pull over, into the parking lot of a golf course. My hands are shaking too much to drive. But also, I want to read the text without distraction. For a second I think of Josh. I picture him staring at the app on his phone, wondering why I've pulled off the road and into the parking lot. Does the app show enough detail for that?

I take a deep breath. I warily read the text.

I hope you haven't forgotten about me. Because I haven't forgotten about you.

The emoji this time is the face screaming in fear.

KATE

11 YEARS BEFORE

May

Dr. Feingold's office is located on the third floor of a medical professional building that sits adjacent to the hospital. The building itself is modern, full of natural lighting and glass. In the lobby, there's a line waiting for the elevator, and so Bea and I take the stairs to the third floor. We say very little as we ascend the steep steps—conserving our breath for the climb—but I can tell from Bea's silence that she wishes I'd change my mind.

I'm dead set on this. I've decided. This is something I need to do.

When we reach the third floor, we walk side by side down the hall. As we close in on Dr. Feingold's office, Bea finally asks, "What do you hope to get out of this?" her words embittered and disapproving. She sets a hand on my arm and forces me to stop, to look at her, and I do.

I can't put it into words what I hope to gain without it sounding ignorant, and so I say nothing. In my silence, Bea asks, "You think he's just going to come right out and tell you he did something to Meredith?"

"No," I say, shaking my head. "Of course not."

"Then what?" she asks. "You're going to ask him?"

"Of course not," I say again, trying to explain that what I'm hoping for isn't a confession, but rather a hunch, some gut reaction, an inner voice telling me that Dr. Feingold did something to our friend.

When we come to it, the waiting room is small but inviting. A receptionist takes my name. She hands me some forms and tells us to have a seat. The nurse, she says, will be with us shortly. I fill out the forms while I wait. I write down my name and address.

Bea glances down at the paperwork as I do. She nudges me hard. "What are you doing?" she hisses beneath her breath, seeing that I've just left my real name and address. Bea rarely gets angry at me. But this isn't anger. Our eyes meet and I see in them that Bea is scared. She's worried I'm getting in over my head, like Meredith did. And now Meredith is gone. I didn't think a fake name and address were necessary. It's not like someone of Dr. Feingold's pay grade deals with paperwork. But clearly Bea thinks it is.

"Go get another form. Start over," she says, but it's too late for that because, a breath later, the door opens and a nurse comes for me, calling out my name into the waiting room.

"Here," I say, standing, and the nurse smiles at Bea on her chair, thinking Bea will stay in the waiting room and wait.

But instead Bea stands. "Oh," the nurse says. "Your friend can come, too, if you'd like."

"Yes, please. The baby's father," I say, "couldn't be here."

I try my best to stay calm. I focus on breathing. Even though it feels like the truth is obvious, Dr. Feingold and his staff have no reason to believe my intentions for being here are anything but genuine. As far as they know, I'm an ecstatic new mom-to-be. And so I slap a silly grin on my face and follow the nurse back into the exam room, where I go blathering on and on about the pregnancy and the new baby and how excited I am to be a mom. I ask the nurse questions. Twins, I tell her, run in my family. Is it possible it's twins? How soon would we know?

She humors me. "Maybe," she says, asking who in the family has twins, and whether my husband and I would be happy with news like that.

"Of course," I say. "Who wouldn't be thrilled?" I tell her I've always wanted a large family.

"Some women aren't," she says. She looks down at my hand when she says *husband*. I don't wear a wedding ring. Bea and I aren't married, not yet, though we have high hopes that one day soon gay marriage will be legal in our state. We talked about going somewhere else to get married, Massachusetts, maybe. But something about it didn't feel right if our marriage wasn't going to be recognized or accepted once we were back home. What I do wear is a promise ring. It's dainty and thin. Some discerning person might see that Bea wears the same thing, a silver band with a delicate knot. We picked them out together, with a promise that when we could, we would get married.

"It might be too soon to detect multiples by ultrasound," she says. "But Dr. Feingold is the expert. He'll know."

She takes my vitals. She asks for information, like the date of my last menstrual period, which I know because I did my research and knew this is something she would ask. I give a fabricated date, one that would make sense with me being newly pregnant, approximately five or six weeks along. At her request, I go to the bathroom and leave a urine sample.

When I come back, the nurse is gone. A paper gown sits on the exam table for me. I change into it. Bea and I wait for the doctor to come.

"It isn't too late," Bea says as I situate myself on the table, staring down at the stirrups, feeling sick to my stomach. I don't know how this is going to go. I don't know what to anticipate, but I also don't know how much it matters. Before too long the

181

nurse will run the urine sample I've left for her. She'll figure out I'm not pregnant. My time with the doctor will be short, before he delivers the bad news, I feign sadness, and Bea and I leave. But at least I'll get my eyes on him before that happens.

"We can still go," Bea says. "We don't have to do this."

"And what would we say?" I ask, thinking it would look strange if we were to suddenly leave.

"That there's been a family emergency."

But leaving isn't an option for me. Not until I've seen and spoken to him. We've come this far.

I close my eyes. I take a deep breath. "It will all be over in a few minutes. Nothing," I say, "will go wrong. As far as he knows, I'm just another pregnant woman. Try and act normal," I tell her. There are magazines on a countertop. I tell her to pick one and pretend to read.

The knock on the exam room door is ungentle. Two quick cracks and then he lets himself in. My own gynecologist opens it an inch before calling into the room and asking if I'm dressed. Only then, when I tell her I am, does she come in. But Dr. Feingold doesn't wait. He stands in the doorway, stern but smiling, the kind of smile that doesn't reach his eyes. It's insincere. He's a tall man. He wears a white doctor smock over a pair of gray pants and a collared shirt. He's about the age I pictured him to be, based on Jeanette's description of him. She said that he was uncompromising. This made him older in my mind, old-school, someone who's been around the block a few times and is set in his ways. He's probably sixty-five, thinking about retirement, about becoming a snowbird, not wanting the Tebows' malpractice case to be the low note he ends his career on.

Dr. Feingold's hair is graying and thin. He, himself, is thin.

"Dr. Feingold," he says. "And who do we have here?" he asks, meaning me, and it upsets me already that he doesn't know my name, that he didn't bother to look before coming into the room. He's businesslike, clinical. My gynecologist is warm. I can't say with any certainty that she remembers me from year to year, but she's never given me a reason to think she doesn't. She sits down on her stool and chats awhile before starting her exam. She asks about my family. She asks about me. It's like we're old friends. Even as a vet, I let dogs sniff me before I start an exam. It's our way of getting to know one another before I touch them.

I tell him, "I'm Kate. And this is my friend Bea." Bea sits on her chair. Her discomfort is palpable to me, though I'm not sure he notices because he never looks at Bea. Her hands are folded together on her lap and she's clutching them so tightly that the skin has turned white. Bea hates the lack of control.

"So you say you're pregnant," he says. He sees pregnant women every day. There's nothing remarkable about it. Not for him, but for a first-time mom it's miraculous. I try to remember this, to remember to be ecstatic, not scared.

"I am," I say, beaming. "I took three of those home pregnancy tests," I tell him, elated, because any other woman in my position—having peed on three sticks and saw a total of six pink lines—would never have a reason to believe she wasn't pregnant.

"And?" he prompts about the home pregnancy tests.

"All positive," I say with a grin, setting a hand on my abdomen.

He looks skeptically at me. "All of them?" he asks, eyes narrowing.

"Yes, sir," I say, shifting my eager demeanor. My smile melts away and I ask, "Is there a problem?" because he's given me a reason to believe there is. I go with it.

He says, "The test we ran was negative."

Silence falls over the room. He doesn't say he's sorry. In no way does he apologize for the bad news. He doesn't break it to me lightly. He stands, watching me, waiting for me to say something in reply.

"I don't understand," I say after a while, claiming ignorance and shock. My voice trembles because I'm scared. It has the desired effect. "But the tests I took at home..." I say, letting my voice drift, letting the doctor infer what comes next.

He's dispassionate. He lectures. "Sometimes we have what's called a chemical pregnancy, an early miscarriage shortly after implantation, so soon in fact that women often assume it's that time of the month," he says, which strikes me as both an archaic saying and a chauvinistic one. I dated a boy in high school before coming to terms with my sexuality. All I had to do was be in a bad mood and he assumed it was that time of the month. He'd badger me about it. Once, after a fight, he gifted me with a box of Tampax. *It's just a joke, Kate,* he said when I broke up with him over it. *Can't you take a little joke?*

"These women never know they're pregnant," Dr. Feingold says. "This could be the reason your home pregnancy tests were positive." He asks if I had any bleeding following the home pregnancy tests, any spotting. I shake my head vigorously. I say no. "We'll do a blood test to know for certain." He tells me a blood test can tell us exactly how much hCG is in my system, if any. He tells me only pregnant women's bodies make hCG. "No hCG, no baby," he says, just like that. He shrugs as he says it, as if what we're discussing is something far less consequential than a life. It doesn't matter that my baby is fictional, that my baby never did exist. That doesn't make it okay. Because to another woman, this moment means everything.

"I wouldn't worry yet," he says, and though the words themselves are heartening in nature, meant to put me at ease, the delivery is anything but. His words fall flat; there's no encouraging smile, not even a fake one. What Dr. Feingold wants, I think, is to forestall any emotion, for me to cry later, at home, alone. Because crying is messy. It's not his cup of tea.

"The blood test," he tells me, "gets sent to the lab. Results will be back in a couple of days. Soon as the exam is through I'll send the nurse back in for the blood. Now, let's take a look," he says, motioning for me to lie back on the exam table.

My breath catches. Under my arms, I begin to sweat. I know that a pap smear and a pelvic exam are routine during a first prenatal appointment. I came across that when I did my research in preparation for the appointment. But I hadn't expected it to get so far. With the pregnancy now nearly debunked, there's no reason for Dr. Feingold to do this until after the bloodwork, until after we know for certain if I'm pregnant, which I'm not. The thought of this man touching me, of his fingers inside me, makes me nauseous. I think of Shelby being murdered, of her naked body dragged to the riverbank and abandoned there.

Did this man do that to her?

"Shouldn't we wait for the results of the bloodwork?" I ask.

Only then does he smile. It's supercilious, predatory. "If I'm going to be your doctor," he says, "you need to trust me. Okay, Katie?" he asks, and I mechanically nod, speechless, not able to correct his blunder. I've never been a Katie or a Katherine. I've only ever been known as Kate. It's the name my parents gave to me, not the diminutive form of something else. "There are changes to the uterus when a woman is pregnant. These can sometimes be detected during a pelvic exam," he says by rote, and though I know he won't feel these changes, any mother-to-be, I think, would do whatever he asked to know if she was pregnant. Any mother-to-be in my position would be desperate for confirmation of the pregnancy.

What choice do I have? I go to lie back, but then I stop myself. I sit back up, propping myself on my elbows. I have questions to ask, and if I'm going to ask them, I need to ask them now. As soon as Dr. Feingold completes his exam and comes back with the bad news—I'm not pregnant—my questions will be moot. No baby, no need for a baby doctor.

"A friend of mine," I say, speaking quickly now, letting my nerves get the best of me. "A different friend, not this one," I say, about Bea. "She had a baby recently. It was awful," I say. "The labor was long. The nursing staff went through three shift changes while she was in labor. She saw three different doctors from her medical practice in that time. It was impersonal, not at all what she imagined about giving birth to her first child. In retrospect, she wishes she had hired a doula. Someone who was there only for her. If she had it to do all over again, she would have hired one, she said. What are your thoughts," I come out and ask, "on doulas?"

Dr. Feingold steps back to the wall. There he reaches inside a box for a pair of latex gloves. He returns, standing before me, sliding the gloves onto his hands.

I don't see a doctor with gloves. I see a murderer hiding fingerprints.

My heart beats hard. Dr. Feingold says, "Unlike your friend's obstetric practice, I'm the only doctor here. If you're pregnant, I will be the one delivering your baby. You can count on that. In my experience, with the right doctor," he says, "a doula is unnecessary."

"Oh," I say, trying to mask my shaky voice. I could be done there. I could let it go.

But there's more to say.

"That surprises me," I tell him, "because I've been doing research into doulas, just in case, you know. Just in case I am pregnant. I've been reading blog posts and stuff. Reviews. Some women really rave about the support and assistance hiring a doula can provide."

He says, "Doulas can be very expensive."

I say, "I've done the math. I think I can afford a doula." Dr. Feingold smiles but he says nothing. I ask Bea to pass me my bag and reluctantly she does. She doesn't know what I've done.

I reach a hand inside my bag. I draw out a slip of paper where I've written names down. I hold the list out to Dr. Feingold. He takes it from me and has a look.

"These were a few local doulas whose names I kept coming across in my research," I say. There are three names on the list. Chloe Nord. Christine Frank. And Meredith Dickey. All three are local doulas. All three are spoken of highly on local moms' Facebook groups, and would be the kind of women I'd look for if I was pregnant and seeking a doula.

I refuse to turn and look at Bea, knowing she's likely pissed.

She'll tell me this was too risky, that I went too far, bringing Meredith's name up. That I crossed a line.

But I'm so close. I can't let it go. I ask Dr. Feingold, "If I did decide to hire a doula, would you recommend any of these women?"

Dr. Feingold takes a long look. He thinks, and I appreciate the attention he gives it, though I don't think for a minute he's being sincere. He's thinking before he speaks, being extra cautious. He doesn't want to say the wrong thing. He tells me, "If you felt the need to hire a doula," he says, with the emphasis on *if*, "either of the first two would be good. But this Dickey one," he says, tapping at the paper with his hand, and I think he's going to trash-talk Meredith at first. "Meredith Dickey," he says. "I don't know her," before passing the list back to me and getting on with his exam.

He's lying. A bald-faced lie. He does know Meredith.

Dr. Feingold tells me again to lie down on the table. It's stern the way he says it this time. Subconsciously I clutch the plackets of my robe together. My mouth tastes suddenly metallic. I lie down flat and defensive on the exam table, pressing my knees together.

Bea sits unconsciously forward in her chair. The doctor, noticing this, says, "If you'd rather, your friend can wait outside."

It isn't such an odd thing to say. If she was my friend, my platonic friend, I wouldn't want her to see me naked. This would be awkward, Bea in such close proximity during a pelvic exam. This *is* awkward, but the idea of Dr. Feingold and me alone, with me naked, his hands inside me, makes my flesh crawl. Bea can't leave.

"My memory is rubbish," I say, swallowing hard and scared, voice trembling. I can no longer control it. "I asked her to come along to remember all the things I'd forget to ask. She has three kids," I say. "She knows a thing or two about being pregnant. This is my first," I tell him, voice diminishing as I say it, taking on the somber tone of a woman who may or may not have miscarried.

Bea shifts her chair in another direction and looks away.

Dr. Feingold motions for me to slide to the end of the exam table and stick my feet in the stirrups. I do, lying spread eagle on the table before him. Dr. Feingold sets his firm hands on my bare knees. He presses my legs wider, before dropping somewhere that I can't see. I'm flat on my back. I can't see what he's doing. I close my eyes, try and transport myself somewhere far from here. My own gynecologist talks me though the entire exam, as if every time is the first time. *A little pressure*, she forewarns. *Just try and relax for me, Kate. You'll hear a click...*

But Dr. Feingold doesn't speak. Before I can process what's happening, his cold speculum is inside me, blades clicking open, and I gasp, not ready for the pressure of it, for the pain. Dr. Feingold moves fast, shifting the cold metal to get a good look inside me. My eyes fly open and I bite down hard on my lower lip, tasting blood.

Before I can catch my breath from the sudden plunge of the speculum, it's out, gone, replaced with his invasive hand and he's feeling around, groping, another hand applying pressure to the outside of me, to my abdomen. It's routine for him, automatic, but it's awful for me, unbearable. Knowing these hands are the hands of a killer makes the heat rush to my face. I think again of Shelby's body there at the riverbank, dead for days. This man may have stolen a life; he may have left a helpless infant without a mother.

There's a sudden ringing in my ears, a blackness spreading from the periphery of my vision so that I think I could pass out. My legs close against my will and Dr. Feingold tells me sharply to open back up, that the more still I sit—as if I'm a four-year-old having a dental cleaning—the quicker he will be done.

"Everything okay, Kate?" Bea asks as tears prick my eyes and I force them back. I mumble an affirmation. I can't see her from my vantage point, but I hear the fear and disgust in her voice, same as in mine.

When he's done, he pulls his hand abruptly from me and he tells me to sit up. "The blood test," he says flatly, "will be more definitive."

"What does that mean?" I ask, struggling to sit up, clutching the robe together at the chest and lap. Dr. Feingold's eyes go there, to my hands, which are shaking.

"It may be too soon to see any changes in the uterus," he says.

"So you didn't see any changes? I'm not pregnant, then?" I ask. "You think I miscarried. Or you think the home pregnancy tests were wrong." I don't have to simulate the fear, the shock, the disgust. It's already there.

"The nurse will be in to do bloodwork," he tells me. "I'm not into speculating. I prefer things to be conclusive. Let's see what we learn from the bloodwork, and figure out where to go from there. You might want to hold off on interviewing doulas until we know more," he says as he leaves.

MEREDITH

April

Shelby Tebow goes into labor two weeks early. The call comes in the middle of the night. It's Jason who calls, from Shelby's phone. Her contractions are close. I tell him to go to the hospital. I say that I will meet them there.

I meet Jason for the first time. He's everything I expected him to be, except that his voice, now that I hear it, is not the same one I heard when I was standing outside their home. That was another man. It calls everything I know about Shelby Tebow into question.

Shelby gets examined first by a triage nurse to see if she'll be admitted or sent home. The suggestion of going back home gets Jason provoked, though it's standard protocol to be examined before being admitted. Jason gets angry with the triage nurse.

"You need to simmer down, sir," she tells him. He stands too close, breathing down her neck as she examines Shelby. The nurse tells him to back away and give her room. She examines

Shelby, who is five centimeters dilated. Her contractions are less than four minutes apart. Shelby gets admitted. She changes into a hospital gown and takes her place in the bed.

In time, Dr. Feingold comes. I've never had the pleasure of working with Dr. Feingold before. But his reputation precedes him. He's overweening and uncompromising. He tries to relegate me to the corner of the room. I won't have it. Shelby is my client as much as she is his.

He wants to check her progress. He jams his fingers inside her cervix, far less gently than the triage nurse. Shelby recoils on the hospital bed. She presses her knees together. She tries pulling away from him.

"You need to hold still," he says. It's apathetic.

"You're hurting me," she whimpers.

He makes light of her pain. "This doesn't hurt," he says, going on. He wouldn't know. He's never had a cervical exam before. Shelby squirms. He tells her to hold still. He says that the more still she holds, the sooner he will be done. It's denigrating. "All done," Dr. Feingold says to Shelby as he yanks the latex glove from his hand. "Now that wasn't so bad, was it?"

She won't look at him.

Dr. Feingold doesn't use electronic fetal monitoring to continuously monitor the baby's heart. Instead, he listens with a Doppler device. Many obstetricians do. Electronic fetal monitoring isn't necessary for everyone, unless they're high risk. But intermittent auscultation is exactly that—intermittent—and requires diligence on the part of Dr. Feingold and the labor nurse. Tonight the hospital is busy. Many women are in labor, including another of Dr. Feingold's patients. The nurse says, "Must be a full moon." There's no truth in that. It's only folklore. Changes in barometric pressure can cause women to go into labor, but not full moons. It's more likely there's a storm coming than that there's a full moon.

Dr. Feingold steps out of the room. Before he leaves, he asks me to step out into the hall with him. He says to me privately as if we're in cahoots about this, "You've got your work cut out for you with this one." He's smirking as he asks, "Is this what they mean when they say *attention whore?*"

I'm so shocked that at first I don't speak. I just stare, wide-eyed and slack-jawed.

"My clients," I tell him when I catch my breath, "are always looking for OB recommendations. I wouldn't recommend you to anyone, Doctor." If I had personal experience with Dr. Feingold before, I would have told Shelby to run in the other direction. I have a growing list of doctors I won't work with, of hospitals I won't go to. He'd just been added to my list. He believes his medical degree gives him carte blanche. It doesn't.

Once he's gone, I return to Shelby's side. She tells me, "I hate him."

"Don't worry about Dr. Feingold," I say. "Just think of your beautiful baby and the life you'll share. You're almost through, Shelby."

Within an hour a nurse comes in to check Shelby's progress. "Already?" I ask when she tells me what she's here to do. It seems too soon for another cervical check.

"Dr. Feingold wants to know." She goes to Shelby. "Let's have a look-see," she says. She motions for Shelby to bend her knees and open up. Shelby does as she's told. She doesn't know that she can say no. She doesn't know what I know. There isn't any good research that says cervical exams are absolutely necessary during labor. They're also not one hundred percent accurate. One person's measurements are not the same as the next, and they need not be done every hour.

"Are you okay, Shelby?" I ask, my hand in the way to prevent the nurse from touching my client without her consent. "Is it okay with you if the nurse checks your cervix? That's when they see how far dilated you are. That's what Dr. Feingold did a little while ago when he was here," I say, because informed consent is important. A person should know what they're saying yes to.

Shelby draws backward on the bed. She whimpers. "Is it going to hurt as much as last time?"

"It might," I say. "And it might not. It's your call, Shelby. If you don't want the nurse to check, she won't," I tell her as the nurse pulls a face. Shelby thinks about it. She decides. She looks to me, and there's an inappreciable shake of the head. "Not now," she says. "Not if I don't have to."

"It's been barely an hour," I say to the nurse. "It's too soon for another check."

The nurse leaves. She's not happy with me.

Shelby asks, "What if she doesn't come back?"

This is the problem. Laboring women don't want to piss anyone off. Because they need them. Which means that sometimes unnecessary things are done to a woman's body during labor, for the sake of convenience or efficiency. Sometimes I'm as much of a bodyguard as anything else.

I promise her, "She'll come back."

Shelby doesn't handle the contractions well. Her threshold for pain isn't high. I sit with her. I try and help her breathe through them. But she's too beside herself to breathe. She asks for her epidural. The anesthesiologist is called, but he's not immediately available. What Shelby wants is immediate relief, but she has to wait.

"What the fuck is taking so long?" Jason asks. He paces the room. I ask him to calm down. I tell him quietly that he's not helping anything by getting upset. He needs to be a calming presence, for Shelby's sake.

The epidural comes. Jason is asked to leave for the placement of it. This makes him irate. I go with him. In the hall, I try to explain that it's a sterile procedure, a catheter being inserted directly into Shelby's epidural space. It's also a liability. Fathers are notorious for passing out at the sight of needles. It takes longer than expected because Shelby won't hold still. This sends Jason off the deep end. I have to physically restrain him to keep him from going back into the labor room.

The epidural slows Shelby's progression. What was quick is now slow.

The relief, though, is immediate. She nearly goes numb from the waist down. I sit on the edge of the hospital bed beside her. I push the hair from her eyes. I offer her ice chips and a massage. She declines both, preferring sleep. Sleep is a good idea. She needs her rest.

As she sleeps, Jason Tebow talks to me. He's cynical, hostile. He swears a lot. But maybe he's not the monster my imagination made him out to be. There's a softer side to him. He's tender toward Shelby. It's endearing. I can see that, though he has a temper, he loves her dearly.

As she sleeps, Jason moves to the edge of the bed. He watches her. He strokes her head. He holds her hand. He tells me, "My father was never around. He left when I was five, got remarried, had another kid. For a few years, I'd get a present at Christmas and on my birthday. After that, nothing." The look on his face is melancholic. "I'm going to do better for my kid," he promises.

"I'm sure you will," I say. He reaches out, touches Shelby's abdomen.

"I'd give my kid the world if I could."

I tell him, "I believe you would."

"Can I tell you something?" he asks.

"Of course," I say.

"I think Shelby's going to leave me. I think she's going to take my kid away with her when she goes."

"Why would she do that?" I ask. I shouldn't have asked. I regret it as soon as I do. It's none of my business. I shouldn't let myself get drawn into their marriage.

"She's cheating on me," he says. "I know she is." I know this, too. At least I think I do. There was a man in their home the day I stopped by. He stood at the top of the stairs, beckoning for Shelby to come. Shelby was desperate for me to leave. It wasn't so that Jason wouldn't see me and get upset. It was so that she could get back to her man. This makes me see Shelby in a different light. Their marriage is far from perfect. But it's not all on Jason, I don't think. They're both responsible for this. I consider the things she suggested about him, the conclusion I drew: that he was hurting her. Was there any truth to that, or was she laying the groundwork for divorce? Things like child custody and alimony would be affected if a judge thought Jason has been abusive toward her. A claim of domestic abuse would swing the balance in Shelby's favor.

But I'm only theorizing. There's no way to know for sure.

I can't stop myself. "How do you know? She told you?"

"She didn't have to," he says. He says that he just knows.

"Have you talked to her about it?" I ask.

He shakes his head. He looks at me. His eyes are a mix of angry and sad. He's sullen. He says, "I know how it is. When people get divorced, the mother always keeps the baby. Shelby can't ever take my baby from me."

"Fathers have rights, too," I tell him, but he isn't wrong. Custody is almost always granted to the mother.

He says, "Every other weekend isn't good enough for me."

"Give it time, Jason. Talk to her. Maybe you're wrong. Pregnancy is hard. You might have misread the situation. Maybe it's the hormones making her distant, not some other guy."

"I'm not a fucking idiot," he says.

I swallow hard. His quick temper makes me nervous. I lower my voice and move physically away, though I've not yet seen him be physical, only verbal in his assaults. "I didn't say you are."

"She's cheating on me," he says. "And there's no way in hell that if and when she decides to leave me, I'm letting her take my baby away."

Later, Shelby wakes. The nurse comes in to check on her. Her dilation and effacement haven't changed much. We wait a while longer.

When Shelby fails to progress, the doctor orders Pitocin. This strengthens her contractions. Soon, Shelby is in pain. Jason wants to know why. "The fucking epidural isn't working. Shouldn't she be numb?" he asks.

"Even with the epidural, the pressure can become more intense as time goes on."

"Call the doctor. Get him to fix it," he says.

"We need her to feel the pressure of the contractions now. It will help Shelby push your baby out," I say, and then I turn my back to him. My energy needs to be spent comforting Shelby, not mollifying him. We try again to work on her breathing, but Shelby is too far gone for that.

When she's reached ten centimeters, the nurse has Shelby labor down for a while before she starts to push, in the hopes that the uterus and contractions will do some of the work for her. But the contractions are unbearable. There's the greatest desire to bear down.

When it's time to push, I talk to Shelby about breathing, about effective pushing. When she screams at me that she can't do it, I tell her that she already is. "You're doing it, Shelby. You are doing it." I smile encouragingly.

When Jason looks like he might be sick, I suggest he step out into the hall for air. He does as I say. After a few minutes, he comes back.

I feed Shelby ice chips during each push. She pushes a long while. First-time mothers who've had an epidural tend to push anywhere up to three hours, sometimes more, which is fine so long as the mother and baby aren't in distress, or the mother too exhausted to push.

By the time Dr. Feingold returns, Shelby is completely spent.

What his patients like about Dr. Feingold is that he's a solo practitioner. He's not part of a big group. There's comfort in that. When his patients deliver, they know just exactly what they'll get. The other groups have upward of ten obstetricians on staff. When it comes to delivery, you might get one you like. You might get one you don't like. You might get one you've never seen before. That prospect worries many. That's why they settle for a no-nonsense man like Dr. Feingold. With him there are few, if any, unknowns. He's been doing this for decades.

The first thing Dr. Feingold says to her is, "The better you push, the sooner you'll be done." That's not necessarily true. It's also patronizing. That the baby doesn't move despite Shelby's pushing isn't her fault.

"I can't do it," Shelby cries out. The sweat drips from her hairline. It rolls down her cheek. "Get this baby out of me," she screams.

Jason, beside me, is incensed.

I pull Dr. Feingold aside and suggest that Shelby can't do this, that she's had enough. Shelby doesn't have any real qualms in having a cesarean. It's not her first choice. But she's fine having one if necessary. And to me, taking her exhaustion into account, the prolonged labor, the fact that things have stalled, it seems necessary. Prudent even.

Dr. Feingold is dismissive of my concerns. "I'm the doctor," he reminds me, loud enough that everyone in the room can hear. He glares at me as he says it. "I've been in practice for thirty-odd years. Why don't you let me decide how this is going to go, unless you have some medical degree that I don't know about."

He walks away from me. He returns to Shelby. "Besides," he tells her, as if he was talking to her all along, "a C-section will leave you with an ugly scar, and no one wants that."

A healthy baby. That was Shelby's only request when we discussed her birth plan.

Instead of a C-section, Dr. Feingold decides to use forceps to help get the baby out. Very few doctors use them anymore, mostly only old-school ones like Dr. Feingold. The use of forceps poses a potential risk. Dr. Feingold doesn't discuss these risks with Shelby or Jason. He only tells her what she wants to hear: that he's going to help get this baby out of her now.

But that's not all. Because Shelby isn't allowed the opportunity to give informed consent before he cuts an episiotomy, using a pair of scissors to cut her perineum instead of having

it tear on its own, if at all. An episiotomy should be an exception these days, not the norm. And it should always come with
a clear explanation of the possible complications, of which there
are many, from painful sex to fecal incontinence. I'm appalled.

"Doctor," I say tersely, but it's too late, because it's done.

He glares at me over my client, where I stand by her side,
trying to comfort her. "Would you like to wait in the hall?" he
asks. I don't move.

He doesn't look at Shelby when he speaks to her. "I'm going
to get this baby out of you. Sound good?" Shelby unleashes a
scream with the next contraction. Dr. Feingold finds humor
in it. "I'll take that as a yes," he says arrogantly. It makes me
irate. The absence of a *no* should never mean *yes*. I've worked
hard to create a culture of consent with my clients, especially in
situations like this, where Shelby is vulnerable and Dr. Feingold in a position of power. There are risks in all manners of
delivery. I know that. But a woman should be made aware of
these risks. She should be given the opportunity to weigh the
options for herself.

I see Dr. Feingold preparing the forceps for use. I won't be
silenced. "There are possible complications to using forceps to
aid in delivery, Shelby," I say, speaking quickly, urgently. I stand
at the side of the bed, leaned into her. I look in her eyes. Shelby
is completely spent. The exhaustion is tangible. She'd do anything for this delivery to be through. "The worst being brain
damage, skull fracture, death. You should know this before—"

Dr. Feingold cuts me off. "Your doula," he says smugly, de-
gradingly, "has no medical training. Are you going to listen to
her or me?"

Another contraction racks Shelby. "Just get this baby out of
me!" she screams.

Dr. Feingold takes that for consent. He applies forceps to the
baby's head. He uses the forceps to first turn the baby's head.
With the next contraction, he instructs Shelby to push as he

drags the baby out. As he does, Shelby screams in excruciating pain, despite the epidural, as if she's being torn in two.

The baby doesn't cry when she arrives. My first thought is that she won't survive.

KATE

11 YEARS BEFORE

May

"You should have told me you were going to ask about Meredith," Bea shouts at me as we make our way across the parking lot and toward the car. The rain is coming down hard, the parking lot riddled with puddles that we step into, sending rainwater everywhere, soaking our legs and feet. We use whatever we can to keep ourselves marginally dry. Bea has slipped out of a jacket and holds it over her head. I use my tote bag, though it's canvas, and doesn't do much to fend off the rain. The rain leaks through. I get wet, anyway, despite the bag.

The medical building backs up to an expressway. Traffic is heavy and loud. The fact that it's raining again only compounds the problem. The rain is as loud as the street traffic. The streets are wet. People tend to drive like idiots when the streets are wet, meaning that every few seconds someone lays on their horn.

Bea isn't shouting at me, though she is angry. She's shouting over the noise.

"Why?" I shout back as we reach the car. Bea and I part ways, me going to the driver's side where I open the door and slide quickly in before the rain has a chance to follow me.

My body is sore from the exam. I feel dirty, sick. I want nothing more than to go home, to shower, change, wash Dr. Feingold's hands from me.

On the other side of the car, Bea slips into the passenger's seat, slamming the door closed. She turns to me and says, "So I could have talked you out of it. You told me you just wanted to get eyes on him, Kate. You didn't tell me you were going to ask about Meredith."

She pauses for breath. "He isn't a nice man," she says, which I know. Even if he hasn't killed Shelby or done something to Meredith, he still wouldn't be a nice man. He's arrogant, insensitive, abrasive.

I turn on the car and begin to drive. Rain pours down from the sky. The wipers whip back and forth across the glass. They can't keep up with the downpour. I have trouble seeing out the windshield as I pull out of the parking lot and into the street. I cut it too close, cutting off another car; the driver lays on their horn for a prolonged period of time, putting me even more on edge than I was to begin with. Usually I'd step on the gas and pull away, but I can't with the streets as wet as they are. It takes time for us to pick up speed.

"Careful, Kate," Bea scolds. "That was close." The other car switches lanes and speeds around us, inconvenienced and apparently immune to the weather.

The window is all fogged up. I rub at the glass with the sleeve of a shirt, clearing a semicircle out of which I just barely see. I turn on both the rear and the front defrost.

"I didn't tell you," I say to Bea, "because I knew what you'd say."

"And what's that?" she asks. She tosses her wet jacket into the back seat.

"You'd tell me not to go through with it."

"You're damn right," she says. "The man is in the middle of a malpractice suit. Meredith is a witness. She was going to expose him. Regardless of what's happened to Shelby or Meredith, you think bringing her name up wouldn't tip him off to something? He knows where we live, Kate," she says. "He knows because you told him. You wrote it down on those forms. If he figures out we're Meredith's next-door neighbors, he'll think we're colluding with her."

"But you saw his reaction?" I ask, fighting through the fog to see. I lean forward in my seat, gazing out that four-inch circle that gradually grows, but not quickly enough for me. I consider pulling over, waiting the deluge out. But more than anything, I want to be home, behind a locked door. I need a shower. I need clean, dry clothes. It's cold in the car and I'm drenched to the bone. "You saw how he responded when I asked about Meredith, didn't you? He lied, Bea. He said he'd never heard of her, when he has. Why would he lie if he hasn't done something to her?"

"I don't know, but listen," Bea says, her tone softening so that she's hard to hear over the pelting rain, which isn't only rain now, but hail. It stabs at the hood of the car like knives. "It's time we stop being amateur sleuths and let the police handle this. We're in over our heads," she says, sounding scared. Bea is the strong one, my fearless leader. I've never known Bea to be scared.

"I know we are," I say, feeling guilty for what I've done, for worrying Bea like this. "I shouldn't have done that. I shouldn't have brought Meredith up. That was stupid of me," I say, though I'm glad I did it. I got the answer I was looking for. I came out of the appointment with exactly what I was hoping to get: a gut reaction telling me that yes, this is a man who could hurt another human being.

The rear windshield starts to clear. As it does, the street behind me becomes minimally visible, enough to see a pair of headlights riding my tail from behind.

At first I think nothing of it. I wish only that the other driver would slow down. The roads are wet. They're slick. I can feel the slipperiness and the unpredictability of the street in my hands as I cling tightly to the steering wheel, going below the speed limit. The rain comes down so quickly that the wipers can't keep up. It makes it difficult, if not nearly impossible, to see. I focus my attention on the taillights of the car in front of me and try to keep in a straight line. But I can't see the markings on the street to know for certain if I'm between the white lines, or if I've glided over them, into oncoming traffic. As we pass the cars that move in the opposite direction of us, I hold my breath, hoping and praying that there's enough space between us because I don't honestly know. I keep at a safe distance from the driver before me. It's safer that way, in case he or she needs to slam on the brakes, and because the spray of rainwater from their tires only exacerbates my visibility problem.

I only wish the driver behind me would do the same. He's close to rear-ending me. The rain brings out the worst in drivers.

I step on the gas, hoping to widen the distance between us, but it doesn't help because this other driver only speeds up as I do, still riding my tail. I can't get a good look at the car. The rain is thick. It's impossible to see through, other than where cars or traffic signals emit light.

"What's wrong?" Bea asks, sensing my growing agitation.

"This idiot driver is riding my tail," I say.

Bea takes a cursory glance in the side mirror. "Just take your time," she says. "He can go around us if he wants."

Bea keeps talking. She's talking about what's just happened with Dr. Feingold, I think, but what she's specifically saying I don't know, because I've unintentionally tuned her out. My attention is honed in on this car behind us. I'm trying not to panic, wishing that this other driver would do what Bea's said: get in the left lane and pass. He's making me a nervous wreck, but I don't feel comfortable speeding up, not that it would necessarily matter because he'd just go faster, too.

I close in on an intersection. I've lost all sense of direction because of the rain. I can't get my bearings, and realize almost too quickly that this intersection is where I need to turn to go home. Without thinking or indicating, I yank on the steering wheel and we sharply turn. The street must be lower in the intersection because the standing water is deep. For a second, the car loses traction and I think we're about to hydroplane. I resist the urge to slam on the brakes, riding it out instead, letting the car self-correct.

Bea falls into me. "What was that?" she asks, panicked, as I regain control of the car. Bea rights herself on the seat, staring out the window to orient herself to where we are.

"Sorry," I say, feeling breathless, my heart racing over what just happened. "I almost missed the turn."

"Yeah, well," she says, "you could have taken another one. You could have turned around in a parking lot. What are you trying to do, kill us, Kate?"

I go quiet. I focus on the road. I hate it when Bea and I fight. She's angry with me. But she's also angry *for* me because of what happened with Dr. Feingold. While I endured his pelvic exam, she was forced to watch. That must have been as awful for her as it was for me. We've both come undone.

Bea knows this as well as me. Her tone softens. She lays a hand on my arm. "You want to pull over and I'll drive? You've been through a lot today, and this weather is the pits. Why don't you let me drive, Kate?"

I shrug her off. "I've got it. I'm fine. Besides, we're almost home."

I glance into the rearview mirror. That same car is still riding our tail. The driver made the same last-minute, ninety-degree turn as me. I become hyperaware. This driver is following us. He doesn't want to lose sight of Bea and me. It's the reason he follows so closely: because he doesn't want to allow enough room for another car to slip in and separate us. I feel it in my gut. I try so hard to get a look at the driver, but his car and his face are fuzzy and indistinct because of the rain. If it wasn't for headlights tailing me, I might not know someone was there.

I say to Bea, "I think that car's following us."

"What car?" she asks.

"The one behind us. Riding my tail."

Bea turns in her seat to look out the rear window. "Who is it?" she asks. "Can you tell?"

"This damn rain," I say. "I can't get a good look."

Bea and I left the medical building together. We were in the elevator alone. No one was with us. Dr. Feingold could have conceivably taken the stairs and followed us out that way. Bea and I were so distracted in the parking lot that we nearly ran to the car, arguing, desperate to get out of the pelting rain. We didn't pay attention to who else was in the parking lot with us. Dr. Feingold could have been ten feet behind and we wouldn't have known. "Maybe it's that car you cut off leaving the doctor's office," she says. "He was pissed. People get road rage."

"That driver passed me," I remind her. "He's gone."

We're still miles from our house. I'm panicking, not wanting to lead this person directly to where Bea and I live, though if it is Dr. Feingold, that doesn't matter because I've already given him my address. How stupid I've been.

I keep driving because I can't think of anything else to do. If this person's intent is to scare and intimidate us, then they've succeeded. I practically lose the ability to drive because I'm so nervous. I drive slowly, hands locked on the ten and two position.

"Just try and ignore him," Bea says, but that's easier said than done. She leans forward in her seat to turn the radio on, a nice distraction. We don't speak. Before I know it, I'm closing in on our home. I'm just a few miles from it, and still not sure what to do. I can't go home. I can't lead this individual to our house. Who's to say what he'll do when we get there, though for the first time ever, I take comfort in the fact that our house likely swarms with workers. Certainly no one would harm Bea or me while witnesses watch on.

It's just by dumb luck that we pass the police station on the way home. It becomes visible through the rain, only because a patrol car, with lights and sirens blazing, comes speeding out of the parking lot as we draw near. Certainly the driver of this other car wouldn't be stupid enough to follow us into the police station parking lot. As I approach the parking lot, I turn my signal on and ease up on the gas. I make the turn into the parking lot as the other car switches lanes and accelerates down the road, leaving a spray of rainwater in its wake.

Both Bea and I try, but neither of us manages to get a good look at the driver or the license plate. It's all just a blur, indecipherable in the rain.

LEO

NOW

On your third day home, you start talking about some kid named Gus. It's by accident that it happens. Someone's playing ball outside. The thump of the ball hitting concrete carries inside. It gets your attention. "It's just a basketball," Dad says, seeing that you've gone white. Ever since you've been home, Dad's neurotic about keeping doors and windows shut and locked, the blinds closed. You can never be too careful. He spends his nights awake. He sits in the parlor and reads. No one's taking you on his watch.

"Gus plays basketball," you say.

Dad looks up from his scrambled eggs and asks, "Who's Gus?"

You tell him. Dad goes white, too. He excuses himself and leaves the room, taking his cell phone with him.

You weren't alone in that basement. Someone was with you. Someone got left behind.

We drive back down to the police station. The lady cop becomes more assertive in her questioning. She no longer tiptoes around you like you might break. Now that we know some-one else is still there, it's time, she says, to get down to business.

She asks what you know about this kid Gus. You don't know much. You can't even tell the lady cop what he looks like be-cause, for all your time together, you never got a good look at his face. You don't know how old he is. You don't know where he's from.

The lady cop looks in those missing kids' databases. She and her henchmen come up with a handful of missing kids named Gus, or some variation of it. Argus. Augustus. Gustavo. They show you pictures, and ask if any of them is your Gus. You don't know. A missing kid from Cookeville, Tennessee, might be, you think. But really, you don't know. You're just trying to please the lady cop by saying something. I probably would, too.

I spent a lot of time on those missing kids' websites when you were gone. Did you know that? Here's the cracked thing about those sites. Not only do they have pictures of the missing kids that they're looking for. Sometimes what they have is found skeletal remains and they're trying to figure out who they be-long to. They call these kids Jane and John. There are a bajil-lion of them, just red and blue dots all over a map, one dot for each unidentifiable body they've found. Cops don't know who they are, but they're in bad shape when they find them, or parts of them, anyway. There's no end to the evil things people will do to one another.

When you were gone, I spent a lot of time online wondering if you were going to be one of the unidentifiable.

I told Dad about these kids. He took my internet away for a month. I never mentioned them again. I wasn't stupid enough to suggest to Dad that you were skeletal remains. Still, I put the idea in his head.

The lady cop asks you a lot of questions. You know nothing. We get nowhere.

When they first found you, a local cop drove you around and around that town, trying to see if you could remember where you'd been. But other than identifying smokestacks and a fence, you were clueless. I looked that town up on the internet, if it can even be called a town. You have to zoom in real close on the map to see it. It's called Michael and has a population of about forty-five. It's five hours from our place, somewhere close to the Mississippi, in an area that's all farmland and trees. Every year it floods.

From the couple of pictures I saw of it on the internet, it's pretty skeevy. Vacant storefronts, with boarded-up and broken windows. Decrepit farmhouses. The only other houses besides farmhouses are tornado bait, aka mobile homes.

Makes me wonder how you ended up there.

Dad's the one who suggests hypnosis to see if that will help dredge up memories, about Mom, about Gus. The lady cop isn't going for it. She says you're not in the right state of mind for that.

It's true. You're shell-shocked. You don't sleep, and even when you do, you have nightmares. You wake up sweating and screaming. You sleep on the basement floor at night because it's the only place you can actually sleep. You can't look anyone in the eye. You're afraid of running water. You shit bricks when the elementary school bus drives by.

"Someone's child," Dad tells the lady cop, "is still missing. Mine is home. I can't have that on my conscience."

MEREDITH

11 YEARS BEFORE

May

The Tebows' baby is covered in forceps marks and bruising when she arrives. Within minutes of her birth, her tiny head begins to swell. Within hours, she begins to seize. A cranial head ultrasound is performed, where doctors discover an intracranial hemorrhage, otherwise known as a brain bleed. The cause: excessive mechanical force to her head, resulting from forceps misuse.

The baby's condition improves by the time she's allowed to go home. But even when she does go home, there's much uncertainty about her future.

The days and weeks pass. The Tebows meet with an attorney. They decide to sue Dr. Feingold for malpractice. Shelby calls and asks if I think it's a good idea.

"Jason says we're doing it, whether I like it or not. He's pissed. Dr. Feingold screwed up."

This isn't for me to decide. "You have to do what's right for your family," I tell her. She has a case. I was there. I saw with my own eyes. I saw him do things to Shelby's body without her consent, things that carried a great deal of risk.

A malpractice suit can't change anything that's happened. Their baby will likely have special needs. A settlement could help pay for the baby's care.

"If I can help in any way, I will. Whatever you and Jason need."

The attorney looks through Shelby's and the baby's medical records. He speaks with medical experts. He decides that the Tebows have a case.

The next week Dr. Feingold receives the medical malpractice complaint. The first thing he does is call me. "Those folks wouldn't know their ass from their elbow. Far be it for them to decide that I did something wrong. You put the idea into their head."

"I shouldn't be speaking to you," I say.

"If you did this," he says, "if this was your idea, I'll ruin you. Do you hear me? I will ruin you." He enunciates one word at a time. I. Will. Ruin. You.

I hang up the phone. My whole body shakes long after I do. For over an hour I sit at the kitchen table, unable to move. My thoughts dwell on one thing: How will he ruin me exactly? Will he ruin my career? Or will he physically ruin me?

Josh comes home with the kids. They're bubbly, loud. Delilah is excited. Their classroom is getting caterpillars. When they turn to butterflies, they'll release them outside.

She hugs me. She's getting taller. Her arms, when she wraps them around me, reach my waist. She asks me, "When can I have a playdate with Piper and stupid Lily Morris?"

"Delilah," I tell her, "we don't call anybody stupid."

"But she is," she pouts.

"Delilah," I warn. My voice is stern.

"Fine. But when can we have a playdate? And does Lily Morris have to come?" she pleads. She sets her hands on her hips. One juts out. Only six and already she has a flair for the dramatic. I smile at her, wishing life could only be this complex. I do feel badly for her. I know how hard it is to be left out.

"Yes," I tell her, "Lily Morris has to come. Because we don't want to leave anyone out. That doesn't feel good, does it?"

Once the kids leave, I tell Josh, "I was just about to start dinner." In the next room, the TV turns on. I haven't so much as thought about dinner.

"How about we order something?" he suggests. I like that idea. I don't feel like cooking. My stomach is in knots. I don't even know that I could eat.

Josh is looking at me. He's incredibly handsome. Josh has always been incredibly handsome. He's dapper. His suit is slim-fitting, navy. He has many suits. While other men collect cigars or license plates, Josh collects suits. Some are tailor-made and others off the rack. He's always trying to impress. He has a likable personality, a gravitational field. People are drawn to him. He's outgoing. His smile lights up a room. Everyone likes Josh.

I should trust him enough to tell him what happened to the Tebows, what's happening with Dr. Feingold and about the threatening texts. But he would be disappointed after the fact. And he would worry. He would want to know how and why I got myself into this situation to begin with. And then he'd want to completely revamp the way I do my work, to some other formula where he believes I'm at less personal and professional risk. But I love what I do. I love the way that I do it.

I put the Tebows and Dr. Feingold out of my mind. Soon it will be through.

LEO

NOW

Around the same time you disappeared, some other lady did, too. They found her. Except that by the time they did, she was already dead.

For a while, cops thought it was all connected. They were wrong. Now the lady's husband is in the slammer. He'll be there for a long time, twenty to life, 'cause they found her bloody clothes in a Dumpster behind where he worked.

That night the lady cop calls Dad on the phone. He takes it into another room because he doesn't want you to hear what she's saying. But when I ask, he tells me. Turns out, the people who took you were dumb enough to use their real names, because there is a real Eddie and Martha Cutter living in Michael, Illinois. Eddie and Martha own a house on Calhoun Street. They've owned it twelve years. The lady cop texts Dad a picture. It's not the nicest house because half of its shutters are missing and there's mildew on the white siding. The trees grow out of control, nearly hiding the house. The inside is ten times worse. It's filthy. The carpet is stained. There's water damage on the walls, turned black with mold. There's standing water on the floor. Dirty dishes pile up in the kitchen sink.

The only problem is that Eddie and Martha are not living there anymore because when the cops went to investigate, the house was abandoned. "Detective Rowlings is trying to locate their family, to see if they know anything about their whereabouts."

I'm wondering what happens if they try and come here.

There are no pictures of the basement. The lady cop told Dad about the conditions they kept you in, but Dad can't tell me because he's too busy crying his eyes out.

Your friend Gus was nowhere in sight. There was blood in the basement.

You get the idea.

There's more urgency about getting your memories back. The lady cop doesn't come right out and say it, but she thinks hypnosis is bullshit. But Dad looked into it and said that if they can relax you enough, you might just remember something your mind has been keeping from you.

The night before the hypnosis, we're all getting ready for bed. You're in your bedroom, Dad's in his. From the hall, I hear you making noise in your room. I wonder what you're up to in there. I go to see. You're not so hesitant when you open the door, like maybe you're getting the hang of Dad and me.

"What are you doing in here?" I ask, looking around. The lights in the room are off.

"Nothing," you say. You're sheepish. You don't want to tell me.

"You must be doing something."

"It's something stupid," you say.

"Like what?"

"Just a game I play."

"What's it called?" I ask.

"It don't really have a name."

"How do you play it?"

You don't want to. But you show me, anyway, after a while of me begging. You think I'm going to make fun of you for it. I don't. Instead, I play your game with you. It's not super dark in your room because of a light from down the hall. So you close the bedroom door, trapping both you and me inside. Still, it's not black. Outside your window the moon is bright.

"It's better when you can't see nothing," you tell me.

"Why's it better?" I ask.

"It just is. That's how the game is played. We got to close our eyes," you say, to make up for the lack of blackness. You tell me to keep my hands at my sides. "It's cheating," you say, "if you feel with your hands first."

We stand with our backs to one wall. The object of the game, you tell me, is to be the one to get closest to the opposite wall without running into it. We can't use our hands.

I try. I fail. I feel like a fish out of water trying to walk with my eyes closed. I can't even walk in a straight line. I plow into the bed frame and give up. This game is dumb, but I don't tell you that.

But I watch as you keep going. You stop within a centimeter of the wall, like you had some sixth sense that it was there.

"How'd you do that?" I ask.

You tell me it's one of those things you got real good at: finding your way around in the dark.

"There wasn't no light where they kept us," you say. "None at all. When someone takes your eyes away from you, you figure out how to get by on other things." So that's what you did. You learned to survive on your other senses and on instinct. It's pretty cool.

"Wanna play again?" you ask.

I don't. Not really. There's a stinging pain in my thigh from where I ran into the bed frame. Chances are good it'll bruise. I don't feel like doing that again.

Still, I shrug my shoulders and say, "Why not?" 'cause I can tell it's what you want to do.

MEREDITH

11 YEARS BEFORE

May

I haven't forgotten about Cassandra. I've been busy. But all the while, she's been on my mind. I want to be a better friend to her than I've been. I've been so busy burdening her with my needs, that I've forgotten about hers. Something is off with Cassandra. I have to know what it is.

On a Friday afternoon, I pick up a Bundt cake from the local bakery. After Delilah is in school and Leo with Charlotte, I walk it to Cassandra's house. I go to her door and knock. She answers with Arlo in her arms.

"What are you doing here?" she asks. Her tone is curt.

I present the Bundt cake. "I thought we could talk. It feels like we never have the time to just talk anymore. I miss you, Cassandra," I say.

She harrumphs, which is how I know that she's really put out about something. "Come in," she tells me. I step inside and out of my shoes. "You want coffee?" she asks. I tell her yes, following her into the kitchen. Cassandra wears a dress, which she almost always does. It's long and cotton and comfortable-looking, but still a dress. She looks lovely in it. I can't remember the last time I wore a dress.

"I'm glad you stopped by," she says as I help myself to a chair. I watch her brew a pot of coffee one-handed, with Arlo in the other. It's effortless. I would have dropped either Arlo or the coffee by now.

"I've been wanting to for a while. Things have been so busy."

"I have something I want to show you."

"Oh?" I ask, thinking it's something having to do with the kids. Something having to do with Delilah, Piper, Lily and their little squabble. I hope that Delilah hasn't done something she shouldn't have, like give Lily Morris a mean picture.

Cassandra brings a book to the table. It's a photo album. People don't keep photo albums anymore. Everything is digital these days. If anything, people scrapbook. Scrapbooks are lovely. But I don't have the time for that.

The album shows its age. The plastic photo sleeves bend. The pictures themselves look old, taken with a 35mm camera. No one has cameras anymore.

Cassandra thumbs through to a certain page. She lays the album flat when she finds it. I see enough red to know what it is. The name of my alma mater is written on almost every T-shirt and sweatshirt in the book. We lived in campus gear when we were in college.

She points to a picture. There I am. There Marty is. My cheeks go flush. I have a hard time swallowing. My saliva is suddenly thick.

Her voice quavers when she speaks, in both anger and pain. She asks, "Why wouldn't you and Marty tell me, unless you had something to hide? I've known for weeks what you two were up to," she goes on without waiting for an answer. "You thought you could get away with it."

She doesn't know that we dated, that we slept together. But

the picture is damning enough. In it, we stand side by side. Marty's arm is thrown around my shoulders. It's casual, comfortable. We knew each other. We knew each other well. That we didn't tell her and Josh looks bad.

"If I told you that nothing has happened between Marty and me, would you believe me?" I ask.

"You could try. But I wouldn't believe you."

I look her in the eye. She looks away. She sets Arlo in his seat, and cuts him a piece of the cake.

I tell her, "Nothing has happened between Marty and me in eighteen years."

She looks back to me. "But something did happen between Marty and you?"

"That was a long time ago, Cassandra. We didn't know you back then. You didn't exist to us."

"But you dated?"

"It was only young love."

She looks aghast when I say this. "You loved him?"

I regret my choice of words immediately. I should have phrased it differently. I never should have said the word *love*.

"I thought I did. I was blinded by all those overpowering emotions that we feel when we're eighteen. But now I know that it wasn't love at all. Cassandra, what you and Marty have is love. That was just naivete. Infatuation. Two stupid kids."

"Why should I believe anything you say," she asks, "when you've been lying to me all this time?"

"I never lied," I remind her.

"You've been keeping secrets from me, keeping me in the dark."

Cassandra is a gorgeous woman. She's elegant and articulate and savvy and smart. In no way would Marty want me now that he has Cassandra. But it's hard to know these things about ourselves. Cassandra feels deceived. "We did it for your sake. For yours and Josh's," I say.

Cassandra sits upright. "Does Josh know?" she asks.

I tell her, "No. I couldn't bring myself to tell him. Not that it mattered either way because there is nothing going on with Marty and me. I swear to you, Cassandra, on my life. On my children's lives. There is nothing going on between Marty and me."

"Did you sleep with him?" she asks.

"Cassandra. Don't do this."

"Did you?" she demands. We've both forgotten all about the coffee and cake. The cake sits beside us. Only Arlo eats it. The coffee has finished brewing. It waits for us in the pot.

"I was eighteen," I say. It's not the answer she's looking for.

"So you did sleep with him, then."

"Cassandra."

"Answer the question, Meredith. Did you or did you not sleep with my husband?" She's yelling now. In his high chair, Arlo gets scared. To appease him, Cassandra offers up another slice of cake. I watch him take it by the handful, shove it in until he's covered with it. There's cake in his hair.

"I did," I whisper, though he wasn't her husband then. But to remind her of that would only make her more upset.

Things go from bad to worse quickly. Cassandra already knew I'd slept with Marty before she asked. Because wedged between two pages of the photo album is a note, folded in half, that I wrote him over a decade and a half ago. I know what it is as she unfolds it and forces it into my hands. I can't bring myself to read the note, though I know what it says. After months of dating, I'd gotten pregnant. The baby was Marty's. I was fully intent on keeping the baby, which I explained to Marty in the note. He could be a part of the baby's life, if he so chose, but there was no obligation.

As it turned out, he didn't have to choose. Because two days later, I miscarried.

"What did you do with the baby?" she asks.

"We lost it at twelve weeks."

"Shame," she says icily.

It terrifies Cassandra, knowing how close Marty came to having a child that wasn't hers. If I hadn't miscarried, Marty and I may have raised the child together. We may have gotten married. The life she knows might not have existed.

"Are you still fucking my husband?" she asks coolly, and I gasp.

"Of course not," I breathe out.

"I'm not stupid," she says. "I know."

"Know what?" I ask, truly confused.

"I know what you and he are up to. His late-night grocery store runs. Those ten o'clock ice cream cravings." She puts it all in air quotes, implying she doesn't for a minute think Marty runs off to the grocery store that late at night because he's craving ice cream. "Do you know that sometimes he thinks I'm so dense I won't realize how he comes home empty-handed? He doesn't even bother picking up ice cream as part of his charade. He just goes and fucks you and comes back, and then he climbs into bed with me, nine times out of ten forgetting to put back on his ring."

It saddens me to think of Marty sneaking out late at night to cheat on her, though I can't say I find it shocking. Not because of anything Cassandra has done or not done, but because the Marty I knew in college was slick. He was a ladies' man.

Maybe he hasn't changed as much as I thought.

What shocks me is that Cassandra thinks that I, too, slip out of my house at ten o'clock some nights, leaving Josh and the kids behind, and go to meet up with Marty.

"Cassandra, if Marty is seeing another woman," I say, "it isn't me."

"And why should I believe you, Meredith? Why should I believe anything you say?"

"I've never lied to you," I say.

"Bullshit," she snaps, again startling Arlo. I've never seen Cassandra so angry. I've never heard her use this language in front of her kids. I don't blame her for being upset, especially if she believes there's something going on between Marty and me. Still, she's taking it to the extreme. "You have lied to me, Meredith. You've been lying to me since the day we met."

"If I did, it was lying by omission and not an outright lie. There's a difference."

"Is there?" she asks.

I say nothing. In truth, I don't know that there is.

"When do you plan to tell Josh?" she asks. It isn't so much a question as it is an ultimatum.

"I'll tell him, if that's what you want me to do," I say. I'll tell him now that Cassandra knows. But I want to be able to tell him on my own terms. I don't want Cassandra to be the one who tells him. "Please let me speak to him first, before you do."

"I wouldn't do that to you, Meredith," she says. "I'm not that kind of friend." It's a slap in the face. She isn't the kind of person who would hurt a friend. But I am.

I rise from the chair. I show myself to the door. She follows. At the door, I turn to face her. "I'm so sorry that we didn't tell you," I say in a last-ditch effort to apologize. "Marty and I thought it was for the best."

"Marty and I, Marty and I," she parrots, her anger tangible. She's red in the face, her poise and aplomb gone. She believes that Marty is cheating on her with me. That if or when he sneaks out of his house late at night to rendezvous with some woman, that woman is me. It's not, of course. My marriage means everything to me. Josh means everything to me. I would never do something like that to him, or to Cassandra for that matter. I'm not that kind of woman.

There's nothing that I can say to make her believe me. It's best that I just leave.

As I step through the door frame, Cassandra barks out, "I hope you rot in hell, Meredith. I hope you both rot in hell."

I can't help but notice how her word choice is a carbon copy of the threatening texts I've been receiving. The language of the texts returns to me. *I know what you did. I hope you die. You'll never get away with it, bitch. I hope you rot in hell, Meredith.*

Cassandra has been the one sending me these texts.

I wheel around to face her. "It was you," I say, more shocked than anything. There's a tremor in my voice. "You're the one who's been sending me those awful texts. You're the one who's been trying to scare the shit out of me."

"Did it work?" she asks, satisfied in herself because she can see that it has.

"Were you following me?" I ask, aghast, thinking of the time a text arrived just as I was leaving the hospital, as if the sender knew I was on my way home and alone.

"If I was," she asks, "would it be anywhere as awful as what you've done? As what you're still doing?"

I consider the threatening, hateful wording of the texts. Was she hyperbolizing only or does she want me dead? Do I have a reason to be scared for my safety, for my life?

"I've done nothing," I say, trying to justify again how Marty and I withheld the information about our past for her sake. For Josh's. We didn't do it to hurt anyone. But I barely get the words out before the door slams closed, a dead bolt slipping into place on the other side.

I won't let Delilah play with Piper. Delilah begs, "Please, Mommy, please." She wants to know why.

When I tire of making excuses, I snap at her, "Because Mommy said so," feeling guilty for losing my patience with Delilah. It's not her fault. It's mine. I can't go outside and face Cassandra, but I also can't trust her to watch my child.

The next day they have Lily Morris over to play. Cassandra must purposefully send the girls into the front yard to rub it in Delilah's face. She sits in the front window and cries, heartbroken that she hasn't been invited, not that I would have allowed her to go even if she was. Piper and Lily dance around the front yard, laughing, holding hands. I'm appalled that Cassandra would stoop so low as to hurt my child in an effort to get back at me.

In the coming days, Leo continues to cry every time I leave him with Charlotte. He clings to me and begs, "No, Mommy. No." I feel awful making him go. I think about calling in sick to work, staying home with Leo. But doing so would only be a disservice to him, because the days he has to go would then be ten times worse.

I make deals with Leo. I bargain with him. "If you don't cry all week, Mommy and Leo will do something special on the weekend. Just you and me." I tell him we'll go to the children's museum together, or to the children's garden at the arboretum if the weather cooperates. His pick.

The mommy guilt is getting to me. I spend time thinking about quitting the yoga studio, about taking on fewer clients, if any clients at all. For as much as I love being a doula, I've been having misgivings ever since the Tebow baby was born. I think of Jason and Shelby often. I haven't stayed in touch well enough. It's hard to do. The baby has suffered irreparable damage. I don't know to what extent. I've started to second-guess the way I handled things in the labor and delivery room. I didn't do everything in my power to protect Shelby. I could have done more. I could have physically put myself between Dr. Feingold and my client.

I call Jeanette. I tell her what happened. We talk it through.

As a midwife, Jeanette is one of the few people I know familiar with my line of work.

"Maybe it's time," I tell her, "that I set my work aside and focus on my own family for a change."

She tells me the same thing I told Shelby. "You have to do what's best for your family. But, Meredith," she says, "you handled Dr. Feingold exactly as I would have. Don't ever let yourself think you're not a good doula, or that you didn't do everything you could for that woman. You're only human."

All the time, I find myself staring out the window at Marty

and Cassandra's house. I think that if Cassandra had the cunningness to buy a burner phone, to follow me around town and send intimidating texts, she's capable of much worse. Are the texts only empty threats? Or do I have a reason to fear for my family and my safety?

LEO

NOW

On your fourth day home, I go back to school. I walk there, taking the long way. I still can't walk by our old babysitter's house
without feeling the need to dry heave, even though last I heard
she and her husband don't live there anymore.

Dad says not to talk to the kids at school about you. If anyone
asks, I'm supposed to say my dad told me not to talk about it.
That goes over about as well as to be expected. During lunch, I
get my cafeteria tray knocked out of my hands because I won't
spill the details of what happened to you.

The tray falls. Dr. Carmichael blames me because by the time
it hits the ground, Adam Beltner is nowhere around. Everyone
laughs. *Look at that idiot*, they say.

Dr. Carmichael makes me clean it up. By the time I do, there's
no time left to eat. I go hungry.

I get nudged during the day. Kids ask questions that I ignore.
They throw things at me. They call me names. Jagoff. Jerkweed.
They stare. They point fingers and laugh.

The effing reporters have snapped about a gazillion pictures of you since you've been home. They're in the paper. They're all over Snapchat and Instagram. Kids keep sharing them on their own stories like what's happened to you is their own tragedy. Everyone's seen the pictures. It's the same picture, taken from ten angles by ten different photographers. In them, you're red, covered with blisters on your arms and face. Bleach burns, the doctors said. Second degree. They'll probably scar. Your clothes don't fit right. You haven't bathed in eleven years; you look like trash.

I overhear some kid call you a burrito face because of the blisters and burns. I go to punch him in the face, but Piper Hanaka gets in my way. "Ignore him, Leo. He's, like, just trying to screw with you. Don't give him what he wants."

Piper Hanaka is your age. She's two years older than me. She's a senior, practically engaged to some guy she's been dating since freshman year. Rumor has it, they're going to different colleges next year. They've decided to break up before they go. Neither wants to hold the other back and, *if it's meant to be*, I've overheard her say, *it will be*. It sounds very mature, and also stupid as shit. But it means that in exactly eight months from now, Piper Hanaka will be single. Not that she'd ever want me.

Do you remember Piper Hanaka? You used to be friends. I don't remember that. She told me once, all cloak-and-dagger-like in the hall. Just sidled up to me at my locker and said she had a dream about you. I went mute. I didn't know what to say. So I said nothing. Then she said, "Do you want to know what it was about, Leo?"

I said, "Okay. I guess."

She told me about her dream, how the two of you were trying to pick all the woolly bear caterpillars up off the street. You did it so the cars couldn't drive over them. You'd gather them in the palms of your hands, then run them back to the trees. You'd set them on the leaves, watch them walk away. By the time they reached the end of the leaf, they were moths. They could fly. In her dream, you were still six.

I thought it might mean something. I thought her dream might be premonitory, like you were dead and you'd turned into an angel with wings, and were flying to heaven.

But as it turned out, it was just a dream. Not all dreams mean something.

She said, "I still think about her, you know? I, like, think about how we used to hang out when we were kids. I wonder if we'd still be friends if she never went away."

Went away, she said. Like you had some choice in the matter. I didn't hold it against her. She's the only one who ever talked to me about you in a way that wasn't brutally honest. She's also one of the few who doesn't give in to the herd mentality and make fun of me.

Piper Hanaka used to live across the street from us. You and she used to ride your bikes on the sidewalk, do cartwheels, play house, climb trees. I don't remember any of it. Any knowledge I have is secondhand from Dad.

Piper and her family moved after everything happened. I don't remember them living there. As far as I know, that's always been old Mr. Murphy's house. But Dad said their house was on the market within five days of Mom being dead. They didn't go far 'cause Piper is still at the same school as me. They stayed in town, just on the other side of it, where they didn't have to look out their window and be reminded that bad things happen to good people every day. It's like six degrees of Kevin Bacon. All the time, we're closer to disaster than we think.

I asked Dad to put our house on the market, too. I wanted to get up and go. I wanted to start over somewhere else as someone new, where no one had heard of Mom and you.

Dad said no, because what if you came back and couldn't find us? As long as you were gone, he would never leave. Time stood still in your absence.

To be straight, Piper Hanaka and I are not friends. Piper Hanaka is way too cool to be my friend. In case you didn't realize it by now, I have no friends.

That said, Piper Hanaka doesn't want to see me get expelled for punching some douchebag in the face. She stands in between him and me until I back down and leave.

KATE

May

The rest of the way home, we're on the lookout for the car. Both Bea and I are circumspect, though I start to second-guess myself, wondering if the car was following us at all, or if it was just another car having as much difficulty navigating the roads as I was. I may never know.

By the time we reach our neighborhood, the rain has let up. Still, everything is gray and nondescript. The streets are empty. The trees hang heavy with rainwater, their branches, what's left of them, anyway, reaching down to touch the ground. The weaker of the twigs have fallen, unable to sustain the weight of the water or the force of the wind. Hail remains, melting on lawns.

I slip down the alley behind our house. Most of the homes in the neighborhood have alleys to provide rear access, because it keeps things uniform and aesthetically pleasing from the street.

The alley is narrow. It's wide enough that two cars, going in opposite directions, can just eke through.

I pull down the alley going slowly. About a hundred feet ahead, Josh returns from wherever he's been. I pull into our driveway and park, and Bea and I get out, making our way to him. He stands by his car, waiting. No one is allowed in the Dickeys' garage because it's been deemed a potential crime scene. Yellow caution tape surrounds the door. I see Bea's eyes go to it, and then move away. It's hard to believe something bad may have happened there.

"I was out searching for Meredith and Delilah," Josh says before we can even think to ask. He wears a button-down shirt, and only half of the shirt is still tucked into the waistband of his jeans. He isn't wearing a belt, and his jeans slip. He grabs ahold of the waistband and hikes them back into place. His eyes are fat.

"I didn't know the search party was headed out again today," I say, feeling guilty that Bea and I weren't here to help. Tomorrow I'm scheduled to work at the animal hospital, so I won't be able to help then, either.

"It wasn't, not with these storms, but I couldn't just sit around all day doing nothing," he says.

Bea asks Josh where he looked, and he rattles off a half dozen locations, mostly parks and other outdoorsy places that Meredith likes to take the kids, though with the weather as inclement as it is, there's no chance they would have been at a park. "Stupid, right?" he asks.

His dog, Wyatt, spent the day alone because Josh didn't have the patience to take him, worried the dog would only slow him down. There are only so many places he could bring a dog. He tells us he needs to take Wyatt for a quick walk, and then go get Leo, who's with the sitter. He's overwhelmed. He's strung out.

"Have you told Leo anything about Meredith and Delilah?" I ask.

Josh closes his eyes. He shakes his head vigorously. He looks at me. "I can't. What would I even say?" he asks, venting about how it's all so tiresome and incapacitating because he doesn't want to walk the dog or get Leo; all he wants to do is be out there, searching for Meredith and Delilah. He hates being home, being idle. It feels shiftless. He should be pounding the pavement, looking for his family.

"Leo is your family, Josh. He needs you as much as Meredith and Delilah do."

"Let me walk Wyatt," Bea offers. "Kate and I will keep him while you go get Leo. Spend time with him. Talk to him. He's a smart boy, an observant boy. Surely he realizes that Meredith and Delilah aren't here. When is he ever without Delilah?" she asks. It's conceivable that Meredith has been at work all this time—she's had back-to-back births before—but other than the few hours Delilah is at school, she and Leo are never apart.

Bea goes with Josh to retrieve Wyatt. I let myself into the house alone, slipping past the workers. They don't stop what they're doing, but I see their gazes fall to me out of the corners of their eyes. Their conversation—spoken in some other language that I don't speak—goes on. I don't know what they're saying.

I climb the stairs and move down the hall for the bedroom. It's dark in the hall; the light from the windows doesn't reach here. I lock the bedroom door, and then slide a chair in front of it for good measure. Ordinarily I wouldn't ever shower with workers in the house, but I can't bear to go another second without. In the bathroom, I undress. I hear the workers in our house. I hear their tools and their noise, rehabbing the second bath down the hall. With the other bathroom inoperative, this is the only one in use for now. It's the one in Bea's and my bedroom, which means that when we're not home, the men are in here, doing their business. It's no longer just mine and Bea's because they leave the toilet seat up, our own towels tilted and wet.

I stand in the shower, letting hot water wash away the memory of Dr. Feingold's hands. I lather the soap onto a loofah and scour my body with it. I pile on shampoo and scrub at my scalp, though he didn't touch my scalp, but as far as I'm concerned, his hands have been everywhere.

By the time I come out of the bathroom and dress, the men are packing up their things and leaving. I watch through the slats in the blinds as they load their belongings into their trucks and drive slowly away.

The earth outside is sopping wet. The puddles are profuse, not even puddles anymore but now flooding. The sky is darkening, though I don't know if it's due to the weather or because night will be here soon. It's hard to say anymore. I can't remember the last time we saw the sun. That alone would be depressing enough, but with what's happened with Shelby, with Meredith and Delilah, things are dire.

Bea and Wyatt are just back from their walk. I watch them out the window as they arrive home, coming up the path and to the front door. The door closes and Bea's voice calls for me up the stairs.

"Be right down," I call as I run a comb through my wet hair. Back in the bathroom, I towel dry the ends of it and throw it into a messy bun. I gather the towels to wash, heading downstairs, watching where I step because our home is covered in rosin paper and plastic sheeting, and sometimes nails or debris get dropped. We have to clean up after the workers leave. Zeus is here somewhere, but wherever he is, he's hiding. He doesn't like having people in the house any more than I do.

Bea changes out of her wet clothes and into something dry. She pours me a glass of wine and brings it to the sofa, where we sit with Wyatt at our feet. Dusk falls and the house turns dark. Bea and I make our way around, turning on lights. We reconvene on the sofa.

"I've been thinking," she says.

I sip from my glass of wine. "About what?"

"Just because Dr. Feingold is a creep," she says, "doesn't make him a murderer."

"Why do you say that?"

"What if he lied about knowing Meredith, not because he's somehow involved in her disappearance, but because of the malpractice suit. Think about it, Kate. If he believed for a second that you were pregnant and in need of a doula, he wouldn't want Meredith to scare you away. Meredith would have bad-mouthed him after what went down with that Tebow baby. It's bad for business."

I consider what she's said. "I guess you're right," I tell her, though this doesn't make him any less culpable in my mind. He's still on the suspect list, as far as I'm concerned.

"I think we can't just gloss over the husband," Bea says. "He and Shelby had problems. He was the only one who knew she'd gone running that night. He had a motive to kill her, and he had the means. And maybe Josh is right—maybe the husband only said what he said about Dr. Feingold to clear his own name."

"But the midwife backed his story up."

"I'm not saying it didn't happen. I'm suggesting the husband had a hidden agenda in telling us. Because let's be honest, Kate, until he did, we were convinced he was a wife killer. But now we're not so sure. He planted that seed of reasonable doubt." Bea is right; he did. Before yesterday there was only one name on my suspect list, and now there are two.

"But we saw Dr. Feingold," I argue, still feeling the way he forced my knees apart, the way he thrust his fingers inside me as if hollowing out a pumpkin. Hours later, I could convince myself that he didn't do anything *unethical*. It was the rote, forceful way that he did it that left me feeling violated and strange—that along with the knowledge of Shelby's murder, with the image of him dragging her cold, naked body out there into the woods and discarding her like trash. "We spoke to him. The man is detestable. He's a swine."

"That doesn't make him a murderer."

"We need to call the police. We need to tell them what we know."

Bea agrees. Her cell phone is on the coffee table. She grabs

233

it and looks up a nonemergency number. The police are conducting their own investigation. They've already questioned Jason Tebow about a bajillion times and are trying to do a deep dive into the contents of Meredith's phone, though without the phone itself, that's proven problematic.

Bea says to whoever answers, "I have some information on the Dickey missing-persons case." She's put on hold. While we wait, I drink my wine, liking the way it both dulls my senses and gives me courage. I ask Bea to put the phone on Speaker so that I can listen in. She does, scooching closer to me with the phone between us. A female detective comes on the line.

"I heard you have some information for me," she says.

"Yes," I say, overanxious to speak.

"And who am I speaking to?"

It's Bea who tells her.

"Okay, Kate and Bea," she says. "What do you know?"

I go first. I start with Cassandra Hanaka from across the street. I feel extra guilty that we've been sitting on this information for over twenty-four hours now and haven't told, but with the discovery of the body yesterday and all the intense emotion that went with it, Bea and I let it slip. I tell the detective about the night Cassandra was up with her son, seeing people in Josh and Meredith's yard late at night. "We were thinking that maybe one of the neighbors has a home security system, and it caught a glimpse of them." Bea and I don't have a home security system. It never felt necessary, until now.

"Unfortunately," she says, "many home security systems nowadays only offer a live feed—they don't record. And those that do only store the footage for a couple of days. But we'll look into it. We might just get lucky. I'll talk to Mr. Dickey, too, and see if he recalls anything amiss that night or the following day. What day did Mrs. Hanaka say this happened?" she asks.

"She didn't," I say. "She wasn't sure. She could only guess about a week or two ago."

Bea goes next. She tells the detective about the Tebows' malpractice suit against Dr. Feingold, because there's another possible suspect to consider besides Jason Tebow. The detective already knows about the malpractice suit. What she doesn't know is that Meredith was Shelby's doula. Bea tells her.

I'm ashamed to admit to our own run-in with Dr. Feingold. I let Bea tell the detective, feeling embarrassed as she does. The detective tells us in the future to leave the police work to the police.

The detective says that she'll be in touch. We end the call.

Bea and I turn on the TV. I drink my wine and try to wind down as another thunderstorm tears through town. But I can't relax. Because I can't stop thinking about Meredith and Delilah out there in this rain, cold and scared and wet. The lightning is rapid-fire. The thunder is so intense it feels like the entire house will give.

And then, suddenly, it's black in the house. The storm has stolen our power from us.

The blackness is so unexpected that my heart nearly stops. Without meaning to, I scream. The low drone of the refrigerator goes suddenly quiet. The dryer, a ceiling fan and the TV turn off. The house is silent, abnormally so. I never noticed the whir of the ceiling fan, but the absence of it I do. The absence of it is deafening.

Wyatt begins to moan at my feet, and I rub his ears, saying, "It's okay, it's okay," but I don't know that it is. I push myself from the seat, leaving in search of candles and flashlights, coming back with as many as I can find.

Until now we'd been one of the lucky ones with power. Our luck has run out, it seems.

I sit beside Bea. I light the candles, setting them on the coffee table. I hand Bea a flashlight, and then use mine to scan the darkest corners of the room. The furniture startles me as I try and make sense of the shadows to understand that they're not human but synthetic. No one is here but Bea and me.

Outside the storm rages. It's more thunder and wind than

anything. Bea and I sit on the sofa with Wyatt, listening for the sound of the tornado siren to warn us to run and hide.

The wind rouses the trees and shrubs. Their limbs scrape against the side of the house, against the window screens, making them rasp.

And then, a door from upstairs slams suddenly closed and Bea and I both scream.

"Maybe it was Zeus," I say, which is ridiculous, because our ten-pound cat could never slam a door like that.

"The workers," Bea says, trying to be the rational one, though I don't know that either of us believe it. "They must have left a window open. The wind blew the door closed," she says, though neither of us has the courage to go see, though if the window is open, it will soon take in water. We scoot closer together on the sofa, clinging to each other.

I'm scared. I feel vulnerable and exposed. I hate feeling vulnerable. I push myself up off the sofa again, and go to the coatrack. "What are you doing?" Bea asks. I don't say. She shines her flashlight on me, watching as I go.

Beside the coatrack is an umbrella stand. I reach my hand in and take out our giant golf umbrella. We may need something to protect ourselves with.

My eyes reach up from the umbrella stand. They move to the window. The windows on our home are ornamental, made to look pretty more than to be practical. Even on the brightest of days, our house is dark; the windows don't let much light in. Now they're lined with rain.

But none of that matters, because no matter how small or ornamental, the thing that catches my eye when I look out the window is that the homes across the street from us are still lit. Unlike ours, they're not dark.

Porch and garage lights are on. Inside the homes, I see people mulling about, backlit by bedroom and living room lights. Across the street, I see Marty, Cassandra's husband, standing in the foyer of his own home beneath a caged chandelier. The chandelier is radiant. Yellow light spills down on him.

"Bea," I breathe out, but my throat is so bone-dry that I can hardly speak. I choke on the words. Tears prick my eyes.

What I need to tell her is that the power outage isn't city-wide. I need to say that the power to our house alone has been cut. Our circuit breaker is outside, that metal box, recessed into the side wall. Someone slipped around the periphery of our home in the dark. They went to the circuit breaker and purposefully turned the main breaker handle off.

The only way to get the power back on is for Bea or me to go outside and turn it on. The circuit breaker isn't easy to find. It's camouflaged, painted yellow to match the house. I only know where it is because the workers use it frequently when they're working on the house, shutting the electricity off here and there so they don't electrocute themselves.

Someone would have had to scope the place out in daylight to know where it is.

My mind goes a step further, preying on my worst fears. Because there's a key to our house just outside the front door, in that lockbox. Anyone who knows the combination to the lockbox could let themselves in.

"What's wrong?" Bea asks, coming to me, patting my back to make the coughing fit stop.

"Look," is all I manage to say as I point a shaky finger across the street toward Marty and Cassandra's house. It takes Bea a moment to process what I'm saying. She sees Marty there in the foyer. She watches as he removes a coat and hangs it on a hook because he's evidently just come home. She sees Cassandra come to him, and we watch as an altercation transpires. Cassandra hurls something in his direction before getting in his face. She's upset; he's apologetic. He reaches gently for her. She shoves him away. Just then, one of the kids comes running in and falls. He begins to cry, breaking up the fight. Marty scoops the boy into his arms and they all leave the lit foyer, Cassandra in one direction, Marty and the boy another.

"What am I looking at?" Bea asks.

What she doesn't see is the bigger picture: that ours is the only house on the block without power. I tell her and though it's too dark to see Bea's expression, I see her back go straight like a scared cat. She stands momentarily taller, taking in what I'm saying.

"Oh God," she says. "What are you thinking?"

"That someone shut off the main breaker to our house."

"Why?" she asks. "Why would anyone do that?"

"I don't know," I tell her, whispering, because if my worst fears are true, then someone has already stolen the key from the lockbox and is in the house with us. The same key fits two doors in our house: the front door, by which Bea and I stand, and a side door, the one we use when we come in from the alley in back, where we park our cars. The workers know this because the side door is wider and a better angle at which to get large panels of drywall in. Anyone keeping close tabs on our house might know this, too.

The side door enters into the laundry room. From there, a person would have access to the kitchen, which would bring them to the servant stairs. From there, they could go anywhere.

Neither Bea nor me wants to go alone to check on the circuit breaker. But also, neither of us wants to be the one left behind.

In the end, we decide to go together. I turn on my flashlight. Bea tells me to turn it off, that we can't be drawing attention to ourselves with the light. We have to go out quiet and blind. We leave our flashlights behind.

I set my hand on the door handle and turn. I peel the door slowly back. Bea stands behind me with a hand on my lower back. Together we take one hesitant step out. I'm hyperaware of my surroundings, though the wind is a distraction. It blows my hair about my face, threatens to tear the door right from out of my hand and throw it open wide. The world is dark and disorienting, making me lose my bearings even in my own front yard. I don't know where things are and I find myself tripping down the porch step, though Bea latches on and steadies me. Lightning flares, not in the distance, but close, right above us. The storm is here.

Bea and I have just made our way onto the lawn, feet sinking into mud, when the heavens open and rain comes flooding down, drenching us both. The rain is cold, debilitating, but we keep going, eyes scanning the yard, searching wildly through the rain for signs of life.

The circuit breaker is on the side of the house. Our neighborhood is old and developed; the yard is full of trees, each of which looks human to me. Bea and I cling to each other as we walk. Bea looks left; I look right. From time to time, we both look behind. My neck stiffens, my sixth sense telling me that Bea and I are being watched, followed, tracked. Is it paranoia only or is someone there? I can't tell. I stop Bea to have a good look, but she tugs on my hand, urging me on. We have to turn the power on so we can get back inside, out of this storm.

Halfway to the circuit breaker, I regret not bringing the flashlight, not for light, but for self-defense. I regret not bringing the umbrella. We have nothing to protect ourselves with.

Bea and I move quickly, nearly running, but our movements are lumbering, the wind holding us back. It blows against us so that Bea and I have to swim upstream, fighting against the wind to get to the side of the house. We trip over fallen sticks. Our feet sink into mud. It splashes up my legs, making them cold and dirty and wet.

We round the corner of the house, Bea in the lead now, dragging me behind. We stay close to the house, using it for wind resistance, for protection from the elements. The rain comes down sideways, straight into our eyes, nearly blinding us.

Suddenly from behind, I hear footsteps. Breathing.

Bea and I are not alone.

I spin wildly, just barely making out the whites of a man's eyes standing three feet behind me. I scream and something sublimi-nal kicks in, an animal instinct. I make a fist. I use the weight of my whole body, driving my fist into the man's abdomen so that he doubles over in pain.

It's only when he cries out that I recognize the voice. It's Josh.

"Oh God, Josh," I say, going to him and helping him stand upright. I've knocked the wind out of him and it hurts. He's bent downward in the rain, stooped, trying to find his breath. His diaphragm is in spasm; he can't breathe. I latch on to him, steadying him, helping him rise back up to standing. "I'm so sorry. Oh God, Josh, I'm so sorry. I thought you were…"

But then suddenly I stop. Because I find myself wondering why Josh is out here in the rain, why Josh is hiding out on the side of our house, so close to the circuit breaker. Confusion fills me and I think of the police officers questioning Josh, of them asking for an alibi, of the blood they found in his garage.

But Josh loves Meredith. Josh would never hurt Meredith.

Or would he?

I step away from him. My pulse beats so fast it makes me dizzy. My legs become weak. "Did you cut the power to our house?" I ask, my voice swallowed up at first by the wind.

"What?" he asks, his own voice barely audible.

"Did you cut the power to our house?" I scream this time.

"What are you talking about?" Josh asks. He pushes against his knees to try and stand upright.

"The power is out in our house. Someone cut the power to our house. Was it you?"

"Kate," he says, still nearly breathless, still in pain, "why would I do that? The power is out on the whole street."

"It's not," I assert, pointing at the glowing homes that stare at us from the other side of the road.

He reaches out to lay a hand on my shoulder. I draw swiftly back. "It is on our side, Kate," he says consolingly. "Our whole side of the street is dark. They must have a different power line than us. Look," he says, motioning to his own black house just twenty feet away, "my power is out, too. A tree fell on a power line. The electric company is working on it. I checked the website on my phone. Power should be restored by morning," he says.

Behind us, Josh's house is black. The homes beyond his are black, too. I couldn't see these homes when Bea and I looked out the living room window because they're in line with ours. I only had a view of the other side of the street.

Josh didn't cut the power to our house. No one did. The power is out because of the storm and I feel like a fool for thinking Josh had plans to hurt Bea and me. It's not Josh's fault that someone scared us, that someone might have followed Bea and me home from the appointment. It's not Josh's fault that I was stupid enough to leave my real name and address, or schedule an appointment with Dr. Feingold in the first place. I put myself in harm's way.

The relief floods me. There on the lawn I begin to cry, all that pent-up emotion finally making its way out. Bea rubs tiny circles on my back, but it's Josh who consoles me. He takes my wet, shivering body into his arms and holds me.

"What's happening," he says, "is destroying me. My life is nothing without Meredith and Delilah. This is hard on all of us—we're all coming undone."

Bea retrieves Wyatt, which is the reason Josh was on his way over: to get his dog. We all go back to Josh's house, where inside Leo sleeps. We stand on the porch, protected from the rain by the roof, though we're all soaked through and cold. I shiver, wrapping my arms around myself to keep marginally warm.

There on the porch Josh tells us, "Detective Rowlings called about an hour ago. The blood in the garage didn't belong to Meredith or Delilah."

I look up sharply. "Then who?" I ask.

"The police don't know. It didn't match anything in their database."

"But maybe it's old?" Bea suggests. "You said the blood was

hard to see. For all you know it's been there for years. Maybe it belonged to some previous owner."

Josh shakes his head. "Forensics was able to determine that the bloodstain is only days' old," he says. After that, we go silent. There's nothing to say.

Something happened in that garage, but we don't know what.

MEREDITH

May

I can't keep concealing so much from Josh. I'm falling apart at the seams, trying to keep the truth from him. It's time to tell him what's been going on. The events of the last couple of months have driven a wedge between us, whether he knows it or not. I want to get back to the couple we used to be. I need to tell him about Marty and me. I can't count on Cassandra not going back on her word and letting me tell him first. If she told him, what would she say? Cassandra thinks that Marty and I are still sleeping together now.

Thursday night I call the teenage girl down the street to stay with the kids. They're in bed when she comes. It will be easy for her. She just needs to be a warm body.

I tell Josh that I'm taking him out for dinner. "What's the occasion?" he asks, grinning at me. It's been so long since Josh and I have had any alone time. With kids constantly at our heels, we can hardly have an adult conversation anymore.

What Josh and I really need is a weekend away. What I wouldn't give for Josh's parents to drive in from Michigan and stay with the kids for a couple of nights. We could book a room at the Four Seasons downtown. We could do adult things: go to a show, sleep in past seven in the morning. We could catch up on all the conversations we never have time for, or those that get interrupted by the kids. It's been a long time since Josh has offered more than a sentence or two about work, about his clients, about his coworkers, because every time he tries, his words are punctuated with kids' needs and arguments. *Can I have more milk? He's touching me. I hate broccoli.*

"No occasion," I say, leaning in to him. "Can't a wife just want to spend a night with her husband?"

I take Josh to an overpriced bar that overlooks the river. The food is good. It's known for its burgers, though the real draw is the view. The restaurant is two floors, with a second-story deck, which is where we sit. The deck has a retractable roof so that when it's cool outside, as it is tonight, patrons can stay warm while enjoying the view. Josh says it's genius.

The place is thriving because Thursday nights feature live music and dancing. With a hand on my lower back, Josh steers me through the crowded restaurant. He pulls out my chair for me. He lets me sit first. He does all those romantic gestures that fall by the wayside when we're shepherding kids around.

We order drinks. I'm het up, but on the outside it doesn't show. Once the drinks arrive, I tell myself, I'll tell Josh everything I came to say. I'll start with Dr. Feingold and the malpractice suit. I'll work my way toward Marty. I'll tell Josh that Marty and I didn't tell him and Cassandra about us because it didn't matter. Because what happened between Marty and me was nothing. I won't make the mistake again of using the term *young love.* There must be skeletons in Josh's closet, too, something he's never told me. If what he's told me is true, he had a half dozen lovers before me. I had Marty and only one other. It's not that bad. The fact that Josh knows him is only coincidental.

The drinks come. The first sip comes as a jolt to my system. It's all vodka and beer. With that first sip, Josh reaches a hand across the table. Our fingers intertwine. It's electric.

"This is nice," Josh says, grinning across the table at me. My heart skips a beat at his touch. Under the table, his leg skims mine. The look in Josh's eye is unmistakable. I know what he's thinking. I know what he wants. I want it, too.

"I can't remember the last time it was just you and me for dinner."

We never thought our family would end with two kids. We imagined more. We envisioned a large family like Josh's, with four, five, six kids. We haven't closed the door on that. Maybe tonight we can try for more. I think what another baby could do for our family, how it could bring us closer. I feel warm inside, flushed in a good way. Maybe it's the rush of alcohol to my system. Maybe it's the way Josh looks at me, like he can't tear his eyes off me.

I won't tell him now. I don't want to ruin the mood. When this moment passes, I'll tell him. I take a long, slow sip of my drink, hoping it calms my frenzied nerves.

"Have you had a chance to look over your menu?"

The waiter is there standing beside the table. He's young. Everyone looks young to me these days.

We haven't had a chance to look over the menu, because we've been so busy staring at one another. That doesn't matter. We've been here before. We know what we want. I go first, and Josh orders after me.

The waiter leaves. Josh raises his beer glass. "To us," he says. Our glasses clink. The sound of it is thin. "Did I ever tell you how lucky I am to have found you?" he asks.

"I'm the lucky one," I say.

We were twenty-five when we met. I was driving down the expressway when some asshole took a glancing blow at me. We were going fast; it could have been cataclysmic. My car spun out of control, smashing into the guardrail on the driver's side before coming to a stop. The driver kept going. Josh was in the car behind me. He was the one who called 911. He was the one who spoke to me, keeping me calm and awake through the broken window until the paramedics and the fire department got there, and I had to be extricated from the car. He was the one waiting for me when I woke up, though he had to lie to the nurse and say he was my brother, or she wouldn't have let him in. Family only. Josh is able to sweet-talk himself into almost any situation.

Suffice it to say, Josh saved my life. By the time I arrived at the hospital, I'd lost a significant amount of blood. I was bleeding internally. I was going into shock.

I mean it when I say that I'm the lucky one.

I watch as a man takes the stage. He tunes his guitar as his band joins him onstage. They start to play. The rooftop is congested. People everywhere, until there are more people than seats. They come up for the music and the view. There is a bar up here. Bodies crowd around it, ordering drinks. It isn't a college crowd. The college kids go to the fratty bars with dollar drinks and moshing, where people dance on tabletops when they've had too much to drink. This place is just expensive enough to keep the college kids out.

"Dance with me," Josh says. His chair skids backward. He stands up. He reaches out a hand to me. I hesitate, looking around. No one else is dancing yet. "Someone has to go first."

He won't take no for an answer.

I set my hand in his. I let him pull me to my feet. The room is unsteady. The bartender was generous with his pour. On the dance floor, Josh twirls me. People clap. Someone whistles and it's reverberant.

When I come back to center, Josh stops me from spinning. He presses his hands around the small of my back, steadying me. He pulls me against him until we're flush. He gazes down at me, giving me bedroom eyes. Butterflies dance in my stomach.

A body brushes past mine. "Excuse me." I feel the mistaken

plunge of an elbow to my side. Before I can reply, Josh's lips press against mine. It's tender, teasing. My body responds.

He whispers in my ear, "I love you more than anything," and then the music begins. I can't hear anything over the sound of it. I wrap my arms around Josh's neck. I rest my head against his chest. We sway. Josh strokes his hands up and down my sides. Everything I came to tell him slips away.

The next song is faster, something pop. We're no longer alone on the dance floor. It's become crowded. Bodies bump into one another. The floor thumps with the vibration of the bass. It's not always a dance bar. But on Thursday nights, that mold is broken. Josh and I draw apart. The music is upbeat, not the kind of music for a slow dance.

And then I'm dancing with some other man that I don't know. His hungry brown eyes leer at me. The man spins me as Josh had. His hand is sweaty, grasping. He spins me once, and then I'm back in Josh's safe embrace.

Forked lightning flashes across the sky. We see it through the glass roof. People gasp. I expect a barrage of rain to fall next. The rain doesn't come. The night stays dry, but charged with electricity.

Back at the table, two fresh drinks wait for us. There's a sheen of sweat on Josh's forehead. He still grins at me, gulping his beer. The dancing has made him thirsty. Our desire has morphed into something giddy, impetuous. We giggle at one another over our glasses.

"Should we ask for the check?" Josh mischievously asks.

"We haven't gotten our food."

"We could always get fast food, if you're hungry."

If we go home, there will be a babysitter and a dog waiting for us. There will be kids to be quiet for. But Josh and I aren't above taking the car somewhere remote.

I grin back. "Let's go." I want more than ever to be alone with Josh.

Josh's eyes go roving around the rooftop for our waiter.

"Hey, neighbor." The voice is singsong when it comes. We look and see Kate sitting at the table beside us, her smile a mile wide. Kate and Bea are here, getting situated in their seats where the host has just sat them.

"What are the odds?" Bea asks, reaching for her menu and having a look.

Just then our food arrives, the waiter skirting around glasses and silverware to deliver it.

Josh and I exchange a disenchanted glance. We can no longer leave.

At Josh's suggestion, we slide Kate and Bea's table closer to ours, make it a table for four instead of two for two. It dampens the mood. It doesn't kill it. The pining I feel will still be here an hour from now.

Drinks arrive for Kate and Bea. Kate offers up a toast. "For Bea." It's Bea's birthday. Today Bea is thirty years old. They came to celebrate. Glasses rise up above the tabletop. Someone clinks too hard, and sticky liquid spills over the edge of a glass and onto our hands. Laughter ensues. Kate scrambles for napkins, apologizing.

Bea asks, "What are you doing out on a Thursday night?"

Josh makes eyes at me. "Do I really need a reason to spend a night with my beautiful wife?"

The food is plentiful. The portions are large. I eat it all because the alcohol has made me famished. Food is delivered for Bea and Kate. More drinks, a round on Josh and me for Bea's birthday. Someone on the rooftop catches wind of Bea's birthday and then everyone is singing happy birthday to Bea. It's cacophonous. It's not pretty. Bea tries hiding her face behind a dessert menu, which Kate snatches away. Bea's not really embarrassed; it's all for show. Bea isn't the type to embarrass easily. When it's done they kiss.

Kate and Bea are opposites. Kate is conventional. Bea is not. Kate doesn't stand out the way that Bea does. Bea is arresting. She's indelible, in the way she looks and in the way she carries herself. Nothing and nobody can touch Bea. Tonight's outfit of choice: black tights with short shorts; a faux fur leopard print jacket over a T-shirt; Doc Martens. Few people could get away with it.

We dance. I'm dancing with Josh. And then I'm dancing with Kate and Bea.

String lights run across the glass ceiling. It's ambient. I lose all track of time. Beneath my feet, the floor moves like the sandy bottom of the ocean when waves roll in and then out.

Josh is here now and we're slow dancing. And then Josh is gone and it's Kate who dances with me. There's a tap on my shoulder, and Josh is back. His face has changed.

"What's wrong?" I ask. We stand beside the table, the four of us. Kate polishes off her drink. Bea's hips still sway.

Josh shouts over the noise. The sitter has called. Delilah had a nightmare and woke up. She's inconsolable. The news sobers me. I'm having too much fun to leave. But Josh says, "I told the sitter we'd be home in a few."

Kate leans in to Bea. "We should go, too." The night is coming to an end.

Bea is tugging on Kate's hand, drawing her back to the dance floor. The look in her eye is pleading. "Just one more song. One more drink. Please, Kate."

Kate protests. "It's getting late. I have to work in the morning."

Bea is pouting now. "But it's my birthday." She dances alone beside us, hands in the air, eyes closed, the music moving her. She's a sight for sore eyes.

Kate is in a bind, torn between wanting to leave, and not wanting to disappoint Bea on her birthday. She confesses to Josh and me that she has surgeries to perform in the morning. Today she spent ten hours on her feet. There was a euthanasia. She's tired and emotionally spent.

I'm the only one who doesn't have to work in the morning. I say to Josh, "Why don't you give Kate a ride home. Check on

Delilah. Get her back to bed. I'll stay with Bea for one more drink."

"You don't mind?" Kate is grateful.

"I don't mind." She hugs me.

Josh's lips press against my ear. His words tingle down to my toes. "Wake me up when you get home. If you know what I mean." He draws back, eyes on mine.

I taste the beer on his lips when he kisses me. I watch Kate and Josh leave, weaving their way through the crowds. Bea takes me by the hand. We're dancing. It's easy to see why Kate is so enamored with Bea.

The music, the alcohol, have a narcotic effect on me. The bartender has been generous with his vodka tonight. "You're a good friend for staying with me."

"It's not every day you turn thirty."

There's a slowness to my words. I feel giddy, euphoric.

We dance some more. The brown-haired man is there. He wants to dance with me. Bea tells him to get lost. We fold ourselves in half, laughing. I laugh so hard my stomach hurts.

Back at the table, the waiter delivers more drinks. The bill comes. Someone pays.

Bea and I are walking toward the parking garage. Neither of us should be driving after all we've had to drink. But I can't call Josh to come and get us because then he'd have to wake the kids. Bea won't call Kate because Kate has to work in the morning.

"Look at that," Bea says, pointing upward. The streets of town are tricked out with a million tiny white lights, like stars.

There's a nip in the night air. Bea clings to me.

We're riding the elevator up. It's slow and creaky. There are soda cans in the corner of it. The floor is sticky. The doors open. We step out and look for Bea's car. It's not there. She starts to laugh. "What is it?" I ask.

We're on the wrong floor. It seems hysterically funny. We're both folded over again in laughter. We get back in the elevator and ride down this time. The doors open and there is Bea's car.

We get inside. Bea turns on the car. She turns on the radio. We're singing. I feel happy, drunk. Bea spins the car down the parking garage ramp and out onto the street.

They say most accidents happen within five miles of a person's home.

I never see it coming.

KATE

11 YEARS BEFORE

May

Three things happen in the coming days. A paternity test, administered by the police with Jason's permission, reveals that Jason Tebow is not the father of baby Grace. The news stuns both Bea and me. As it turns out, monogamy was neither Jason's nor Shelby's cup of tea.

A day later, a nurse from Dr. Feingold's office calls with the news: the blood test results came back. "I'm sorry, honey," she says over the phone, "but it's not good news. You're not pregnant." I pretend to be sad as I mutter my thanks and hang up the phone.

The search for Meredith and Delilah continues and then stalls. Josh's grassroots effort waxes and then wanes as people start to lose hope. They give up. Their lives move on while Josh's, Meredith's and Delilah's don't. For a while, the police augment the search with dogs and divers, searching the woods and the river for Meredith and Delilah. The state police become involved;

soon after, Meredith and Delilah become national news. Still, they're not found. The weather doesn't help. Almost every day the search is called off because of unsafe river conditions and the threat of more rain.

And then one morning, I wake up to the ping of my phone, an incoming message on the group chat. When I look, there on my phone is a photo of the back end of a car and, on it, a close-up of a license plate number.

I'm still out of focus from sleep. It takes me a moment to process what I'm looking at. When I do, I see that the photo is of Meredith's license plate. It's Meredith's car.

I sit suddenly upright in bed. I shout for Bea but she's outside in her studio working again. Over the next few seconds, the group chat becomes a flurry of activity. Meredith's car has been spotted by a member of our group in the parking lot of a motel two towns over. The police have been notified.

Bea sees the text, too. She comes running in to find me. Unshowered and undercaffeinated, Bea and I decide to drive Josh to the motel. He's been in touch with the detective, but refuses to stay home and wait for news, though that's exactly what she told him to do. He's understandably worked up and in no state to drive himself. The three of us drop Leo off with the babysitter on the way; while Josh walks him to the front door, I call my office and ask them to reschedule my morning patients. Josh, Meredith and Delilah need me now.

The drive feels long, though it can't be more than twenty minutes. All the way, we don't speak, each lost in our own thoughts, thinking the very worst.

The motel is located off a two-lane highway in an unincorporated part of town. There isn't much around it other than a handful of industrial buildings and open land, much of it for sale and underwater. When we arrive at the motel, there is an obvious police presence in the parking lot. We don't see Meredith's car at first, but we're drawn there by the circle of officers that surround it.

Josh throws his door open while the car is still moving. He leaps from the car and runs toward Meredith's. The doors, the trunk of it, are open and police are looking inside.

I can't find Meredith or Delilah. "Do you see them?" I ask Bea, glancing around the parking lot.

"I don't," says Bea. She looks, too, but all we see are a handful of bystanders and police.

I pull into an empty spot. The parking lot is not large. I park the car and Bea and I make our way toward Josh. We don't get far before we're stopped by police, and forced to wait a good thirty feet back, away from what the officer calls a *crime scene.* His words make my throat go suddenly dry and I'm certain they've found something inside Meredith's car. A body, more blood. Bea grabs my hand as he says it and together we stand, rooted in place, waiting anxiously for Josh to return with news.

The motel itself is somewhat skeevy. It's dilapidated and small, a single-story building with doors that enter from the outside. In the parking lot, a 1970s neon sign flashes Vacancy, advertising rooms for just fifty dollars a night or two hundred a week. I'm guessing much of the clientele is homeless. They live here.

This isn't the kind of place the Meredith I know would ever go.

"What did they find?" Bea asks when Josh comes to stand by us.

"The car," Josh tells us breathlessly, "is empty. No sign of either of them, though there's mud all over the driver's side. Blood in the passenger's seat. An officer went inside and spoke to the clerk. He was told that Meredith checked in on the same day she disappeared. She paid cash. She rented the room for the month and declined daily maid service. The police are going to search the room." He stops there, dragging his hands through his hair. His eyes are exhausted but hopped up on adrenaline. They don't look right. "I'm supposed to sit tight and wait, but..." His voice trails.

Two things flash across Josh's face in that instant: hope and despair.

Bea reaches for him. We stand together like that, the three of us in a row, holding hands.

The officers step inside a room and close the door behind themselves. It takes too long for them to return. With each passing minute, my concern grows exponentially. I fidget. I can hardly stand still, but I force myself to for Josh's sake.

Josh asks things like, "What do you think is taking so long?"

God bless Bea, she comes up with reasonable explanations that put Josh at ease, like, "They'd want to talk to her. They'd have questions for her if she was there."

But I think that if Meredith and Delilah were there in the room, the officers would be back immediately. But they're not. Too much time passes as we watch from behind the barricade tape, staring expectantly at the closed motel door.

A few officers remain to keep watch on us. They speak to one another through walkie-talkies, though the voices are muffled and low; we can't hear what they say. But then, as we watch, two of the officers leave and move toward the room. They're let inside by someone we can't see. The door closes. There is a window in the room, but the curtains are drawn. We can't see anything.

"What's happening?" Josh calls out, but no one responds. The number of bystanders has doubled since we arrived. Cars on the highway slow down as they pass, staring out their windows at us.

I swallow hard when the first officer emerges from the room. The day is overcast, though there's no rain. Today, shockingly, there isn't even a threat of rain. Somewhere behind the dense clouds, the sun fights to get through and at first I thought it was propitious—sunlight after all these days in the dark—but now I'm not so sure.

The officer holds his hat in his hands. He moves across the parking lot and toward us, his head hanging low. The female detective follows behind, three steps back.

Beside me, Bea grips my hand tightly in hers. No one says a word. No one breathes.

When the detective arrives, she asks Josh if she can speak with him. Josh quickly obliges, stepping beneath the barricade tape. He follows the detective. They go to a spot far enough away where no one can hear but everyone can see. There they speak. It doesn't take long.

As a dozen spectators watch on, Josh falls to his knees in the parking lot. He cries. His plaintive sobs are audible even from this distance, as he lets out a desperate, elongated, "Noooooo!" that will stay with me my whole life. His movements become feral, rabid, as he smacks at the gravelly parking lot with his bare hands, then looks skyward begging, demanding to know why. "Why?" he screams. "WHY?"

MEREDITH

11 YEARS BEFORE

May

My eyes are closed. I'm belting out the refrain to a song. I don't know the words. I make them up as I go. They sound perfect to my ears. Bea and I laugh, giddy, euphoric. We drive so fast the car becomes airborne. We fly.

We've left downtown. The lights are behind us now, the streets dark.

Bea must see something because there's an inappreciable gasp a second before impact. I hear it later, only in retrospect.

The impact is pronounced, a dull, heavy thud, and then it's quiet.

When it happens, I jerk upright in my seat. I'm stunned. My eyes go wide. Bea tries slamming on the brakes. But because of the speed of the car, we don't immediately stop. We go forward another few feet. The car jounces, running over whatever we've hit. Bea brakes harder. This time we stop. My seat belt locks, pinning me in place. She slips the car into Reverse, going backward. Again the car jounces.

I fall silent. I gaze into the darkened world beyond the windshield, seeing nothing, only stars.

Beside me, Bea keeps saying, "Oh shit, oh shit, oh shit."

All I can ask is, "What was it?"

Foxes scavenge the neighborhood at night. Coyotes, too. There are many of them. The neighbors are always warning people with outdoor cats and little dogs to watch out.

Bea doesn't tell me. She just says, "Oh shit, oh shit."

She slams her hands against the steering wheel.

The mood in the car has changed. It's deathly quiet.

Bea gets out of the car. Her movements are stiff. They're robotic. She leaves her door open. She steps around the front end of the car. I sit in the passenger's seat, watching, still pinned in place by the seat belt.

Bea is all aglow in the light from the headlights. She looks angelic.

I'm buzzed. Things happen in slow motion. My depth perception is off. I feel disconnected, but still cognizant because the buzz is wearing off.

Bea and Kate have a cat. They foster things. Bea would never intentionally hurt anything. She's beside herself with guilt. She folds herself in half, puts a hand to her mouth and cries. It happens only momentarily. Bea isn't one to cry.

She snaps back up. She wipes her eyes. She rushes to the car.

As she descends into the driver's seat, she's chillingly composed. She's hatched a plan.

The first thing she does is slam her door closed. The car fades to black. She kills the headlights. The street before us also turns black. Our streetlights are lanterns. They're more decorative than practical.

"What are you doing?" I ask. If the animal is dead, there's nothing we can do for it. If it's still alive, we can call Kate. Kate could help.

Bea turns to me. She grabs ahold of my arm, so tightly it hurts. Her nails dig into me. "You can't tell anybody about this. Do you hear me, Meredith? You have to promise me that. Do you promise?" she says.

I quickly sober up, because she's scaring me. People run over animals all the time. It's why there's a word for it. Roadkill. I'm not insensitive, but these things happen.

"Get a grip, Bea." My voice is light when I speak, an insouciant whisper. "People hit animals all the time. It's fine. Is it still alive?"

I try to free my arm. Bea won't let me. If anything, she holds more tightly. My forearm begins to throb.

The light in the car is negligible. I can just make out the shape of her, though the details are imprecise.

"Promise me," Bea demands. Her voice is unshaken. But there's something off about her eyes; they're not quite right.

At her behest I do. "I promise, Bea. I won't say a thing."

I tell her that whatever ran out into the street did so before she had a chance to react. She can't beat herself up over it. It's the thing's own fault. "When I was sixteen I ran over a whole litter of raccoons. Babies," I tell her. I'd just gotten my license. I was driving at night. I never saw them, yet the guilt ate at me for months. I felt awful about it.

"It wasn't a fucking raccoon, Meredith!" Bea screams.

In all the time that I've known her, I've never known Bea to lose her temper. I've never seen this side of Bea. She's tough, she's iron-willed. But this is a Bea that I don't know. This is a Bea that's reactive.

Silence fills the car. She stares at me, wild-eyed, her hair falling in her eyes.

I can't hear my own panicked breathing, but I can feel the way my chest rises and falls.

"Bea," I say. It comes out as a breath. "What is it? What did you hit?"

Her silence terrifies me. She lets go of my arm. She relaxes back into her seat, staring ahead.

I get out of the car. I stagger to the front end of it. I have to see what it is.

I prepare myself for the worst. Roadkill is never pretty. Decapitation comes to mind, as does limb loss. Something horrific has happened here. Something that's shaken Bea to the core.

And then I see, in the faint glow of the nighttime sky.

It's not an animal.

The horror washes over me. My heart palpitates. My legs are like rubber. My palms sweat. I stand frozen at first, gaping, my sweaty hands pressed to my mouth to hold a scream back.

It's a person—female, based on the hair length and body shape. She's lying facedown on the street, a barely perceptible pool of blackness spreading beneath her. Her arms are up like goalposts. It's the same way Delilah used to sleep as a baby, on her chest with arms up and over her head. This woman's long hair surrounds her. Her legs are tucked beneath the car.

Bea steps from the car. She comes to stand beside me. "She should have been wearing reflective gear. A fucking headlamp. She should have been on the sidewalk."

My legs finally give. I drop to my knees, not by choice but out of necessity. The gravel from the street digs into my skin. I reach out for the woman, but Bea says, "Don't touch her," as I do. Her words are sharp. They startle me.

"Why?" I ask, dismayed, looking over my shoulder at Bea. "We have to help her, Bea. She needs our help. We can't just leave her here."

"Of course we're not going to leave her here. Help me," she says, dropping down to the other side of the woman. Bea wears gloves now. They must have been in her car, remnants from the winter. My hands are bare. Bea tells me to bury my hands in my shirtsleeves so we don't touch her with our hands. I don't think to ask why. I just do.

We try to turn her over. She doesn't weigh much. But she's

limp, sagging, all dead weight. At first we can't pick her up. We have to roll her onto her back. In my head I think that we shouldn't be doing this. You're never supposed to move someone who's injured. We should leave her where she is and call for help. But that thought never leaves my head. It stays where it is. I listen to Bea. I go through the motions mostly because I think I'm in shock. This isn't happening. I'm not here. I've dissociated myself from what's happening and though, physically, some part of me kneels on the street, turning this woman over onto her back, the rest of me watches, horrified, from a distance.

It's only when she's flat on her back that I get a good look at the woman. The alcohol inside me rises up, and I find myself rushing into nearby bushes to be sick. I begin to howl. In an instant, Bea is there, in my face, taking me to task. "Shut up, Meredith," she snaps, more panicked than anything. "You'll wake the whole fucking street."

She presses a hand to my mouth and holds my cries in. I have to fight her off to breathe. Bea is scared, I know that. She's panicking. I am, too.

The woman on the street is Shelby.

I push past Bea. I rush back to the car. I dig inside my purse for my phone. No sooner have I found it, than Bea is there. She snatches it from my hand.

"Give that back," I say.

"What do you think you're doing? Who are you going to call?"

I grapple with her for my phone, but Bea is bigger and stronger than me. She wins.

"I know her, Bea," I say, and I explain. Bea's face falls, but to her, it changes nothing. "We need to call 911," I insist. "We need to call for an ambulance. She needs help."

"We're *drunk*," Bea chastises, "and she's dead, Meredith. She's *dead*. I checked for a pulse—there's none. There's nothing we can do for her. I'll go to jail if anyone finds out about this."

"So what do you want to do?" I ask. "You want to just *leave*?"

It's unfathomable, leaving Shelby here in the middle of the road for someone else to find.

Bea shakes her head. "Of course not, Meredith," she says, "We can't just leave her here," and I'm relieved at first. At first I think Bea plans to do the right thing. But then she says, "We need to get rid of her," and my heart stops.

"What do you mean?" I ask, aghast.

"We need to take her somewhere secluded, where she won't be found for a while, if ever."

"No," I say, my head jerking wildly back and forth. "No, Bea. Why would we do that? You're out of your mind."

"Listen to me," Bea says, her voice controlled. She grips my head in her hands, forces me to look at her. "Just listen to me. I know you're upset. I get that, Meredith. I'm upset, too. But think about it for a minute. Just stop and *think*. This woman is dead. There's nothing we can do for her. If she was alive, Meredith, I'd call an ambulance. I'd take her to the emergency room myself. But she's dead. She's fucking *dead*. Nothing we do now can change that. But if we turn ourselves in, we're fucked. *I'm* fucked. We can't save her but we can save ourselves."

"We leave her here, then," I say, decisive. "We leave her here and we make an anonymous call to the police."

If the alternative is hiding her body, it's better to leave her here.

"We can't do that," Bea says.

"Why? What difference does it make?"

Bea's response is thoughtful, swift. She's two steps ahead of me. "Because if we leave her here, the police are searching for the driver of a hit-and-run by morning, at the latest, if not tonight. If we get rid of her, they're looking for a missing person. It's different. Don't you see that, Meredith? For all we know there are tire impressions on her body, paint on her clothes. Evidence that connects her to me. We have no other choice," she says. "I know this is hard. But we have to get rid of her."

I shake my head frantically. The tears come. They're inaudible, falling from my eyes. "I can't. I can't be a part of this," I rant. I turn away. I set my hand on the door handle. I think about leaving. Where would I go? What would I do?

Bea grabs me before I can leave. I try shrugging her off but can't. I turn back to her. "Stop it, Bea," I say. "Let me go. I won't be a part of this. I can't have this on my conscience. We should call the police. You should turn yourself in."

"Snap out of it," she says as she slaps me hard. I fall silent, shocked. My cheek stings. My hand goes to it as I choke on a sob. "Haven't you figured it out yet?" she asks. She has the presence of mind to keep her voice quiet. "You're no innocent bystander," she says. "You're already a part of it. What do you think Josh would say if he knew we plowed down some woman in the street? You think that husband of yours would ever think the same of you?"

Shame and fear wash over me. What would Josh do if he knew? Running into Shelby was an accident. But would he judge me for getting in the car with Bea when she was so obviously drunk?

"I don't know," I say frantically, shaking my head. "I don't know what he'd do."

"Get out of the car, Meredith. Now. I can't carry her alone."

She's firm. We're no longer on a level playing field. Now Bea is in control.

We get out of the car. We go back to the body. With Shelby on her back, she's easier to carry. Bea slips her arms under Shelby's underarms, and lifts her upper half. She has to slide her out from under the car first, before I can take her feet. All the while I sob, my body in spasms. Bea tells me to be quiet, to walk faster. It's only a matter of time before someone comes.

I go through the motions. I do as I'm told. This isn't happening, I tell myself. This isn't real. I keep waiting for myself to wake up. This is all just a dream, a horrible nightmare.

I never wake up.

We haul Shelby to the back end of the car. She's as limp as

a ragdoll. There's a mark on her head from where she landed on the concrete. It's swollen. It bleeds. Blood comes from her mouth. Whatever caused her death is far worse than skin-deep. Head trauma. Organ failure. Internal hemorrhaging.

Bea shuffles her into one hand so she can pop the trunk. It's awkward and ungainly. Shelby's head sags backward, practically snaps. As Bea opens the trunk, a negligible light comes out. But on the dark street, it might as well be the sun. Bea panics. "Hurry," she says, nearly throwing her half of Shelby into the trunk, beside jumper cables, a box of cat litter.

There's a dull thud when Shelby's head hits the inside of the trunk. It sickens me. I won't do the same. I carefully, tenderly, lay Shelby's lower half inside and rearrange her so that she's comfortable.

Bea doesn't like this. "Hurry up, Meredith. Just put her in."

Her eyes appraise the street. There are houses. Most are dark. Most everyone has gone to sleep. Of the few homes still lit, the windows are empty. No one's watching.

I step back from the trunk. As Bea is closing it, I swear I hear Shelby moan.

My blood curdles. Only Bea felt for a pulse. I never checked.

"What was that?" I ask, panicked. "Open it back up," I say, but Bea just looks at me.

"It's time to go, Meredith." She starts to walk away.

"She made a noise. I heard her," I insist. "We have to see."

What if she's still alive?

What if Bea is mistaken?

Bea says, "I didn't hear anything."

"Please, Bea," I beg. "Please open it so that I can check."

"Get in the fucking car," she says, walking around to the driver's side and getting in. I follow suit, only because Bea tells me that when we get where we're going I can see if she's still alive. She starts the car. She doesn't turn the headlights on.

"If she's alive, we take her to the hospital," I say. "Promise me, Bea. Promise me we can take her to the hospital if she's alive."

"She isn't alive."

"I heard her. She made a noise."

"You're hearing things."

Bea pulls away. I don't know where we're going or how long it will take to get there. If Shelby is alive, I pray there's enough oxygen in the trunk to last awhile.

But what about the exhaust pipe so close to the trunk? Does carbon dioxide get in?

And if she's bleeding internally, how long until she bleeds out?

It's only after we've gone a block that Bea turns on the headlights.

"If you heard something," Bea says after a while, "it's because bodies make noises when they die."

Bea keeps her eyes on the road. She won't look at me.

Rain begins to fall in big, fat glops. It splatters against the windshield. If the weathercasters are right, this is the first of many rains to come.

"Can't we just check?" I ask a few miles from home. The hospital is nearby. If we check and she's alive, we can take her there.

"Shut up, Meredith. Just please shut the fuck up!" Bea snaps.

I fall silent. I think of Shelby in the trunk. I think of what we've done. I think of Jason and her baby at home. I think of Josh, at home in our bed, waiting for me to come.

We drive for miles. We drive through town and then keep going. The road turns wooded. It cuts through the river's floodplain, on the outer edges of a forest preserve. The houses disappear. The road turns narrow, gravel. The trees close ranks around us, scratching on the hood of the car.

That's where Bea stops the car, in the middle of the abandoned gravel road. We get out. "We can't do this. I don't want to do this, Bea."

"I'm not going to jail," she says. She's hell-bent on that. I've never seen this side of Bea. I don't know who this woman is, but I know this woman is as scared as me, even if it manifests itself as anger and control. Bea is a good person. She's not a psychopath. But she's backed into a corner, desperate for a way out. This is that way.

She opens the trunk. I brace myself, not knowing whether we'll find Shelby dead or alive.

Shelby is dead. She has no pulse. Already the earliest stages of rigor mortis have begun to set in. Her face is fixed in a terrifying grimace. The coloration of her skin has changed.

But she's shifted positions since we laid her in the trunk. This bothers me.

Was she alive and deliberatively moved inside the trunk, trying desperately to get out?

Or was she dead and kinetic energy moved her?

I can't stop thinking about it, obsessing over it.

But other than to assuage my guilt, it doesn't matter. Shelby is dead.

I've lost all track of time. I don't know how long ago the accident was, or how long we were driving.

The rain is steady. As we carry Shelby deeper into the woods, she slips. Her ankles, in my wet hands, are like sardines. They're hard to hold on to. The ground is soft, wet. We trip over tree roots. We sink into the mud.

Here, we don't have to worry about being quiet.

We go a couple hundred feet, deep into the trees. I hear the river flowing in the distance. It moves fast. My first thought is that Bea is going to toss Shelby's body into the river.

But then she stops short of the river. She sets her half of Shelby on the ground. It's ungentle.

With her gloved hands, Bea starts digging into the softened earth. "You just going to stand there and watch?" she asks. I gently lower Shelby's legs to the ground. I drop to my knees. I start carving away at the dirt, with my hands still covered by my shirtsleeves. Shelby's body lies beside me, watching. My actions are reactive, unconscious. I go through the motions, because I don't know what else to do. I can't leave. Bea is the one with the keys. She's calling the shots. I cry as I dig. For a minute my whole body heaves. I try to get control of myself but I'm so overcome with emotion. Shock, horror, guilt, fear.

It takes forever to dig a hole big enough for Shelby's body. It's sloppy at best. It's not nearly deep or wide enough. We don't have a shovel. But at some point Bea finds an ice scraper in her trunk and we take turns with that. We find tree limbs and use those, too, to chisel away the dirt.

Before we bury her, Bea strips her of her clothes. She savagely tears her shirt from her head. She yanks her pants down. She leaves her underwear around her knees.

Naked, Shelby still carries the baby weight. She hasn't lost the extra pounds that worried her so. Her breasts are huge, sagging. They fall out of the bra that Bea tugs from her arms.

I watch Bea as she takes Shelby's shoes. I think of the shame and indignity of being found naked. One final disgrace. I look away. I can't watch.

"Why, Bea?" I ask.

"If she's naked, it implies something sexual happened here. The police will go searching for a man."

We drag her into the hole. We use the dirt and the mud that we've unearthed to cover her up. We canvass the forest, gathering whatever detritus we can find: leaves and sticks. We lay those on top of the mud. Shelby's body shows as a protuberance from the earth. But it's slight. With any luck, no one will find her here.

At some point in our drive home, it stops raining.

Bea stops just short of our houses, pulling to the side of the street.

"What are we doing?" I ask.

Bea kills the engine. She says only, "Follow me." We get out of the car and start moving down the sidewalk. We're both filthy, caked with mud. It's on my clothes, my hands, my shoes. It's in my hair.

Bea asks if I have bleach. I tell her I do. By now the rain has washed Shelby's blood from the street. It's no longer visible. No one will know it was there.

But Bea's trunk still shows evidence of blood. That needs to be cleaned.

"Where is it?" she asks, walking fast. Her legs are longer than mine. She doesn't wait up for me. I have to jog to keep up.

"In the garage," I say. It's where Josh and I keep all the cleaning supplies, so that Wyatt and the kids can't get into them by accident.

We come to my house. It's surreal, standing outside it at this time of night. I don't recognize my own yard. "Go get it," she says, about the bleach. "I'll wait here." She stands in the yard. The yard is wooded. The neighborhood is hundreds of years old. Some of the trees were here before the homes. They provide coverage. No one can see us, we think.

My house is dark. The porch lights are off. Josh must have forgotten to turn them on for me. He often does. It has to be the middle of the night. If Josh were to wake, he'd be worried. But Josh is a sound sleeper. The odds of him waking up are slim. It's far more likely one of the kids would wake up and come looking for me.

I wonder about Jason. Is he sound asleep like Josh, or is he awake, worried, wondering why Shelby isn't home from her run?

I slink into the garage. I leave the lights off. I move by rote. I find the bleach and return to Bea. It's cold outside. Only now, as the adrenaline slows, do I notice. I start to shiver. It's slight at first, but then turns considerable. My body jerks.

Bea takes the bleach from my hand. "I'll take it from here," she says. "Go take a shower and go to bed. And remember, not a word to anyone, do you hear? Not a word."

I offer to help Bea clean. She doesn't want my help.

Before she leaves, she makes me strip naked.

"Why?" I ask.

"Just do it," she says.

On my own front lawn, I stand and strip down to my underwear and bra. I'm too devastated to be self-conscious. Bea takes my clothes from me. "What are you doing with those?" I ask. They're covered in mud, in blood.

"I have to get rid of them. They're evidence," is what she says, and then, "Go home, Meredith. Go home to your husband and kids. Forget all about what happened tonight."

She starts to walk away from me. I grab her arm. "And if I can't?" I ask, knowing I'll never forget this night.

"You need to," she says as she shrugs me off and leaves.

LEO

NOW

I don't go to the hypnosis. I go to school because Dad makes me go. He's worried I've missed so many days that I'm starting to fall behind.

The day sucks as school days do. When I get home, you and Dad are in the kitchen. I come in and overhear you tell Dad that you're sorry. I hang back, by the door, watching you, wondering what you're sorry for. You look so small. You stare down at your hands, picking at hangnails that you've torn and bitten off.

Dad's bought you clothes of your own and, even though they fit right, they're not right. Girls don't wear clothes like that these days because Dad had to shop in the little-girls section and not the one for teens. There's a panda bear on your shirt. It has rainbows for ears. A girl like Piper Hanaka wouldn't be caught dead wearing that.

"I'm sorry, sir," you say again.

Dad tells you, "There's nothing to be sorry for. You didn't know. How could you have known?"

There's a quaver to Dad's voice. I know it by heart. He just barely manages to keep the valve closed so the waterworks don't begin. As I watch, Dad puts his arms out like he might hug you. You shrink back, banging into the countertop. Dad gets the point. He puts his arms down, knowing you're more of a trauma victim than his daughter. You may never be the daughter he used to know.

Dad hasn't gone back to work since you've been home. He's on what's called FMLA. He isn't getting paid but that doesn't matter because we have money. Dad's a workaholic. After you and Mom left, he would rather have been at work than home with me. We never went on vacation or did anything fun. He thinks he's undeserving of nice things. His car is a twelve-year-old Passat with a hundred thousand miles on it, when he could easily afford the same Mercedes-Benz the neighbors just got.

"It's not your fault," Dad says.

I close the front door and let my backpack drop loud enough that you know I'm home. I go to the kitchen. "How'd it go?" I ask. I help myself to an apple, sink my teeth into it. You and Dad are mute. "The hypnosis," I say, with a mouthful of apple, because no one's answering me. "How did it go?"

"Good," Dad says, busying himself making dinner. He takes ground beef from the refrigerator, a skillet from the cabinet. He sets the skillet down lightly, careful to keep noise to a minimum for your sake. "It was very informative. We learned a lot. I'm glad we did it."

Talk about beating around the bush.

I look from Dad to you. You stand with your shoulders rounded, your head slumped forward. I take another bite of my apple. My question this time is less open-ended. "What did you find out?"

It's quiet at first. Everyone's disinclined to tell me. I wait it out and, in the end, you're the one who does.

"Gus ain't real," you say. You shuffle your feet, staring down at them so that your hair falls in your eyes.

My jaw hits the floor. "What do you mean he isn't real?"

You're red-faced when you say it. "Gus is pretend. I made him all up."

This gets a rise out of me. After all that Dad has done for you, you go and do something stupid like this. You got Dad and the cops all worked up about some kid who didn't exist.

"Why would you do that?" I ask.

"I didn't mean to."

"What do you mean you didn't mean to?" I'm mad because a person doesn't just go and invent another person by accident. You did it for attention. For a reaction.

"Leave it be, Leo," Dad says. His voice is stern. He frowns at me.

But I won't leave it be. "She's a liar, Dad."

You pull a face. Dad does, too. I might as well have hit you.

"Don't call your sister names."

"But she is," I say.

"She's not."

"Then what is she, a schizo?"

It's out of my mouth before I can think better of it. I don't mean to be a jerkweed. I just am. But I'm pissed. Because I thought you and I were getting close. I thought you were opening up to me. Turns out I was wrong.

Dad slams a wooden spoon on the countertop. The sound is loud. "Damn it, Leo! Just shut up. You don't know what you're talking about."

In all my life, Dad's never told me to shut up. You freak out, because of the noise. You're shaking. You start to cry. Or maybe that's pretend, too. Maybe you're making that up just to dupe us.

Dad coaxes you into a chair. He gets you something to drink. He gets you one of those pills the shrink prescribed for you.

If I lied, Dad would take my internet away for a month. You lie and he babies you.

After you're done shitting your pants, Dad goes back to his

ground beef. I stand there watching the whole thing and then leave.

No one asks about my day.

MEREDITH

May

The next morning I'm sore. My whole body aches. I wake to Josh's lips teasing mine. My eyes open and there he is, suspended above me. "You were supposed to wake me up when you got home," he razzes me. "We had a date."

"I'm sorry," I say. My saliva is thick, my mouth like cotton. It's hard to swallow.

"Don't tell me you forgot."

"I'll make it up to you."

I have trouble getting out of bed. It takes time. The room spins. I have a headache, one that creeps up the back of my neck.

Josh, watching me, laughs. "Looks like you and Bea had fun after we left."

My cheeks flame. Josh doesn't know the half of it. All he knows is that Bea and I stayed at the bar and had another drink after he and Kate left. He thinks I'm hungover.

"What time did you get home? I tried staying up for a while," he says, and I tell him that I don't know, that we lost track of time.

"Bea didn't want to leave," I say.

What I wouldn't give to go back to last night, to go home with Josh instead of staying with Bea.

I push myself from bed. I think that when Josh looks at me, I must look different, changed. Last night, after I let myself in, I showered in our first-floor bathroom. I couldn't risk waking him or the kids. I went to bed with my hair still wet. That was only four or five hours ago. If he looks closely enough, he'll see it's still wet.

"You want coffee?" Josh asks, standing at the mirror, fixing his tie. I say yes, though I'm not sure I can hold anything down. "Just give me a minute. I'll brew a fresh pot."

I'm no sooner on my feet than I have to rush past Josh and to the toilet. I fall to my knees before it, grasping the seat with clammy hands. The three or four drinks I had last night are not enough to make me sick. It's what came after that lays waste to my insides.

"Wow," Josh says, coming up behind me. He stands in the bathroom doorway, smirking proudly as I wipe the vomit from my mouth with the back of a hand. "That was a heck of a birthday celebration. You sure showed Bea a good time. She's lucky to have you."

I'm not known as being the life of the party. I'm more of a wet blanket when it comes to nights out. I'm typically the first to want to go home. This is uncharacteristic of me. Josh is relishing the idea of me being hungover because it doesn't happen often.

He fetches a washcloth from the vanity. He soaks it in cold water and hands it to me. As I take it, I see mud still buried beneath my fingernails, despite my scrubbing last night.

I hide my hands from Josh. My telltale heart is beating.

Word begins to spread later that day. It starts on Facebook. It starts as a plea. Shelby and I are Facebook friends, as I'm Facebook friends with many of my clients. Shelby is tagged in another friend's post. That friend is looking for her.

That evening, Shelby makes the local news.

Josh and I watch together. The kids are in bed; it's the ten o'clock news. I freeze up when the story breaks, barely daring to breathe as the anchorwoman talks about Shelby. I should tell Josh that I know her. I should tell Josh she's a client.

But I get cold feet. I hesitate because I've never been much of an actor. I worry my reaction would come off as unauthentic and give me away.

And then, because I didn't do it right away, I can't tell him later. Because he'd want to know why I didn't tell him before. It's the same as what happened with Marty. As the days go on, I can't tell him about the malpractice suit or Dr. Feingold or any of it, because it would all look so dodgy and dishonest.

I brood over the police coming by, asking if I know Shelby, and me having to decide whether to lie. If I lie, I'd never get away with it. But if I told the truth, it might get back to Josh, and then he'd discover the lie by omission. It's a catch-22. I can't win.

The next day, Bea comes to the house. I'm alone when she comes.

"Should we be seen together?" I ask when we're behind closed doors.

"Why would that matter, Meredith?" she asks.

"Because of what we did," I hiss under my breath.

"And what was that?" she asks. "Go to the bar and have a good time?" She tells me that to avoid suspicion, I have to act normal.

I recoil, offended. "I am acting normal," I say, though I'm not. I'm far from it.

Bea asks what I would do if a client of mine ever went missing. "I don't know," I say, controlling the sudden urge to cry. Bea, before me, is impassive, tall. She looms over me in the foyer of my home. She didn't bring an umbrella and so she's wet. She drips onto my entry rug. "It's never happened before."

"Don't be stupid," she says, deadpan. It comes as a slap to the face. "*Theoretically*, Meredith, what would you do?"

I swallow hard. "I'd call her husband. Express my condolences. See if there's anything I can do."

"Then do it," she commands. "Do it today."

She leaves the same way she came. I walk to the front window to watch her go, to be sure she's really gone.

Outside the world is charcoal gray. It's foggy. I can only see to the other side of the street. The world beyond evanesces into clouds.

In the coming days, police descend upon our neighborhood like snow in winter. I watch from a distance. No one comes to our house asking questions, though I obsess over what I'll do when and if that happens.

What we learn, we learn from word-of-mouth and the news.

Josh is all worked up about it. "How does a grown woman just disappear?" he asks no one in particular. He's pacing the house. He tells me that he doesn't want me out after dark for anything, not until they find the person who did this to her.

"You're going to drive me to and from my births?" I challenge. "Wake the kids up in the middle of the night and make them come?"

He thinks it through. His answer to this is, "You'll take a cab. The driver can drop you off and pick you up at the hospital door."

"You're being ridiculous," I say, trying hard to control the tremor in my voice. "You do hear what they're saying, don't you, about the husband? How he killed her? I think I'm safe, unless you have plans of killing me," I say, fleeing the room. I'm more contrary than I should be.

The guilt ravages me. Not only Shelby's death, but that Jason may take the fall for it.

"Are you mad?" Josh asks when he finds me later in the bathroom getting ready for bed. "Did I upset you?" He comes up behind me. He lays a tender hand on my lower back. He wraps around me from behind, so that his arms circle my midriff. He knots his hands. He lowers his chin to my shoulder. He says, "I couldn't live without you."

I don't deserve Josh after what I've done. Josh is a good man.

I can only stand it a few seconds before I free myself of his hold. "What's wrong, Meredith?" he asks.

"Nothing," I snap at him. "I'm fine."

"You don't seem fine."

"I am fine."

I find myself searching things online. How exactly does one die in an auto-ped accident? Head trauma is often to blame. So, too, is organ damage, internal bleeding, damage to major arteries. I get sucked down a rabbit hole of information. Shelby's body should have ricocheted off the hood of the car when we hit her, because of the force of impact, and because of Newton's laws of motion. She shouldn't have toppled over in front of it. This leads me to believe she wasn't standing upright. That she was hunkered down, doing something as innocuous as tying a shoe. Who'd ever think you could be killed while tying a shoe?

Another thing I look up: Do corpses make sounds after death? The answer is yes. When a body is moved after death, the air left in the windpipe can escape. The result is a groan or a moan.

I obsess over this. I try to replay the sound I heard as we laid Shelby in the trunk of Bea's car. Was it the contents of her trachea leaving? Or was she still alive?

Did Shelby ricochet off the hood of the car and land in front of it? Or, like a domino, did she fall over?

It doesn't matter. Either way, she's still dead.

The rain won't let up for anything. I'm tormented by images of Shelby cold and naked, lying in the rain, shivering, soaked to the bone. I can't stand it.

One morning, I stand at my closet looking for something to wear. My mind screams at me to pick something. *Just pick something.* The indecision paralyzes me. It's like this every day. But it isn't just the clothes. It's every one of the seemingly million inconsequential decisions I make every day. The kids are at my feet, arguing. I don't have the energy to react. Their voices sound muffled, as if I'm underwater and they're up above, as I stare into the endless abyss that is my closet. It's all too much.

I settle on something. I get in the car. I take the kids where they need to be, though Leo begs and cries as I leave him with Charlotte. I can't go on with this guilt. I can't live like this, thinking of nothing but what Bea and I did. All day and night I replay the moment of impact in my mind. I feel it still, the car crashing into her, and then, seconds later, the repulsive sensation of driving over her body, not once but twice.

I'm snowed under by what-ifs. What if I'd gone home with Josh? What if Bea and I hadn't had that last drink? What if I'd insisted on driving? What if Shelby had been on the sidewalk? What if her shoe hadn't come untied, if she hadn't been bent down tying it, if that's even what happened.

The guilt is a heavy burden to bear. I feel battle-scarred.

I go to the store. I no longer enjoy driving. I'm overattentive. I drive below the speed limit. I step on the brakes when I see even the slightest movement in my peripheral vision. My heart races the entire time. It's not that I think I will be hurt. It's that I think I will hurt someone else. My hands on the steering wheel are slick. I can't get a good grip of the leather. Cars honk at me. I've become a danger, because of my extreme caution.

At the store, I buy a blanket. It's plaid and fleece. I take it to the woods alone, where I last saw Shelby. I have to search awhile because the trees, the riverbank all look the same to me, though the river is higher than it was the last time I was here.

The days have become squally. We no longer see the sun.

I find Shelby. It's been days since her death. The sight of her wrecks me. She's still mostly buried, but the rain has washed much of the forest floor away. I see parts of her. A single bloated leg, lying on a bed of miry leaves. Strands of her dyed hair.

I wear gloves as I take the blanket out of its packaging. I use care not to touch it. I go to her, lay the blanket on what's visible of her body. I don't want to look. But I can't tear my eyes away. What I see is unspeakable. Where the blood has settled, Shelby is purple. Gravity has taken its toll, pulling the stagnant blood down. Her lower half is entirely bruised. The flies have discovered Shelby's body. They buzz around; they land on her. I try to dispel them. But they're not scared of me. They leave, and then they come back.

When I look closely at Shelby's body, there are maggots.

What I don't think about is my shoe prints left in the mud. I see them only as I'm leaving. I've seen enough cop shows to know that this is how people get caught. For a split second I think about leaving the footprints there. Then it's out of my hands. If I'm meant to be caught, I will be.

I think somewhere deep inside that's what I want: to be caught.

But I can't do it. I step out of my shoes. I retrace my steps. I sink to my knees, smear the shoe's tread away with my gloved hands, moving backward. By the time I'm done, I'm bathed in mud. I let the rain rinse me clean. I carry what remains into the car with me.

Halfway home I have to pull to the side of the road to hurl.

Now when I think of her, she's alone, but at least she's not cold.

It's the only thing that gets me through the night.

LEO

NOW

Before bed, Dad comes into my room where I'm doing algebra. Algebra is about the only class I like because there's a right and a wrong answer, and no in-between. There's no gray area, unlike in life. Life is all gray area.

"Can I come in?" Dad asks.

I shrug. "It's your house."

"Don't be like that, Leo."

"Then how do you want me to be?"

I'm not usually so stubborn.

He comes in and sits on the edge of my bed. I turn my back to him.

"I want you to listen. To hear me out. You're not giving her a fair shake."

I turn around in my chair. I look at him. It's a swivel chair. I can go back to not looking anytime I want.

I tell him, "I'm listening." The way I say it is petulant. All my life I've had to be a grown-up. It's nice acting like a child for a change.

Dad ages every day. He aged about a decade when Mom died. He's aged another now that you're home. His hair is gray. He has a paunch. There are dark circles under his eyes because he doesn't sleep. He's always tired. He doesn't eat much, either, not real food, though he's taken to feeding his depression with potato chips and beer. It's the reason for the paunch. He was an athlete once. I was a skeptic when he told me he competed in a marathon before I was born. I called bullshit. He showed me the medal to prove it. The only reason he ever runs now is when there's been a potential sighting of you.

I don't remember Dad before. But there are the pictures, the home videos. In them, he's pretty jacked. He's a stud. He has brown hair, and plenty of it. His hair wasn't thin like it is now. It wasn't gray. His smile wasn't bogus back then, either.

He's let himself go.

"The way the psychiatrist explained it to me," Dad says, "being isolated in the dark for as long as your sister was drives people to the brink of insanity. It impairs their sense of time, their sleep cycles. Without being able to see, they suffer sensory deprivation. It fucks them up, Leo," he says. I go rigid because Dad just said *fuck*. Dad doesn't swear.

"This friend of Delilah's was a hallucination. But to her," he says, "he was entirely real. Where she was kept, she had no one to talk to. She couldn't see anything in the dark. In the absence of all other stimuli, Leo, her mind kept working, and it created Gus, who, to your sister, was as real as you are to me. She wasn't lying. She's not a liar. She believed one hundred and ten percent that Gus was real. It's possible that Gus was the only thing that got her through all this."

When he says it like that, I feel like a shithead for calling you a liar and a schizo.

Dad doesn't make me apologize. I do it, anyway.

I get an idea then. I ask Dad to drag out the home videos and we watch them. For just a little while, it's like you are you again and Mom is still alive.

MEREDITH

11 YEARS BEFORE

May

I can't keep going on like this. Josh can tell that something is wrong. He asks me about it. He saunters up behind me when I'm at the stove or the sink. He massages my shoulders. As he does, I tense up. It isn't that I don't want Josh touching me. It has nothing to do with Josh. It's that Shelby is on my mind all the time. I see her when I'm awake. I see her when I'm lucky enough to sleep. The memory of her lying naked on that bed of leaves makes my flesh crawl. It will only be a matter of time before the animals find her, if they haven't already.

Josh says things to me like, "Hey, babe, everything okay?" and that trite old saying, "Penny for your thoughts," because he can tell I'm being pensive.

I shrug him off when he does, tell him I'm fine. He says that he's beginning to hate that word. *Fine.* The tension between us grows exponentially.

Bea comes by almost every day. She skulks over when I'm

home alone. She must monitor my comings and goings, or keep an eagle eye on my car in the driveway.

When she comes, I ask her things like, "What did you do with my clothes?" and, "What did you do with Shelby's clothes?" I feel breathless all the time, in a constant state of panic. What makes it worse is having to hide my feelings from Josh and the rest of the world. Only when Bea is here can I speak freely.

Bea, on the contrary, is always composed. She tells me not to worry about it. "I took care of it," she says, about the clothes, which doesn't answer my question. Took care of it how?

"You didn't go to work today," Bea says accusatorially. "You had a class to teach at nine. I saw it on the website. You should have been there."

"I'm not feeling well." It's not a lie. Guilt isn't only emotional. It manifests itself in very physical ways. My head aches. My back aches. My stomach is in knots, and I'm constipated. I could never stay focused through class, much less make it through without that overwhelming urge to vomit or cry. I spend so much time ruminating about what Bea and I did that night, second-guessing the choices we made, the choices I made. I can't get away from it. I'm obsessed. My mind is in a constant state of flux. I can think of nothing else but what happened that night. I don't sleep. I barely eat.

"You need to act normal, Meredith. *Normal.*"

I'm not particularly religious. Josh, the kids and I go to church on Easter and Christmas, but that's all. Still, there's a Bible verse that's been running never-ending through my mind since sometime last night. *The truth will set you free.*

It sounds so simple. I make the mistake of telling Bea.

"We'll make the police see it was an accident, that you didn't mean to hit Shelby," I say. "It was unpreventable. They'll understand."

Bea stares at me, incredulous. "Have you lost your damn mind?" she snaps. "They'll just fucking *understand*? I didn't step on a bug. I killed a person. We, Meredith," she says, "*we* killed a person."

I plead with her. "Please, Bea. I can't go on living like this."

"You have to," she says. "You have to figure it out." She takes a step closer. "I was drunk, Meredith. And you knowingly permitted me to drive the car home. It's your fault as much as it is mine. You'll go to jail, too, you know, if we're ever found out. How do you think Josh and the kids would fare while you're rotting away in jail for years?"

I've thought about this. I have an answer ready. "It's not like they can do a breathalyzer now. It's too late to prove anything and, if you weren't drinking, it's a much lesser offense, like a misdemeanor."

For a second she just stares. And then, "Are you really that dumb? Since when did you turn into a lawyer, anyway?" I see now that Bea isn't hamstrung by the same guilt as me.

The Bea I know isn't cruel. She's compassionate. She's outspoken but kind. This Bea is scared. "We're not just talking manslaughter anymore, or a misdemeanor," she says. "Because we also carried her out to the woods and hid her. That's concealment of a homicide." She pauses for effect. "It's time you set your fucking conscience aside and think about your kids."

After she leaves, I collapse into an armchair. I don't move until six hours later when I hear Josh and the kids come home. I hear them outside first. I try and make myself look busy before they come in.

LEO

NOW

Back at school, Piper Hanaka comes up to me. "Hey, Leo. Can I show you something?" I'm at my locker, trying to open it for the third time because Adam Beltner already slammed it shut on me twice. I let it slide both times. He called me a wuss for it. If I'd have fought back, he would have exterminated me. I can't win, no matter what I do.

You're lucky you never got to experience high school. High school is pretty fucked up.

I tell Piper, "Sure. Okay. I guess."

It's game day, which means the cheerleaders wear their uniforms. The skirts are short enough that Piper is all legs. It barely covers her crotch. I learned the hard way that I'm not supposed to look at her legs because if I do I get called things like *peedy* and *perv*. So I don't look at her at all. I pretend to be looking for something in my locker.

"I saw Delilah's picture in the paper."

"Yeah. Me, too."

"It's all so sad."

"Yeah. I know."

"Except it's supposed to be happy, too, because she's, like, *back*."

I don't know what to say so I say, "What do you want to show me?"

I've never had a girlfriend before. I've never even had a girl like me. Freshman year, someone told me in gym class that some girl named Molly liked me. I still have nightmares about it. It took me three days to get the guts to ask her to the homecoming dance. Turns out it was all a hoax. Kids laughed their asses off at my expense when she said no. Molly already had a date, a junior on the varsity football team, built like a linebacker because he was.

Piper says, "My mom, like, made me get rid of everything-Delilah after she disappeared. She didn't think it was healthy to have it around. It sucked. Like, I used to have half of a best-friends necklace that I shared with Delilah. My mom made me toss my half in the trash. She was all, like, 'It doesn't mean anything without the other half.' I cried over it. So she went and bought me a new best-friends necklace and told me I could give it to anyone I wanted. I might have been six but you don't just, like, forget your best friend."

"Who'd you give it to?"

"Lily Morris. Do you remember her? She doesn't even live here anymore. She moved to, like, North Carolina when we were twelve."

I shake my head. I don't remember her.

"Doesn't matter. Lily was never a good friend, anyway. In fourth grade she started a rumor that I, like, peed my pants when I laughed."

I want to ask her if it's true. If it is, I'd find it endearing.

"Anyway, my mom let me keep one picture of Delilah, though."

"That's cool," I say, though it was a dick move for Mrs. Hanaka to make her get rid of everything that reminded her of you. Dad, on the other hand, kept everything. Your rainbow glitter shoes are still by the door and have been for eleven years. You've probably noticed.

Piper shows me the picture. You're a little kid in it. It's a close-up of yours and Piper's faces smashed side by side together. You're smiling. Half your teeth are missing. You're all red hair and freckles, happy like the kid I saw dancing around on Dad's home videos, not scared like the person you now are.

"It's just that, I was, like, digging around on the internet, trying to figure out if cleft chins are one of those things that just goes away, you know? And they're not."

No matter what kids like Adam Beltner say, I'm no idiot. I know what Piper means by this. What I don't know is how to feel about it.

Piper cut out the picture of you in the newspaper. The Hanakas might be the only people in the world who still get the actual, physical newspaper. She sets both pictures side by side, the one some asshole photographer shot yesterday, and the one of you when you were six. They're mostly similar—red hair, green eyes—except for that cleft chin. I never noticed before that you had a cleft chin. It's not something that's super obvious. It's on the small side as cleft chins go, the kind of thing you might not notice unless someone else pointed it out for you. But now that I know it's there, it sticks out like a sore thumb. Except that on the picture taken yesterday, there's no cleft chin. None at all. Not even a small one.

The bell rings. I look around and the halls are empty. We're late for class.

Piper is backing away from me. She hugs her books to her. "Don't be mad at me, Leo," she says before she turns around and runs.

MEREDITH

May

"I have a confession to make," Charlotte says. She's on the other end of my phone. Her tone is somber. It's evening. Josh and the kids have been home for hours. They're in the next room, watching TV together on the sofa. Josh has a book open on his lap, but he's laughing at the TV. It warms my heart, that a thirty-six-year-old man can find humor in preschool TV.

Charlotte says, "Something happened," and there's the sense that she knows what Bea and I did. I go into a flat spin. I'm losing control. I'm in the kitchen when it happens. I've just finished washing dishes and wiping down the table. I pull out a chair and sink into it.

"What's that?" I ask. I'm short of breath. My heart pounds in my chest.

She says, "Someone has been picking on Leo," before her voice cracks and she comes apart at the seams, saying, "Oh

God, Meredith, I'm so sorry. I feel awful about it. I should have known."

My mind doesn't change course so quickly.

"How would you have known?"

"It's my job to know these things. Especially after you called about the bruise. I should have paid more attention after that. I should have put more stock into what you said, but instead I cast it off as kids being kids. I'm so sorry, Meredith. I wish I'd known sooner that he was being picked on."

"Picked on how?" I ask, still breathless. "And by whom?"

"Brody Parker," she says.

The name doesn't ring a bell. "What did this boy do to Leo?"

"Well," she says, chastened. "I'm ashamed to admit this, Meredith. I hope you'll forgive me, but this afternoon he locked Leo in the outdoor toy chest."

I picture our own plastic toy chest. It's maybe two feet high by two feet wide by three feet long. Leo, at his last exam, was thirty-eight inches tall. If Charlotte's toy chest is about the same size as ours, that means Leo's little legs wouldn't have been able to stretch fully out inside it. He would have had to bend at the knees. But is there enough width inside the toy chest for that? And what about the toys inside it? Was he lying on them, too, or did this Brody Parker have the decency to remove those before forcing Leo in?

My mind is racing. But all I can say is, "It's raining outside, Charlotte. They were playing outside?"

"Brody asked if they could get the Nerf guns and bring them in. I said yes, because with all this rain, we're running out of things to do. Brody asked if Leo could help him carry the guns back in. I said yes. Then one of the toddlers wet herself, and I got all caught up in changing and washing her clothes. I didn't know that Leo hadn't come back in. Brody," she says by way of explanation, "goes to the elementary school. We walk and pick him up, same as we do Delilah. We didn't get home until close to three-thirty, and then the kids wanted a snack before they played, so…" Her voice drifts. She's holding something back.

"What are you saying, Charlotte?" I ask.

"It was less than an hour that he had Leo locked inside that chest of mine," and I gasp, imagining Leo trapped in a dark, cold toy chest all alone for an hour.

"What grade is Brody Parker in?" I ask, imagining him as a kindergartener, like Delilah.

"Fifth," Charlotte says. This would make him ten or eleven. What kind of eleven-year-old boy picks on a four-year-old? I wonder if Leo was lured into that toy chest, if he was double-dog dared, or if this little hellion picked Leo up and forced him in.

"Why wouldn't Leo just get out of the chest?" I ask. Leo may be shy, but he's a capable boy. He could have just climbed out.

"It has a lock on it."

"Dear God," I say, pressing a hand to my mouth. I wonder if there are air holes in that toy chest, how much oxygen it holds. And then, because I can't get her off my mind for anything, I go back to Shelby in the trunk, and whether she was dead before we put her in, or if she died inside.

Charlotte says, "When it came time to clean up, I realized he was missing. Leo is always the first to clean up. He's such a good boy, Meredith. But Leo's puzzle never got put away, and that's when I knew something terrible had happened. I want you to know, I've already called Brody's mother. I told her he's not welcome here anymore."

LEO

NOW

Over dinner I stare at you, wondering if the cleft chin only shows its face sometimes. But for as long as I stare, I never see it. It's not there.

That night I do some digging on the internet. I see the same thing Piper saw. The only way to get rid of a cleft chin is through surgery. That costs about two or three thousand dollars. I seriously doubt those meth heads forked over a couple grand for a chin implant for you. I'm also doubting there's a plastic surgeon anywhere near Michael that could have done it.

I compare the two pictures side by side. There are far more similarities than not. Most of the differences could be chalked up to time, like the way your nose has widened or your face narrowed. That happens as we grow up. Your hair is also darker. The sun lightens hair. Where you were at, there was no sun.

But then there's that cleft chin, also known by the internet as the incomplete fusion of the *symphysis menti* during fetal development. In layman's terms: a butt chin. It's rare. It's genetic. It's gone. You don't have it anymore. It isn't that you lost it.

It's that you are not my sister.

I don't know what to do with this information. Do I tell Dad and break his heart? Or let him go on believing this pipe dream of his? The odds of my sister ever coming home now are slim to none. As long as Dad thinks you're her, he's happy. He can get on with his life. He can have closure, albeit phony. You, whoever you are, who lived locked in someone's basement for eleven years, can have a better life. Dad will take care of you. He'll give you everything you need.

Except that you probably have your own folks out there. Maybe you have a kid brother, too. They're probably missing you.

I wait two days before I show Dad the pictures Piper showed me. At first he flies off the handle, mad mostly at me for making shit up.

But the longer he stares at those pictures, he sees.

"The DNA test, Leo," he says, "was conclusive. The DNA test confirmed that she's Delilah. DNA tests don't lie."

That is a major question mark. Because DNA tests almost always get it right. There are rare errors that can be chalked up to the quality of the sample or the way the sample was handled, or the results interpreted.

We go to the police station. With you in another room, Dad corners the lady cop and one of her henchmen. He shows her the pictures. She's dismissive at first. "You can't just think she'd look the exact same as she did when she was six. People change, Josh. They grow up. That baby fat disappears and features become more defined. That's all that's happening here."

She ascribes Dad's fears to some form of PTSD, thinking that after all these years of missing Delilah, he has anxiety over losing her again.

It's not that simple. I printed out the articles online that say cleft chins don't just vanish; they're here for life. She reads the article and her face goes white.

"What if the DNA test got it wrong?" Dad asks.

"DNA tests are lauded as extremely reliable, almost one hundred percent."

"I'd like to see those results," Dad says, thinking the lab fucked up. There are things called a false positive and a coincidental match.

The lady cop doesn't move. She holds stock-still.

"Carmen?" he asks. "I'd like to see the results, please." Though why, I don't know, because it's not like Dad, an investment banker, can make heads or tails of a DNA report.

"I can get it," the henchman says.

"No," the lady cop says quickly. "Let me." She walks away. Dad's eyes follow her. She's not that bad-looking, for an older lady. Like Dad, she's got to be pushing fifty, though she takes better care of herself than Dad does. She looks like she works out, eats healthy and all that. Under her clothes, she's probably ripped.

When she comes back, she's shaking her head. Her hands are empty. She says decisively, "It wasn't there."

"Ma'am?" the henchman asks.

"It wasn't there. The DNA report wasn't in the file." She is phlegmatic. Her voice is flat. She stares at the henchman, then Dad, unblinking.

"Maybe you missed it. Those papers have a tendency to stick together. I can double-check, if you'd like, ma'am."

"It wasn't there. I didn't miss it." She's pissed now, for two things: one, that the report is missing, and two, that the henchman second-guessed her in front of Dad and me.

"Yes, ma'am," he says.

The henchman offers to pull up the report online. "I can do it myself," she says. We follow her to a desk. She sits at the computer, fingers pecking away on the keyboard. Neither Dad nor I can see what's happening on the screen because we're on the wrong side of it.

She stops typing. Her fingers hover above the keyboard.

"What's wrong?" Dad asks.

"I just…" she starts. "I forgot my password, that's all. Just give me a minute." We do. It doesn't help. A minute later she still can't remember her password to whatever software cops use.

"Let me try mine," the henchman says, reaching past her for the keyboard.

"Don't," she snaps at him. "Just don't." It's loud enough that people stare. Some other cop walks over and asks if everything is all right.

Detective Rowlings is the undemonstrative type. She's seen everything there is to see in her line of work. She's become desensitized to all things bad.

But still, you can see a tiny breach in her shell. It's visible.

She looks at Dad. "We've been together from the very beginning, Josh. All the ups and downs of this case. I've watched you cope with the unbearable loss of your wife and child. I've seen firsthand your hope and resilience every time you thought there was a lead as to where Delilah might be. You never gave up on her." Her voice cracks. "You were hell-bent on searching until Delilah came home, and I told myself long ago that I was in this for the long haul. If you weren't giving up, neither was I. I grew fond of you over the years, Josh, and wanted more than anything to bring your little girl home to you. This wasn't just a case for me—it was personal. I should know better than that. You're never supposed to let it get personal. There's a line. You don't cross it. I did.

"And then I got the call we'd been waiting for for eleven years. I was so certain she was Delilah, Josh. She checked off all the boxes. She looked like her. She said she was her. Unlike the imposters we've seen, this one was one hundred percent legit. I could feel it in my bones. We'd done it. We'd found Delilah. I saw the relief and the euphoria in your eyes. This meant everything to you.

"And then the results came back. Negative. Not a match. I was incredulous. I was devastated. It was impossible. It couldn't be. I thought of how I'd tell you, the words I'd say. I practiced.

But when the time came, I couldn't do it. I just couldn't do it. I couldn't take her away from you again. I'm so sorry, Josh. In some inane way, I thought I was doing the right thing, for you, for her. I thought if no one knew the truth, what harm would it do?"

Dad openly cries. I can't bad-mouth him this time because I feel it, too, a black hole inside me.

The one question remaining now is why you thought Dad was your dad when he's not.

We go into the room with you. It's like taking that long final walk to the execution chamber. I sit down in a chair next to you. Dad sits across from me. He can't bring himself to look at you. The lady cop doesn't come in with us. After her confession, she was led away by some superior officer with her head hung low. There will be some form of discipline for what she's done. Not only did she lie, but she tampered with police records. She'll probably get canned. Maybe have charges pressed against her, too. I don't know.

Instead of her, it's someone else asking the questions now, a man cop. He doesn't sit at all. He doesn't beat around the bush. "What made you believe this man is your father?"

There's a tremor to your voice. "He's not?"

Your face falls. You're helpless, confused. Your eyes go to Dad, who's crying. That's your answer.

"No. He's not."

You blink over and over again like there's an eyelash in your eye. You're mute at first. You pull your legs into you. You rock on the chair. It's raw, primal. It's hard to watch. Tears pool in your eyes and then slip down your cheeks. That's how I know you're not lying. You honest to God believe him to be your dad. You say to him, "You are. You are my daddy," and then even I'm crying, too.

MEREDITH

11 YEARS BEFORE

May

In the middle of the night, Delilah cries out for me. It's a stran-
gled cry, and then she's sobbing, gulping through her tears. I
spring out of bed. I rush to her room, where I find Delilah sitting upright in bed, eyes like saucers. I go to her. At first touch,
I know what's wrong. Delilah has spiked a fever. She's sweating
through her sheets, despite the fact that she shivers violently.
"Oh, sweetie," I say, stroking her damp hair. Her skin is clammy;
her pajamas stick to her.

Delilah's eyes are fixed on the corner of the room. I look, but
there's nothing there but a lamp. The lamp is a kids' floor lamp,
tall, with three acrylic shades that look like balloons.

Delilah's hand rises up from beneath her soggy sheets to point
at it.

"What, baby?" I ask, dropping down on the edge of the bed.
"What do you see?"

"Someone's there," she says, voice hoarse. I look again, feeling my heartbeats quicken, though of course no one is there. It's Delilah's fever speaking. What she sees is the floor lamp, and she's mistaken one of the balloon-shaped lampshades for a head, the tall, narrow tube for a body.

"No one's there," I assure her. "It's just your lamp. Want me to turn it on and show you?" I ask as I press up from the bed and make my way toward the lamp. I don't wait for her to answer, because Delilah is looking at me strangely. I reach a hand out for the switch. Delilah coughs. It's a barky, croup-like cough. Delilah has had croup before.

I turn on the lamp. Yellow light floods the purple room. I look around, glance under the bed, inside the closet, make a big show of saying, "See? No one's here. It's just you and me."

Delilah sounds so sure when she says, "They left, Mommy."

I know that can't be.

"Who was it?" I ask Delilah, humoring her. She blinks at me, unspeaking. Her stare is vacant, glassy-eyed. She doesn't say. Her red hair droops. Along the hairline, it's dark with sweat. I let it go, knowing no one was here. I reach a hand back out to turn off the lamp switch.

I retrieve the thermometer from Leo and Delilah's bathroom, and the children's Tylenol from downstairs. I take Delilah's temperature first. It's nearing one hundred and three degrees. I double-check the dosing on the Tylenol, and then give it to her. Delilah has sweat through the sheets. I make her get out of bed long enough for me to change them. She gets back in. I lie beside her.

I stay with Delilah until she falls back to sleep. Then I go back to my own bed. I slip in beside a still-sound-asleep Josh. Josh has the ability to sleep through anything. I don't wake him because Delilah gets sick all the time. She's our germ magnet. If someone in her class is sick, you can bet your life Delilah will be, too. Delilah's fever isn't breaking news. I can tell him in the morning.

As I lie there, I notice that our bedroom window is open a

crack. Josh runs warm. Even in the winter, he wants to open the bedroom window at night, otherwise he overheats. The cool spring air wafts in, blowing the gauzy curtains into the room. The rain falls lightly outside. The sound of it is peaceful. If not for thoughts of Shelby that torment me, it would be anesthetizing. But instead I lie there dwelling on how Grace Tebow will never have a mother to tend to her at night. It's all my fault. It makes me sick to think of. It makes me sick to know that, while I lie in my soft, warm bed under the weight of my husband's arm, Shelby lies alone in the woods, her body being devoured by maggots and flies.

I've reached the end of my rope. I can't keep living with this secret. I need to go to the police. I need to tell them what we've done, and suffer the consequences. I deserve that.

My own guilt aside, Jason deserves closure. He needs to know what happened to Shelby. I've been following the investigation on the news, and it's not good. All roads lead to Jason. Jason has been rumored to have been having an affair. It's damning. I'll never be able to live with myself if Jason gets convicted of murder. If that were to happen, what would happen to the baby? Who would raise her? Who would care for her special needs? Would she be institutionalized?

At some point I must have drifted off to sleep. Because when I wake up, Josh is gone. Beside me, on the nightstand, is a tepid coffee. The bedroom smells of his cologne.

He was here. But now he's not.

I get out of bed. I go downstairs to see if he's there, but he's already left for work. Back upstairs, in their bedrooms, Delilah is still sound asleep but Leo has begun to stir. Delilah won't be going to school today. I debate keeping Leo home. There's really no reason for him to go to Charlotte's if Delilah and I are home.

But he's been having such a hard time at Charlotte's of late. It would be confusing to him if I were to keep him home. Tomorrow he'd cry twice as hard. And besides, Charlotte promised me that that Brody boy wouldn't be there. The thing Leo hates most about Charlotte's is gone. I can't just keep him here to catch Delilah's germs.

I go into Leo's bedroom. He's out of bed, playing with his toys on the floor. I sit down beside him and pull him into my lap. "Hey, baby," I say, kissing the top of his head. His hair is mussed up. He smells like sleep.

We play with his toys together for a while. It's a firehouse playset. He's the fireman while I'm the Dalmatian. There's a fire on the other side of the bedroom. Our fireman and dog hop in the toy fire truck and Leo pushes it across the floor to put the fire out.

After a while, I say to Leo, "Miss Charlotte called last night. She said you've been having trouble with another boy at her house." I pause, wait for Leo's reaction. "A boy named Brody." Leo's whole body stiffens at the sound of this boy's name. His face turns red, his eyes fill with tears. I wrap my arms around him. "I wish I had known that this boy was being mean to you, Leo. I would have liked to help," I say. It isn't an indictment. I'm not blaming Leo for not telling me about the abuse. But I want Leo to know he can tell me anything. "Miss Charlotte says that Brody won't be coming back to her house to play. It's just you and the other kids from here on out. How does that sound?" Leo shyly smiles. He likes the sound of that.

Delilah wakes up. Her fever is back. She looks glassy-eyed. Her voice is rasping and she holds a hand to her throat like it hurts. I take her temperature. Again it's one hundred and three. I give her another dose of medicine. I help her down the stairs to the sofa and get her something to drink. She has no appetite. She watches cartoons while Leo gets ready to go to Charlotte's house.

Delilah waits in the car when I drop Leo off. I tell Charlotte that Delilah won't be coming after school because she's sick. "It's just Leo," I say. Leo steps up to the door. He looks inside. He doesn't cry.

Back at home, Delilah returns to the sofa. She's all tuckered out from the quick drive to the sitter's house. This fever has gotten the better of her. I sit beside her for a while, with her head on my lap. In time, I get up to look for my phone, to let Josh know that Delilah is sick. I take a lap around the house but don't find it. I must have left it in the car when I took Leo, along with my purse. I peek on Delilah before going to the garage to get the phone. She's sound asleep.

The garage is detached. It's a good fifty feet from our house to the garage door. The day is wet. I step out the back door and into the weather. I pull the door closed. I don't like the way I feel as I turn my back to it. But Delilah won't be alone long. I'll be back in thirty seconds if I'm quick. I run through the rain. The yard is covered in puddles. I step in them and they splash, soaking my lower half. I'll need to change my pants when I get back in. The lower-lying parts of the yard have begun to flood.

I go in through the side door, not the roll-up door. I step inside and go to the car. I yank open the passenger's side door and there it is: my purse. Except that I'm in a hurry. When I go to pick it up, I grab from the bottom. The contents of the purse spill onto the floor mat. "Shit," I say as I lean in to collect them. A tube of lipstick has rolled beneath the seat. I lower myself down, stretch my arm beneath the seat to get it.

"Good morning, Meredith," I hear.

The sound of her voice throws me into an even greater state of imbalance. I jolt upright. I wheel around to face her, standing behind me. "Bea," I say, putting my hand to my heart. "You startled me." I'm on edge all the time.

Bea comes fully into the garage. "You don't look good," she says to me. I haven't showered. My hair is thrown into a sloppy bun. I'm wearing sweats, which I wore to drop Leo off with Charlotte. If not for that, I'd be in my pajamas still. Other than the coffee Josh left, I haven't had anything to eat or drink. I feel weak, small in comparison to Bea. My heart thumps. It's dizzying, loud. I'm certain Bea can hear it. "Are you all right?" she asks.

"Every time I close my eyes, I see her," I confess. "I can't keep doing this. I can't keep going on like this."

"You need to keep your shit together, Meredith," Bea warns, "for a little while longer. We are so close to getting away with this."

"I'm done," I breathe out. "I can't keep this secret anymore."

"The husband is already guilty, according to the court of public opinion. He'll be arrested soon. Then our lives can go on. Everything will go back to normal."

"Normal?" I ask, staggered. What even is normal anymore? I will never be normal again. I tell her, "They won't arrest him if they don't find her body."

"What do you know, Meredith?" she asks reproachfully.

"Without a body, how can anyone be sure she's even dead?"

She picks holes in my theory. "People have been convicted of murder without a body before. All they need is enough circumstantial evidence to convince a jury she's dead."

"Circumstantial evidence?" I ask. "Like what?" The details of the investigation are hush-hush. We only know some. There were dogs looking for her. They didn't find her, or else we'd know.

Bea says, "Her bloody clothes."

"What did you do with her clothes?" I ask. I think of the way she wrenched Shelby's clothes from her body that night, letting her head drop, unsupported. It was ungentle.

Bea doesn't say what she's done with Shelby's clothes. But from her silence, I surmise.

"You're going to frame Jason. You're using her clothes to frame him." My hand goes to my mouth in disbelief.

"Since when are you and he on a first-name basis?" she asks.

"Have you forgotten that Shelby was a client of mine?" I ask. "I know Jason. I know him well enough. He has a child, Bea. A baby girl. She just lost her mother. She can't lose her father, too. I won't let you do this to him," I say, and for the first time, I'm sure. Killing Shelby is one thing. But letting Jason take the

fall for it is another, because that's premeditated and purpose-
ful. I can't get Grace off my mind, imagining her growing up
without a mother's or a father's love. "I'm calling the police."

The conviction in my voice is unmistakable. I see a change
come over Bea. She's bemused at first. She stares, openmouthed.
"You can't do that," she pleads with me. Her voice changes, becoming less domineering, more desperate. She softens and for
the first time since we killed Shelby, I see that tough exterior
crack. "Please, Meredith. Please think this through. I beg of
you," Bea says. "I can't go to jail. I wouldn't survive it. I'm not
as strong as you are."

"No, you're not," I tell her. "You're stronger."

She shakes her head. She doesn't believe that she is stronger
than me. "If I go to jail, Kate will leave me. She'll move on
while I'm gone. We'll have nothing when we finally get out. You
and me. Not one fucking thing, Meredith." She's begging now.

I close my eyes. I imagine a world ten or twelve years from
now, when Bea and I are finally released from prison. Delilah
and Leo would be teenagers by then. They'd be in high school. I
wouldn't get to see them grow up. They might hate me because
of it. They might be resentful, embarrassed, ashamed. Would
Josh bring them to visit me? Would I even want them to come,
to see me incarcerated? Josh, in my absence, might find and fall
in love with another woman. It kills me to consider these things.

"We'll get a good lawyer," I tell her. "Josh has clients who
are defense attorneys. We'll find one who can help us. Think
about it, Bea. We have no prior criminal charges. Neither of
us has been charged with a prior DUI. We can work out a plea
bargain."

"And what would that be?" she asks, miffed. "Five years instead of ten? Do you have any fucking clue what five years in
jail would be like? We wouldn't survive five minutes."

It doesn't matter what the consequences are. I can't live with
Shelby's death on my conscience. I don't want to live like this.
Shelby will never see her daughter grow up. Why should I?

"I'm sorry, Bea. I have to do this."

Another change comes over Bea. She turns hard. "The hell you are," she says. Suddenly I'm a liability. I am the only thing standing between her and her freedom.

I go to leave, but Bea is in my way, blocking me from leaving. I'm wedged between the car door and the garage wall. There's hardly any room to scoot past.

I ask, "What if I told the police that I was the one driving the car that night? What if I said that you had too much to drink, and I offered to drive? *I* was the one who ran into Shelby. It was my idea, taking her out to the woods, hiding her. I did it while you were passed out drunk in the back seat."

Her tone is flat. "No one will believe you," she says. She steps toward me. The lights in the garage are off. The only light comes from outside, though the day is gray. Hardly any light gets in.

"Why's that?" I ask. I'm not a good liar. But the police have no proof to the contrary. It would be my word against theirs. They'd have no choice but to believe it.

"Because you couldn't have pulled all that off without me. You weigh like a hundred pounds, Meredith, sopping wet. There's no way you could have moved her all on your own. There's no way you could have buried her."

"I did my part," I tell her. "I pulled my weight that night."

"But you couldn't have done it without me. No one will believe you. We'll still both go to jail."

I remind her, "We killed a woman, Bea. We took a life."

My phone is there on the car's floor mat. My eyes fall to it. I lean down and reach for it before she can stop me. Bea sees what I've done and she comes at me, trying to take the phone out of my hands. She'll never let me call the police. The battery icon shows red. Soon my phone will be dead.

We tussle over the phone. She tries to rip it out of my hands. I pull back; I shove her. I don't mean to. I just react. Bea reels back, into the sheathing, which is riddled with exposed nails. Josh and I talk about them all the time. We talk about how those nails on the garage walls are a hazard. We worry about the kids cutting themselves on one. We worry about things like tetanus. Josh has talked about using the bolt cutters to cut the nails back, but he never did.

Bea falls into them. They lance her arm. She's bleeding, but I don't think she knows that she is. She's slowed down because of the fall. I use it to my advantage, to move quickly. I have to get away from her. If I get to the house, I can lock the door behind myself. There I can call the police. I'll confess to what I've done. I'll let Bea decide what she wants to confess to when the police come looking for her.

But I only get as far as the other side of the car. She's quick. She catches me there, grabbing me by the arm. "Give me the phone," she snaps, clutching my arm so tight it hurts. "Give me the fucking phone, Meredith."

I try to pull my arm away, but can't. I spin around to face her. Bea's eyes are enraged. I'm about to tell her no, that I won't give her the fucking phone. But the words get stuck in my throat. Bea now wields a hammer. Josh's hammer, which she must have grabbed from his workbench on the way past.

"What do you think you're going to do with that?" I ask.

"Just give me the phone and I'll put it down," she says. I almost believe her. Bea doesn't want to hurt me. I know this. Until what happened with Shelby, Bea bore no malice toward me, toward anyone. She was benevolent.

But the Bea I see now has her back to a wall. I have no idea how far she's willing to go to protect herself and her freedom.

She holds her free hand out. "Give me the fucking phone, Meredith."

I tell her no. I can't do that. I glance down at my phone and find the keypad.

She hoists the hammer above her head. "Don't fucking test me," she screams.

"Or what?" I challenge. "What will you do to me, Bea?"

She says nothing. I call her bluff. Bea is my friend. We've

known each other for years. It's not like I'm Shelby. Bea didn't know Shelby. She had no affinity toward her. It was far easier to do what she did to Shelby than to hurt me.

I turn away from her. I'll go back to the house and call the police from there.

But as I turn, I'm shocked to see Delilah standing in the open garage door, watching us. She holds the TV's remote control in her hands. Her hair spills across her face. Her eyes are punch-drunk with fever and fear.

"Mommy," she says. Her tiny voice wobbles, seeing Bea with the hammer just steps behind me, listening to Bea and me fight.

It all happens at the very same time.

Delilah's eyes turn to swimming pools. They fill with tears. "Mommy. The remote doesn't work," she says as I feel the immobilizing pain of the hammer striking my head from behind. It's more shock than pain. I try to speak, to tell her to run, but my words are suddenly slurred. My legs collapse and I'm falling. The garage spins. The cold garage floor catches me, and then, all there is, is blackness.

LEO

The cops brought you back to our place just long enough to pack up your stuff. The rest of us wait downstairs while you go up alone.

We're all guilty of assuming you're pretty much helpless. We've forgotten you're the same girl who survived eleven years in some hellhole, who crafted your own shank to stab a man with and set yourself free. Not many people could do that. You're stronger than we think. You're stronger than you think.

This is what the cops came up with at the police station: there's something called false memories. They feel real like real memories, but they're not. People's minds can deceive them, or they can be tricked into remembering things that never happened in the first place. Memory can be manipulated. Ideas can be implanted inside a person's head. That's what they think happened to you.

As the cops continued to pry, you remembered being read to from a newspaper, seeing Dad's and Mom's pictures in that paper before your world went dark. The cops dug up an old article from the paper online and Dad's picture was exactly as you described it: Dad standing in front of our blue house. There was another picture inset into the text. This was one of Mom. The caption: *Suburban mom found dead of apparent suicide.* The article had been added to the AP newswire, which meant it ran in papers almost everywhere.

For whatever reason, Eddie and Martha found the article. They made you believe you were Delilah, and that the people in the pictures were your dad and mom. There's no saying why, not unless the cops find them. But the man cop guesses that Eddie and Martha were obsessed with Delilah's high profile case, or they were copycat criminals. They got off on taking you. They either pretended or believed that you were that elusive missing girl who captured the attention of the world and quickly earned celebrity status: my sister.

It's taking a long time for you to pack up your things. But no one wants to rush you because you're going through a lot of heavy stuff right now. You need a minute alone. We sit in the kitchen and wait. Dad gets everyone water.

The good news is that your DNA is a real match to some missing kid in the database. Your name is Carly Byrd and you're sixteen years old. You disappeared about a week after my sister did, from some place near St. Louis. You got snatched off your own street. There's no saying why someone deemed my sister's story newsworthy and yours not.

After about a half hour of waiting for you, Dad goes to see if you need help.

Almost immediately, he starts hollering from the top of the stairs. "She's gone. She's gone!"

I take the steps two at a time to find that the room is empty and the clothes Dad bought for you still in their drawers. You've run away. The window is open. My sister's bedroom is on the second floor, but there's a roof and a trellis just outside. Desperate times call for desperate measures. And you're desperate.

MEREDITH

11 YEARS AGO

May

My hearing returns to me first, to a limited degree. What I hear is spotty, sporadic. Slurred words. Wind rushing through a tunnel. Drumsticks tapping a snare drum. I can't make sense of it. I press my eyes closed, avoiding sensory input. It's too much. Vomit rises in the back of my throat and I swallow it down. My head throbs. It pulsates in my ears, my temples, the backs of my eyes. Someone hums.

I don't know where I am or why I'm here. I must have been dreaming.

I force my eyes open to see the world hurtling past. It's dizzying, disorienting. My vision is blurred. It comes and goes, clouding over with fog before clearing. Rain falls, everything a monochrome shade of gray. I'm cold. I shake.

Things beside me start to take shape, my world coming slowly into focus. I see a child's board book, a dog leash. A booster seat thrust to the floor, my feet on it. Gray and red with a pink water bottle angled in the cup holder. It's Delilah's water bottle. It's Delilah's booster seat. Plastic covers hang from the headrests of the front row seats, to protect the fabric from little feet.

I'm in the back seat of my own car.

I sit slowly up, my body sore. I find that I'm bent over a car seat, the knobby parts of it pressing into my skin, leaving marks. There's the imprint of the chest clip on my arm.

It's Leo's car seat.

I sit fully upright, looking desperately around. Where is Leo? Where is Delilah? Why am I here? The car is in motion. It's going fast.

Disequilibrium overwhelms me. I grip the first thing I see to steady myself.

Bea is in the driver's seat. Bea is driving my car. Her window is open an inch. It moves her hair. Somehow or other the rain doesn't get in. The radio is on. Bea speaks to herself, something agitated, incomprehensible.

It all comes rushing back to me then.

Bea and me arguing. Bea with the hammer. Delilah standing scared in the open garage door. After that: nothing. Blackness.

The first words out of my mouth are, "Where is she?"

My words are garbled when they come. My lips are sluggish, unable to form words. The pounding in my head intensifies when I speak. I press my hands to my head, drill my palms into my eye sockets. It helps nothing. I pull my hands away.

I try again. "What did you do with her?" This time, words form.

"You're awake," she says, glancing over her shoulder at me. As she does, she tugs on the steering wheel by accident. The car swerves. A car horn blares. Bea looks back ahead. She rights the car before we get hit.

"What did you do with Delilah?" I demand.

Bea doesn't say. Her lack of a response makes me frantic, desperate. I need to know where my daughter is. I need to know what she's done to my child.

I grab for the door handle, try and force open the door. My first thought is to jump from the moving vehicle and make a run for it. But I can't because the door doesn't budge. The child locks have been activated. I don't know how long I was unconscious. Long enough for Bea to do something to Delilah, to get me in the car and drive. I look out the window. I try and orient myself as to where we are. We haven't gone far. We're only a few blocks from home. If I can just get out of the car, I can get back to Delilah. I can see if she's okay.

"Did you hurt her?" I ask. I'm terrified that Bea has done something to her. Delilah watched as she hit me over the head with the hammer.

Delilah saw too much. Bea couldn't just let her go.

I slide to the other side of the back seat. I try and open that door. It, too, is unopenable. I go to put the power window down, but it's locked. Bea has thought of everything.

Desperate, I smack my hands against the window to try and draw attention to us, to myself, trapped here in the back seat of my own car.

Bea snaps, "Stop it, Meredith. What the fuck do you think you're doing?"

"Let me out of here," I say, feeling like a caged animal. "You can't do this, Bea. You can't do this to me."

The only thing I can think to do is lunge into the front seat of the car. To forcibly gain control of it. A rush of adrenaline counters the pain in my body and head as I, impetuously, press myself into the narrow space between the two front seats and start to go.

But then I see it, sitting there on the passenger's seat: a knife.

Bea grabs for it at the same time as me. She gets there first. I go rigid.

"What are you doing with that?" I ask, terrified that she already used the knife to do something to Delilah.

"Just do what I say and no one gets hurt." Her voice is controlled.

I sit back in my seat. I have no other choice. My mind is in flux, trying to figure out how to get out of this. I come up empty, despairing because of it. What is Bea planning to do to me? What has she done to Delilah?

Bea drives through town. We turn right, then left, then right again. It isn't aimless; she's hatched a plan. We leave our town and enter another, and then another, where it's less populated, more industrial than residential.

"Take me home," I beg as she drives. "Please just take me home. We can forget this ever happened. I promise you, Bea, I won't go to the police. What happened to Shelby stays between you and me."

She ignores me at first. But I keep pressing until she snaps. "Shut up, Meredith. Please just shut the fuck up." Her tone is cold, direct.

She pulls into the parking lot of a run-down motel just off the highway. The building is ochre in color. It's single story. There is a Dumpster in the parking lot, picnic tables, a vending machine. She parks my car in the nearly empty lot.

Bea grabs my purse from the floor of the car. She tells me what's going to happen. "You're going to go in there and get a room. For a month. Pay cash," she says. She goes through my wallet and then hers, gathering dollar bills. She leans into the back seat and presses them into my hand. "Check into your room. Get the key," she says.

"And what if I don't?" I ask, though I watched with my own eyes what Bea did to Shelby. I've witnessed the cover-up, the lies. Hard-pressed, Bea is capable of anything.

"You don't want anything to happen to Delilah, do you?" she asks, and there's a glimmer of hope: Delilah is alive.

Unless Bea is lying to me.

Bea gets out of the car. She tucks the knife into the back pocket of her jeans, and hides it beneath the hem of her shirt. She comes around the side of the car and opens the door for me. It takes me a minute to get to my feet. I'm unbalanced, my head still throbbing.

"Don't do anything stupid, Meredith. I will be just outside watching. Remember, I'm the only one who knows where Delilah is. Don't test me." I swallow hard. I don't know what Bea has done with Delilah. But if she's alive, I have to get back to her. I have to do what Bea says. I have to behave, for Delilah's sake.

Bea follows me to the motel office. She stands far enough back that security cameras, if the motel has them, wouldn't reach. The clerk takes my cash and hands me a key. She doesn't look up long enough to see that I'm not right.

Bea and I walk to the room. She tells me to unlock the door. With shaking hands, I do. She tells me to turn on the light, to close the blinds. She touches nothing. I'm sensitive to this.

"What are you going to do to me, Bea?"

She doesn't say.

The motel room is squalid. The carpeting is stained. The plaster flakes off the walls.

"Delilah is sick," I tell her, pleading now. "She's overdue for medicine. Her fever will be back by now. She'll be burning up. She'll need Tylenol."

Bea says nothing apropos of this. Instead, "I need you to find paper and a pen." I do what she says. I don't ask. I go rummaging through drawers to find what Bea needs. But this isn't the kind of place to have free paper and pens. Instead, I come across an outdated phone book in a drawer. I tear a page from it. Bea has a pen. She wipes it on a sleeve before passing it to me.

"Write this down," she says. "Write *Delilah is safe. She is fine.*"

I look at Bea, not understanding. "Just do it," she says when I hesitate. "Write down *Delilah is safe. She is fine.*" I'm not quick to do it. Why would she want me to write that down? She reaches for the knife in the back pocket of her jeans, holding it to me. "I'm not messing around, Meredith. I need you to write it down. If you do what I say, I'll go and get Delilah for you. I'll bring her here. But you have to do this for me first."

"Okay," I say, acquiescing. I write the words down, because of her promise to bring Delilah to me and because of the knife at my throat. I don't know that I have another option. All I can think is that Bea plans to leave us in this dingy motel for the month that we've paid for. She's going to make Josh think we've run away, which will buy her time to figure out what to do. It's not a bad plan. I could survive a month here.

What I don't understand is why Bea didn't bring Delilah and me at the same time. She must have a reason. But maybe the two of us together was too much to manage.

When I'm through, I hold the paper out to her to take. "Set it on the dresser," she says. I do. "You understand, this needs to look like a suicide," Bea says.

I hear her words. They reach my ears, but they don't get interpreted by my brain. They don't make it that far. I don't have time to comprehend what she's said. I don't have time to react.

A second later I feel the excruciating sting of the knife blade slicing across my wrists. I scream, backing away from her.

"I'm sorry to be so direct," she says, following. "But you did this to yourself, Meredith. If only you could have kept your mouth shut, this wouldn't be happening. I warned you. I told you to just let it go, to forget about what happened that night. You couldn't. I never wanted to hurt you or Delilah," she says. "You left me no choice. I told you so many times—I can't go to jail. What did you expect me to do?"

She lashes out. Again the blade scores my wrist. It bleeds. I press my palm to it to try and control the bleeding. I try backing away from her in the room, but the room is small, boxy. Bea, with the knife, stands between me and the door. There's no way out. The motel is vacant or nearly vacant right now, the parking lot empty. If I were to scream, no one would hear. No one would come.

This is how she plans to do it, then. Bea plans to make the world believe I slashed my own wrists. That I was a desperate woman. Suicidal.

I hide my arms behind myself, thinking that will buy me time. I don't expect her to have an alternative plan. But then, in an instant, I feel the knife plunge into my gut. I watch in horror as Bea yanks the knife back out of me. It's so spontaneous. It knocks the wind out of me, makes it almost impossible to breathe. As I watch, the redness spreads from my center. My hands go to the blood, holding it back. Bea takes an inappreciable step backward. She watches me flounder, knife at the ready in case once wasn't enough.

She says, "I never wanted it to come to this. You were my friend." She cries. Standing there, watching me struggle, tears drip from her eyes. "Why couldn't you just leave it be?" she screams.

The shock sets in, replacing pain. My legs lose the strength to hold me up. I stagger, reaching out to her for help. "I'm sorry," she cries. "I'm so fucking sorry, Meredith." She steps away from me. She turns her back to me. She can't watch me die. She presses her fingers into her ears so she can't hear.

I collapse onto the motel floor. The floor catches my body, and I think what a relief it is to lie down. I'm so tired. For the first time in days, I think that I could sleep.

KATE

NOW

Bea and I are in the kitchen when the doorbell rings. I've just gotten home from work and am telling Bea about my day while she makes chicken enchiladas for us for dinner. Bea chops a pepper while the chicken browns in a skillet on the stove. My mouth waters. My day, as always, was incredibly busy so that I didn't have time to sit down for lunch; I ate on the go instead, a nibble here, a nibble there, between patients.

Today was difficult. I had to put down a dog I've been treating for a long time. No matter how many times I do it, it never gets easy or routine. I euthanize patients almost every day. Even harder than that are the days I get vilified by clients. The animals I adore; their humans are another story.

"Are you expecting someone?" I ask Bea at the sound of the doorbell.

"I don't think so," she says, turning the heat off under the chicken. I carry my wine with me, following her to the front door.

It's early evening, just after five o'clock. Outside the day is still bright. Bea pulls the door open and there stand Josh and Leo on the porch, a couple of uniformed police officers on the porch step below them. Concern lines their faces. There are tears in Josh's and Leo's eyes. The likeness to that night eleven years ago renders me momentarily speechless as I picture Josh with little Leo by his side, arms wrapped around Josh's leg, the storm raging in the background. The night their nightmare began.

Eleven years later, it's still ongoing.

"What is it?" Bea asks. "What's wrong?"

I set my wine on the coffee table. Josh says, "She's gone. She's run away," and it's all so similar to the night Meredith and Delilah first disappeared that I'm caught off balance, left open-mouthed. Josh doesn't look like himself. He hasn't in quite some time. Our friendship has waned over the years. We see each other far less. When we do, Bea and I have to be cautious to censor what we say. We don't ever mention Meredith or Delilah.

It's been just about a week since we heard the incredible news that Delilah had finally, after all those years, made a safe return. I'd given up hope of her ever coming home. For as much as I wanted to see her, I didn't want to impose on Josh. Bea and I had made the decision to wait until the media left, until the hoopla died down, to go and welcome Delilah home.

But now Josh is here in our doorway telling us she's gone, that she's run away, and all I can do is stare openmouthed while Bea does the talking. My heart is breaking for him inside. Not again. Please, I silently plead, don't let him lose her again.

"Delilah ran away?" Bea asks.

Josh says, shaking his head, "Yes, no, yes. It's a long story. Have you seen her? The girl?" and that's the moment I know that this girl, living inside Josh and Leo's house for the past week, is not who she claimed to be. Josh has been duped again. He looks broken.

Standing beside Josh, Leo looks lost. "Carly," he utters beneath his breath. And then, more pronounced: "Her name is Carly."

One of the police officers steps forward. "Would you mind

if we take a look around your property for a missing child?" he asks.

"Of course," Bea says. "Whatever you need."

Bea and I slip into shoes and follow them out in case we can be of any help. The reporters, I see when we do, are having a field day with this. They don't step onto our property, but they stand at the edge of it, camera-ready in case something news-worthy happens, which it already is.

I catch up with Josh and take his hand into mine. I can't imag-ine what he's going through, after all these years of searching, to think he'd found his daughter only to have her taken away again. For the past eleven years, he and Leo have lived a quiet life, a private life. I wish I'd been a better friend to them over the years. We tried early on, but Josh was so snowed under by grief that it was hard. He pushed us away. We gave up. We didn't even invite him to our wedding because it didn't seem right to force our happiness on him, who was sad.

I should have tried harder. I should have done more.

There are police cars outside Josh and Leo's house. There are a half dozen officers on foot, each searching in a different di-rection for this missing girl.

We walk our property. It's not large by any means, but there are towering trees with branches and leaves that hang low. There are also hedges where a person, if she wanted to, could conceiv-ably hide. The police officers search the hedges. She's not there. We make our way around the side of the house, following the concrete walkway into the backyard. One of the officers investi-gates the shrubs. Another asks, "Mind if we search the garage?"

He goes to it, sizing up Bea's music studio from the outside. The studio is a near-replica of our house. It's smaller, of course, a story and a half tall with a storage space on the upper floor. We don't use that storage space; we don't need to. If anything, Bea keeps old recording equipment in there. Between Bea and me, we don't have many belongings, and what we have can eas-ily fit into the spare bedroom in the house.

Bea goes to the studio and jiggles the door handle. She stands taller than the police officer by an inch or two. I stand, watching her in her jeans and her black T-shirt and her sneakers. She looks troubled. Like Josh, Bea changed significantly after what happened to Meredith and Delilah. I suppose we all did. Bea became less relaxed, less carefree, more overburdened. She spent more time in solitude working on her music, though she never produced much. She lost interest in having kids.

"The door is locked," she says to the police officer. Bea always keeps that door locked. She has expensive equipment in there, and nearly everyone in the neighborhood knows exactly what she uses the space for. It isn't so unlikely to think someone might try to make off with her equipment when no one's looking.

The officer asks, "Do you mind opening it for us?"

Bea says, "It's been locked all day, Officer. No one could have gotten inside."

There's something about Bea's response that lies heavy on me. Bea is right; short of telekinesis, there's of course no way a person could have gotten through the locked door. There's one window on the building, and it's upstairs. There's no easy way up, aside from scaling the yellow siding.

And yet, if I was Bea, I'd open the door and let the police officer see for himself that no one is there.

"Are you saying you won't open the door?" he asks, staring Bea down. Josh no longer holds my hand. He's let go, moved closer to Bea and the officer.

"That's not what I said. I just don't see how anyone could have gotten inside. I'm worried you're wasting your time," she says, and then I realize that she's not being insubordinate and unwilling; she's trying to save them from a pointless search. Bea is helping.

"Bea," Josh says. "We don't know how long the girl has been gone—"

"Carly," Leo interjects again. He hovers somewhere behind

me. "Her name is Carly." This time when he says it, he enunciates each word at a time.

Josh swallows hard. "We don't know how long Carly has been gone," he says, putting emphasis on her name, "or how far she could have gotten by now. Please, Bea, please just open the door and let them see, so we can get on with the search."

"Of course," Bea says, offering Josh a faint smile. She looks embarrassed. Bea doesn't embarrass easily. She didn't mean to be a burden, but from the looks of things, she has been. I offer her a sympathetic smile, knowing she was only trying to help. "Of course," she says again, dropping her eyes. "I was just trying to save you time. I'm happy to open the door, if that's what you need. Just let me go get the key," she says as she steps past the rest of us and makes her way to the concrete walk, rounding the side of the house for the front door, which we left unlocked. The rest of us wait, unspeaking. The day is hot. Sweat drips from me, from all of us, though we're standing still. The trees block the sun, though there isn't the slightest hint of a breeze. It's stifling hot, a muggy Indian-summer day. The mosquitoes and bees buzz around, attracted to our sweat.

It takes an eternity for Bea to come back. Josh and the officers get anxious. "What's taking her so long?" someone asks, looking to me expectantly, as if I have the answer.

"Maybe she's misplaced it," I suggest. There's a mirror in our entryway with brass pegs where we keep our keys. It wouldn't be hard to find. "I'll go check on her."

I head in the same direction Bea went. The front door, when I get to it, is open a couple of inches as if she tried to slam the door closed behind herself, but it didn't latch. I gingerly push the door open. I step inside the house and close the door behind me, feeling like a fish in a fishbowl with the reporters watching from just outside.

I call out for Bea. There's no response.

I try again. "Bea!"

Only silence follows.

My eyes go to the brass pegs that outfit the bevel-edged mirror in the entryway. Only my keys are there.

I slip out of my shoes, dashing up the stairs in my bare feet. I try our bedroom first. It's empty, though one of Bea's dresser drawers has been pulled clear out and overturned on the floor. She was looking for something. I check the bathroom, the spare bedroom. All empty.

Running back down the wooden steps, I slip, my feet sliding out from beneath me. I land on my backside, feeling the pain of it radiate through my tailbone. I curse out loud at Bea, blind to what she's doing, but knowing it's something reckless and rash, something that leaves me in a bind.

I'm mad. I'm scared and confused.

I press myself up from the steps, rubbing my backside. I limp to the kitchen, where our half-made dinner sits abandoned. Through the glass door I see Josh, Leo and the police officers in our backyard, still taking stock of Bea's music studio.

My cell phone sits on the kitchen counter. I pick it up and try calling Bea. She doesn't answer.

Only seconds after I've ended the call does she text.

Forgive me. I didn't mean for any of it to happen.

My heart races wildly inside me.

Forgive you for what? I type immediately back, punching each letter into the keypad.

My question goes unanswered.

Where are you? I ask.

She doesn't reply.

I try calling again. It rings once before going to voice mail. I call again and again, feeling frantic now, wondering what Bea has done that she didn't mean to do. What am I to forgive her for, other than leaving me in the lurch like this?

What is she running from?

I hurry barefoot, back around the side of the house, my bra

strap sliding out from beneath a sleeveless shirt, falling down my arm. I force it up. It falls again. My heart is beating hard inside my chest. My mind is restless, reeling. Where did Bea go? What is she up to?

My hair hangs in my eyes, wet with sweat. "She's gone," I tell them, breathless, when I return to the backyard. My chest hurts. I can't catch my breath.

"What do you mean she's gone?" Josh asks.

"I don't know, Josh. I don't know. The house is empty. I looked everywhere for her. I tried calling her. She texted this," I say, forcing my cell phone into Josh's hands.

He looks at it, at Bea's disclosure, and asks, "What does this mean?"

I shake my head. "I don't know."

Josh passes the phone to the officers. Bea's car is parked in the alley beside mine. Wherever she went, she went on foot. She can't be far.

"Can you let us inside the garage, ma'am?" one of the officers asks. There's something in there that Bea doesn't want the police to see. Stolen audio equipment is all that comes to mind. But Bea and I have enough money. She could buy anything she needs.

"I don't know where the key is," I admit. "There's only one. It's gone. Bea must have taken it with her when she ran off," I say, ashamed for many reasons, but mostly that Bea cut and run and left me in the dark like this. It's so unlike Bea.

I go on to explain, my eyes moving between Josh and the officers, "I never go in there. It's Bea's space. It's where she works. I don't like to intrude." I'm spinning, remembering how I used to have a key to the studio. But then many, many years ago, Bea told me how she thought someone had tried to break in; she installed a new handle on the door herself, something more secure and foolproof. She boarded up the one window with plywood, though the only person getting up there without a ladder was Spiderman. It seemed excessive and a bit paranoid, if I'm being honest. But I told myself at the time that, if it made

Bea feel more safe, so be it. I didn't argue. It was shortly after all that happened with Shelby Tebow, Meredith and Delilah. The whole neighborhood was on edge. It was understandable that Bea might want to take extra security measures to feel safe.

The new lock, she said, only came with the one key. She told me she'd have another made for me. Now that I think about it, she never did.

One of the officers asks, "Do we have your permission to knock the door down?"

Without hesitation I say, "Yes. Of course."

I need to know what Bea has been keeping from me.

The officer goes back to his vehicle. Minutes later, he comes back with a battering ram. It doesn't take long. The door busts violently open, ricocheting off the wall. From where we stand, I see Bea's equipment. Nothing looks amiss.

I release my pent-up breath.

The officers step heedfully inside the studio. One has a hand on the weapon in his holster. Josh makes an attempt to follow.

"Sir," one of the officers says firmly. "You need to stay put."

Josh does as he's told. He, Leo and I stand together, waiting. It's all so like that day they found Meredith, when the female detective told Josh, there in the parking lot of that seedy motel, that Meredith was dead of an apparent suicide, which was later confirmed by autopsy. He fell to pieces on the concrete lot. The rest of the day was a blur for all of us. I don't remember much.

From where we stand, I just barely see the officers probing around Bea's space. It doesn't seem like they're finding anything of interest to them.

Suddenly the officers stand at attention. One of them points upward, to where the attic is. The three move to the stairs. They start to climb, their movements in sync. After a half dozen steps, they drop from view. I can't see them anymore.

There is a door at the top of those steps, I remember. It must be locked. The officers don't ask this time; instead, I hear the unmistakable sound of them breaking it down.

The scream that reaches my ears as the door bursts open is shrill, terrified, female. A girl. The girl Josh and Leo are looking for. But why? For what reason would Bea shelter this girl in her music studio? I can think of none.

My knees buckle. My legs give. I sag onto the lawn. Josh breaks into a run, but Leo tries stopping him, tries holding him back. Josh is stronger than Leo. With Leo hanging on to his arm, he drags Leo across the lawn and toward the studio door.

I'm frozen to the ground, horror-struck as the police officers return with the girl. Except that when she emerges, she is not the same girl that I've been seeing on the news. Bruised and battered, malnourished, skittish.

She is the spitting image of Meredith instead. Flaming red hair, fair skin, freckles, eyes the same as Meredith's mineral green. She's Meredith in her mannerisms, in the way she carries herself, in the way she stands. She's clean, well fed, seemingly unharmed. She is no longer a cherubic little girl. She's developed into a lovely young lady who takes my breath away.

Josh falls to his knees at her feet. "Daddy," she cries out, lowering herself to the ground, collapsing into him. Leo, at first hesitant, rushes to them and together they hold each other and cry.

Delilah.

It's Delilah.

I feel ashamed, deceived, horrified, hurt. Confused. How did Delilah come to be here in Bea's studio after Meredith killed herself? For eleven years she's been here, in my backyard, and I didn't know.

I don't have to wonder for long. Josh also wonders.

"How?" he asks. "How did you...?" He's at a loss for words, unable to grasp what's happening. Meredith left a note when she killed herself. Something to the effect of: *Delilah is safe. She is fine. You'll never find her. Don't even try.*

The realization stuns me. Meredith chose Bea to watch over Delilah after she was gone. She entrusted Delilah to Bea. Bea was making good on a promise to Meredith; she was honoring Meredith's last request.

But why? Why would Meredith ever keep Delilah from Josh? My thoughts are derailed with Delilah's next words.

"I was there," Delilah says, "when she killed Mommy."

The world falls silent.

And then I hear, "No," vehemently at first and then screamed again and again, with more passion, more fury, "No! No! Noooo!"

It's only when all eyes fall to me that I realize those are my words. That I'm the one who's screaming.

Later, after the police have completed their investigation, which includes interrogating me, they let me into Bea's studio. I don't know what to expect as I ascend the steps and let myself into the upstairs attic where Delilah was kept for eleven years. The sole window is boarded up with plywood, except for a small circle, carved just big enough for an eye, out of which Delilah could see. For eleven years she watched her father mow the lawn, watched Leo toss a ball to Wyatt the dog until he died. She watched flowers bloom and snow fall, but never felt the sun on her skin.

She wasn't treated unkindly. Delilah has told the police as much; the stacks of books, of toys, of art supplies, the plentiful clothes suggest the same to me. And yet Bea took her childhood from her. She stole years of Delilah's life that she will never get back. She took her from her family. She stole her innocence and her freedom. Why? Because Delilah was witness to what Bea did to Meredith.

As it turns out, Delilah didn't see Bea kill Meredith, though for eleven years she thought she did. What she saw was the commencing act: Bea immobilizing Meredith with a hammer, and Meredith falling unconscious to the ground. As Bea held her hand to Delilah's mouth and carried her running from the Dickeys' garage to ours, little Delilah was sure her mother was dead. Bea never told her otherwise. Delilah doesn't remember much from that day, though she remembers that when Bea came back, after leaving her alone for what felt like an eternity to a six-year-old, she had medicine and ice cream.

The upstairs of the garage is tiny and cramped. With the window boarded up, it's always gloomy, if not dark. The roof is a gable roof. Only where the edges meet to form a ridge could Delilah, at seventeen years, stand fully upright. When she first came to this place at six years old—an impossibility that devastates me again and again, how Bea kept a child in here for *eleven* years—it would have been different. Then she would have been able to stand anywhere without hitting her head.

There is no room for a bed. Instead, there's an air mattress where Delilah slept. It's covered with pink sheets and a pink comforter, suggesting that Bea was considerate of what Delilah liked, and yet there's no bathroom other than the folding steel commode, the kind of thing meant for the elderly who don't have the capacity to walk to and from a bathroom. The space smells of urine. Every so often, according to Delilah, presumably on days I worked, Bea would clean the commode out. She would fill buckets of warm, soapy water for Delilah to sponge bath. She would help her wash and braid her hair.

I don't know that I'll ever be able to sort out this Bea from the one I loved.

That same day that Delilah is found, the other missing child, Carly Byrd, is found hiding out near an abandoned dam in Dellwood Park. She's safe, she's fine, waiting at the police station for her family to come and take her home for good.

Three days later, the couple that kept Carly captive is found when they stupidly return to their own home. They confess to her kidnapping and captivity. They'll be going to jail for a long time. She will never need to live in fear of them again. They were copycat criminals, inspired by Delilah's story. They wanted the same notoriety that Delilah's captor—Bea—had. They wanted full media coverage, attention, a nation in fear.

326

I try to understand it but can't, because what they did falls outside the realm of any rational thought.

A few days after that, Bea is captured by police when she tries to procure a fake ID. At her arraignment, she pleads guilty to first-degree murder, vehicular homicide, concealment of a homicide and aggravated kidnapping. I don't go to the arraignment. Josh goes and tells me later.

It was Bea's blood the police found in Josh's garage.

Bea kept Delilah all those years because she couldn't bring herself to kill her. Delilah knew too much. Bea couldn't let her go home to snitch. She had only two choices: kill or hide her. She chose the least bad option.

Nothing will bring Meredith back to life, but perhaps restoring her reputation is the best that we can do. Leo has spent his life feeling neglected by her. Now he knows that his mother loved him fiercely.

With Bea's confession, Shelby Tebow's husband, Jason, gets released from prison after erroneously serving eleven years. He goes home to nothing. His wife is dead, and the child he once believed they shared now lives with her real father. It's tragic. The consequences of what Bea did are overwhelming. She didn't just hurt one person. She hurt so many. She ravaged so many lives. It deeply disturbs me, not only because I feel guilty by association, but because the woman I loved, the one I thought I knew, the one I made a life with, has turned out to be selfish and cruel. Bea is a kidnapper. She is a murderer. She hid Delilah under my nose for eleven years; she let Josh and Leo search for her in vain; she let an innocent man rot in jail for over a decade of his life.

I cry myself to sleep every night. I don't cry for me. I cry for all the lives Bea shattered.

Only once do I take her call from prison. "What were you planning to do, keep Delilah there for the rest of her life?" I ask, still finding it unfeasible that Bea kept a human being in there for eleven years. If she hadn't been caught, would Delilah still be there eleven years from now?

Did Delilah ever try and escape? Did she scream? It wouldn't have mattered if she did; the garage is soundproof. I wouldn't have heard.

"I didn't have another choice. If I let her go, she would have told," she says, and I'm sorry I asked because knowing this makes it feel worse. Bea takes a deep breath and says, "I didn't mean for any of it to happen. I fucked up, Kate. I panicked. It was one colossal mistake that spiraled out of control. I never set out to hurt anyone."

"But you did," I say. "You hurt *everyone.*"

I hang up before she can say more. I refuse to accept any more calls from her.

In the evenings Josh and I share a beer on his front porch sometimes. We watch Leo and Delilah together, doing things that brothers and sisters do. Kids are more buoyant than adults. They're quicker to bounce back. Even though Josh says there are times that Delilah shows a strange affinity toward Bea—wishing she could talk to her, that she could tell her something—she's adapted well, slipped right back into her old routine of teasing and taunting her brother. It's brought life back into Josh's eyes. Their home is a joyful one.

They say time heals all wounds. Josh, Delilah and Leo are evidence of this.

As for me, I'm patiently waiting, but hopeful that my time will come soon.

★ ★ ★ ★ ★

ACKNOWLEDGMENTS

Thank you to my phenomenal team, without whom none of this would be possible: My editor, Erika Imranyi, for always being so very diligent and perceptive, and for pushing me to make my words the best that they can be. My agent, Rachael Dillon Fried, for being the most incredible advocate, cheerleader and friend. And my publicists, Emer Flounders and Kathleen Carter, for working tirelessly to promote my books.

Thank you to HarperCollins Publishers and Sanford J. Greenburger Associates, and to the many booksellers, librarians, bloggers, bookstagrammers and readers who have championed my books over the years, especially the incomparable Mary O'Malley, for her passion and dedication to authors and books. I'm so fortunate to know you.

Thanks to my earliest readers for your friendship and your indispensable feedback, including Janelle Kolosh and Vicky Nelson, and Nicki Worden and Marissa Lukas, who also provided insight into the doula experience. Thank you, thank you, thank you to

Karen Morrison, Adrienne Campf, Robin Krieb, Jackie Simon, Aaron Buldak, Carlie Peterson and Hannah Peters for being so willing to do a favor for a stranger in a pinch. I'm so grateful.

Finally, a huge thanks to my family, especially Pete, Addison and Aidan, for your love and support.

QUESTIONS FOR DISCUSSION

WARNING: CONTAINS SPOILERS!

1. Of the main narrators—Kate, Meredith and Leo—which spoke most to you? Was there one you connected with more than others?

2. Meredith tries to find a work-life balance while having two young children and a very unpredictable schedule as a doula. How do you feel about Meredith as a mother and how she raises her children?

3. Leo feels a great deal of resentment toward Delilah when she returns home. Is this anger and resentment justified?

4. How do you feel about Josh as a husband and father? Did you ever consider him to be a suspect in the disappearances? Which characters did you consider to be suspects?

5. The suburban Chicago weather is as volatile as the story itself. How does the stormy spring weather add to the atmosphere of *Local Woman Missing*?

6. This novel discusses obstetric violence and abuse. Did it surprise you to learn of the things Meredith has witnessed as a doula or to read about Shelby's experience giving birth?

7. Keeping secrets from friends and loved ones is a recurring theme in this book. Have you discovered something surprising or even shocking about a friend, family member or neighbor that made you see them in a different light?

8. Discuss the choices that Bea and Meredith made in the car the night of the hit-and-run. Do you think Bea is a cold-blooded killer or a desperate woman with no other way out? Was Meredith as complicit as Bea?

9. At the end of the novel, there are many victims: two women killed, a man sent wrongly to prison, a child kept in captivity, another being raised without her mother and father, and more. Who suffered the most throughout *Local Woman Missing* and why?

WOMAN
LOCA
cal Woman Missing
Woman Missing
oca
LOCAL WOM
CAL
Local Won
WOMAN MISSING
WOMAN MISSING
WOMAN MISSING
ocal
WOMAN MISSIN
WOMAN M
n Missing
LOCAL
AL WOMA
WOMAN MI
Local